PIG IN THE PARLOUR

LENA KENNEDY

GW00468158

Published by Kindle Direct
IBAN 9798558294088

The Pig in the Parlour was a story my mother wrote
after a trip to Ireland, but it never got finished.

The Inspiration came to complete the story, when
I looked into her old family photograph album and
found photographs taken during the 2nd World War.

Angela Kennedy Smith
(Lena`s daughter)

**This book is dedicated to
My mother Margaret Murphy
and my Nephew Alan Kennedy
-so proud of his Irish heritage.**

3

PROLOGUE

The Legacy

Islington is a very dreary spot, even on a sunny day. On a wet and windy November day there are few words to describe the air of gloom that surrounds these tall three-storey dwellings with six stone steps going up, and ten stone steps going down to a dreary basement. The original owners were the stalwart Victorians, who kept their servants trotting up and down at the slightest pull on the bell, it being a very high class respectable locality in the good old days.

In this present day the mixture of population is of all kinds and colour who had inherited these relics of old Regency that were let out as one-room flats, and all with mod cons. It did nothing to add to its fading beauty.

My abode was on the top floor consisting of two attics, where the ceiling sloped almost six inches from the floor, forcing me with my long lanky shape to remain perpetually in the centre of the room, unless lying down. This I did, and spent most of my leisure lying on a narrow bed staring at the litter that surrounded me of past hobbies taken up with great enthusiasm; then the sudden loss of interest: old cameras, stamp books, nude magazines and bits of antique junk and piles of returned manuscripts to keep me company.

I was just beginning to wonder how much longer I could mentally survive when one cold, grey morning a buff envelope was slipped under my door, having been retrieved from the front door mat by my kind thinking Pakistani neighbour below. I slowly opened it and a bright shaft of sunlight seemed to penetrate the general air of gloom. I had been left a legacy; Mick O'Hara, orphan and derelict layabout, had come into some money.

This very legal looking document informed me of the demise of my old Aunt Bridie, and if I would kindly call at their office in the Strand on Monday morning, I would be told further details that were possibly to my advantage. What words - those lovely, beautiful 'words'.

I dashed jubilantly up and down the long flights of linoleum covered stairs at great risk, as I was constantly sliding down the polished garish brass rod fittings; three steep flights, calling on my many neighbours to come and drink to my health with cups of Nescafe, and informing them that I had come into money. All gathered in my apartment, but because of the difficulty of talking in another language, they got the impression that I had won the 'Pools' and immediately I became very popular.

On Monday, before nine, I sat waiting, cold and shivery with the excitement of it all, at Blunden and Compton, for the family solicitor to arrive. He was definitely most kind and helpful, explaining that as sole heir to my Aunt Bridie's estate I had inherited a sizeable properly in Ireland, with a cottage and land attached - not much in the way of ready cash, only two hundred pounds, but the property was mine, lock, stock and barrel. Aunt Bridie must have been getting on, I faintly remembered a visit to Ireland after my mother died, but that's all, but it was a step in the right direction. I was now a man of property, and I was allowed an advance of fifty pounds to go to Ireland and inspect my estate.

I returned to my lodgings, gave away a few possessions, packed my suitcase and started out for my estate in Ireland, lord of all I surveyed: Mick O'Hara at twenty one, never having a bean except that which he gained by the sweat of his brow. So I had quit my job, distributed my few possessions amongst my friends, said goodbye to those dreary lodgings, and was soon on my way to the Emerald Isle.

. . .

The journey from Paddington to Fishguard was uneventful, except for a slight punch-up in the train corridor, when one big Irishman put a half nelson hold on another, and various other passengers fought to part them. I got used to being continually shoved aside; a long line of hefty chaps pushed backwards and forwards to the restaurant car, their breath almost knocking me unconscious, so full of whiskey they were. I did in the end manage to get a seat in the corner and sat there unobtrusively, being a nervous sort of chap. I never fancied my chances with these hefty Micks' going home on leave to their families. So, by the time I got to Fishguard, my stomach was hitting my boots – to get aboard the 'Enniskillen'- which one had to brave the dangers of- being pushed off the gang plank into the raging sea. It was like a stampede of elephants, so my cautious nature got the better of me and I decided to wait until last.

When I did chance it the harassed official informed me that the ship was full to bursting - point and no more passengers were going on that trip. If I wanted to get there that night I must get on the mail boat called the St. David that went to Rosslare, not anywhere near Cork. Well, as they say, any port in a storm. Did I mention the word 'storm'?

The waves were a mile high, dark green, and horrible white topped waves like galloping horses came roaring over me. Unfortunately, I am not a good sailor and the harbour light could still be seen when I hung over the side wishing I could die.

At dawn I sat with others on the top deck feeling ghastly and longing for the sight of land. The salt sea had washed the dye from my navy socks and my best flannel pants were blue and halfway up my leg. A hot cup of tea at the station revived me slightly, but the long wait for the train and my being afraid to leave the platform as I had not been quite sure of the time of its arrival, plus the official with a brogue as thick as butter who did tell me, but was incomprehensible - did not help.

I suppose you could call it a train, but it was the oldest type still running - the original 'choo choo' of my childhood. If you have travelled in a slow train from Rosslare to Cork you will not need to be reminded of the discomfort of this slow journey - a long wait at every station, while milk churns were unloaded and cows were taken on board, and the wooden seats were hard and smooth, and as the journey progressed you travelled from side-to-side. I was beginning to wonder if I was in danger of arriving at my destination with no seat in my pants that were already blue, halfway up my legs and damp, and cold, and clammy.

Once - we stopped for quite a while, to wait for the driver to chase sheep off the line and finish a heated argument with the fellow that owned them. There was one moment very early in the morning when we passed through a place called Dungarvan. There lay a stretch of snow white sand beside a very blue sea, inhabited by sea birds, and behind me I beheld a range of mountains in the early morning sun. They shone a thousand ever changing colours. It was a truly wonderful sight as I have never seen mountains before and resolved to come back one day to walk on the lonely beach in sight of those beautiful snow capped mountains adorned with rainbow colours.

At some little town women got on board loaded with shopping and they all chattered loudly in some unknown language and passed bread and black sausage around. They kindly offered me some but my tummy had not yet recovered from the ravages of the Irish Sea.

Eventually I arrived in Cork City and after a wash and brush up I changed out of my two-tone coloured pants and treated myself to a slap up meal. With roast beef, spuds and cabbage, whiskey and two beers inside me I was a new man and ready to take over as lord of my

Irish manor.

. .

BANTURK

Ch.1

There was still a little way to go; another train out of Cork passing the famous castle of Blarney and on towards the lake of Killarney, but not so far was Banturk where my journey ends.

There is a sort of cool greenness about the countryside in Ireland, a damp mistiness, but so different from London mist; it is crisp and fresh and I was beginning to feel excited by the scenery as the low hills and cool meadows rushed past the train window.

I was the only passenger to alight at Banturk, just me and a couple of milk churns; there was nobody on the platform, not a soul in the ticket office. I walked outside the station and there was not a person in sight, so I left my heavy luggage and took a light suitcase and went to find a taxi. Outside, the quite sandy road led up to a hill and there seemed to be some sort of building at the top. I was halfway up when I saw an old chap coming down on a bike. With one hand he wiped his bushy whiskers, with the other he steered the bike. He pulled up level with me.

'You missed it, sir,' he said, 'no matter, not many trains today.'

It was then I realised I was addressing the station master. 'Is it possible to get a taxi?' I asked. 'I have heavy luggage in the station.'

Two very vivid blue eyes weighed me up from beneath bushy eyebrows. 'Aah,' he said at last, 'you must be the 'O'Hara boy.'

'My name is Mick O'Hara,' I replied. 'Could you tell me where my aunt's place is?'

He got off the bike and drew closer; beer fumes mixed with strong tobacco swept past my nostrils. He looked closer at me before answering. 'I knows' the place, why, I'd be raised out in Inshallalee.'

'Is it far?' I asked a bit exasperated.

'Inshallalee, now there's Daneen who be out there. No, my mistake, he be gone on the booze since your aunt passed away, God rest her soul.'

'But how do I get there?' I muttered impatiently.

Now he held up his hand. 'Wait a bit, laddie, I'm thinking. Best thing you can do is come with me to Davy Joe's, if we can find Davy Joe, won't be another train till six when she comes back, luggage will be safe enough.'

So back up the hill we went, the old chap pushing his bike very energetically until we reached a small village at the top. It reminded me of a cowboy film set: a few dwellings, a bar and no one in sight, just two dogs playing in the middle of the road.

We entered the bar that had a green sign outside decorated with shamrock. It swung back and forth with a strange creaking sound in the wind that was beginning to rise. Silence descended as we went inside. All the young farmers leaning on the bar turned to look and the old men in the corner stopped their gabble as we came in. The buzz of conversation ceased and all eyes fell on us as though waiting for something to happen. I felt very embarrassed and stared at the sawdust floor, waiting for the next move. Then I realised they were waiting for me to order a drink and once I handed the old fellow a pint of porter and downed mine, I immediately felt better. Conversations resumed and all apparently lost interest in us.

'Where's Davey Joe?' asked my friend, of the old boys in the corner.

'Won't be back 'til three o'clock,' one said, 'down the farmer's club he be.'

'We'll wait,' he said, sitting down with the old fellows and making room for me.

In the next hour I discovered that the station master was called Paddy Mac and Davey Joe was his son-in-law, and between them they transported everyone in and out of Banturk.

The table was continuously stocked with pints of porter and conversation drifted from Gee Gees to beer and back to Gee Gees again. I also discovered Paddy Mac and Davey Joe were my relations and that I was a descendant of the great chieftain 'O'Hara who was a big shot, years before, but not only Aunt Bridie, but a majority of the population was O'Hara and all considered themselves related to me.

It was quite a blow, me being a lonely orphan, having found out that I not only had blue blood in my veins but was snowed under with relatives, but the strength of the beer subdued the shock a bit, so by the time Davey Joe arrived outside in a battered old Bedford van, I never knew if I was coming or going trying desperately to keep my feet from going in a different direction.

My luggage was already in the back of the van. They seemed to have their own sort of Bush telegraph and by 4.30 I was on my way to my new estate in Inshallalee.

The old van bumped along the country road and Davey Joe, red and robust, looked me over, like I was a kid out of school.

'The old fellow has baptised thee well,' he chuckled, 'beer's a bit strong round here, but you'll get used to it.'

I tried to focus my eyes on him through my horn-rimmed spectacles, but for some reason they would not go straight. He stared down at my long, skinny legs.

'Put a bit of weight on you will, could do with it.'

And so I sat and looked daft and said nought. It must have been nearly five o'clock that afternoon as we did the rest of the journey to Inshallalee. It was getting near evening; the sun had already begun to set. There was a rosy glow in the sky and a silver glint of a river in the distance. Either side there was a cool emerald green meadow: such a moist deep dark green and hordes of cattle roamed or sat chewing the cud.

'It's lovely scenery,' I remarked to Davey Joe.

'It's fair enough in the summer,' said Davey, 'but lonely out here in the long winter, but old Bridie liked it.'

Soon we left the road in the direction of a neat pair of thatched cottages. They stood in the middle of green rolling fields completely isolated, a very green, dark, damp bog-land, not a house or a tree or even a haystack in sight. In front of them a swift flowing river and behind them Blue mountains.

'Here we are,' said Davey Joe, 'here's Aunt Bridie's foine place out here,' he said, 'pity she never cultivated it, she was a hard case was Aunt Bridie. I'm your cousin by marriage, you know,' he added cheerfully. He looked towards the river. 'Got the fishing rights out here, many a time I've seen old Bridie out there in the freezing cold hooking a salmon.'

I stared, amazed. Here was I with two isolated cottages, a river and a mountain, and a Tarzan of an aunt who fished for salmon. It was not my idea of a country inheritance.

'So long,' said Davey Joe, 'I'm away, got to meet the six o'clock train.' He dumped my luggage on the path.

'How much do I owe?' I asked.

'Get away,' he said, 'I owe old Bridie a few favours, God rest her soul,' and the next minute he was gone.

MY NEW ABODE

Ch.2

I stood there stunned, sick with disappointment. My Irish manor had turned out to be two dilapidated cottages in the middle of a bog and God knows how many boozy sarcastic relations.

Feeling pretty desolate, I looked for the key. It was strange what tricks the memory plays, it was then and only then that I remembered I had been here before. The key on a big iron ring hung over the door lintel and someone some time had taken it and opened the door; a memory flashed through my mind of a big buxom woman with short red hair who did the same thing. My Aunt Bridie, of course - I had been here as a boy to spend a holiday with her. I remember how she frogmarched me to the church on Sundays, her large bosoms swaying from side to side. I recall after that going back to London and being sent to a boarding-school run by the 'welfare'.

I felt pretty lonely and desolate as the heavy door swung open with a protesting whine, and I was in a fair sized hallway at the time these two cottages had been made into one. A fox head on the wall stared at me out of the twilight, and big red eyes of a fish in a glass case glared at me. As I advanced towards a living room I went on feeling for the light switches, but then realising it was lit by oil lamps. I saw one in the centre of the table covered by a red table cloth. I got out my lighter and after a struggle, got a nice bright yellow gleam from the lamp.

I began to inspect my new abode as I looked around, and realised who I inherited my untidy habits from - my Aunt Bridie. All over the room were glass cupboards, tables and whatnots; all were littered with various oddments: fishing reels, bits of string, thousands of magazines and newspapers, various jars empty and medicine bottles. There were plenty of bottles under the table and under the chairs, but there was a nice big brick fireplace laid with logs and peat blocks stacked at the side. I soon got a nice fire going.

It wasn't so bad, nice and cosy – a home of my own at last, more than I'd had since my mother died. I began to cheer up. I looked in the sideboard hoping to find a drink, but hundreds of birthday and Christmas cards shot out onto the floor, rejects of eighty years of birthdays and Christmas's.

The living room was getting nice and warm but there was a peculiar smell about it, a sort of mixture of lavender polish and moth balls. I rummaged in another cupboard and found a bottle of Guinness and a tin of sweet biscuits.

It had begun to get very dark outside and there was a sort of uncanny silence. Think I'll settle round the fire tonight, no sense in rummaging around in the dark, so with my beer and biscuits and my overcoat to cover me I banked up the fire and was about to start on my supper, when from the direction of the back door came the most unearthly noise, a kind of scratching, squealing, thumping all at the same time. My heart nearly stopped beating. Oh my God, what was it? I sat quiet, then it came again, this time louder than ever, a squealing, howling, scraping. The back door rattled on its hinges, so something or someone was trying to get in. I'm not a very brave fellow, but managed to nervously grasp the poker and crept towards the back door and lifted the latch.

Something rushed at me, knocked me to the ground, tramped over me then rushed straight to the sitting room and sat in front of the fire. Pale faced and stunned my mind on pixies and giants I lay on the floor and then quietly got up onto my feet, crept to the door and peeped. In the sitting room was a hairy pig with a most ridiculous expression of contentment on its face, toasting its snout by the fire. I was filled with a mixture of emotion, first astonishment, then a kind of creepy fear, thinking of witches and their unpleasant familiars. The pig uttered a soft kind of shush and getting louder as he continued to ignore me, then getting closer, I lunged out with my foot right in its ribs.

'Get away!' I shouted, but the darned animal turned its head and almost smiled at me, as though the kick were some form of endearment, and wriggled up closer to the fire. I wondered what to do next, and got suddenly nervous wondering whether there was a herd of them out there, so I quickly went to shut the back door.

I could deal with one pig, but not a dozen, but this pig was not going to be so easy to deal with, smiling smugly as he stared into the fire. I know very little about pigs, but I could see he was not young, a sort of middle-aged pig and certainly a male. He was a dirty grey colour with a black patch on his back. He took no notice of me, just simply drooled with pleasure as he stared at the fire.

I crept back to the Windsor chair by the fire, still holding the poker. I was not taking too many chances; his small curly tail wagged like a dog's as I approached. He seemed friendly enough, so I stood and stared at him and he just opened one red eye and sort of sneered. So I gave him a shove with my foot again and he showed a line of yellow teeth in a positive snarl and moved over out of my reach, then proceeded to doze off to sleep.

Well, he's not going to move, I thought, he seemed determined to keep me company so I left him alone. By this time clouds of steam rose out of him as he roasted himself by the big fire, it mixed in with other smells like an old coconut out drying in the sun. He was not going to budge so I suppose even an old pig is better than no company.

So I started on my supper, reached for a bottle and he watched me; his small beady eyes had a kind of sly look in them. He watched me as I moved around the room. Bent over, with my key ring I took the top from my bottle of Guinness - it came off with a loud pop.

The effect on my piggy friend was startling; he rushed at me and butted me in the stomach with his long hairy snout. As I tried to regain my breath he started on the fallen bottle of Guinness and proceeded to gobble up the liquid as it poured out of the bottle. I could not believe my eyes and before I could stop him he had spotted my box of biscuits and was making short work of them.

'Why, you swine!' I yelled. 'You bloody swine!' My four letter words had no effect on him, but he showed his yellow teeth in a sort of devil grin and pushed the lid off the biscuit box and consumed them all, paper as well. Having enjoyed my supper, he then turned back to the fire, his nose uplifted to the heat. It was then the humour of the situation descended upon me. I started to laugh, long and heartily, and believe it or not the pig seemed to join in. He rolled over on his back, just like a pet dog does, waving his trotters in the air and inviting me to stroke his tummy. I dug him with my foot in a non – too - gentle manner, saying, 'Get out, you old rogue, you can't sleep here all night,' but he had no intention of removing his smelly old carcass from my fire.

'Alright, mate, I don't know about you, but I'm going to have a kip. Pig or devil, whatever you bloody, well are, stay if you feel inclined, but it's been a long, hard day for me.'

I found my grey overcoat, covered it over my knees and closed my eyes. The smell of the pig, the old coat combined with a string of odours, moth balls and lavender floor polish, lulled me to sleep.

. . . .

I woke in the grey light of dawn cold and stiff, the cold winds from the river had blown down my neck all night. The light had entered the window when I was awakened by another terrible racket, squealing and scratching; this time it was my friend the pig trying to get out. I opened the back door and helped him on his way with a push of my foot, and turned and found my way up the winding stairs to a cosy bedroom, and of all things - a goose down bed. It had been a long journey to find this place and little peace since I was here, so I just collapsed into the bed and was lost to the world.

I woke later in the day feeling very relaxed and I had a luxurious sort of feeling, having slept on a bed of soft down after that hard mattress in my lodgings, but it had been a deep slumber void of dreams and now I felt so refreshed, so different from the bleary eyed Mick, who often slept all day in bed too tired to get up for work. The sun came in through a small leaded window and green leaves of a climbing plant tapped on the panes, and in the low eaves the birds rustled and twittered in their nests. It was not so bad at all in the daylight, a kind of softness in the air and a silence that I was quite unused to: no traffic noises and no gabble of Pakistani voices as my neighbours got ready for work. Yes, it was good, I thought. I'm going to like it after all, you fell on your feet at last, Mick - I told myself.

It was a nice bedroom with old polished furniture and a patchwork quilt on the bed. There was a film of dust on it, but that was soon shifted. It wasn't a bad little pad really. I went to the window, my intention to take a long deep breath of clean fresh air. I opened the small window and looked out at the mountain scene and held my breath at the beauty. In a long, blue shadow, it dominated the landscape and all around was green fresh meadowland, and in the distance the silver gleams from a river. It was certainly very picturesque. I looked down into the small square paved yard in the middle of which was a pump, old fashioned with a large handle, and round it waltzed the pig.

He was almost human, seemed to be trying to turn it on. A strange grunting noise came forth and his little squiggly tail went backwards and forwards. At the sight of me he raised his snout and set up a terrific squealing. I covered my ears with my hands and yelled at him. 'Shut up, you darned old swine!' and I closed the window rapidly. Oh dear, I mused, he must live here. I suppose I have to feed him, I wonder what he eats?

I stared out the back door, not a sight or a sound of another human being. Cows mooed, birds sang and that blasted pig was now furiously charging the water pump and kicking up a frightful racket. I was beginning to think I was marooned and likely to starve to death, when I heard the clatter of a horse drawn cart. It drew up at the gate, and out of it dashed a boy with a big mop of tousled, ginger hair, carrying a bucket and running like a mad man down my path. He stooped half near the pump and sloshed the bucket of stuff into a trough and the old pig dived almost head first and positively wallowed in it.

I shouted over, so pleased was I to see another human.

'Can't stop!' shouted Ginger. 'Only came to feed Oikey. I've got to bring letters and papers from the village,' then he darted back to the gate, leapt onto the cart cowboy-fashion and rattled away. I was more hurt than shocked at such treatment, but at least Oikey got some breakfast. So that was its name, that was what that swine was called, I wondered if old Bridie kept him as a pet? Seemed as though it did live here I suppose, must have inherited the bloody beast.

Nonchalantly I wandered to the front door and in a basket on the step, was a fresh baked loaf, and a dozen eggs and a pint of cream, also a kind of covered can that contained milk. Well, who the devil put them there? I looked about me. Not a soul in sight, it must have been Ginger, wonder I never saw him.

I wandered about poking and prying, trying to get some law and order in the downstairs sitting room. I counted all the pots of jam on the larder shelf, fifty seven all old. Outside it looked silent and still, old

Oikey was snoring in his sty. I made scrambled eggs, and found the tea caddy at last, then, having eaten my fill I went to inspect my estate.

Under leaden grey skies the wide river flowed swift and silent. I walked about fifty yards, the green meadowland that looked so inviting through the window was bog land and I sank ankle deep in icy water, it filled my thin shoes. In front of me was a small mountain, a dark sombre shadow, not a cottage or a cow in sight. I turned up my coat collar against the bracing wind that had seemed like a calm breeze from inside, and plodded back to the house, passing Oikey snuggled down in the straw of his sty.

'Hallo, you old son,' I said, but never even received a grunt of acknowledgement. There was a long kitchen garden and a hut on it at the very end, but this I never bothered to explore, having had my fill of fresh air.

I lolled by the fire for a few hours, wondering what to do. There were no books or newspapers and I soon got sick of reading birthday greetings to Aunt Bridie. There was miles of fishing tackle and tangled lines, and the huge stuffed trophies seemed to stare insolently at me.

THE KENNEDY STORE

Ch.3

At midday the sun came out, so putting on an old pair of Wellingtons miles too large for me I trudged off down the road in search of civilisation. Down a long lane, then up on the hill, I immediately recognized Davey's, where the inhabitants gathered. The shamrock sign looked very inviting today, so in I went. Inside it was just the same: the lounging labourers holding up the bar, the same old men circled the table and Paddy Mac also held up the bar. No one seemed surprised or pleased to see me; they seemed to have lost interest. I got my glass filled and sat with the old fellows, who talked all the time. Only some of it I understood. It was mostly talk of the weather or the Gee - Gees. I did remark that it was a long walk from Inshallalee, only to be asked: 'Has not Daneen come back with the old banger?'

I shook my head, having no idea who Daneen was, or his banger. They began a heated argument among themselves, the gist of it being that Daneen had gone off to Cork City on a real right bender.

At three o'clock when my head and my tummy felt heavy with the weight of the ale, I walked out into the pale sunlight, feeling lost and rather dazed. The scene outside was still reminiscent of a cowboy film set: an empty street, a dirt road, line of shacks and a feeling of watching eyes. I then spied a little shop. Over the door was written: 'The Kennedy Sisters' – 'Groom and provisions'. I cheered up. At last I'd go and buy cigarettes and stock up my cupboard. I am very tall, six foot two in fact, and rather narrow and have always been nervously conscious of this.

When I got inside this small expanse of space, I did not know which direction was likely to do less damage. The little shop was stocked with packets and tins all stacked very neatly and very high, but hardly any room to move around. Overhead ladies smalls swung like flags. I bent to enter the array and almost jumped out of my skin when I heard the long clanger and jangle of bells attached to the door. I turned and hit a stack of packets that came tumbling down, and then turned to pick them up and got tangled in a row of frilly knickers linked together, that settled on my head. Then I staggered frantically into a pile of tinned soups that ran over the floor like live things.

The three Kennedy Sisters stood looking in amazement as I wrecked their shop. I stood before them involved in a forest of small ladies' bloomers and baby pants that hung over my head. I moved them aside, knocked off my spectacles, bent to retrieve them and in a matter of seconds there was chaos as I staggered into a pile of boxes and was assailed by packets of cornflakes. I managed to pick up my specs, and my red and confused face stared apologetically through the legs of a baggy pair of bloomers that seemed to have settled on my head.

Three very startled ladies, who stood behind the small counter, gazed in horror while I wrecked their shop further; although, they soon began to laugh very heartily. My face got redder and I looked for the entrance ready to make a run for it, until one lady lifted up the flap of the counter and said: 'Why, if it isn't Mick O'Hara arrived in style.'

Well, I was relieved at last that someone welcomed me, and Mae, one of the sisters said: 'Glory Be to God, what's he doing to the goods out there?' and a chorus of giggles rang out as they stacked the boxes back up.

'Come along in, Mick,' a pleasant voice urged, 'get inside, man, before you do any more damage.'

Soon I was installed in a cosy room, a cup of tea and hot potato cake beside me and in their rich, hearty voices the Kennedy Sisters bade me welcome.

There was Mae, Babs and Lillie, all looking very much alike, their ages ranging between forty and fifty: red - gold hair, freckles and lovely teeth, and the most pleasant personalities I had so far met.

'We are cousins on your mother's side,' they told me. 'We never married, no one ever asked us, all the men we knew went off to England.'

I spent a very pleasant afternoon being stuffed with tea and potato cakes, while they explained, that I was a second cousin of theirs on my mother's side, descended from a great chieftain called O'Hara, and so was half the rest of the population.

'Tis always grand to see an O'Hara come home to roost,' said Mae, 'aye, there's many 'O'Hara's in these parts.'

'Tis a foine tall boy ye are, Mick, Bridie would have been mighty proud of ye,' added the one called Babs.

I gave them a big order for food, as they insisted I needed all these goods.

'Shall I pay now?' I asked. They looked amazed.

'No,' said Mae, 'Bridie paid only on settling up day, we will go on the same way, Mick.'

So, all cash was refused. It seemed they carried on a sort of exchange and barter system. Bridie, not wishing to bother with all her relations, held a family party once a year and every one settled up. I begged them to explain and was astonished to hear that Aunt Bridie was related to most people in the village and only bought from them. Not wanting to be bothered with visitors, she had one day a year, settling her debts, when she threw a kind of family party. It sounded like the middle ages, but at least I would not starve. They told that she had been eighty two, and still standing in the river fishing most days of her life, before she died: the sight of her in an old trilby hat and mackintosh was one of the landmarks of the district.

'She lived out there all alone?' I asked.

'Except for Daneen,' replied Babs, but Mae put a warning finger to her lips and the conversation flagged, no one seemed to want to talk about this mysterious Daneen. I was beginning to wonder why? Davey Joe would bring up the groceries, I was told and, as I expected, he was also a cousin and between them Davey Joe and Paddy Mac handled all the transportation of visitors from the station, Paddy Mac being in the important position of station master.

Well, it had certainly been a rewarding afternoon. I plodded back up the road in my two large Wellington boots. Perhaps it was not going to be so bad after all, how could I be lonely with all those relations in the village? Feeling more optimistic, I felt my way down the path as it had now begun to get dark.

THE ELUSIVE DANEEN

Ch.4

Just inside the house I stumbled over something. Things moved under my feet. I got up and went down several times, and eventually I struck a match and saw that a big sack of potatoes lay in the path. The top had been ripped and half eaten spuds lay everywhere.

'It's that bloody pig,' I muttered, 'wait 'til I get my hands on him.'

I staggered as the potatoes rolled under my feet. Down on my back I went, shouting and swearing. As fast as I struggled to get up, these objects crammed my path and down I went again. In the end I scrambled on hands and knees and lit the lamp and all around me were these potatoes; half chewed ones rolled everywhere and I sat there wondering how the sack of spuds came to be there. Stumbling into the living room, I was wondering who had put the spuds there and went over to the fire that had been freshly made up, and there was a new peat block stacked at the side. Who the devil was this, an invisible thing – a pig could not replenish a fire.

I sat brooding, for whoever it was avoided me like the plague, and might be the mysterious Daneen that I had heard mentioned. By hell, tomorrow I was determined to find out. The fire blazed brightly and suddenly, in rushed Oikey fussing and fretting like the white rabbit in 'Alice in Wonderland'. He's going to start looking at his watch in a second, I thought, then pulled myself up quickly. 'Blimey, I'll go barmy if I stand much more of this.' I struck out at Oikey with a big foot. 'Scram you fat, stinking swine!' I said viciously, but Oikey only settled closer to the fire. 'Ate all the spuds, didn't yer,' I gave him another kick, but his small eyes looked wickedly at me. So I moved back nervously and went looking for something to drink. I found a bottle marked 'potato wine' that looked, and smelt and tasted like whiskey.

'Ah, well, I suppose a bloody pig is good as anyone,' and I settled down to drink from the bottle. 'What are you, pig or bloody devil?' I said to Oikey. It was all too much. Pigs don't light fires, even if they enjoy the comfort of them. Someone was mooching about here and did not want to meet me, one to one, but why?

In the early dawn I came back to life – the potion had proved too strong for my own constitution. I had relapsed into complete oblivion spending the night huddled in the wooden armchair. I was stiff all over and the back of my neck had the most painful crick in it. My companion Oikey had managed to ram the back door open as he returned to his warm sty, leaving me to wallow in the cold wet mist that floated in and out of the bog once the fire died down. I walked stiffly towards the pump, and having doused my head with the ice cold water, hurled many a curse into the direction of Oikey's sty.

Wanting to refresh myself in the morning air, I went for a walk and sat by the long winding river and later walked around the old stone cottages and the church, but there was little else to see. There was a drizzle of rain in the air. As I passed the farm workers they waved, but I seem to have travelled in a circle, for in no time I was back at my own front door and down in the bottom of the garden a tall, lean figure was digging the ground. At last I had come upon the elusive Daneen.

'Good morning!' I called out.

Daneen turned and stared.

'You must be Aunt Bridie's helper,' I said, feeling embarrassed at the man's stare. With that, he turned away, his head down. 'It's a nice day,' I remarked cheerfully as I approached him, but his only response was a sort of grunt and, without looking up again, he continued to dig.

'I'm Mick 'O'Hara,' I continued. 'I've inherited this land from my Aunt Bridie. I believe she was a friend of yours.'

'Aye, a friend for some,' was the doleful answer. I stood looking at this handyman I had inherited. He was very tall, thin, with skin the colour of dried bark. His eyes were small and close set and streaked with tiny red veins. Too much booze, I thought. As I stood looking, he took not the slightest notice of me, his clothes were very old and earth stained, and about his neck tied in a sailor's knot was a red handkerchief- his dark hair streaked with grey hung out over his collar and a battered felt hat completed the picture. Slowly and deliberately he turned the earth, bringing up large white skinned potatoes.

'Lovely looking spuds,' said I, trying to make conversation. No response. He just put down the spade and from his pocket he brought out a little black pipe and a small tin, and his earthy fingers rammed the dark shag into the bowl while he stared at me all the time without uttering a word. I began to feel very uncomfortable, slightly hot and embarrassed, while his eyes peered straight into mine with a hostile expression.

'Well,' I said, 'I'll go have a cup of tea – like to join me?'

His words came out deep and hoarse from a mouth that was just a slit in his face. 'Don't take tea,' he said. 'You're the master, I'm the labourer. Keep to your end, and I'll stick to mine.'

Feeling rather dejected, I said: 'Okay, suits me,' and I turned and went back inside the cottage.

Now, what to do, I was not sure the day was young yet. So I tried to tidy the sitting room; a hopeless task, and the books on fishing I burned and watched the fire blaze merrily. I was beginning to get dry so I resumed my seat beside Oikey, his smelly old company as good as any, I suppose. I was feeling very fed up and it was then that I remembered the potatoes in the cupboard and decided to have some. Oikey watched me with his usual arrogance.

'Hop it,' I said, 'it's not evening yet,' and I moved my bottle carefully out of sight, but Oikey just sneered and settled smugly on the mat. After one or two more goes at the bottle I began to feel sorry for myself. 'Here you are, Mick,' says I, 'stuck in this God forsaken hole, where people treat you like a leper and only a dirty, smelly pig for company. I wonder who would buy a bog and half a mountain.'

So I sat drinking and commiserating with myself feeling a little frustrated, nothing much seemed to happen around here, no noise, that deathly silence outside. I began to long for the roar of the traffic and the hideous gabble of Pakistani neighbours in London. Any life was better than nothing – and that bloody smelly pig.

I must have dozed off for a while and it might have been the effects of the potent wine, but I awoke feeling aggressive, and looked down at Oikey sleeping like a baby snuffling and grunting in his sleep.

'It's all - your fault,' I snarled at him, 'never sell this place while you're here.' I looked at him again. 'No, I won't have your death on my conscience. I'll take you and lose you or push you in the river, that's what I'll do.'

Oikey was oblivious to my threats; just went on snoring, so I sat racking my brains on the best way to dispose of the horrible pig. The potato wine was very strong, in fact it tasted just like whiskey, and after several more cups full I began to snarl and swear at Oikey, poking him in the ribs, viciously. At first he did not protest, but when I was unprepared for his onslaught, he grabbed the leg of my trousers and with an evil grin ripped them down from the knee, then with a satisfied expression he waddled out.

'Why, you bastard!' I roared, trying to get up, but the potent wine had taken effect. I could not rise; my legs seemed to have detached from my body. So I continued to drink, singing songs, and my voice sounded very distant, swearing that in the morning I'd take Oikey to the knackers yard, sell this bloody bog-land and go to the States. Shortly after that I passed out, waking once more cold and stiff, realising it was morning. I had spent another night at my Irish manor

THE OLD BANGER

Ch.5

My head felt like a big pumpkin, so I tried putting my head under the pump - with one hand I pumped the handle and with the other I threw cold water over my head and onto my face. But Oikey, who was wandering about the yard as always and seemed to think, it was some new kind of game, came joyfully over and butted me in the backside. With my head hanging, he sidled back and forth between me and the pump until I was soaked. The water got in my eyes and I could not find the towel or my spectacles. Eventually I kicked Oikey all the way back to his sty and put on my specs, then to my amazement outside the front gate stood an old Ford Estate car. I waited for someone to step out of it.

I whistled and called, but no one came, and I wondered if this was something to do with Daneen, but I did not want to go near him again. It was not a bad little car and I wondered who owned it.

Furtively looking from side to side, I got in and turned the key. She started off first go. Then, feeling like a highway robber, I revved it up and cruised down the lane out onto the road, and went on a merry jaunt in my stolen car, realising suddenly that I was out of gas. Near the pub was a little shop with one pump outside, and from a workshop at the side emerged my cousin, the red robust Davey. He came out with shirt sleeves rolled up and oil on his face and hands.

'Hallo there!' he called loudly. 'Got the old banger back, I see.' I stared at him for a moment wondering guiltily if he was the owner, while he began to fill the tank, still talking all the time. 'Got the old banger back, I see, dry as a bone she is. Don't know why old Bridie didn't get a decent car, all the money she had.'

'You mean to tell me it's Aunt Bridie's car?' I gasped. 'So, it's mine?'

'Must be, Bridie left you the lot, didn't she?'

I sensed something spiteful, but made no comment.

'Look here,' I said, 'where's it been?' In the back of my mind I wondered, if that- Daneen, had brought it back.

'Daneen took it up the city - must have got it back last night.'

So it was Daneen after all who took the car, what a cheek. He didn't even have the audacity to mention it. These people had a funny way of going on.

'I saw him up the garden,' I remarked to Davey, 'he did not seem to have much to say for himself.'

'Oh, he'll be alright once he's sobered up,' said Davey nonchalantly.

Davey went back indoors, and I felt chuffed with the car and returned to Inshallalee, resolving in my mind a plan to rid me of that pig. The old Ford was just the job for transporting pigs, being an old type Estate it had a wide back door. I'd lure him into it and if I could not get the butcher to have him, I'd dump him in a field, miles from nowhere.

It was a bit early for Oikey, he usually arrived at dusk, but I stoked up the fire and rattled bottles and saucepans to induce him to come in. He came at last covered in mud and grunting with pleasure at the sight of the fire, settled himself before it, clouds of steam rising from him as he dried off. But the trap was already laid. In the centre was a large round table and on it reposed a dark red cloth: sort of very thick material and a line of bobbles round it. I placed this carefully on the floor and tied string to its four corners, then, putting some of Oikey's favourite biscuits in the centre, I sat waiting patiently. At first I tried persuasion.

'Come on, old boy,' I said, 'Come Oikey, nice cakes.'

But he only eyed me scornfully and still sat browsing by the fire. Then I pretended to go out of the door and as soon as I 'went' he got up and waddled under the table and snorting and shuffling, consumed the biscuits. I was on him fast. I pulled the strings tight and brought him down with a rugby tackle. The noise he kicked up was indescribable. He rolled over and over and I kept pulling the strings tighter, then with much hard endeavour I dragged him all trussed up out to the old banger and aimed him inside. I leapt in and revved it up, and feeling very pleased with myself, set off down the road to find the knackers yard, or a nice deserted spot in which to dump him.

EILEEN KENNEDY

Ch.6

It had just begun to get dark - a kind of pink grey twilight, and later along the road a white mist rose up. I was not expecting to see anyone on this usually uninhabited stretch of country road, so I swerved madly, nearly ending up in a ditch, when a white clad figure stepped out almost in front of me; hand raised as though wanting a lift, and a voice as sweet as an angel said: 'I'm sorry, Mick, I startled you, but I want a lift down to the school house, I'm late for the music lesson.'

Startled was not the word, I just stared stupidly as this lovely apparition got in and settled herself beside me. I peeped slyly at her long red-gold hair and the fine chiselled features, and when she turned her head and smiled, those dimples and white even teeth made my heart hit the roof of the car, and this lovely being, real or unreal, had called me by my name.

'Don't stare like that,' she protested with a giggle, 'I'm Eileen Kennedy. I live at the farm.'

In her smart short white mac and perfect fitting tight trousers she looked lovely, and I would never have taken her for a country girl. 'How do you know me?' I stuttered.

'Oh, everyone knows you, you're Mick O'Hara, Aunt Bridie's nephew,' she kind of scoffed at me.

So I lapsed into silence – another close cousin, how disappointing. I had forgotten Oikey and took little notice of the grunting and scuffling in the back until he thrust his hairy snout in between me and this lovely young girl, and in a soft, sweet voice she said: 'Oh, Oikey, darling!' and delivered a kiss on his face. Well, you could have knocked me over the steering wheel, I was so disturbed.'What is oo doing Oikey, darling, out for a ride with your new daddy?' asked Eileen of that rotten old devil, and he protested and grunted as though trying to inform her of my treatment of him.

I had never been very good at chatting up girls, and here I was with this beauty sitting right next to me, her golden hair shining in the sunlight, and I was finding it difficult to get any attention – that rotten pig was getting it all.

I could see her stroking those long, pink ears, she was treating him like a pet dog, and that gormless expression on his face, why, it was pathetic.

'Have you been a good boy?' she whispered to him, resting her face on that rubbery snout, and I saw her full mouth ripple with laughter as she booed and cooed at him.

I looked at her white skin above the neckline of her blouse as her mackintosh gaped open, at those high little bosoms and I could only listen, completely captivated as she told me about her life on the farm. I was beginning to change my impression about this place, knowing I had a neighbour such as her.

Feeling jealous, I narrowed my eyes at Oikey, telling myself that all I had to do was get rid of him, then I'd have Eileen all to myself, but now I knew I had to dismiss any thoughts of pig trotters for tea. 'You're stuck with the beast,' I muttered when I suddenly felt a sharp jab in my back from him, and had to suppress a string of swear words.

'Now stop that, Oikey,' cried Eileen, pulling him back. 'Mick is trying to drive.'

Then I had to witness him being gently scolded. 'Now, now, Oikey,' she said, wagging her finger, 'you must calm down.'

Calm down? I thought. I'll calm him down alright.

When finally I did get her attention, she turned and watched me drive and I felt those Celtic green eyes looking me over, full of questions.

'You must get a little lonely out at the cottage. It gets very dark at night around here.'

'Oh, I've got Oikey,' I replied, forcing a smile, 'he's great company.'

'Can you drop me at the school gates?' she asked, as the car bumped along the stony uneven road towards the village.

The journey was difficult, the car cutting out in places and the pig making a racket, and I felt myself getting worked up as I turned the key several times trying to get the car to move. It had come to a halt on the hill, but Eileen took it all in her stride.

'I'd say Daneen has worn the old banger out now,' she said in good humour, 'I see him up and down this road, off to the pub.'

I was amazed how everyone seemed to know what went on. Was there no privacy? Then one more rev and the car started.

'Hoorah!' she said to Oikey, who oiked with a kind of answer. 'Have you seen Daneen?' she asked me.

'Sort of,' I replied, wanting to say, 'what, that old misery' but, dared not.

'Can't understand why he even lives there,' I remarked, showing my irritation. 'No one seems to explain it to me.'

Eileen gave a little twist of a smile. 'Typical Irish, that is,' she said, 'I'm best to stay out of it.'

So even the lovely Eileen was being evasive, but I let it pass, for I was fascinated by her lovely golden freckles, her bare arms that came so close as she stroked Oikey, and the faint smell of lavender came from her presence.

We reached the other side of the hill: there was a cold mist and an East wind blowing.

Eileen spotted the Kennedy farm in the valley. 'That land,' she said, looking out across the fields with a warm light in her eyes, 'that's our farm! We Kennedys have been here for generations, there's, a lot of us in these parts, like the 'O'Hara's. My father works all that land. See that field yonder?' she pointed towards my place, 'that was once old Bridie's field, but she leased it to my father.'

'You mean that's my field?' I asked her. I was wondering whose sheep were grazing on that high ridge. I was relieved they were not mine.

'So,' Eileen said coyly, moving a little closer, 'it's all your land now, Mick 'O'Hara,' and for the first time I was feeling like a landowner. 'But, I'd say,' said Eileen, as if she wondered whether she should say it or not, 'even farmers have to keep their place a little tidy, for I couldn't help noticing the other day when I came that Oikey had the whole bag of potatoes out over the floor.'

'It was you, then!' I exclaimed with surprise.

'Of course, who do you think it is now who's been lighting your fire?'

I could only thank her and apologise for the mess.

'But it was Oikey,' I found myself saying like a naughty school boy telling tales.

'I know that,' she giggled, 'but are you coping with him, that's what I'm saying? 'Cause, I know your Aunt Bridie spoilt him, he was more like a pet dog.'

'I can see that,' I told her, 'he likes to sit around the fire every night, and pushes me out,' I confessed.

'Well now, we can't have that,' said Eileen, and she gazed at Oikey in a silent reproach that made him back off nervously.

Good, I thought, glad he had got told off, and I smiled jubilantly, it was almost like a competition between us. You're being ridiculous, I told myself, but couldn't resist telling Eileen how the pig ate my supper. 'I did shut him out, but he came charging back in again, it was all I had in the cupboard.'

'Oh dear,' Eileen said with a smirk, 'I'd say that old Oikey has got it in for you, Mick, you must have rubbed him up the wrong way.'

Rubbed him up the wrong way? I wanted to shout, and I wished she wouldn't talk about the blighter like he was human.

'Even my brother, Ginger, said Oikey was kicking up a fuss.'
So it was her brother who was bringing the supplies, it seems the Kennedys were everywhere.

'So I was thinking,' said Eileen, sitting on the edge of her seat as the school house came in view, 'I don't mind giving you a hand with old Oikey.'

That was the best thing I'd heard all day, to have this beautiful creature come and rescue me from this beast.

Eileen started to wave to a young boy as I pulled up outside the school. He was waiting by a square stone building, its chimney stood lopsided in the skyline; the hazy sun twinkled in the red bricks.

'Hi, Tommy,' she called, 'I'm just coming! I'm a bit late with his piano lesson,' she informed me. 'I teach part-time here, but if you like I'll come and help you with Oikey on my day off. I know his ways, in fact Aunt Bridie was going to mate him, perhaps that's what he needs, a wife. That will soon keep him in hand, won't it, Oikey, dear,' and she giggled, patting his head farewell.

'Will you really come and help me?' I stammered.

'Of course,' she said, and looked at me with some amusement, then gently reached and gave my hand a quick squeeze. 'See you next week,' she said, slamming the door, and went off to meet the young boy who stood impatiently by the school fence under a tall display of hollyhocks. I watched her go; how silent it all seemed without her, she was like a whirlwind. With her arm over the small boy's shoulder, she walked briskly up the path, disappearing out of view under a red tiled porch. I found myself sitting there, waiting like a dumbstruck schoolboy for a little wave, and when it came - I waved frantically back through the open car window.

'It's me she waved at,' I sneered at Oikey, not caring, for now I could have it out with him, and I jabbed him in the ribs. The pig snorted obstinately, then scampered to the back of the car, but at last I felt that things were changing, and relaxed with a sigh. 'Calm down, you old beast,' I said to Oikey, 'you've got a reprieve, if Eileen's coming to help me with you. You've got your uses after all, mate.'

The pig grunted, but would not settle down. I didn't care, I was happy thinking of Eileen. I turned the car around and headed back, whistling a little tune, and saying to Oikey, 'You stay out of my way, mate, and I'll stay out of yours.'

LOVE TAKES OVER

Ch.7

The next week Eileen came to the cottage. I had been lounging around reading, the remains of a meal left on the side, bottles of beer - and cold ashes, lay in the fire: the place was a mess.

'Top of the morning to you, Mick,' she said, her red cheeks glowing from the fresh air. She looked me over with a radiant smile. 'Now, how are you, Oikey?' she said, looking him over. He had pushed his way between us. 'Why, Oikey, you look as though you need a good wash.'That was an under- statement, that pig had wallowed in the mud and traipsed it over the mat.'Now, you can't have him in the house all the time,' she moaned, showing him the door, and I couldn't believe how obediently he went.

All around the room there was a layer of dust. Eileen turned up her nose as she looked the place over. 'Well, I won't ask you what you'll be doing, Mick O'Hara, I can see there's plenty to do here.'

I stood there gaping, not taking my eyes off that lovely presence.

'And you look as though you need a shave for a start,' she said, rolling up her sleeves and, picking up the bottles, she aimed them into the bin with a resounding crash, then picked up the broom, and brushed down the cobwebs that were in the corners. 'You need taking in hand,' she said with some amusement.

Before the day was out, she had the cottage spick and span, with Oikey looking all pink and glowing after a rub down. I was amazed at her energy as she cleared the grate and proceeded to put in order the disarray, while she hummed an Irish tune.

As the weeks passed she started to say: 'I've made you a little supper this week.' Then one day when I came in, she said: 'I'm taking your washing back to the farm to do, it all needs a good soak,' and off she went with my bundle of dirty clothes. I used to feel a bit embarrassed, but it was her way of taking over. It wasn't long before she was looking at the old wallpaper and paintwork and screwing up her freckled nose in disgust. 'It's about time you did this place up.'

As the months went by I longed to see her more and more. What a pleasure to have that cheerful little body bossing me and Oikey around, and there was always a nice peat fire blazing, with a cooked meal with a plate over it, kept hot on the stove. It was usually a weekly treat of spuds in their jackets, boiled bacon and cabbage, or sometimes stew cooked on the aga with a note on the side saying: 'I've taken a bowl up to Daneen' but I didn't find that so pleasing as he was still as ignorant as ever.

Sometimes I would sit at the window waiting for her weekly arrival, so pleased to see her coming across the field, her golden hair blowing, swinging her basket that was usually filled with cheese or butter from the farm. She always walked so quickly, and I would climb quickly away from the window in case she saw me looking.

I was beginning to fall for her, and would stare at her as she spoke, looking into those large green eyes that used to seem to me as deep as the lake of Killarney. They were forever changing colour.

'What you looking at, Mick O'Hara?' she would say with a little grin, and I would feel myself going red. 'Not enough work to do, that's your trouble, and she proceeded to dust around, giving me a knowing glare.

'You need to get out in the fresh air,' she said one day as I watched her going about her chores, those hips moving from side to side, but she soon put me in my place, getting me to follow her out into the small walled garden to do some work. In her sun hat she worked away at the vegetables, gently digging out the weeds with a hoe, while I was told to clear up the rubbish - old bikes and tools, putting them in the shed. It took a while, but once it was all cleared, she brought plants from the farm and planted rows of potatoes and cabbages in the small plot, then stood with pride at the kitchen door, looking it all over: her long hair tied up in a knot on top of her head, her hands blackened with the earth, and she rubbed them over her scruffy apron and smiled jubilantly, her eyes roaming with pleasure over the little garden, and I felt I wanted to grab her and kiss her there and then.

'You have a smudge on your nose,' I said to her, coming closer, but she only wiped it with the back of her hand and in her bossy way said: 'Keep Oikey off the plants, and you'll have to make sure you keep the gate shut.'Once Oikey was mentioned, my ardour was crushed. 'And make sure,' she continued, 'that you give them plenty of water. I know what you're like, Mick.'

So I was not surprised when one day she suggested I did some work for her father over at their farm. She had been standing in front of the sink washing the dishes and the house was quiet, except for the rattle of plates as she stacked them in the cupboard. 'Got a nice steak for your tea tonight, Mick,' she said, turning and giving me a warm smile. 'I've been thinking, seeing as you don't seem to have much work, you might like to help my pa with the potato crop.'

Goodness, I thought, how do I get out of this one? I felt more than obliged, these Kennedys had looked after me, but I dreaded the thought of digging for spuds.

'How long is it for?' I asked tentatively. 'I like to do my journal in the afternoons.'

Eileen raised her eyebrows and tossed her hair. 'Well, I'd say that it will get you nowhere writing in that book, sitting in that stuffy room.'

I felt a bit hurt by this remark, but she seemed to soften. 'Well, you can't live on dreams, Mick,' she said more tenderly. 'And you'll be well paid,' her soft brogue went on, and a sweet smile hovered on her lips, 'you could even get yourself some nice things for this cottage.'
So how could I refuse? 'Okay,' I said, 'if it's only for a few weeks.'

'Oh, Mick,' she said, coming over and putting her arms round my neck.

I found myself looking longingly down on those full red lips.

She stood on her tip toes, being that I was so tall. I wondered what to do next, when she quickly planted a big kiss on my cheek. 'You won't regret it, she said, pulling quickly away, just as I was going to grab hold of that lovely little body and squeeze her tight.

So I ask you, how does a man stand a chance? 'Tell your dad I'll start on Monday,' I told her.

MY LOVE

Ch.8

So, stuck with the job, I was soon out in the early morning before daylight, working in the fields. My back ached when I got home, and one week's work had led into another, as after the potato's came the cabbages, then the carrots, then I was asked to help clean in the cowshed. There seemed no escaping these Kennedys.

In their large farmhouse kitchen I would be invited at about eleven o'clock for a cup of tea, pleased to go into the warmth and have a break, but this particular day there was a group of ladies from the 'Village Guild' sitting on the sofa under the big window that looked out across the fields. Mrs Kennedy was doing her best to entertain them, and on seeing me at the kitchen door, said: 'Come on in, Mick,' and she introduced me to the ladies as Eileen's boyfriend.

'Oh,' said one grey haired lady with a florid complexion, 'she's a fine lass, you be courting.'

'Now, sit at the table, Mick, and have your tea,' said Mrs Kennedy, 'we'll not be interfering with you.'

The women sat around making lace and talking quietly, while I looked out the window half dreaming and sipped my tea. I could see several cows, and a bull had wandered over, and was right outside this window. The bull suddenly mounted a cow and proceeded to make a groaning sound that was becoming very unpleasant. I could see him moving up and down on the cow's back, his big black head over hers. I was wondering whether the women realised what this noise was. I could see their ears pricking up and one or two were looking around anxiously. As the cries of mating could be heard, they chatted away, but as the groans got so overpowering, faces changed, and the conversation flagged; a silence descended: the only other sound the chink of tea cups. Poor Mrs Kennedy looked very embarrassed.

As the groaning noise from the bull was slowly getting louder and louder as he tried to reach a climax, I felt myself going red too, and it seemed that all eyes were on me, being the only male in the room. Two of the ladies started tittering behind their hankies. I didn't know whether to titter myself, but some warning looks were coming from some of the ladies, right at me. I couldn't think why they were picking on me – because I'm the male here, I suppose.

Then suddenly from the bull there came a long roar like a lion's, which was enough to unnerve anyone. One old lady fell off her chair, and they had to hoist her up again. Very slowly this roar subsided into a long, slow simpering. I breathed a sigh of relief - it seemed the old bull had finally made it. I was glad he got there, even if I never did, but while this simpering was going on, it was getting all too embarrassing in the room. These sounds   now resembled a tune played on a trumpet.

'I think I'll have my tea,' I said, breaking the silence. I was feeling very uncomfortable.

I was relieved when the farmer rushed in with one Wellington boot on, the other still in his hand. 'My goodness,' he said, unabashed. 'Did you hear that old bull?' and the ladies faces broke out in faint little smiles. 'I tell you, I wouldn't trust that old bull as far as I could throw him,' he said.

Mrs Kennedy looked relieved it was all over, and came over to lift my tea cup away. 'What did you think of that?' she said with a saucy wink.

I shrugged, not knowing what to say.

'Well,' she whispered, a slow smile hanging on her lips, 'I thought that old bull sounded just like him on a good night,' and I looked at Mr Kennedy and wondered. I was a bit surprised at the buxom Mrs Kennedy, but then Eileen could be straight talking.

'We're close to nature, us people', Eileen had said. 'Earthy.' And evidently Eileen's mother was too. She wiped over the table top, then, put her fingers to her mouth. 'Of course, don't tell the 'Ladies' Guild'

I said so.' And she tittered. 'More tea, ladies?' she called.

As I left, I could see the group was now restored. The ladies spoke in whispers, laughing amongst themselves, but I avoided going in there for my tea in future. It had all been a nervous strain, they were certainly very frisky the animals round here. Strange creatures, women, I thought, and I wondered if I understood the old bull more.

I knew I'd be relieved when the work finished at the farm, I was getting fed up with the early starts; I was nearly always late. But I went to please Eileen, and I was so eager to impress her. I loved it when she would stay on some evenings waiting for me to come home and greet me with a warm, sympathetic voice.

'Well now, our Mick's been working hard all day, so get away from the fire, Oikey, and give him some space.'

I was surprised one evening coming in exhausted to find she had filled the bath-tub in front of the blazing peat fire and told me to get all my clothes off and get in. I wasn't sure what was going on.

'It's alright, Mick,' she said, her hands on her hips, 'I won't bite,' then she turned her head away behind a huge towel, holding it up with a little smile hovering on her lips.   'Now get in that foine hot water before it goes on you, and give me a shout when you've finished, but if your back is after needing a rub, I'll do that too,' she teased.

'It's all right,' I found myself saying, 'I can manage.'

I could hear her chuckling as she sailed out of the parlour, and although I was anxious to prove my manhood, I suddenly felt I was not in control. 'I'll take your dirty washing home!' she called out.

I was beginning to feel like a stripped patient, but laid back into that steaming hot tub for a long soak, thoroughly enjoying it, except for the fact I could hear Oikey snorting as he leaned up against the side of the bath for warmth.

'Your turn next, you old git,' I hissed at him, then, chucked a handful of water over his snout, leaving him shaking it off with an unfriendly grunt.

Afterwards I was served some hot kippers on a little tray and then I lay stretched out in front of a nice log fire, watching the smoke curl up the chimney. I felt like a king with Eileen sitting on the settee beside me. We talked about my day on the farm, about ideas for doing up the cottage, and I was getting such a longing for her. I could not help constantly looking at her high bosom as she leant forward, and I watched those shapely legs as they crossed, one knee over the other. She wore neat green shoes with ankle straps, and I wanted to reach out and touch that slim ankle. I was beginning to feel very uncomfortable and suddenly sat up. I could feel beads of sweat on my brow.

'Don't you think you're sitting a little close to that fire?' she said, looking at me curiously.

So I got away from the fire and sat beside her. She was looking at me so deeply with those green eyes, and I felt a tremor run between us. It was then that she smoothed her hand over my forehead. 'Why, you need an early night, Mick 'O'Hara, I think you could have a cold coming on.'

I knew something had come on, alright, and it wasn't a cold, and she wasn't making matters any better by placing her soft, slim hands upon my forehead. I found myself suddenly grabbing that white hand and holding it to my lips, smothering it with kisses, then suddenly realising what I'd done, and immediately let it go

'Whatever were you doing?' said Eileen with a giggle. ''Tis a foine thing you kissing my hand, Mick, but if you want to kiss my lips - it's okay by me,' and she smiled coyly.

Just what I thought and something stirred deep within me. She was now pouting her lips and closing her eyes. I immediately pressed my lips onto hers, holding her tightly in my arms. The kiss went on for a while then she slowly and gently pushed me away.

'That will be enough for tonight now, Mick.' But I could see her eyes were smouldering and wanted more. 'Why, Mick,' she said, getting up, her round face red like a polished apple. 'You've made me feel all funny.' I felt more than funny myself, and didn't want her to go, but she waved a warning finger. 'I must get home,' she said in a hoarse whisper, reaching for her coat. I was relieved she was not annoyed. She even seemed quite pleased, I thought. 'I'll see you on Tuesday,' she said, 'and perhaps I'll stay for tea.'

When she left I wanted to jump for joy. 'She likes me a lot!' I cried to old Oikey, who only opened one eye and looked very bored with the situation.

All that night I could not sleep for thinking of her.

COURTING STRONG

Ch.9

Within six months we settled down to a relationship. Eileen would stay on some evenings and we would canoodle on the settee, passionate kisses were often acceptable, but I would get carried away and reach out and caress those small bud-like breasts, then Eileen would pull away, her cheeks flushed, and hold down her skirt.

'You behave yourself', she would tell me, and I would sulk for a while thinking what a tease she was. But then she had said very gently, 'I shall stay a virgin for the man I marry,' and at times I was almost on the point of asking her to marry me, but something held me back. I wondered if it was because I'd been on my own since my mother died, and I was quite at home in my own company, and could I cope with all the demands a woman would make?

There won't be any more lounging about all day, I knew that.

One evening as we sat quietly on the settee, I asked her if she ever heard of my mother.

'Oh, yes,' she said, 'it was before my time, but I remember,' she smiled, 'there was always a little story about her . . . you know how stories came through the generations.'

'Tell me,' I said, putting my arm around her.

'I heard that she ran off to London with Tim O Hara, who was Bridie's brother, he brought her to live on the farm. When they did get married, it was only for a short while, as his plane was shot down and he was killed. I thought it was sad,' Eileen continued, 'falling in love, then, he was killed. So, I guess that man was your father then, Mick. He must have been a foine man.'

'Yes,' I told her, 'but he died when I was very young, hardly knew him,' and I went to the sideboard drawer to get the medal my mother had given me.

'Look,' I said, handing it to her, 'this was his medal.'

'It's beautiful,' she said, turning it over in her hand, 'you must be proud.'She was thoughtful for a moment; her long lashes veiled her eyes as she looked at the medal.

I watched her, and caressed her hair, but I was remembering the photograph of Tim 'O'Hara: it was always on our dresser when I was a lad, and I would stare fascinated at the gold wings, embossed on the medal. "It's the spitfire badge", my mother used to say, clutching the photo with tears in her eyes. As I got old enough I asked her if he was my father, but she never gave me a direct answer, just said: "Your father was a brave soldier", giving me the medal to hold as if it would comfort me in some way. So I would look at that photograph, study that short figure in a uniform with his long sideburns and thick red curly hair, and I used to think that I never looked like him at all.

I was brought back from my reverie, as Eileen's hand clutched mine. 'Now cheer up, Mick.' She smiled and snuggled into my chest. 'That story has made you sad, but it was no secret, I thought you knew.'

'But I never knew my mother worked on the farm.'

'Yes, it was a working farm this place, when your grandfather ran it. Your mother was the milkmaid, I hear, and they used to employ lads to work on the land. Why, that's how Daneen came to live here, it's the only real home he ever had, I heard.'

'So he was here too, then?'

'So they say, but wasn't your mother a nurse?'

'Yes, she told me she wouldn't like to work on a farm, and assumed she hadn't,' I said, 'and she trained at the London Hospital.' And as I spoke of her, that old melancholy feeling came sweeping over me, and I remembered how my lovely mother used to come in so tired in that nurse's uniform, working long hours on the night shift in the hospital.

Eileen snuggled up to me. 'Don't be sad, Mick,' she said, 'you have me now.'

'Yes, my little darling,' I said, pulling her close, and we began to kiss, long hot kisses, and my hands roamed over her white neck and she gasped as if her heart missed beat.

Breathlessly she came up for air and I could feel her hot cheek on mine. I moved my hand softly over her knee, with my head on her bosom and a hot passion surged within me. I began to feel that I had to have her . . . when suddenly there was a loud noise and Oikey came joining in, rubbing his head on her leg and making the strangest noises.

My head was just nicely resting on Eileen's bosom, her body moving restlessly beneath mine, and I was becoming lost in passion, but there it was again, that noisy pig in the background – the sound was impossible to ignore. How I wished he'd go away, it was so embarrassing. Of course, I didn't want to interrupt anything. I was just reaching for her most intimate part, just feeling that beautiful hot flesh and little cries came from her, but Oikey's cries got even louder. I gave the frisky beast a quick kick with my foot, not wanting to move from the position I was in, but it did not put him off; he was not going anywhere and it turned out that he was making such a to do that in the end I heard Eileen splutter with laughter, as though she could hold it no more. She pulled herself up with a red face, wiping little tears of laughter from her eyes, and quickly did up the buttons on her blouse, and tidied her rumpled skirt.

'Whatever were you thinking, you mad pig?' she said to Oikey. 'I'll chuck a bucket of water over you in the yard.'

So I just gave up. Trust that pig to spoil it, I thought. Half dazed, I glared down at him. I could have crowned him: he had ruined my love making.

'Goodness,' Eileen said, pulling Oikey towards the back door. 'I was getting all carried away myself. I'll open the back door, get some air in here and you'd better have a cold, quick shower, by the looks of you.'

'Okay.' I shrugged, trying to get over my disappointment. 'Lock that pig outside,' I snapped. 'He's got himself all excited.'

'And he's not the only one,' she said. 'Come on, Oikey, out in the yard!'

A ROMANTIC WEEKEND

Ch.10

In the spring the Pat Kennedy suggested I took some time off from the farm. 'You'll be pleased to know, Mick,' he said with a knowing smile, 'that, I'm laying you off for a while.'

I tried not to show my joy, for of late I was getting fed up with the early mornings and often didn't arrive until lunchtime

'All the planting's done,' said the farmer in a brisk tone, 'and our Eileen looks as though she needs a holiday.' His sharp face studied Mick quizzically. 'Well, lad,' he added, 'so, why don't you two love birds take a trip away?'

I had the strangest feeling they were pushing me onto Eileen.

'She's such a hard working girl,' said her dad, 'why, she's done wonders with that house of yours.'

Or perhaps, I began to think, this was a reminder that I should put a ring on her finger. I wasn't sure, but decided to go along with it. I was more than pleased when farmer Pat Kennedy informed me that his wife had agreed to have Oikey. 'She's going to mate him with some other pig,' he said, 'so you'll be glad of some peace from him then, Mick.' It crossed my mind for a moment, as I felt myself go red at the thought, that possibly farmer Kennedy knew Oikey was interfering with the courtship. He certainly had a wry grin on his face.

'Can't say I'll be sorry to lose him,' I confessed, and I got to dreaming of me and Eileen lying in front of the log fire together without that pig interfering in some way.

The following week we went off to Kinsale for the weekend. Eileen had been saving for a trip ever since I had been working, taking every week from me a few pounds and putting it in a jar. I was amazed how it had mounted up. We travelled down by train, not having the car anymore: Daneen had taken that over – I got fed up with putting petrol in it for him to use without a word of thanks.

Kinsale was a resort with a pretty marina. We booked into a hotel by the river, and from our room we could see the many smart yachts moored there. There were also many fishing boats that adorned the wide green river, and we walked arm in arm around the jetty watching the fishermen pull in their haul. Eileen found it all very exciting.

'I've never been to a real marina,' and she smiled, watching the fish wriggle from the nets. She looked lovely in a new styled trouser suit one of the Kennedy Sisters' made for her. It was emerald green with a check lining. The colour suited her golden complexion.

In the evening, after a meal at the hotel, we walked to the high cliffs, taking a long winding path that led upwards and over the cliffs. We talked and laughed in the fresh, crisp air. There was a strong hazy sunlight, and I could see the sun in a ball of fire throbbing over the horizon.

'Look,' said Eileen, 'the sea is glowing with a kind of crimson light. It's all so beautiful.'

I thought how happy she looked, and I knew in my heart that this was the time to tie the knot. You've been dragging your feet long enough, Mick, I told myself – there had been many a Saturday night when we had almost done the sexual act, the heavy petting getting almost out of control.

As we walked on, breathing in that fresh sea air, I stroked her hair that shone like burnished chestnut in the twinkling light of sunset. She buried her head in my neck and I could feel the passion rising between us even as we walked – the flush on her face, the way she shivered as her cheek brushed mine, and I could feel my blood pumping. We'd reached the top of the dark cliffs, and stopped to look down on the grey sea seeping in and out of the caverns below.

'Somewhere here is where the Lusitania went down,' I told her, remembering one of those wartime stories, but Eileen only hung around my neck. She seemed so eager to be loved and I was relieved that Oikey wasn't around.

Eileen gave a little shiver and said: 'I love you so much, Mick' and my beautiful Eileen threw her bonnet to the wind and pulled me closer to her. 'I have never felt this way before,' she uttered and moved her body in unison with mine, for Eileen was revealing the hot passionate women she was.

I could hear the sound of the sea crashing against the rocks and the gulls swooping overhead as Eileen gave herself to me. I knew then I would never want to leave her and afterwards we lay close together, caring little for the cold or the dampness of the grass.

The next afternoon, listening to the Irish folk band at the hotel, we joined in the Irish jig, but having two left feet, this dance was beyond me, so I sat and watched Eileen cavorting in a line with the other guests. Afterwards we enjoyed tea and cream cakes, brought around on silver trays, although I was looking around for the bar to open, really fancying a glass of Guinness.

'When's the bar open?' I asked a waitress.

'It's a private function today, sir, the bar's not open 'til six,' but the kind waitress was soon offering us a glass of champagne with a friendly smile.

'A private function,' I said to Eileen, 'mean to say we've been eating all their cream cakes?'

'Yes, Mick, it's an engagement party, didn't you know?

It was then I looked into those deep green eyes. They looked a little sad for a moment, so I put my arm around her and took her hand gently in mine

'Shall we come here for our honeymoon, Eileen? I like their cream cakes.'

'Oh, Mick,' she gasped, throwing her arms around me, 'do you want me to be your wife?'

'Of course I do, darling!' I said, and held her tightly in my arms. From then on it all happened very quickly, for on our return Eileen could not wait to get over to the Kennedy farm to tell them the news.

WEDDING PLANS

Ch.11

Before I knew it there was a big knees up arranged at the village hall, with banners flying for the engagement of Mick and Eileen and the villagers arrived with gifts, even Daneen turned up drunk, shouting about the Irish protests in Derry and how he was going on one of the parades.

'I'll be chucking a few bricks,' he shouted, although no one was really interested as the attention was directly on me and Eileen, and once we had named the day, Pat Kennedy could arrange with the priest the ceremony. The Kennedy's were content. I felt I'd been swept up in a whirl wind, everybody deciding what I should and shouldn't do, and in the end just let them get on with it.

'I know Dad has a way of taking over,' said Eileen, sitting on my lap and rustling my hair, 'but you know little about an Irish wedding and he will sort it all out for us.'

For the next six months, till the day in spring when I was to marry Eileen, the Kennedy's were constantly calling, with guests lists, catering ideas and what kind of flowers for buttonholes. What a fuss, and then there was the dressmaker calling to fit the bridle-gown, there did not seem a minutes peace, even the pig had been returned, but now with another pig 'Selena' who they decided to mate with Oikey.

At least a gate was put at the back door so as to keep Oikey out of the house, but he was happy courting, coming out only for his bath under the pump. Having given the pigs their breakfast, I preferred to stay out of the house, after hearing the sound of Mrs Kennedy`s voice arriving with more wedding plans. So I reached for my old work boots from the shed and decided to do some work, anything was better than listening to them debating the guest list. I`d hear enough about that. They were now up to about a hundred guests and I wondered where they were all coming from. But don`t forget I reminded myself, you are one of the O Hara`s now, and there is a lot of them in these parts, so I guessed I must be related to some.

So as I walked up through the 'High Fields' a name they had given to this recent land I had ploughed up, I noticed the pale green shoots appeared in the furrows and a thrill ran through me, for here was something that I had planted myself and it actually grew. I bent to touch it, for never before had any green thing done that for me and I walked along proudly and carefully, looking around at the land. 'King of all I surveyed'.

MY BEAUTIFUL WIFE

Ch.12

Mick sat looking at the river. Little green whirlpools fussed and frothed as the river ran swiftly, boosted by the spring tide that was bringing the salmon back from the sea to their natural breeding grounds. Every now and then the sun glinted on a silver film as the king salmon nosed its way through the shallow water, seeking the deep rocky pools where he and his mate would wait until their young were born, then it was back to the freedom of the open sea. Strange things about nature, Mick was thinking, the pattern does not change.

He sat on a mossy hillock, his son peacefully sleeping in the pram beside him. The black and white collie raced up with a stick that Mick had thrown into the water. He stood dripping, his long, pink tongue lolling out, waiting for him to repeat the game. Mick was not sorry he had returned to the home of his ancestor, the great 'O'Hara, he had found his lovely Eileen. He surveyed with screwed up eyes the grey, Blue Mountains in the distance. He stood just as 'O'Hara had done a thousand years ago looking for game to hunt so that his family could live.

Why can't you settle down? He remonstrated with himself. What is it you want? You own all this land. You are the father of a three month old son and a beautiful energetic hard working wife. What more do you want? Maybe this was it, Eileen so lovely and so willing to get out of bed before dawn to work on the farm, and the scorn of her looks as Mick pulled the blanket over his head, determined not to move until the baby woke him. Then he would rise to take care of Shamus – that was one job he never minded, but the rest of the chores Mick did in a very half-hearted fashion, so there was trouble in the home and Mick sat dreaming on the mountain side, not sure what to do about it.

Mick 'O'Hara's, appearance, had changed quite a lot, since he had lived in Inshallalee. He remembered when he arrived at Aunt Bridie's cottage a few years ago, tall, lanky and terribly nervous, his eyes blinkered perpetually behind his big spectacles, his shoulders hunched as he walked. Now he stood up and stretched his arms, no stoop now, not even any specs. It was marvellous how his young wife had persuaded him he would see better without them, and she had been right.

His mind wandered off to that first office job he had when he left school up in the city – it was strange how far London seemed now. He recalled how the other boys used to steal his glasses when he washed in that dirty little cloakroom, and Mick was convinced he could not see and would shout and scream in a panic, and earned himself the title of mad Mick. God, how nervous he was and how those boys bullied him.

Amid this beauty the terrible sad days crept back to him of when he was in adolescence and his mother was pale and very sick, but always insisted on getting up to make him something for breakfast – not that there was ever much to eat, but cornflakes filled that hole in your tummy until lunchtime, and you then sat out in the school yard behind the office with a pack of bread and margarine, worried in case one of the horrible boys would notice the emptiness of your sandwiches. Then there were the sad days, when a neighbour said: "Your mother's been taken to hospital, Mick", and the heartbreaking sobs as he stood in the hospital corridor, his head pressed to the cold marble wall that felt like, and always has reminded him of - death.

He sat and pulled his knees close to his chest as he recalled the time the welfare took him off, to board at a school in the country, and at weekends when the other kids' parents came to visit, he would hide himself under the blankets in the dormitory, for he had no one to visit him. Later, when he came of age, Mick was glad to see the back of 'Little folks home', as they called it, and waved goodbye with only a small suitcase of possessions.

They did find him lodgings and a job in the city, but he kept himself to himself, afraid the other boys would find out he was an orphan. So, alone and sometimes hungry, he watched the other boys with their girlfriends, being too shy and too poor to participate. Grief overwhelmed him as he stood looking towards the sun.

With a loud yell, Shamus awoke. Mick pulled himself together and went to the pram. 'Alright, darling, Daddy's here.' With the collie running beside him, he pushed the pram over the soft grass towards home.

You've got to get your finger out, Mick told himself, life has been good to you, look what you have now to what you had a year or so ago, but grief still hung over him and melancholy showed in his blue eyes, an inborn thing he found so hard to forget.

As he approached the thatched cottages, two of them lying close and snug together, he saw smoke rising from the chimney. Eileen will be home, he told himself. I wish I'd cleared up the breakfast things. As usual, Eileen had done them, the kitchen shone with her clean, efficient energy, and with her sleeves rolled to her elbows and her golden hair flying in the wind, she was hanging the washing on the line.

'Well now,' she said in her soft brogue, 'if it isn't the lord of the manor himself finished his dreaming on the mountain side.' She picked up the baby and briskly walked past Mick into the house. Mick knew she would nag, also that she had good reason to, but his courage deserted him and he sat outside on the oak seat, head hanging and never said a word.

DANEEN TO THE RESCUE

Ch.13

In the garden was the tall figure of Daneen digging up the potatoes, his face as brown as leather, his eyes red-veined with drink. Mick watched him. He stood up, leaning on the fork and surveyed the landscape; his black untidy hair needed cutting and the dirty red choker still adorned his neck. Mick in his disconsolate mood was not anxious to tangle with Daneen which he often did. It was one of the unsolvable mysteries of Inshallalee, why Daneen stayed around so long. He seemed to hate Mick, and the dislike had grown mutual – he never held a conversation with him. Daneen greeted him with just 'yes' or 'no', whatever served his purpose, and during his drinking sessions he became positively insulting.

'Bloody Cockney bastard,' he snarled as he passed Mick.

Many a time when Mick decided to sack him, it was Eileen who tried to keep the peace in spite of her temper. But she always protected what was her own and Mick was her husband and woe - betide anyone who said anything about her Mick. So Daneen kept well clear of Eileen.

After they got married Daneen arrived in the middle of the night roaring drunk.

'Come out, you Cockney git!' he yelled drunkenly. 'Come out and stand up and fight like a man!'

Mick, in bed, had no intention of going out in the cold to fight anyone, and pulled the sheet over his head, muttering, 'I'll get rid of that swine in the morning. I've had enough of him.'

'I'll go down to him,' said Eileen, 'and you leave him be, Mick O'Hara, or else you will hear from me.' He heard her gentle voice persuading Daneen to go to bed, which he did.

'Oh dear,' sighed Mick, 'will I ever get to know these people?'

At that moment, when Mick felt the end of the world was nigh, Daneen was down the garden staring malevolently at him, then slowly sticking the pitch fork in the ground and leaving it, he wiped his hand across his lips as he frequently did and came down the path towards Mick.

Mick stared, panic inside him, but sat rooted to the seat, his nerves not allowing him to move. Daneen came slowly down the path until he reached, Mick, then slowly and very deliberately he sat beside him and without a word he produced a bottle from his pocket, wiped the top with his hairy hand and offered it to Mick. Mick was astonished, but automatically took the bottle, took a swig from it and handed it back. Daneen slowly took a swig and put it back in his pocket, then the hatchet jaws opened and real words came.

'I'd be thinking,' he said, 'I do sometimes,' and Mick thought he was going to start about the riots in Belfast, as only this morning it was on the news that petrol bombs had gone off and the crowds were still protesting. These Irish struggles for independence, were a constant thorn in the side in many of the local people and of late, and Daneen had been threatening to go to Belfast and join his old Sinn Fein pals in the riots, complaining that the soldiers were dropping smoke bombs. Mick only wished he would go to Belfast, for everyone was fed up with Daneen raving about Ireland being a Free State.

'You wait and see', he had said, 'it will come about. The struggles have gone on long enough'. But this was of little importance to Mick and annoyed Daneen even more and he would often complain in Mick's presence, about getting the British out of Northern Ireland. So Mick wasn't sure what Daneen was going to say now.

'I suppose you think I'm going to go on about old Ireland's

troubles?' he said with a twisted smile and Mick was not sure if he was supposed to answer, so he just inclined his head to let him know he was listening and was relieved and somewhat surprised to hear Daneen talk of the Land.

'Well now, that land yonder,' Daneen pointed to the meadow near the river, 'that's good farmland, take oats and barley.'

Mick looked interested. 'You mean, plough it up and plant on it?'

'I do. Old Bridie, she was too bloody worried it would all scare the fish and spoil her fishing, but the fish, they're just the same bloody blighters - deaf, noise of tractors won't hurt them.'

Mick smiled, he was wondering what had come over old Daneen.

'Where would we get a plough?' he asked.

'Leave that to me,' said Daneen, 'you help with the work, laddie, and I'll do the rest.'

So that was it. Daneen knew that Mick was too lazy to go to work for his father-in-law and he was finding a way out for him. Well, good old Daneen, as Mick thought he hated him. He turned to thank him, but Daneen was already shuffling down the path back to his potato digging, and Mick went in to face his beautiful Eileen.

She sat by the fire rocking the babe in his little crib, a far away expression on her fair face. Mick stood in the doorway and thought of the picture he had once seen of a golden Madonna and her child. He went forward and down on his knees and placed his head in her lap. 'Forgive your lazy old man,' he said, and she stroked his hair and then their lips met and they sat on the rug together and all despondency had fled and Mick 'O'Hara was happy again.

He told her about Daneen, the drink, and the offer to help with the land.

'Poor old Daneen,' said Eileen, 'think he wants us to be happy`and he loves the baby.'

'Well, what do you think of the idea?'

'You mean, become self-supporting? What about it, Mick, can you do it?'

'With Daneen's help, I don't see why not. You see, darling, I don't know anything and I know your old man is good to us, but I make such a bloody fool of myself over there.'

She put her arms around him. 'Oh, I know, Mick, they would be your own mistakes here, I do understand, but can we make it pay? It's a long winter if you get nothing in the bank.'

'Don't worry, love, let's have a go. we need the money`, think your old man will mind?'

'I'll handle him,' she said with confidence. 'I think I'll get some hens, I might even get Oikey a young sow.'

'Oh no!' said Mick, 'not more Oikey`s ' and together they rolled on the rug laughing, young and healthy and full of plans for the future.

THE KENNEDYS

Ch.14

In the evening, being Saturday, they drove over with the baby to Kennedy's farm. Grandma and Grandpa liked to see Shamus on Saturday, that was when they gathered and relations came from all directions to eat their fill and see the great 'O'Hara, the new grandson. Mick who had previously been the 'Belle of the Ball' last year, took a back seat for his son, also quite sure that his popularity had waned when he found the bed so alluring, and he never got to the farm until all the work was done.

Weekends they all sat in the best room, the long wide comfortably furnished sitting room, and high tea was served in the kitchen. Cold chicken and ham and plenty of hard boiled eggs were served – there was no stinting in hospitality at the Kennedy's farm. There was plenty of beer and whiskey for the men, and cards were played, while the women sat around knitting and gossiping.

At first Mick, after his lonely childhood, had found this life warm and comforting and the talk lively and refreshing, but lately, he felt hemmed in having to do the same things each Saturday and listen to the same stories. So little happened in this out-of-the-way-place that stories went around and you heard the same story several times, but etiquette demanded you listen, for these people loved to talk.

Eileen at home was her old vivacious self, the baby passed from hand to hand and presents were brought for him. His mother-in-law, an almost complete replica of Eileen, only at a different age level, chattered and lashed out lavishly with the food, and Mick sat silent and remote wondering if they should not fast for a week before visiting the Kennedys. He usually managed to upset someone if they engaged him in conversation – a sore point was religion – if it came to an argument over religion the fat was really in the fire.

Once he'd had the audacity to suggest that Darwin might be right, that men could have come from monkeys. The horror and aggravation it caused was beyond him, he came from a town where you expressed your views and no one cared. So, poor old Mick often sat silent not knowing what to talk about. The worse set had been when Mick talked of Communism and remarked that to those people who believed in it, it was a kind of religion. A bomb could not have achieved such results; they all chattered at once of heathens and God fearing people. Mick tried, but could not swallow the Catholic religion as they did. They swallowed it whole, word for word, and his scientific mind would not allow him to, so this caused trouble with the in-laws. Mick had not been to Mass since Christmas Eve, then, it was because he was too drunk to argue.

When they arrived this Saturday, the atmosphere was cool. The Kennedy Sisters from the village shop were visiting, bringing all the gossip. His mother-in-law was always nice to him.

'Leave him be, Pat,' she'd say to her husband, 'is he not Shamus's grandson, your old friend. You'll join him in heaven that's for sure, if you're good to young Mick.'

But tonight Mick was ready for them.

'Now, Mick,' said Eileen, 'you stand up to me pa, don't let me down, he's like an old bull – stand up to him and he'll back out.'

After tea she said brightly, 'Mick's going to plough up the meadow land at Inshallalee.'

They all stared. 'Mick's going to do what?' retorted her father.

'Go on, Mick, tell them,' she nudged him.

'I'm putting in oats and barley,' he shouted loudly, because he was so nervous.

They roared with laughter. 'Be jabbers, Mick, you must be getting uncomfortable in that double bed of yours,' said Davey Joe.

Eileen, her face as red as fire, got up. 'Do you mind!' she shrieked, pointing at Davey Joe. 'That man is insulting my marriage bed, I demand an apology!'

'Hush,' said her mother, 'it was only a joke.'

But Eileen was off in a temper and there was no stopping her. 'Either he leaves this table, or I do, and I'll not come back!'

'Alright,' said Davey Joe, still smirking, 'I've had me tea, I'm going.'

Eileen started to cry and her aunts and mother fussed over her, then the baby joined in.

Mick sat looking down, feeling a headache coming on. Why the hell did they have to have all these scenes? Surely it would be better to keep their business to themselves. No, it was customary to toss it to the family like a bone to a lot of hungry dogs.

The table was emptying, the women making a shocking cackle, and Mick's father-in-law motioned him to go to the sitting room for a drink.

'That's better,' he said, as they downed the whiskey.

'I'm sorry about all that,' Mick said.

'Sorry? What for? The women love it, makes a bit of excitement and our Eileen's a proper Kennedy she is - like my mother. Never had a party in our house without *her* - God rest her soul, starting some rumpus or other.'

Mick felt it was all a waste of time. These people seemed so set in their ways, he wondered if he would ever get used to them.

'Well now, what's all this?' said his father-in-law, 'better tell me, Mick, before all those old hens come back in here.'

'I don't know that it was such a good idea, all the ruckus it's caused,' said Mick despondently.

'Don't matter, tell me.'

In spite of the fact that his father-in-law was big and very dogmatic, Mick had a hidden admiration for him, he was a successful farmer and he kept his head fanatically above water, whoever else went under; now he strode up and down sucking his pipe, his shrewd eyes seeming to see right into Mick's brain.

'Alright, out with it.'

'Well, Daneen suggested it - that, we start on our own, become self-supporting, not relying on you for our livelihood.'

He looked very surprised. 'Daneen? Well, I suppose in some ways he's entitled to it, but is he going to help you, that's the point, or start something then go off on a bender?'

Mick did not understand the part of the reply, why should Daneen be entitled to anything, but the rest seemed correct enough. 'Well, to tell you the truth, I was wondering too, he's an awful drunkard, but it's strange that since the baby's been born he seems to have improved a bit. He loves little Shamus, sits near his pram minding him when Eileen is busy.'

'Oh, he would,' said farmer Pat Kennedy, but what you going to sow, Mick, oats and barley? Tell you what, I'll send a tractor and young Ginger to give you a hand, and if you make it pay I'll let you have the land back I leased off your aunt for grazing, might chuck in a few cows.'

'Well, that's good of you,' said Mick.

'Got to make a start somewhere, lad, no good getting lazy. Eileen's not been brought up that way, she'd soon get sick of a bum.'

Mick looked away in shame. They had a way of making him feel inferior.

Eileen and her mother came in, having got rid of the aunts.

'It's alright, Mick,' said Eileen, running forward to kiss him, 'Mum's giving me hens and a few geese, and we got Oikey back, she's fed up with him.'

So, after a good night drink they went back in the old Ford and to their little homestead called Inshallalee.

. . . .

THE HOMESTEAD

Ch.15

By April the little homestead had settled down. Daneen kept to his part of the bargain and gave Mick all the help and advice he needed. Young Ginger told all the Kennedys, it was so funny up there, as the March wind blew and Daneen occasionally got drunk. He never left his post but he did start the day with a wee dram to keep the cold out, and increased the dosage as the day wore on, and sometimes he rode on the tractor thinking it was a British tank and over the hill were the Jerries, swearing in English and Hindustani. He shouted and charged till Mick and young Ginger rolled on the grass laughing.

A new companionship had sprung up between Mick and Daneen: they talked of London and of France, and India that he seemed to know well. He had been a Sergeant in the Irish Guards stationed out in India. Mick looked at Daneen's dried stick-like appearance. He was certainly tall, but Mick tried to visualise him with sturdy shoulders and wearing a busby and found it impossible – and for the first time he heard from Daneen about his life in the shack.

'I have lived there a long time, before you was born, boy,' he said.
One day Mick asked: 'Do you remember my mother when she was
young?'

A strange look came into his eyes. 'Perhaps I do, perhaps I don't,'
he said. 'I'm turning in,' he muttered, taking a swig from his bottle,
and he disappeared over the hill and was not seen for days, but the job
was done and Mick was well pleased with himself, also he felt very fit,
better than he had done for a long time.

Sitting by the cosy open fireplace that evening, the peat block threw
out a good warm heat. Mick leaned back in his chair, pipe and
slippers handy. This was the life.

Eileen returned from putting the baby in bed. With her she
brought a book. 'See this, it's our account book, we will keep accounts
of all we spend and all the profit we make and in no time we will be
rich.'

'Of course, darling,' said Mick lazily, making no attempt to even
open the book.

But Eileen was persistent. 'Now, come on, Mick, let's spend our
time getting things in order.' She opened the ledger in a very business-

like manner. 'Here's what we started with. So far I've had the hens giving me eggs, and the cockerel has done well, and I've got one broody hen and I should get chicks soon. I scrounged a mate for Oikey from Paddy Mac. I called her Selena. Paddy will miss her, you know, but I promised Paddy Mac a couple of piglets. I've put in strawberries down the bottom and plenty of cabbages. . .'

But Mick was sound asleep. 'Oh, Mick,' she said, looking disappointed, but she kissed him and sat at his feet with the ledger on her lap, dreaming of a host of hens and maybe some turkeys later. The fire blazed brightly and the black velvet night outside wrapped their cosy nest like a warm blanket.

In the morning Mick got up to make the tea; he idly looked through the book, at the assets, which was not much – a hundred pounds and a car from Aunt Bridie, but the funny thing was that after a year of married life they had seventy five pounds in the bank and still had the bit of money put by that Aunt Bridie had left. How did she manage this? It was beyond Mick who had no head for figures. He looked at the outgoings: not much, a few household expenses and the doctor when Shamus was born. I wonder who pays old Daneen's wages?' he thought. Eileen never did, if she did it would be written down.

He carried up a cup of tea and the baby's bottle. She sat up in bed, the child beside her. Mick held the bottle for his son, which he sucked lustily.

Eileen sat sipping her tea, looking at the old fashioned patchwork quilt, which was a variety of colours and the pretty curtains at the tiny window. It was a nice little bedroom, Mick thought.

'Who pays Daneen his wages, Eileen?' he asked suddenly.

Eileen's blue eyes opened wide. 'Don't you know, Mick?' she said, looking shocked.

'No, dear, I don't, he was here when I came, he never asked for money so I presumed someone paid him, thought it might be your old man.'

'No, Mick, he gets about twenty pounds a month from Aunt Bridie's legacy, that's all, but he seems to manage to get drunk on it.'

'What was he to Aunt Bridie?' asked Mick. He wanted to get off his mind things that bothered him.

'Well, it's a bit of a mystery. I was away at school, so I only know by the bits of gossip. There was some sort of funny connection between them, don't think it was sexual because old Bridie was more like a man than a woman, but it was something - they were close. Everyone here seemed to think the land would be left to Daneen. They say he was very disappointed. He got drunk and shouted abuse. All she left him was the old shack and five pounds a week as long as he stays here and worked for you, that's all I know, Mick.'

'Don't seem fair, does it, how he can live on that much money and he's like a damned, tied surf, being forced to work for me. Don't like it.'

'Can't alter it, Mick, and no one can discipline Daneen.'

'Anyway,' said Mick firmly. 'I'm going to find him tomorrow and offer him some more money, if it's only two pounds a week and he could eat with us, then the booze won't take so much effect if he's well fed.'

'We can't really afford it, Mick, but I know how you feel, so go ahead and I'll find a way. I might do a deal with the Kennedy shop with the eggs.'

'My careful little darling,' said Mick. 'Oh well, back to work.'

He pulled on his farm boots and went out to mix the hot mash for Oikey and the pig's new 'wife'. Oikey's attitude to Mick had not changed much, he still looked at Mick with a sort of human leer and was very jealous of his attention to his wife, Selena. As Mick bent to say hello to his sweet, pink young sow, Oikey butted him in the backside and Mick landed in the mud.

SINN FEIN

Ch.16

Daneen was in the doldrums as he sat in his shack, his head drooping and out of the corners of his mouth a cigarette hung, miserably. He was thinking Mick had everything and he had nothing. 'I'm just like a bloody - surf,' he muttered to himself. He was also remembering how Bridie used to say: "I will always look after you my love". But that was all gone now, and he knew it was his own fault, he had lost her after all what he did and remorse tugged deep in his heart.

Pull yourself together, he told himself with a sigh, Bridie`s has left

Mick everything. Getting up he stumbled to the dresser, and picked up the photograph of himself and Bridie, sitting bare-back on a horse. Her soft gold hair blowing in the wind, she was grinning in that mischievous way and he would never forget her soft blue eyes, that were flecked with green. They had been only young and her arms were tight around him. Must have been about twelve, he thought, but even then everyone said, they would one day marry. They were always together and it seemed the most natural thing in the world, to marry: but now that was only a sad memory. If only he had stuck with Bridie - how different his life would have been. . .

He started to think back down the road to when they grew up together. And the happy times they spent on the farm, were filling him with sweet nostalgia, for he could almost hear those words "Up the Irish", and as he closed his eyes, he could see the men raising their fists in unison. For Ireland was going through a very a troubled time and the sounds of the rebel songs of Ireland were ringing in his ears. It was that time in Ireland, after the East rising in 1916 and people were fighting more than ever, for Ireland's independence and many volunteer organisations were starting up, sympathising with Ireland's cause.

At the time Daneen lived with his grandfather, a ruddy cheeked man with a slow drawl, who had taken him in as a small lad and was like the father he never had. No more did he have to put cardboard in his shoes, for his grandfather made sure he always had good strong boots to work in the stables.

Granddad was also, a man very loyal to the cause of Ireland and the founder of the Tipperary Brigade: a voluntary organisation that began in the stable at his farm in county cork. At first, there was only a handful of sympathisers, but the organisation grew daily and Daneen as a boy would watch them training, marching around with guns and firing them into the air and even join in, and when he became an expert shot, Granddad put the cloth cap on his head and a bandolier to wear across his chest, that was all part of the uniform.

Granddad was known to the locals as Granddad Spud, as he was raised on a farm that grew solely potatoes, but after the potato famine, his parents turned it into a stable, to raise fine horses. Daneen loved working alongside Granddad Spud at the stables and they became known as 'Old Spud' and 'Young Spud' by the locals.

Each day Daneen would muck out the paddocks, laying down clean straw, then brush the shiny backs of the horses whispering in their sensitive furry ears and not far away at his anvil, Granddad would be making the horseshoes, being that he was also the local blacksmith and each day Granddad would give him a riding lesson, showing him how to jump a fence, then trotting along the leafy lanes; relishing the silence all around, telling him all he knew about horses.

'You`ll be a fine horseman', he would say. Then one day, Granddad hitched the chestnut mare to the horse cart and they rode to Bantry, for the County Horse Fair. There they watched the thoroughbreds in the ring and listened to the noise and clatter in the beer tent, where men did private deals and talked of nothing but horse flesh.

That day there was a 'Steeple – Jack' event taking place, and after a few drinks in the beer tent, Granddad entered Daneen, and put his name on the board.

'Now don't forget all I taught you', said Granddad, 'hold tight the reins, you can do it boy', and handed Daneen his old riding whip. Granddad was too old himself at sixty for the jumps, although he still liked to dress in his high velvet riding hat, that he wore over his greased, grey head and the old high leather boots and britches for the occasion.

His big red face, beamed with joy when Daneen won the race, for he had leapt the chestnut mare over the fences leaving the other riders behind. 'I've taught you well', he said, talking about it on the way back to the farm.

On the road, they would also pass the dairy farm where Bridie lived with her father, Shamus 'O' Hara, who was also a member of the Tipperary Brigade. Their farm was only a horse's gallop across the field from his grandfather's and Bridie was often bringing messages over from her father Shamus; especially - if the auxiliaries were in the village, standing on the street corners, stopping people to search them for weapons, for the auxiliaries were against the volunteer groups that were gathering around Southern Ireland and would confiscate any weapons. Although, Granddad would complain that the Tipperary Brigade, only had a few old shotguns as weapons.

This often came up at the meetings of the group and Shamus would rant and rave about ambushing the army barracks and stealing their weapons. These discussions at the meetings of the Tipperary Brigade were held in the stables, with smoke and whiskey fumes, till late into the night, when they would argue politics. Some were tough muscle men, others local farm lads - all with their loyalties to old Ireland and

Daneen and Bridie would make themselves comfortable in the hayloft above, nestling in the straw, listening to the group of men making plans for their next attack.

Together young Daneen and Bridie, went on marches with the brigade, carrying posters, backing the demonstrators, who called for a Free State, and join the crowd throwing stones at the army.

It was a way of life and the political struggles for old Ireland, was all around them.

Granddad Spud didn't like the English. He felt invaded by their presence and would fight tooth and nail to have Ireland back for the Irish. 'It's our country', the old man would say, banging the hammer down as he repaired the horseshoes. 'I'll see old Ireland free from British rule, before I'm done'.

It was 1917 and Granddad Spud and Bridie's father, being Sinn Fein followers would travel all around to hear de Valero speak. In the square in Limerick, big crowds gathered, but a plan had been hatched by the Sinn Feins to blow up the hotel and Granddad had agreed to make the explosives, while Shamus walked into the hotel and lit the taper, and even though the auxiliaries tried to put the fire out, the hotel was burned to the ground.

Shamus 'O' Hara was a daring, impetuous young man, all the things that made up a rebel, with his chirpy grin, lithe figure and shock of curly red hair; despite the fact he was a hard drinking man. He had lost his young wife to tuberculosis and he was left to bring up Bridie and her younger brother alone,. `look after young Tim ` he would say and go off to the pub and when he came home drunk, he would be storming off about the Irish cause. 'I'll kill the bastards!' he would yell, then throw his dinner up the wall. Bridie would guide him off to bed. So Bridie at a young age, a motherless child, learnt to stand up for herself and it all developed her strong character to the full.

While Shamus was the one who would be firing off, often he could be full of hot air. It was Granddad who made the bullets for the guns, as the Tipperary Brigade was very short of weapons and he would make bullets from lead, moulding them in his blacksmith's yard for the few old shotguns and revolvers they possessed.

Bridie's dad would often send the youngsters down to the village with a message: 'Tell them to get the arms out of their houses. Tell them the troops are coming', and Daneen would jump on his horse with Bridie on the back, and the pair would ride bare back across the farmland, trying to keep out of sight, as they made their way to the village to warn the family.

During those political times in Ireland, the groups of rebel volunteers had become much stronger, and fought the struggle of Ireland for independence. This was at a time, not long after the First World War had finished and men came home from war looking for work. Some got work at the ship building industry and others the mines, some answered the adverts from the British Army asking for men to help defend British Territory and fight against the IRA. These were the Black and Tans: men who did not fight through loyalty to their country, but were paid ten shillings a day by the British Government.

Daneen could still hear his grandfather's voice. "Beware of the black and tans, boyo, they're nothing but mercenaries, they'll soon have you up against the wall".

As the youngsters grew, they considered themselves to be young Sinn Feins, fighting the good fight for Ireland. So far they had survived by ducking and diving and fooling the British Troops, but these daring pair were getting known and also by the auxiliaries. Bridie's father thought it about time, she learnt to protect herself, and became the best shot, shooting at a line of beer bottles on the wall.

'That will keep the lads in tow', said her father with a grin, and everyone knew, Bridie was a toughie and the boys would all say, "Don't get fresh with Bridie, she's got a punch like a prize-fighter", for she would take no nonsense from any boy, although, she didn't look the most attractive girl in the village, with her short sturdy frame and dressed in ragged jeans and Granddad would say on the side with his quite humour, 'She's more boy than a girl'. But Bridie longed to be more feminine, and would look down at her short, strong legs and wish they were long and slim.

Granddad Spud's farm was also a safe house for the IRA to hide, and Daneen and Bridie would ride out on horseback to deliver written messages to other members of the brigade. 'Better we take the back roads, keep out of the way of the British Soldiers', they would agree, but many a time they got through the road blocks, for the British Guards, never suspected a young girl. Daneen also loved to fool the British Guards, at the road blocks. It gave him a buzz.

` 'How did it go?' Granddad would ask.

One day when they returned, they were laughing, saying how the soldiers called for them to stop and they rode so quick, they couldn't catch them.

'It's not a game', Granddad told the two youngsters, 'now go and rub down the horses and give them a good groom. There may be more tasks that you may have to take more seriously, if you're going to be good brigade members.

'What you got in mind?' Bridie said, as she sidled up to Granddad, hands on hips, wanting to know what it was. Granddad had to smile at her pluckiness. 'Let's have it', she said, pushing her curls from her oval face. Her golden hair hung down her back, and although her features were uneven, she had lively bright blue eyes and rosy cheeks, but she would sometimes look at you sideways with a deep frown, as if she trusted no one.

When Granddad told them both about the plan to take the horse and cart to the coal mines to pick up explosives, Bridie's face broke into a sudden grin, for this was something different. Granddad went on to explain how his friend, who worked there, was allocated explosives each day to blow up the mine, but instead he was going to give them a share.

'It's only a small piece', said Granddad, 'you can hide it in the cart.

It might be delicate, so wrap it well and keep on the smooth road. The youngsters agreed.

The following week, they rode off to Killarney, close to where the mine was situated. They went quickly, to catch the friend after his day working down the dark mine, whipping the horse as they hurried to the coal mine to pick up the explosives, taking the horse and cart high into the hills. The coal shaft could be seen overhead as they rode upwards - and below the winding road in the valley.

The explosives were collected, from the harassed miner who came out with black coal dust still on his face. His black dusty hand had reached for the explosives that he had hidden in his helmet.

'Be careful with this stuff', he told the youngsters and rushed back to the mine.

It was then wrapped in the soft blanket and placed in the back of the cart, hidden amongst the straw bales. Then it was a slow ride back, to County Kerry, keeping the explosives still and the horse steady.

They took the flat road, hoping there would not be soldiers.

Granddad was waiting for them, wiping the sweat from his brow with a big handkerchief and was relieved when they returned, beaming a big smile, that they were safe. 'You're doing a foine job', Granddad would tell them. Then he would take the explosives and hide them in the stables, where later, they would be used to make hand made bombs. Once Granddad had heard all about the job, Bridie would return home to her own farm, riding her horse across the field, to tell her father, that the explosives had been collected from the mines.

'My smart girlie', Shamus 'O' Hara, would say, picking Bridie up and swinging her around, and her golden hair would swing out from her bonnet. 'You've got the 'O'Hara colouring', he would say. 'Your hair is your crowning glory', and Bridie's cheeks would glow red, for she loved this hard drinking father who shouted, 'We will bomb the lot now', and laugh out loud.

Often the two young people would be sitting around the grate, watching the glow of embers in the fire, listening to Granddad, with some of the Tipperary gang and their plans, and as time passed Daneen and Bridie became more involved with the brigade's missions.

Daneen got to wearing a bandolier and cloth cap, wanting to look a real member of the gang, but his grandfather told him it was better he didn't, as the black and tans were stopping people in the streets and he would be recognised as a brigade member.

Bridie's father would call most days with news and bring orders back from other Sinn Fein gangs that were set up in mountainous regions. 'It's guns, they need', and although Granddad in the blacksmith yard, would be making ammunition for the old revolvers, Bridie's father would moan.

'It's not enough to make a stand. What we need is gelignite to make more grenades and blow up the barracks', and talked through his plan, laying out a map, whilst the group gathered around the table.

This is the British Barracks in Dublin', said Bridie's father pointing to the map, his tall figure leaning over the table; his vivid blue eyes staring out from under his red hair that fell over his forehead and his cap balanced on the back of his head.

'You're not thinking of blowing that up', said one elderly member, 'surely there's a better way to get guns'. But Bridie's father, who had big ideas, tried to convince them, they could blow the barracks sky high.

'But first we would break into the store room to steal the weapons', he said, 'and hold the British Soldiers, ransom'.

'Don't be such a hot head', said Granddad, butting in, 'there'll be no need for that, for there is more than one way to skin a cat', and all the men agreed.

The impetuous Shamus, didn't want to listen and became loud and bombastic, waving his big hands. 'I`m telling you, we need to take it over. We'll use grenades, blow them up'.

The others members shrugged, looking from one to another, for to blow up the barracks was very risky, with many soldiers inside. Shamus continued to try and convince, walking around hands in pockets looking very superior. He had been drinking all the afternoon and was bleary eyed, and even Granddad knew he had to be careful of Shamus`s temper.

Granddad looked at the clock wearily and scratched the bald patch, where his hair had receded over the years. Even the men were whispering amongst themselves, disagreeing with Shamus's ideas, until Shamus grabbed his map off the table and walked out, saying, ye haven`t the guts, none of yis`.

'he`s acting the maggot` said Granddad, in his calm way. The arguments and debates continued until Grandad told the other members that he knew the lad who runs the quarter masters stores at the barracks. 'I used to go to school with his grandfather', he informed them, 'and he is a real sympathiser'.

So the next evening Granddad called another meeting. 'I've negotiated a deal', he told the men. 'The boy who works in the barracks, tells me he has plenty of ammunition in these stores and is willing to do a deal and hand over a box of fifty rifles'.

'But how will we get them out', asked one member.

'Well that's where the canal comes in', said Granddad, sucking his pipe with a pleased expression, 'because, there is a canal that runs at the back of these barracks and it goes across the border and all the way down to Limerick. The plan is', he explained, 'that the lad will smuggle the rifles onto a narrow boat and his friend will bring them down the canal to a place where we can pick them up. But, the destination will be kept secret for now. So what do you think lads?' he asked, as the men were looking very interested and nodding approval. `aye lads, we will have rifles` said one man, 'to protect our own', and raised his arm.

'To be sure`,cheered the other members, all agreeing the British were shooting at their people and burning down their villages.

'All we have is a few old shotguns', said another raising his cap.

'We have no choice, but to fight back', said Granddad.

So with this plan arranged, all the men talked and drank irish moonshine discussing the date when this would be done. Daneen and Bridie were all ears as they sat at the old piano, taking it all in, and Daneen suddenly stood up, saying, 'I'll go and get the rifles'.

Bridie piped up, 'I'm up for that too'.

'But it could be a dangerous', said Granddad, 'not sure you youngsters are ready for such a task'.

But Bridie was adamant. 'Let me do it', she said, 'me and Daneen, together. We never get stopped, we can hide it in the cart', and she folded her arms obstinately, linked through Daneen's and a very determined grin.

'It's a responsible task', said Granddad, and looked around at the men for approval, who all agreed the youngsters would be less suspicious and had no objections.

So Daneen stood upright with pride, wanting to be chosen, for he was keen to impress the brigade. 'We can surely do it', he said. 'We take explosives around all the time from the mine'.

So it was agreed and Bridie linked her arm through Daneen's 'As long as I am with you', she said, 'I have no fear of anything'.

It was agreed again that the youngsters should go, and Daneen and Bridie were full of questions for Granddad, who started by telling them the name of the boat. 'It's called 'Starry Night' and you will have to be at the canal dock with the horse and cart to collect the rifles'. Then showing the youngsters a map of the area, he pointed – 'It's where the canal meets and the lad will then go, straight back to Dublin once he has given you the drop. If you get caught with the load, it could be dangerous', he warned them, in a low anxious tone. 'Watch out for the troops and black and tans on the journey. But Galway is not so far, head for it quick once you have the guns'. So he told them to look for the green and black boat. 'And the lad's name is Milo, he's short and stocky with black wavy hair.If the boat doesn't arrive', he added, 'just get yourselves out of there, it will mean the handover has gone wrong'.

It was the next morning the old man drew a map of the bridle paths he knew on the way to Galway, and told them of an unknown route through the mountains that lead to the Tipperary Brigade camp, based in the mountain range. 'At the foot of these mountains is the great lake of Lock Derg', he said tapping on the map, 'and the lads' camp is in the mountains, they will be expecting you'.

Eager to know where they would be picking up the guns, the old man pointed to a humped back bridge. 'Just here is where the canal ends, and the lad will be waiting there under the bridge with the guns. Can't miss the place - it's by Shannon Harbour, called Griffith Bridge'.

'Isn't that where the Grand Canal, meets the Brosna?' said Bridie, who had travelled many times on the canal with her father.

'That's right girl, it's known as the Brosna route and it's a good place to meet, 'cause the lad with the boat, won't go over the great lake - reckons the old narrow boat won't make it'.

So it was arranged that the youngsters would take the horse and cart to County Offaly, cutting across farmland tracks and then through the village, keeping as close to the mountain range as they could, for Daneen knew the ropes, having travelled all around the mountain range with his grandfather visiting members of the IRA, and on his travels, often witnessed a village house set on fire, and many a local lad taken off to prison.

When the young couple left in the cart, the old man stood watching from the door, confident they would look after each other on this important mission. He watched until they were out of sight, with Daneen urging the horse on, cracking the whip: no one could catch him, the speed he rode and knew he had taught the boy well, for there was nothing Daneen didn't know about horses, and was sure he could handle them well; even climbing the rocky mountain paths, he was sure of that - but the mission in itself, he was not so sure of.

So the old man, tired and dusty, with the same faded overalls, would stand at the anvil, making lead bullets for the old revolver he owned. But this day, by his side, he kept the old shotgun, for he knew that if anything went wrong the British could be here to arrest him, and he wasn't going to taken without a fight.

There was talk amongst the brigade of a reprisal. As friends had been shot at a football match between Cork and Tipperary, an occasion that the brigade had been looking forward too, but as the locals gathered, enjoying the game, cheering the players on, the Black and Tans arrived, carrying rifles and without warning opened fire, shooting at the crowds, that ran with terror, as the bullets whizzed through the air and men lay on the pitch injured, some lay screaming in pain and it was a sight not to be forgotten. So the brigade got together and worked out a plan, to ambush the british troops as they transported gelignite from the barracks, it would be a good reprisal, the gelignite was much needed by the British, to blow up the quarry to build a new road.

The plans to blow up the quarry, whizzed around in Grandad Spudds head, how he hated what the black and tans did, he was still haunted by the event. A few tears trickled down his cheek and hung on the end of his hairy moustache, but he wiped it away with his grubby sleeve and reached for the bag of fertiliser on the shelf above. With a snear, and a vengeance he poured it into a bucket, for he knew, just how to make a grenade. The British won`t like this, he grinned to himself and knew he had to have just the right amount of ingredients of fertiliser and semtex to make it work. He also knew, it could explode in his face, but he wasn't thinking of any danger to himself, for his mind strayed to the youngsters who were on their way to meet the boat, and of the weapons they would be collecting.

Firstly, they had to get there, and he was imagining them as he mixed the ingredients, going along the road to County Offaly, the horses in a gallop. He knew Daneen would go fast, he was a good horseman, nobody could catch him when he was on a horse, he knew that. He hoped they would get plenty of rifles, but whether they could get the ammunition, that would remain to be seen, so he would do his part, work all day at the anvil, making plenty of lead bullets and the time would go quicker, for he could not wait for the day to end, when the youngsters would arrive home safe.

THE CANAL

Ch.18

On the way to the canal, Daneen rode the horses at a quick pace. All the time Bridie watched along the roads for the British, as often they would put up road blocks and they didn't want to be questioned. They soon passed farmland, where farm labourers were going home, wet across the fields, walking wearily after their day's work.

'It seems a bit quiet,' said Daneen, and Bridie looked around nervously.

'Let's take the old bog roads', she said, 'you never know when the troops will be coming this way, so they turned into a narrow, muddy road, where peat piled either side and although the horses had to slow up they were feeling safer.

As they passed groups of cottages in small hamlets, they waved to villagers who outside a white thatched cottage chopping wood, looked around them all the time, as many village houses were being raided at this time by the Black and Tans, who were searching their homes, and any weapons were being confiscated. There had been less and less weapons available to the volunteers struggles, since the Easter rising, as the British Army had barred them and they were no longer able to carry a gun in the street.

This caused rebellion and village houses were raided by the Black and Tans, searching for weapons. They would think nothing of pulling the occupiers out of bed, even the old grandmother, pushed up against the wall, her shawl wrapped around her and terrified, as they were lining up against the wall and the young men threatened. They would search the houses, pulling the place to pieces and threaten the family, telling them they were supporters of the IRA and asking questions, but none would talk and often got bashed, but they all knew what happened to informers: they would be shot; often close range with a Smith and Wesson revolver.

But this particular day, it was peaceful, passing through the villages. It was autumn and lovely rustic tints were on the leaves. A cold grey sky formed the background and the horses cantered along at a steady pace.

'We are on time,' said Bridie, guiding Daneen onto the back roads to meet the canal passing across a little stream, then turning into a long shadowing lane, with muddy tracks and hedges either side. They came to the river and could see the green boat was soon coming along. And there in front of them was the bridge at Griffith: It looked a quiet place with patches of woods, ablaze with golden primroses, little clumps of them under the trees. There was no one else around, and the boat was under the humped back bridge half hidden. They pulled up the horses, close to the water's edge. The bridge was right in front of them and a big built lad came walking towards them, with a sailor's rolling gait.

'Get on here,' he said, summoning Daneen to his boat. They were soon inside the cabin and Bridie waited nervously, before the two appeared again, carrying the boxes of rifles.

The lad looked nervous as he handed them the rest over. 'If you get stopped, keep your mouths shut,' he said meanly and shook his big tousled head like a shaggy dog. He was obviously glad to see them on the road again and shot off back to his boat, moving swiftly down the canal.

'There's five boxes of good rifles,' said Bridie looking inside one of the boxes, but Daneen had no time to examine them, as he rode the cart quickly away, all the time looking around. 'We will go back on the same old bog road,' said Bridie covering the rifles over on the cart and sitting in front again with Daneen.

'It's a lot slower the bog road,' he moaned.

'Yes, but it's far better to be safer,' said Bridie, but it was a bad mistake, because although the bog road through the village had been clear an hour back, now there was uproar, as the British Troops were there. It was when they were going towards the cottage, where the old man had been chopping wood outside that they could see there was a group of men with arms.

'It's the British,' said Daneen, 'we had better stop. They've spotted us now, can't turn around.' And they could see a trooper walking towards them and waving his gun to and fro.

There was no way out.

'Just go forward,' said Bridie, her young face hard she grabbed a rifle from the back, 'I'll shoot our way out if I have to,' and hid the rifle beside her. And Daneen with a swipe of the horses went forward hoping the troops would not stop them. But as they came towards the gathering outside the village house, the trooper came with, cautioning them to stop. It looked a dangerous situation as there was a whole family of kin folk stood up against the wall, stood shivering in the frosty air. There were only a handful of troops, and one stood guard over the family outside the house, while the rest of the troops searched inside it.

As Daneen slowed up, he tried to see what was going on. There was an old lady, holding a shawl around her shoulders, he could see her feet tapping together and anger rose in him as the soldier prodded her with his rifle. There was shouting and screaming coming from the house and he wanted to go and help, but Bridie put a soothing hand on his shoulder, `be still` she whispered the trooper in coming over. This trooper carrying his rifle with a couldn't care less expression, came beside there wagon, waving the rifle:

'Get down from the cart,' said the trooper, who had one eye on the scene at the house, as well as asking them what they were doing there.

'Just come to visit some friends at a cottage along the road,' but the trooper looked suspiciously at them both and ordered them to get down from the cart, and Bridie knew he was about to search the back of it, and she was having none of that and she suddenly pulled out the rifle and shouted: 'Let's go!' to Daneen, as the butt of the rifle came down on the trooper's head. He fell flat to the ground. It was then that Daneen charged the horses off, leaving the man unconscious on the ground, and Bridie stood, trying to balance herself, shooting the gun in the air deterring them from following.

'But they'll be following soon,' said Daneen, charging the horses forward. 'We've got to get some speed up.' But looking behind they saw fire bellowing from the house where the troops were searching and Bridie said: 'Perhaps they will be too busy to follow, perhaps someone's thrown a grenade'.

'Hope it's at the troops,' said Daneen. 'By the way, well done, darling,you put the officer out cold, what a gel I've got.' And Bridie smiled, as Daneen had said, she was his girl and that was all she really wanted to be.

'I hate the British Army,' she said, 'I'll put them out any day.'

'That's my gel,' he laughed, and swung the riding whip to and fro until his knuckle glowed white and the horse galloped at a tremendous speed. 'No one will catch us now.'

They went through a dirt road, through the town and then over open countryside and soon they were heading to the mountains, taking narrow tracks that led upwards, where they looked down on the swift flowing river, as it wound its way to Limerick; shining like silver in the distance. They made their way towards the IRA stronghold that was hidden amongst the caves in the crevice of the mountain, where it had good views down the mountainside.

Bridie wanted to stop for a minute to relieve her bladder behind a tree and for a moment after, she looked around at the damp, cold mist that crept over the mountain and gave a little shudder.

'We will be safe in the cavern,' said Daneen, hurrying her along. 'It's like a fort up there,' he told her. They knew that the IRA was waiting for them to bring the rifles, although Bridie kept checking to see if anyone was following.

'Perhaps they won't come after us,' said Daneen, whipping the horses to go faster, staring straight in front of him. They passed a small farm at the foot of the mountains that towered in front of them, with purple heather, bright on the mountain slopes. Daneen knew the ins and outs of these narrow pathways up into the mountain and the IRA stronghold was well hidden and he remembered the route Granddad told him, and taking that, it led straight out to what looked like a large historic stone and suddenly it lifted up, like the entrance to Aladdin's cave and a tall man, with wide shoulders, pointed a gun straight at them.

They were soon told to enter and followed the man into the smoky cavern, where a whole world new existed and a hundred men, lived. Huddled around a camp fire was a band of men, crouching on the stony ground and Daneen recognised the uniform of the Tipperary Brigade, beside them shotguns - and he knew he was in the right place. As order came, the men ran up the stone steps to the entrance of the cave and quickly brought the rifles down, working like an army of ants, lifting them below, then disappearing into the deep crevices of the cavern to a hiding place.

It was Bridie's task to unleash the horses, while the cart was taken off, and hidden in a barn and it all happened very quickly. Soon a man appeared on a motorbike handing the youngsters two helmets, all the time the man looking around, his gun ready to fire, with one eye down the mountain slope for any intruders.

'Go safely,' he said, this bike will get you down   quicker.` As Daneen and Bridie got on the motorbike, they headed over the mountain and down the other side, going back along the   narrow pathways. It all happened in about fifteen minutes and they knew that if the armoured car ever got there, the IRA stronghold had the guns well hidden in the caves.

So when the two youngsters pulled up at Granddad's farm on the motorbike he was there with arms open and a wide grinning smile. The message had soon reached him by pigeon that the guns had been delivered.

'By George,' he said, 'you did it! And they are good guns. The brigade will be over the moon. There's, over fifty rifles here.But how did you get on?' the old man, asked, as they sat in the kitchen and warmed themselves by the aga. 'I hear the troops have raided a house on the bog road, I was worried you got stopped.'

'We did,' Daneen told him.

And Bridie told him the story of how she ended up coshing the trooper with the rifle buck. 'Daneen's a good horse rider,' she said, 'how he ever got us away at such a speed I don't know.'

'Well the pair of you together is a good team', said the old man, and patted Daneen on the back. 'Don't know what you would do without such a gel beside you.'

'I know,' said Daneen, 'she's a fine girl. She's not scared of no – man.'

'And that's sure true,' laughed Bridie, jumping onto Daneen's lap and was kissing his face.

'Behave yourself,' chided Granddad, supping his beer, his moustache dripping with the brown liquid, his face scrunching up into a grin as the two youngsters larked about together.

So Bridie and Daneen grew in the movement of the Tipperary Brigade, going on to do more and more missions: like the time, they helped in the ambush at the quarry, when the Tipperary gang confiscated the gelignite, and the new road the British were building, never got finished. They handled many a mission, including when car bombs were used to blow up an armoured truck.

The missions of the Tipperary gang became a way of life. They aided in many and became known as the daring pair.

Growing up together, they had been close, like brother and sister, but as they grew older, Daneen could not help noticing how her blouse got tighter and her bud like breasts showed beneath it. When they were not on missions, they would be training the horses in the paddock, or go riding across the sweet meadowland and often stop at the stream to watch the fish and listen to the birds, and watch the deer roam past. Often they took just the one horse, mounting it together to ride bare back, and Granddad would say they were joined at the hips. He loved to see them together and would watch them with a grin.

They made a fine couple, but sometimes, Daneen would look at Bridie with a disapproving air; for her behaviour was more like a boy's, carrying her rifle on her shoulder, the Tipperary cloth cap, covering her pretty hair.

'Ain't you got a skirt?' he had said, but Bridie told him, she was one of the gang and clutched him around the shoulders with her strong arms, and although Daneen would always feel safe with Bridie, she would drag you into political arguments, making statements about law and order and be forever forcing her will on him.

'She's got too much jaw', Granddad would say, as Bridie went on about the emancipation of women. 'Goes on about women getting the vote', he would moan, 'but men will always be stronger'.

Daneen wasn't sure about that, but Bridie certainly had a lot of jaw on these subjects.

One day when they were sitting in the high field, watching the horses graze, she was laying down the law over Ireland's freedom, with a clenched fist.

'Don't be so aggressive,' said Daneen, and threw his weight on top of her and over and over they rolled. But however strong Bridie was, she was struggling to get up.

'Get off me you brute,' she started to laugh, but Daneen sat on top of her holding her arms either side of her head and as they lay on the cool grass, when he pressed his lips onto hers, a little shiver of excitement ran through her. She had never felt this way before. Her blue eyes soft and loving, she lay her head on his shoulder.

From then on, she seemed to have a healthy glow about her skin and felt sure that they belonged to each other.

Time rolled by and although the 'cease fires' came into being, as talks of a peace treaty would be signed, raids on the barracks continued. In the villages the houses were set on fire and there were reprisals and more bombings over the years.

Then one day as Grandad Spud waved the youngsters off, as they went off to a mission, his world fell apart. He was just toddling off to the stables to feed the horses, puffing at his clay pipe and whistling an Irish tune. His mind as usual was on the youngsters, who were delivery guns to the brigade in Tipperary, when suddenly he was attacked from behind.

`Get down on the floor, an English voice threatened and from the corner of his eyes grandad recognized the uniform of the black and tans and the tall figure was ramming a gun in his back

` let me go`, granddad squealed as he lay on the floor, trying to get free, but the man stood over him, with his foot in his back.

What you want you bastards shouted Grandad who had plenty of spunk, but they only laughed, pulled his beard and tied him up. Then soon found the many guns that were stored in a box under the horses straw. Grandad was kicking and yelling laying there on the stable floor, with only the horses to hear him and as much as the horse s kicked there hind legs out trying to break down there paddock, there was no one around, as the black and tans were off to search through the house, pulling everything out until they found the explosives they wanted. It was all hidden at the back of the fridge. `got it they said, bringing it to show the old man, who denied knowing anything about it, but they took him off to the station jail, treating him with humour and the occasional slap as the old boy called them `mercenaries`

When Daneen and Bridie got back, the house had been set on fire and the horses had been set free onto the fields.

Daneen searched the house, the stables, black smoke was bellowing out, he kept calling his grandfather name `the black and tans have got him` said Bridie, `I just know it`. But Daneen ran around like a headless chicken, in and out of the fire looking for the old man. When Bridie discovered the Rifles were gone, she pulled daneen away, ``theyve got the guns she said, `granddad is probably in the police station` and Daneen couldnt wait to get there, picking up his grandfathers old gun, that lay on the sawdust, saying he would shoot his grandfather out of there.

`we have got to get the horses in` said Bridie, seeing them running wild around the fields, and grabbing Daneen lasso, was quick to hand it to him. `get them together, she said, before we loose them. So daneen went over the fence and into the field, jumping straight onto the back of one of the horses,just like a rodeo star and with the skill of one, lassoed the horses, one by one, bringing them to heal and tied them under a tree, bridie put there feed boxes before them.

`I`m going to get granddad said Daneen, his gun in his hand`

'Don't be stupid,' said Bridie, 'they will kill you', and called her father, who was just coming into the farm, having seen the fire. And shamus, together with a farm hand, grabbed the shotgun from Daneen as he tried to get away and held him down until   heartbreaking cries escaped from Daneen's lips. For to think of his old grandfather being held by the constabulary, and pushed around, was too much too bear.

'They won't get any information out of the old boy,' said Shamus. 'Try not to worry.' But Daneen was afraid for him.

But not long after, with two black eyes and a broken nose, the old man was sent off to Cork Jail. Now the farm had been burnt to the ground and Daneen no longer had a home. So Bridie took him in, on her father's farm, and that's where he stayed, but he would keep up the good fight for Ireland, and continue the work that his grandfather had taught him. He missed the old grandfather being there, being like a father to him, with his hearty laughter and telling one tale or another, but Granddad Spud remained in Cork Jail, despite Daneen trying to convince him to escape.

"I'm too old and had my time and I am not having you risk your life, boyo", the old man had said to him. Daneen settled for visiting the old man, who, over the years became thinner and his face paler as he lost his ruddy complexion. "I'm alright, son", he would say, still with that hearty laughter. "Me and the other volunteers, cause havoc in here, half of them, are on hunger strike".

'Don't want you doing that,' Daneen had said, with an anxious tone, but Granddad would grin from ear to ear, hiding the tears that formed in his watery old eyes and laughed out loud, talking of the famous hunger strikers who were in the cell next door. As the winter passed Grandad got weaker, he would never stop his fight for Irelands freedom, even in jail and became an advisor to many a political young prisoner. Daneen missed his presence, especially on early morning rides out on the marshland, where grandad took him as a boy and trained him in the art of riding. It was spring time and the marshland was full of flowers, gold masses of marsh marigolds, full of purple iris`s and delicate blue and pink flowers mingling in the long grass`s bordered the dykes that ran down to the river. He would still dream up plans as he rode, to get Grandad out of the cork jail, but time ran out and eventually, grandad passed away. It was a bereft Daneen, who would never forget all he taught him about horses and the politics of Ireland. He thought much about that last visit at the jail, when the old man took his hand and said: "You must take the reins now my boy".

During the following years, Tipperary was more a peaceful place and Daneen settled at Bridie's father's farm, taking much work off her father, old Shamus, as he had got injured by the British Army. This happened, during a plan, to spring a captured man from a train. It was a dangerous mission, but the Tipperary Brigade, would go a long way to free one of their men, that the British had captured. The British, had been after him, for some time, ever since he had shot a black and tan in cold blood and one day when he came out of the cinema, the British were waiting to capture him and take him off to cork jail. They were transporting him on a train to cork jail, but the Tipperary brigade, had been tipped off.

`well get him off that damn train` said shamus wielding his shotgun, there not taking our man to cork jail`.

So as the train stopped at Kanturk station, the brigade jumped on and took the prisoner off, cutting his shackles with a chopper and beating the constable. Then suddenly from out of no where the irish constabulary arrived, firing ammunition from their armoured car. The Tipperary gang didnt stand much of a chance and they ran in all directions, firing back and trying to get away.

Shamus was one of the first to be hit and lay beside the prisoner, on the station platform, until two of the brigade, lifted them to there feet and frogmarched them to safety, before the british got across the line.

`Dirty bastards` old shamus was calling out as he limped along, while the armoured car was still firing bullets from its guns.

Many got shot and they all asked themselves, how did the british know, as they went off in a car. But Shamus had taken several bullets in his leg, that he never really got over, and resulted him being in a for the rest of his life.

It was not until 1922, after the peace treaty was signed, that some peace came to Ireland. There was a truce, as the Irish 'Free State' was now created, with a breakaway government, declaring independence for Ireland, and the people celebrated in the streets for days. There was dancing in the village hall and the men drank irish moonshine and got very merry. The women drank wine. They all sang songs and danced a jig or two, and tales were told of the folk they knew, and family stories of wakes and weddings. Even the priest dropped by and slyly partook of the strong irish moonshine. Everyone was in good spirits and no one down at heart, and no one mentioned the arrests that were taking place, as the young men were taken off by the constabulary to jail.

Daneen and Bridie danced around the floor, although she clomped around in her boots, and was a hopeless dancer, as she was usually behind the times, whether dancing or fashion. But she would sing out loud to the Irish songs and drink back a pint of ale with the boys. Often talking of her father, who was a hero, since he was wounded when rescuing one of the Tipperary brigade from the train, `my poor dad, she would say, tears in her eyes, he will never walk again. And then filled with anger, she would run the british down, for what they

did, often referring to the political statements, she had learnt from
her father. `Get the british out` she would shout`,

  "She ought to be the next Sinn Fein leader` they would laugh. As she
was always up front with the rebels, knocking down her pint and talk
talk of old Ireland gaining strength, and if any drunken lad said a
wrong word to Daneen, she would knock him out with her fist.

  Together Daneen and Bridie worked the farm, building the place up.
A ram and some sheep were brought at market, then put to graze on
the high field and in the spring many a lambs was born.
`Aye now, take the money from the bank` old shamus would tell bridie
`Tis foine, get a stable built for Daneen, he will make a fine business`.
`you wont be sorry Bridie would tell her Pa her blue eyes lighting up
with joy, she would kiss her fathers wrinkled brow. His mop of red
hair was now thin and his injured leg withered.
 Each morning she would give him a blanket bath in his wheelchair
and he would grin mischievously, wanting to know any gossip that
went on in the Tipperary Brigade, for in his heart he would always be
a sinn fein and although, his body was failing him, his brain was still
as alert. He would watch from the window while Daneen trained the

horses,

 often going to market and bringing home the wildest horse, but Daneen would soon have the horse baying.

So with a new stable block, built for boarding many a thoroughbred horse, the farm became a success.

During these successful years, Daneen also taught Bridie's brother, Tim to ride. He was younger than Daneen, with a mop of red hair and always glued to the TV set watching the cowboy films

`your not a cowboy now`Daneen would tell him, `bit old for that` and snatch the whip from Tims hand as they galloped the horses across the farmland.

 Together, they would go to horse fairs and steeplejack riding and he had a good home there on the farm and he and Bridie, were a good team, looking after the livestock, growing new crops.

She was often out on the tractor ploughing the land, while Daneen took over the stables. Bridie tended the sheep, breeding lambs in the Spring and even sheared them herself, making a fine profit. They employed farm labourers and grew freshly cut crops for the market to sell; despite the fact, Daneen on market days, would slope off to the bar and often drive the cart home drunk. But Bridie didn't care, she would sing along merrily with him as the cart wobbled from side to side, along the dirt tracks home. And anytime Daneen disappeared to the country club, for a pint with Davey Joe, Bridie would soon follow and join him, drinking porter by the pint, with the rest of the lads.

'She can drink me under the table', he would tell them, but after a few too many, they all had to listen to Bridie's political arguments, in her loud persistent voice.

As time passed, there were political stirrings in England and a man called Mosley with a following known as the `Black Shirts` gave talks on the street corners about the Nazi`s, and talk of war grew and no one knew whether it would blow over. Bridie was still waiting to become a bride and one day said to Daneen, 'Don't want to miss the boat, you might be dragged off to war and we will never be married,'. So Daneen agreed and they became engaged, but Bridie was not the kind of girl who would be gathering for her bottom drawer, she was much happier out on the land digging or rounding up the sheep.

Tim her younger brother, had grown into a fine young man and one day, he told Bridie, of his girlfriend. 'I am sure you will love her,' he said, and when he brought the raven haired beauty to the farm, all the family were in awe of her.

'She's a ray of sunshine,' old man Shamus said, 'but I can't imagine the gun in her hand like Bridie.' For Nora was delicate, and they felt a little sorry for her, as her parents had been killed in the First World War and she was left an orphan. It was a convent education she had been given, often her hands folded in pray, they were white and soft, unlike Bridie's rough hands that dug in the clay with a pitch fork planting the vegitables. `

'You'll have to toughen her up,' old Shamus said, `work on the fields, do her good`. but Tim only wanted to protect his young love,. It was not long before she came to live there on the farm and old Shamus told his son: 'She will have to help out`, she can work in the cow shed. Teach her how to milk the cows, boy.'

It was Bridie who had that task and was not very patient as she sat Nora down on a stool in the cow shed, showing her the cows' udders. She eventually got the idea of how to milk, although, Daneen would see her most days struggling with the chore as he passed the milk shed to go to the stables.

`Tis a foine Job your doing` he laughed out loud and when she looked at him with those enormous blue eyes, her skinny legs either side of the stall, he would stand a while watching her - as if mesmerised. But when Bridie came along, he would soon scoot back to the stable and she would stand over the girl in an impatient manner, her arms akimbo, then show her again, just how to milk the cow.

So life at the farm carried on, despite it was a time of political trouble, and war was imminent, young men were leaving the village and going into the army and navy. Young Tim had always wanted to be a pilot and went off to england to enlist in the R.A.F. He hated to leave his love, Nora, and said he would send for her. 'But you'll be alright on the farm here, for now,' he told her, 'for Bridie and me father will look after yis.' He shook Daneen's hand saying, 'Keep an eye on my girl,' and the girl smiled coyly at Daneen and he wasnt sure how he was going to handle her. Despite the talk of war that went on in the village, Bridie was busy planning for her wedding at the church, and some said, `a war might not last long`, although, there was now a dark cloud hovering over her plans and knew that she could be left to look after old Shamus and Nora and keep the home fires burning, if all the men went to war.

Some afternoons Daneen and Bridie would ride out on horseback, like they used to as youngsters, - Bridie up close behind him on the back of his horse. On the way home they stopped by the river to fish for salmon to cook for tea and share some moments of love. They found a shady nook, where honey suckle and wild rose entwined and she took his hand, `lets rest here`, she whispered in his ear and together they lay on the bank, savouring the scent of the honey suckle that pervaded the air and listening to the birds in the trees. With a little teasing smile, she looked down on him as he lay, his arms resting behind his head and piled her long yellow hair up on her head, securing it with a pin, and let the little wisps of curls hang onto her face, `my pretty girlie` he said, looking into her mischievous blue eyes.

`I know just what your after having` he smiled, pulling her towards him.

and her hot lips came down on his, as she could never say no to daneen., once his hands rested on her, it was like a strange quivering that rippled inside of her. To her it was like the sea to the shore, the most natural thing in the world, for he was her man and always would be and as he kissed the back of her neck and his passionate kisses overwhelmed her, she was soon caught up im that swift hot passion, that always carried them away.

Afterward they lay side by side, at peace, listening to the flow of the river. Her face was flushed and her hair array, but she didnt care, as long as she was with her man. But there was a questioning look in her eyes as she said,

`if you go to war,  I will wait for you`, knowing there was a war on and wondering, if he could be called up`

`They will take the young men first` Daneen laughed, pulling her towards him `I`m just an old batchelor`.

`not for long` she smiled, and `and I`m soon to make you mine`

`Oh be sure, he grinned, I`ve always been yours, `have we not always been known as a couple and people say we were made for each other.`

`True enough` she smiled softly, but as they sat on the hillside together looking down at the rolling river, a tear trickled from the corner of her eye. and there was a hurt expression in her blue eyes.

`when you come home, she murmured, we will have the biggest wedding,  `I want it to be just right, with all the Kennedy family and the `O`Hara`s of course.

`I don`t want you to go` she suddenly said and wiped a tear, that ran down her face.

143

`but I may have to` he returned, `its war``and pulled her to him
`I`ll cope she said, `Ive always had to be strong`.
`you are my strong girlie`, Daneen said, clasping her hand, `the times
you have rescued me over the years` and she started to smile, as long
as she was Daneen`s girl, she would be alright and nestled in his arms.

Bridie had become a little more feminine since the peace time in
Ireland; abandoning her gun from her shoulder, although the
shepherds' crook seemed to go everywhere with her these days. But
her hair was always glowing and clean from her swims in the river,
where on hot afternoons she would go naked and lay on the bank to
dry out, inviting Daneen to lay beside her.

The sexual act was nothing new to the couple these days, and
afterwards, Bridie would lay purring like a cat, but as that summer
passed on the farm she seemed to need him even more, until Daneen
said, as they lay in each other's arms one day, 'You don't want to be
left pregnant, I might be called to war`.

'We are already like husband and wife.' Perhaps that was true,
Daneen agreed, but his love for Bridie, never seemed fuelled by the
need to get her into bed, it was more a caring, loving feeling that they

both shared. 'But if I get pregnant,' she said, 'I know you'll be mine forever,' but there was a sadness in those usually lively blue eyes, and Daneen knew she was wondering if she ever could have a baby, for so far, it had not happened and they had taken many chances. 'when the world is at peace', she said, giving his knee a pat and lifting her face to be kissed, 'we can have that big wedding.' And that lovely safe feeling of belonging, that she gave him, was always there.

Within two months, the young men were disappearing from the local farms: very few worked on the fields, for they were going off to war, but that didn't stop Daneen and Bridie, who were always busy with the chores. Bridie was mostly up in the high fields tending the sheep; the sheep dog by her side. She would blow the whistle and he would round up the sheep.

Nora was always fretting over Tim being away and would say with tears in her eyes, 'I hope my Tim will be home soon'. Her little girl ways, used to annoy Bridie, who wished she would get on with milking, the milk churns were always half empty, but instead she idled away around the farm, picking flowers, watching the pigs and imitating their noises, or would wander into the stables to watch Daneen groom the horses, asking all about them and saying how she would like to learn to ride. This usually fell on deaf ears as Daneen mucked out the stables.

'Need any help?' she would ask, stroking the horses shiny backs, but Daneen was usually pretending to be too busy to look up, for each time she looked at him with those enormous blue eyes, it sent a shiver inside of him.

'You had better get back to the milking', he would say, 'for Bridie will be on the war path'. He could see the brown and white cows, lumbering along the muddy lane, lowering painfully as there udders over flowed with milk.

With a coy smile, Nora picked up her milking stool and swinging her hips she made for the milking shed, then, sat astride the small stool, the cow's soft udder in her hands. She nodded at Daneen, and produced a soft chuckle that rippled along the old milking shed.

Some days she would dress very prettily, taking off the little white cap that the dairy maids wore, letting her hair hang loose, then with a mischievous glint in her eyes, twist, her hair up in a little knot on the top of her head. In a low cut dress, her young white bosoms could be seen like two mounds of ice cream as she bent at the tap to fill a bucket with water, then turn with a tender smile, showing the fascinating dimples that appeared both sides of her cheeks, asking Daneen, if he needed any water for the horses.

'No thanks'. He would reply, almost haughtily, as this young girl did not seem to know how beautiful she looked.

One day Bridie came back from the field, striding as she always did into the stable, her strong physique, erect and her boots muddy from the river. 'How you doing?' she asked Nora. 'How many buckets of milk you got from the cows today?' But Nora would go all shy and stare cow - eyed, looking bewildered, and whine how difficult she found the job and slope away.

'She's a lazy little cow,' Bridie said, 'just floats about in a pretty dress and doesn't like getting her hands dirty.' After that, Bridie put Nora digging in the vegetable garden, but that only made her complain that the shovel made her hands sore.

But Daneen was glad Nora was out of his sight, although he had to admit to himself, he missed the feeling that her presence gave him.

Then one warm afternoon, he wandered down to the stream and there sitting on the bank was Nora, her skirt hitched high and her feet in the water. He was surprised to see her sitting there and as she looked up, her lovely black hair was blowing in the breeze and her lips curled up in a wide smile, and his heart began to beat quickly. He wanted to reach and touch her beautiful thick mane of hair that hung to her waist over the flowery, summer dress, which clung to her figure.

'Oh,' she said, as if startled and began to get up. 'I expect Bridie will be looking for me,' and her sharp little face studied him quizzically. But Daneen could not answer. He felt suddenly dumbstruck by her presence and could not help looking with admiration at her long white neck and smooth bosom. 'I better go,' she stood staring at him, but Daneen rushed past her and down the track beside the stream, feeling that he had to get away.

AFFAIR IN THE COWSHED

Ch.19

It had been an affair that changed a lot of peoples' lives, as affairs often do, but this one, involved four people who were related in one way or another. At first it had only been a harmless flirtation, when Nora would smile coyly at Mae Kennnedy and say, what a handsome man Daneen was.

'Now you beware of him', Mae would return with a grin, 'Bridie will be after you', as Mae was Bridie's close friend, and often at the farm visiting as the district nurse to attend old Shamus.

There wasn't much that Mae missed, and Eventually, she noticed that Nora was hanging around the stables a bit too much and began to side track her into coming to church,   telling her to stay away from Daneen. 'After all, you are engaged to Tim, so behave yourself while he is away'.

'But we are not doing any harm', Nora would say, in her girlish manner, although, she would dress very prettily just to milk the cows, often a low neck, showing her white bosoms, that would tempt any man, and there was a pink glow about her face.

Each morning as Nora die her chores, she rushed to the stables, her heart would be singing, for she needed to be near Daneen, for everywhere she went, she felt his presence and would constantly talk

149

about Daneen, not being able to get him from her mind.

Mae would notice the flush to her neck as she spoke his name and tried to warn her to keep away. But Nora could not stay away and would sit in the stable watching Daneen; his strong, bare arms, brushing the horses with the grooming brush. She became almost mesmerised as he brushed them till they shone and when he turned to look at her with a roguish smile, she would blush coyly.

'Still here are you?' he would say with a grin. 'Bridie will be back soon from the field and want to know how much milk is in the churn'.

'I will get it done', she said, getting up and twisting around, her skirt swinging out as she danced around and he could not help noticing her high breasts and a small waist.

He got to look forward to her visits to the stable and was feeling such a pull to this girl, it was like two magnets attracting, and it wasn't long before he could not help himself anymore, one day, when she came in wearing a pink silky dress, its low neckline frothed with frills. She had stood beside him as he groomed the horse. Her small white hand smoothly swept strokes across the horse's flank.

'This mare is a beautiful horse,' he told her.

'Do you think I'm beautiful?' she asked in a childlike manner and came closer, lifting her face up to be kissed. He could feel her breath on his face and his lips brushed her long white neck.

'Now behave,' she said with a tease as her body leaned towards his and he bent her backwards as his lips kissed her gently and his dark moustache tickled her white breasts. She was lost in passion and he wanted her more than anything. With her arms around his neck, he untied the silky dress, that slipped from her body and onto the floor and he bent down in homage. 'Darling,' he gasped, and as he kissed her breasts, she stroked his hair in a whimsical manner.

'You are my man,' she whispered, and their lips met in a passionate kiss, as her legs wrapped around him. He could hold back no more and suddenly with a thrust, he entered her hot body and she gasped with passion.

Afterwards they lay side by side in the sweet smelling hayloft.

'I've never felt about any woman, like I feel about you,' he whispered as she snuggled into his arms.

So began this love affair, they both knew would hurt others. 'But where will it all end?' whispered Nora as she got herself dressed, but

Daneen didn't have an answer, he only knew that any minute Bridie could walk in through the stable door, and there would be hell to pay.

All that summer the affair continued, as they could no longer stay away from each other and would meet secretly in the cornfield. There they would make love, then lay naked in the shimmering sun, laughing and talking like lovers do. Then there came the time, when they suddenly heard the village church bells chiming loudly and saw people running towards the church. `whats going on`, said Daneen, grabbing her hand and her lithe body skipped and jumped as they chased across the field towards home and found out that the Prime Minister had declared war on Germany and giving a speech. On listening to the words, Daneen saw a chance to join up, men were needed to fight this war and his face brightened, as he wanted to travel and see the world and if there was a chance he could work with horses, decided he would be go. That week the men enlisted and began to go off in different directions around the world, and many young men gathered in the village square, talking about the war and queuing at the recruitment office. When Daneen told Nora that he had enlisted for the Irish guards in India she came at him with the yard broom, screaming that he was a

bastard for leaving her. But Daneen was going, for no women had been

able to hold him as yet, not even Bridie and Nora would be no

exception, but he took Nora in his arms, and held her till her tears

subsided. `what an irish temper` you have he told her and stroked her

hair, till she calmed down. But after that they went there seperate

ways, as Nora suddenly left for England. It was Bridie who told him, that

Nora had gone to join Tim, who was stationed in england. Daneen was

finding it hard to look at Bridie as she spoke of Nora and was hoping

that Bridie would never find out about his affair.   As he told Bridie he

was leaving, tears filled her vivid blue eyes, and she threw her arms

around his neck.

`I need to go` he said, `its an opportunity` I want to be in a cavalry

regiment and see the world.

So she gave him her blessing, for she knew how he loved his work with

horses, he was getting well known for training many horses in the

county.

`you are my man` she said, drying her tears, `I will pray you keep safe,

and `I will be here waiting for you to return`.

So Daneen packed his haversack and left on the next boat in Cork harbour, sailing for Liverpool. It was some months later when he got news of Nora. It was when his battalion was being posted out east. There were crowds of soldiers on the dock and they stood in rows waiting to board a ship, then by coincidence, all those miles from home, he bumped into Pat Kennedy from the village. He had joined the same regiment as Tim. He was just getting off the ship, everyone was pushing and shoving down the gang plank and there was little time, but Daneen asked how Nora was Pat told him, with that humorous glint in his irish eyes, that Tim was on compassionate leave, to be married to Nora and that they were expecting a baby. Daneen tried not to show his surprise, thinking she didnt waste much time, but deep in his heart knew it was for the best, and that he had Bridie to consider, although, Pat Kennedy had to put his pennyworth in. `and I`d leave them alone` he said in a gruff tone, cause there very happy`. For a moment Daneen wondered if Pat knew anything about there affair, but was soon moved on, as impatient soldiers pushed past.

Ch.20

BRIDIES HEARTBREAK

Later that year, when the men had gone to war, the only one at home was old Shamus sitting in his wheelchair and Bridie was left to look after him and the farm. The war was progressing fast: there was talk of air-raids in London and shelters being built.

Mae called at the farm on her way back from her rounds as a district nurse, riding her bike along the dirt road to the farm. It was old Shamus's bath day and her and Bridie always managed to get him into the bath, although old Shamus ranted and raved, saying he was clean enough and didn't need a bath. Bridie greeted her friend with a warm hug and went to the kitchen to put the kettle on the hob.

'There's a letter on the mat,' Mae told her, untying her blue bonnet, with the red cross, whilst Bridie dashed to pick up the hand written white envelope, tearing it open.

'It's from Tim,' she gasped, dropping down in an easy chair and read it aloud.

No 57768 - RAF base, Essex.

Dear Bridie,

I hope you are well and coping with the dangers of war. I have been flying my spitfire over Germany most of this week, avoiding old Hitler.

I am writing to let you know I am alright. The flat in Paddington with Nora, is in a dreary tenement, but at least it's a home of our own and we are happy.

I wanted you to be the first to know, about our happy event, for my lovely Nora is to have our child and we are both over the moon. I would have written sooner with the news but I get leave once every few months. Nora loves the flat and is working at the London Hospital, as a probationary nurse, but for how long, we are not sure. But I will keep in touch Bridie, and hope all is well on the farm. Give our love to Daneen if you hear from him. We heard he is stationed in Calcutta, India.

With much love
Your brother
Tim.

P.S. our address is flat 26, Vauxhall road, Paddington.

Thank goodness they are safe,' said Bridie, going into the conservatory that was warmed by the afternoon sun as it shone through the glass. They looked out on to a hazy sky and across the green hills, as Bridie was keeping an eye on a flock of sheep that grazed on the high field.

'I worry about Tim flying that spitfire,' Bridie tugged off her boots that were muddy from the fields. She was dressed in a check skirt and britches and her golden hair, hung down untidily in strands with streaks of silver. Her rosy cheeks had faded over the years and her waistline not as slim. 'Hope the war doesn't go on too long,' she said, 'and they are back for the wedding, I have the church booked for a May wedding next spring.'

'Mae sat listening, wondering what to say, she was very fond of her friend and would often moan about Daneen, acting like a batchelor boy and taking his time to get married, but now he was making an absolute fool of her.

Mae had never married and cared only about a successful nursing career, she had forged for herself. At school she had been very studious, passing her exams with top marks, despite the fact she was short sighted. Her hair was a dusty ash colour. It was always well trimmed with a straight fringe above the heavy black spectacles she wore. She was always known as a plain Jane and certainly didn't want to be bothered with any man. But Bridie was different, and in an unusually animated mood, talked on about her marriage to Daneen.

'Well it won't be long now,' said Bridie, 'I have my dress all ready for the big day.'

'It's about time,' said Mae, clicking the knitting needles, 'that you got him down the aisle. You know, a man can go off the boil very quickly.'

'My Daneen has always too busy with his horses, to worry about women,' laughed Bridie, but Mae knew exactly what had kept him busy and that was Nora in the cow shed.   Mae sat listening to Bridie. 'Me and Daneen, have been together since we were children,' Bridie went on, 'and that's when you know a man inside out.' Mae wasn't so sure about that and sat with her lips set in a grim line, feeling that Daneen was making a fool of everyone. 'And now,' declared Bridie, in an excited fashion, 'I am to be an aunt, now that Nora is having a baby. Our Tim will be so proud to be a father.

Mae could not help wondering who the baby belonged to, knowing of the love affair between Daneen and Nora, thinking that there was a possibility that the baby was not Tim`s and that Daneen could even be the Father. These thoughts buzzed in her head, but she tried to push the doubts aside, telling herself, there was no proof, and a voice kept saying`it`s none of your business`.

For a while they sat sipping tea and looking out onto the spring lawn, primroses were shooting up amongst clumps of pansies, and leaves were blooming on the row of peach trees.

Bridie flipped through the pages of a bridal magazine on the kitchen table showing Mae in an excited fashion the dress she had chosen. 'It's got a lovely flared skirt, don't you think,' and then she swung around in the kitchen imagining wearing it. But Mae was looking at her fuller figure, as she had put on weight.

'Better make sure it's the right size, Bridie.'

'Oh, I'll be losing weight for the wedding,' she said, her face lighting up and her eyes rolling dreamily.

'Well, all I can say,' said Mae in an irritated fashion, 'it's about time. You make sure you get Daneen down the aisle. He has certainly dragged his feet.'

'It's, nerves that's all,' said Bridie.

'Some men are like that when it comes to getting married. I`ve mentioned it over the years, she confessed,

always seemed afraid of making the commitment, think it might have been that insecure childhood of his, left an orphan, had no one really, till Grandad Spudd took him in. `

`Oh your too soft`, said Mae, thinking she was always making excuses for him, he was just a blaggard, doing just what he wanted and played the field with Nora.

 How cruel, she thought, her face blushing scarlet and tears clouded her grey eyes as she thought of poor Bridie, who was so happy about marrying him.

'What's the matter with you?' said Bridie spotting the tears, and put on the kettle for more tea.

'I'm alright,' said Mae, 'just glad your tying the knot at last.'

And as Bridie buttered some hot muffins she talked on about the guest list she was sending out and the big wedding she was planning.

'Might be better to wait till the war is over,' warned Mae.

'If it's not, he will get compassionate leave,' said Bridie, as if nothing was going to stop her. Had a letter from him, she continued, `telling me he volunteered for the British Indian Army and left the irish guards. It was when an opportunity came up to train horses for the Burma jungle, but he had to be sent to barracks in Calcutta. Shame, about the irish guards, she said, but I could never imagine him sitting on a horse for long, with a busby on his head, he likes a bit of action, my Daneen.

But Mae wasnt interested in Daneens military career, she was thinking about poor Tim and what a 'cuckold' Nora was making of him.

The blush on her face was now on her neck and her knitting needles clicked furiously, until she dropped a stick. She was hot and bothered and wanted to just blurt it out, to put Bridie right, for Daneen was nothing but a scoundrel and it seemed had got away with it; for he was now far away in India and he deserved to be horse whipped.

Bridie glanced at her friend as Mae scooped the stitches back on the needle with a long face.

'It's about time you got yourself a man,' she said looking at her friend, whose mouth was full lipped and looked very sullen. She was wondering if she was a little jealous, that she was not getting married herself.'I think every woman should be a bride, at least once in there lives.'

'Not me,' said Mae, adamantly. 'You know me with men,' she added, her eyes downcast, and watched her needles click, for she could not bring herself to look Bridie in the eye. 'I got let down years ago, as you know,' continued Mae, 'never trust a man again. In fact I've joined the women's trade union. 'I'm also becoming a feminist.'

Bridie laughed out loud, for in her heart, she knew Mae would never change. They then went into a long discussion about women's equal pay, as they were both keen pioneers for the emancipation of women and Emmaline Pankhurst, who had founded the national society of women and this was their favourite subject, and all the great suffragettes, who had fought for the vote. So for the rest of the afternoon talk of the wedding was dropped and Mae was relieved, feeling she had heard enough about that for one day.

'I'm thinking of joining the strikes,' she said. 'Women are still on low pay, but at least there is work for the war effort. Women are being employed in the ammunition factories, so that's a good start,but still not good enough. It's, men's work and they should get a man's wage.

Why do you think the suffragettes fought for us, all what they went through.' Mae's face was as red as beetroot and Bridie was wondering why she was getting so worked up.

'Women have always been kept down. Slaves to men it seems,can't say I feel a slave to men,' said Bridie, with a grin and carried on making the bread to bake for dinner.

'You're forgetting how women have been kept down,' Mae went on. 'At one time they were only allowed to be domestic servants and now we have got us the vote, we must fight all the way for a better working life for women. Look at those suffragettes, how they suffered for us.' She put her knitting needles on the table with a huff, then, banged her fist on down. 'Women must not settle for the low pay and repetitive shift work. We are still treated as inferior.'

'Don't know what you're getting in such a fluff about,' said Bridie looking at Mae's flushed face. 'You're now qualified as a midwife, what an opportunity, to help these young women, left alone, there men at war.

`Why don't you leave district nursing, not much happening in this village, and go off and join the war effort, work at one of the hospitals.'

'I intend to,' said Mae, 'but I'm still joining the women's strikes.'

'Okay,' said Bridie, trying to please her friend, 'I'm willing to come to a few meetings with you, but remember I've got this farm to run and my invalid father to look after, as well as a wedding to arrange.

But Mae was miles away, thinking of the strong women of the Suffragettes movement and how they chained themselves to the railings and went on hunger strike. Then there was poor Emily Davidson, who got killed by a horse. How brave they all were and yet, she didn't even have the pluck, to tell her best friend the truth; put her right and let her know of Daneen's betrayal. It was burning inside of her, but she knew how nasty Bridie could be: she was well known for using a shotgun in the Irish revolution, and still carried a gun around the farm. Most people avoided arguments with her.

'I'm so pleased about Tim`s Baby continued Bridie, who herself would love to be a mother, but it had never happened, 'but at least I am getting married, a bride at last`. Perhaps I can help Nora with the baby. That girl, she don't seem to be able to cope with much, she could not even milk a flaming cow`.

No, thought Mae, *too busy with Daneen in the cowshed.'*

'She`s a bit delicate,' said Bridie.

'Delicate,' huffed Mae. Was that what she was? For Nora, was nothing but a little tramp as far as she was concerned, sleeping with Bridie's bloke. If only she knew.

'Don't be too hard on her,' said Bridie. 'Remember, she was an orphan and brought up in a convent, this is the first real family she has had.'

And a fine way she treats them, thought Mae. 'This baby, is Tim sure he is the father?' she suddenly blurted out.

'Of course he is,' said Bridie, staring at her in puzzlement. What do you mean by that?'

'Nothing particular,' Mae shrugged, and tried to hide her hand that shook with anger.

But Bridie stared at her coolly. 'I don't know, what's got up your nose today,' she said.

And Mae bit her tongue, afraid of telling her the truth. 'Well all I can say is,' said Mae changing the subject, 'Nora would make a hopeless suffragette.' So for a while the conversation went on about the brave Emily Davidson, who was killed by a horse, but the discussion, became heated as they disagreed about the event. Bridie thought, Emily Davidson was standing up for what she believed and showed great courage, but Mae pulled a face, disagreeing with whatever, Bridie said.

'But you have to stand up for whatever you believe,' continued Bridie, 'in whatever way you can, just like the champions of the Irish Revolution. Look at the brave Delavero who wasn't afraid to stand up for the cause, and there is an old saying:

"When they took the Jews, I said nothing.

When they took the communists, I said nothing

When they took the trade unionist, I said nothing

When they came to take me, there was nobody left".

'Don't fire quotes at me,' snapped Mae, with irritation, 'I'm fighting for women's equal pay and backing the strikes, for we need progression. No good keep hankering about the past, for women need good jobs now and careers, like men, it's not fair.'

'But at least, in war time,' returned Bridie, 'theres work in the ammunitions factories`

'Yes, but women still need to fight for better jobs`

'Just like Emily Davidson did,' said Bridie, who could have a romantic turn of mind, saying, she would have loved to have chained herself to the railings.

'Don't be so ridiculous,' said Mae, in an argumentative tone, 'and you won't even stand up to your man.'

'What you mean by that?' asked Bridie with a quizzical eye.

'He gets away with murder, that's why,' snapped Mae, who was soon wishing she had not said it, as Bridie was looking annoyed.

'I don't know what you mean by that either,' she said, 'and I'm fed up with you running him down. My Daneen, is loyal and strong, shame you can't find yourself someone.'

'Oh don't worry,' said Mae, in a sarcastic manner, 'I wouldn't want a blackguard, like him.' Mae was sick and tired of Bridie having the wool pulled over her eyes. It was about time she woke up.

'Well,' said Bridie, coming up and standing right in front of Mae, her arms akimbo, 'if there is anything you got to say about him, you better spit it out 'cause you obviously don't like my man.' And Bridie was glaring straight at her, close to her face.

Mae shuffled back in the chair, her back against it and picked up her knitting. Fear rippled over her.

'Just m . . . meant', she stammered, 'you . . . you should keep an eye on him, that's all.'

But Bridie wasn't letting go, she was sure, Mae was making an accusation and she sat down opposite her, her elbows resting on the table and they were eye ball to eye ball.

'Come on, let's have it,' said Bridie, her lips taking a mean curl, and that's when nervously, Mae, burst into tears and told her how she had seen Daneen in the cow shed with Nora.

'What!' screamed Bridie, gritting her teeth, 'you're a liar, you better take that back!'

'No it's true, and you shouldn't marry a man like that. I'm just trying to protect you.'

For a moment, there was a shocked silence, then, Bridie flew into a rage, and banged both her fists on the table, getting up and shouting in Mae's face, at such a terrible accusation.

'You're making it all up,' she stormed. 'You're just jealous, because I'm getting married and you're not!' But Mae was shaking her head from side to side, fear rushing through her as Bridie screamed into her face, it was untrue and her eyes were like blue fire.

'How long?' she shouted. 'How long has this supposed to have been going on?' and her hands were shaking, as she lit a cigarette, then stormed up and down the kitchen. 'You better tell me!'

So Mae gathering her courage, wiped her eyes and told her how she had seen them flirting one afternoon and then going off to the cowshed, coming out all bleary eyed and dishevelled.

Bridie was silent and listened, but her eyes were red rimmed, with unwashed tears.

'I saw them from the window,' continued Mae-'

'And you . . . have known about this all along and not told me,' Bridie accused.

'Mae looked down, afraid to say, for it was all like a thunderbolt to Bridie who yelled and threw the teapot up the wall and burst into floods of tears.

Mae rushed to pick up the broken pot and clean the mess.

'Leave it!' yelled Bridie and fired one question after another at Mae, wanting to know the ins and outs of this affair.

And Mae told her all she knew as the tears rolled down Bridie's face.

'And now she`s pregnant,' said Bridie, her face twisted in bitterness.

'But it does not mean, its not Tim`s baby`' said Mae softly, but Bridie looked with sad eyes and cried so hard, she was inconsolable. It was as if her whole world had fallen apart.

'I thought I needed to tell you,' said Mae, `especially now you are to be married,   and gently putting an arm around her shoulder as heartbreaking sobs escaped from Bridie's lips. 'I just didn't know how and you were so happy.

I don't want you to make a mistake by marrying him - and poor Tim,   I don't want to see him fooled, as Nora as been so unfaithful to the poor man.

Bridie put her head on her arms on the table and wept: the salted tears rolled down onto the floor, and whatever Mae said, Bridie did not answer, and her eyes were blank, so Mae crept from the room and closed the door quietly, leaving her friend to her heartbreak, for there seemed, there was nothing else she could do.

Soon after that time, Mae kept away, spending long hours working as a district nurse and was waiting for a transfer to England as a midwifery sister at one of the hospitals.   As for Bridie, when she cried at her father's feet, telling him all about it, he attempted to get out of the wheelchair and get his gun, saying how he was going to kill Daneen.

'But he is in India, Dad, you can't get him, none of us can.' The old man cried with frustration, saying how his son must never know. `and what about the child` he asked, his old eyes filled with tears and gave his nose a hard blow.

`It may not be Tim`s said Bridie, with a sad shrug. `

'But there's many a cuckoo in the nest,' the old man said, choking back his tears 'I don't want Tim to have the pain of knowing what Nora has done. `whoever is the father, he added, `be Better Tim brings the child up, as his own.' Bridie listened to her father's wise words and promised him, she would never tell her brother of the affair.

'No, Father, I will not,' she promised, resting her head on his knee`, `I would have liked a baby, she said, but somehow I was not bless, it dont seem fair, somehow.

`life isnt fair, girlie he said, as salted tears ran down her face.

'It's for the best', the old man added, stroking her hair, but deep inside of him, there was an anger that was seething.

'But I never want to see that Nora here again,' said Bridie.

'That's fair enough,' her father said. 'You better write and tell her not to show her face. Because, even I might be tempted to slap her pretty little face, better we don't see her here again.'

So, when Bridie's tears were dried up and she felt there was not another tear left for Daneen, for now there was only hate, she sat and wrote that letter to Nora;taking out the old letter from Tim, that the address was on.

Dear Nora,

You know what you have done, and the pain you have caused, so never show yourself in Ireland again. My father and I do not want Tim to know, if the child inside of you, does not belong to him. We do not want him to see him hurt, so you can be sure your dirty secret of your affair will be safe with us. But the deal is Nora, you stay away from Ireland, and my brother will never be told, as we never want to see you again.

You had better tear this letter up as soon as you have read it.

Bridie.

So life went on for Bridie, without her dream of getting married. In fact when her wedding dress arrived, she ripped it into threads and never breathed Nora or Daneen's name again.

The villagers all said that she had been left on the shelf a bitter woman, for Bridie had lost her warm smile and that lively spirit that was always ready for a political argument. She worked hard on the farm and looked after her father until he died that year. His health had deteriorated quickly and his dying words were: "Take care of Timothy".

Bridie would listen to the news on the radio about the bombings and the spitfires that attacked the German planes and thought of her brother and the dangerous missions. The war was getting worse in Europe, Jewish people were put in ghettos and people said, this man Hitler was trying to take over the world. This brought out her fighting spirit and now her father was gone, there was nothing holding her - and too many bad memories. She would leave the farm, close it up and perhaps one day build it up again, but for now, she had to get away. So the next day, she went and signed up for the Women's Royal Artillery.

THE LETTER

Ch.21

While Eileen was baking bread in the kitchen, Mick sat in the armchair reading the Irish Times, the collie at his feet and now and again looking over the top of the page, to see what mood Eileen was in, for Mick did not want to move from his cosy spot, where he could watch his son Shamus, who was a fat toddler in his playpen and look out of the window as the evening sunlight shone through the open door making the windows gleam silver. Outside the autumn sent a carpet of red and brown leaves, over the garden and as the autumn breezes gave way to the frost of winter, Mick was kept busy chopping wood for the fire and Eileen would push him out in the frosty mornings, into the pale morning mist, to fetch the wood as the wind rustled in the tall trees of the forest.

In the spring, they ploughed the fields and Daneen was as unreliable as ever and on the first day out in the high field cutting the crop of corn, it

had not been a successful day, for when it came to lunch time, Daneen
had deserted the tractor in the middle of the field, and could be seen
heading off across the fields to the Inn.

'Can`t do much now,' young Ginger, had said, 'got to wait for Daneen',
and sat on a mound of corn eating his sandwiches.

'So the top field is hardly started then?' asked Eileen as she stood over
the aga stove; the heat from the oven making her sweat on this
summer`s day.

'No, but I`ll get a good day in tomorrow.'

'You're going to have to pull your finger out, Mick,' frowned Eileen,
'especially now, we'll have another mouth to feed.'   Mick looked
anxiously at her, but Eileen patted her high stomach and said with a
note of pride. 'Perhaps we will have a girl this time. Now, Bridie would
be a fine name.'

The back door opened and in strolled, Oikey, followed by his fat wife,
Selena.

'Oh no,' said Mick, 'those flaming pigs again, I forgot to shut the gate.'

'Leave the pigs,' said Eileen `they will amuse young Shamus,'who, on
spotting the two pigs cried out in glee, pulling himself up from his

playpen and reaching out his jammy fingers towards the pigs, but the two pigs were more interested in hovering around the aga; their snouts twitching at the smell of the bread cooking.

There was now a large kitchen at the cottage, ever since Pat Kennedy and Ginger, had come in and knocked the parlour wall down. Eileen had insisted on having a modern kitchen diner and the two pigs paced up and down on the new black and white linoleum floor, from the aga to young Shamus, who proceeded to rock up and down on those chubby legs - his damp nappy hanging between them, he started to make the strangest noises that sounded like oink- oink, drawing his breath in and out, screwing his face up.

'Whatever`s the matter with him?' asked Mick.

'Oh, he is trying to copy the pigs,' she answered.

'Don't want to do that, Son,' and the boy grinned mischievously. Eileen smiled warmly at the pair of them, taking the hot bread from the oven, then proceeded to slice it up, the pigs twitching their noses beside her while young Shamus reached out between the bars for Selena`s tail, pulling it with a deep chuckle.

'Now stop that,' Eileen told him as she spread the butter on the hot bread, which immediately melted. 'You must not be spiteful.'

Young Shamus let go of the squiggly tail, but his brow knitted in a cross expression at being chastised by his mother and he aimed his bottle at Selena, that bounced off her fat shape, for she was also pregnant and Oikey was to be dad to many piglets.

Three hot steaming loaves stood on the round table on a wire rack, while the rest of the family were handed slices to eat. Mick having homemade jam on his, and young Shamus licked the butter off the top, trying to copy the pigs beside him, who licked their slices on the floor.

'Take one of those loaves for Daneen, tomorrow,' said Eileen. 'It's a shame he won't come and eat with us, he is an obstinate old stick, but at least he is working with you now Mick.'

'Yes, when he is not drunk,' was Mick's caustic remark.

'Well, you'll have to be firm with him, Mick, make sure he does a good day's work 'cause you're going to have another mouth to feed soon.'

Eileen wrapped the warm loaf in a tea cloth and put it in Mick's bag with a flask of tea for the next day.

'Now don`t forget to give Daneen the loaf,' she reminded him.

She stood for a moment by the open front door, looking out at the sunset, the shadowy Blue Mountains, lined in the distance.

'Why, there is a beautiful red glow right across the sky,' she said. 'It looks like good weather tomorrow, so there will be no excuses Mick O`Hara, you should be able to get a good part of that field cleared,' her voice rose excitedly for she was determined to get the produce to market in two weeks.

Later that week, Eileen busied about the house, trying to organise some space, she was anxious to make provision for the new arrival in the family. For not only was she pregnant but also was Selena. An old ottoman was put outside in the pen, turned on its side and straw was put inside, making it a little den for the sow to have her piglets, and Selena went inside to investigate. Eileen decided that the carved wood sideboard of Aunt Bridie's that stood in the hallway, was old fashioned and with a lick of white paint, could become a cupboard for the new baby's clothes and toiletries.

One evening she had Mick dragging the sideboard into the kitchen diner.

'It's a real eye sore this thing,' she said, trying to pull open the two doors.

'I'll get the key,' said Mick. 'It's all Aunt Bridie's old bits and pieces, she kept it locked.'

'I thought you were going to clear it all out,' Eileen moaned, and turned the key tentatively.

Mick knew she was going to grumble, but it was just another job he avoided doing.

'Why? Look at all this rubbish!' she exclaimed looking inside.

'Well, I don't know what to do with it`, he said, 'felt a bit rotten throwing all her personal little bits out.'

'Don't be so daft,' said Eileen, being practical minded, 'you can't keep what's rubbish and most of it is. You should have sorted through it all.'

`You do it,' he said with a pleading look, 'then anything you think I should keep I will.'

Eileen sighed, with a deep frown, 'As if I haven't got enough to do.'

But that evening sitting on the floor she went through Aunt Bridie's sideboard, pulling out the old Christmas cards, briefly reading through them, keeping only a few of the bigger ones, that she placed in a cardboard box, together with any personal letters, taking only moments - deciding what was worth keeping and what was not. Then items were quickly tossed in the pile, to throw away. On coming across a post card from Mick as a boy, she handed it to him,

'Why look, Mick, you sent this to your Aunt Bridie. It's from Brighton, do you remember going there?'

He turned the card over, looking at the date. 'It was fifteen years ago. I remember that holiday, me and mum went together.' Eileen could see he had gone all quiet sat, and staring at the view on the front.

'Now don't get upset,' said Eileen almost snatching the card from him. 'I'll keep that one for you,' and methodically placed it in the cardboard box. At the back of the cupboard she pulled out wool, knitting needles, medicine bottles and packets of tablets.

'Don't know what she kept all this lot for,' and on coming across a bound pile of old newspapers directly chucked them on the heap. 'These go back to the war years,' she said, 'ridiculous keeping them.'

'Perhaps there is some interesting articles,' whined Mick, not liking to see them chucked away.

'Interesting articles,' she snapped, 'well, you're crazy if you think I am going through them. Why Mick, you'd be as much a hoarder as Bridie was, if I let you.'

Opening the other side of the sideboard, she came across old tins, filled with all sorts of objects: old fishing reels, needles and cottons, a collection of tea cards, old broken reading glasses and pens.

`What a mess!' she exclaimed. On searching in the back of the cupboard, she pulled out old bags, purses and half darned socks, flinging them over her shoulder and onto the pile, as she went. Then holding up some lace cushion covers exclaimed: 'They'll come in handy. Only need, a good wash.'

There was also a nice collection of enamel brooches.'I'll share these out amongst the Kennedy Sisters, they`d like those.'

'Ok,' Mick mumbled sleepily, as he dozed lazily in the chair, only half hearing the loud exclamations of Eileen as she came across different items. But Oikey heard and woke up twitching his snout coming over to see what was going on, poking and prying into the pile of unwanted goods beside Eileen on the floor.

'Now don't make a mess,' Eileen warned the pig, giving him a little push. But Oikey remained like a stoic bull - his beady eyes watching.

Eileen continued her sorting, and came across something else, at the back of the cupboard: a large brown envelope addressed to Bridie and inside was a roll of material. The date on the front was war time and on the back was Daneen's name and address of the barracks in India. She pulled it out and unravelled it. It was so beautiful this silk material, oriental, designed with birds and trees, and the edging was fringed and she thought it would make lovely curtains. It was so unusual and she was remembering that Daneen had served in the army in India. How lovely she thought, a present from India, from all those years ago and decided, that this was worth keeping and she would make something from it. So, just as she was going to put it aside, she rolled the material back up, and something fell out of the folds, and as she reached down for it, she saw it was an old envelope bag.

'This must have been pretty at one time,' she said, turning it over and looking at the design of coloured beads, it also had an oriental design, but now a lot of the beads were missing; some hanging untidily in amidst strands of crinkled cotton, and the silk pink material was faded. 'That's a shame,' she muttered, quickly looking inside to check for any contents, then, aimed it on the pile. But this item interested old Oikey and while Eileen was examining a pretty crocheted shawl she'd found, wrapping it around herself, Oikey was having a game with the envelope bag, tossing it into the air and tearing at it with his pointed little teeth. He shuffled the bag around in a circle.

Eileen gave, Oikey a push. 'Out of the way,' she cried out, and tried to retrieve the bag from his snout. A tug of war proceeded, but he eventually let go, with a splitting rip to the lining.

'What's this?' said Eileen, noticing a white envelope sticking out of the torn lining of the bag and aptly slipped it out, giving it a quick glance. She was about to throw it back in the pile of rubbish when she noticed the postmark was England way back in 1950.

`Its an old letter,' she said to Mick, looking at it curiously and wasted no time in opening it, but when she saw it was from Mick's mother, she was silent for a moment as she read the words.

1STJune l950
4, Peabody Buildings, Shepherds Bush, London W2

Dear Bridie,
Thank you for the money you have sent for Mick at Christmas, it will

buy his new school uniform, for the secondary school. He is studying for his eleven plus, he is a clever boy, but I don't think he will pass, as he is a nervous child. Nevertheless Bridie, you have a fine nephew and whatever you still think of me, he is a son that Tim would have been proud of.

We have moved to Shepherds Bush now, as Mick and I have at last been housed. It's a second floor flat with a balcony and overlooks a park. It's not easy bringing up a child alone, although, I still have full time work at Paddington Hospital. There's lots of night work, so I`m there when Mick comes home from school, but I might not be able to work much longer, because the Doctor at the hospital examined me yesterdays and tells me my TB has reached a stage, where it has become, more or less untreatable. So Bridie, I am not sure how my health is going to be in future and I am writing to tell you this, as Mick needs to know he has others who care about him. I was wondering if he can come for a holiday to Ireland. He has been worried about me lately and looks a bit pale, thought the country air would do him good. I hope you will agree. The school holidays in August would be a good time.

I have kept my word to you Bridie and not returned to Ireland, so I hope you will keep your word to me, but Mick is a growing lad and may need his Irish relations.

Mick sends his love.

Nora

Eileen put the letter slowly down, she had gone a little pale, the freckles on her face stood out. Slowly she got up and went and sat on the end of Mick's chair. Oikey was now raking over the pile of rubbish, making a mess, but Eileen did not care, she was more concerned about Mick and what he would think about this letter. Mick looked sleepily up at her and smiled. 'Now what's this?' he asked, reaching out for the letter that she held in her hand, 'something I sent, Aunt Bridie?'

'No Mick, I think you had better read this carefully, it's from your mother.'

His eyes opened wide with surprise as he took the crumpled letter. On reading the words, Eileen watched his pensive face and the pig scuffed his trotter up and down on the floor, like a horse, shaking his head, having got a fishing reel caught round his rubbery nose, but nobody took any notice.

'My poor mother,' he mumbled, 'she must have known she was very ill. She died that year,' his voice croaked and he looked on the verge of tears.

Eileen's arms went around him. 'Don't be sad, darling,' she said, 'your mother loved you so much,' but Mick was thinking about that holiday in Ireland and how sick his mother became when he returned. 'That's was why she sent you to your Aunt Bridie's,' Eileen cajoled him. 'She was looking out for you.'

'Looks that way,' said Mick, but added a little bitterly, 'I can't remember hearing much from Aunt Bridie after that holiday.'

'What, not even when your mother died?'

'No, they just carted me off to the boarding school and Aunt Bridie didn't ask me to Ireland again.'But then he recalled how she used to send pocket money each month to the school. 'The headmaster used to call me in to the office to collect the postal orders,' he said, smiling at the memory.

'She must have been fond of you, Mick.' But he only stared down at the letter and spoke of his mother.

'So what does all this mean? Why did my mother never return to

Ireland? Was it because of, Aunt Bridie? I don't understand,' he said miserably. 'It sounds like they had some kind of pact.'

'Now, that I don't know,' said Eileen and wished she did, for she knew this would trouble him. She wondered if she should ask the Kennedy Sisters about this.

'Don't you remember your aunt?' she asked, as she started to clear way the pile on the floor, as Oikey was shuffling it all around the room. 'Get away,' she grumbled, pushing the pig with the broom. 'Now Mick, you must remember something?' she repeated.

Then with a faint smile, he recalled that time Aunt Bridie took him fishing. 'I remember sitting on the river bank, and she taught me to fish - never did nothing like that in London. She helped me throw the line in and when I suddenly caught a salmon, I was terrified. It wriggled and pulled and she stood there laughing, leaving me to pull the line in alone.

'Now, that`s a foine memory,' smiled Eileen coming to sit beside him and he rested his head on her shoulder.

'I remember,' he said, 'watching Aunt Bridie get the hook out, but then she bashed it on the head and I got very upset. "Begorrah, Lad, she said, Don't be such a cissy`,

'They say she was bossy,' said Eileen, suppressing her laughter, for Mick had a serious face.

'It must have been late August,' he continued, 'the corn was being cut. I remember sitting in the tractor beside the driver and how I loved it, he even let me drive it across the field, while he tied the hay in bundles. Oh, how good it smelt,' he said softly, as if he was back in that very spot.

'Perhaps that was Daneen,' declared Eileen,

'It was not him 'cause I remember now, she told me someone called Daneen, used to drive the tractor, but he went off to join the Guards and that she hadnt seen the blaggard since`.

`I remember she seemed upset about this.`

Mick kept reading the letter over and over, one minute his face sad, then happy, as he recalled memories of that holiday. 'I remember sitting around the fire with, Aunt Bridie at the cottage,' he suddenly declared, 'and she got out the photograph album. There was loads of relations that she pointed out and a photograph of my father, but I declared, how short he was and she did not like that and said, "And Heaven knows where you get those long legs from Mick 'cause your father's were short", Then, there were the other Irish relations who kept saying, where's his bright red hair, all the O 'Hara's have that?I was beginning to wonder,' admitted Mick, 'if there was something wrong with me and I felt like coming home.'

Eileen could see how offended, he must have been as he sat brooding, with a deep frown.

'How was I supposed to know,' he stated, 'that this father of mine had bright red hair? "

'What a lot of fuss,' said Eileen, 'you do take things to heart. Sure, it's true, a lot of the O`Hara's are copper knobs, they say it comes down from the "Great Chieftan 'O'Hara" himself, but sometimes the red colouring, skips a generation.' Then putting down the broom she went to the cupboard and pulled out an old print, of 'O'Hara, himself.

'Look,' she said, 'that's him, in his suit of armour. It looks like a metal skirt, with high metal boots,' she giggled, and went on in an excited manner. 'Can you see he has red hair and a bright red, curly, beard? They say he was a great warrior, and look, there is his shield,' and pointed out the coat of arms.

Mick stared at the picture in dismay. 'I'm glad I don't look like him,' he said, 'I don't wear no, metal skirts.' Eileen tittered with amusement, but Mick only continued to moan about his Irish relations, saying they made him feel, like some kind of mongrel, `I was beginning to wonder whether I even was an O`Hara`.

The next morning while Mick was sleeping late in his bed, Eileen got up to do her chores and went out into the fresh morning air to feed the pigs. The hazy sun had come up over the Blue Mountains In the distance and she deeply breathed the air in. She could hear the pigs squealing and carried the heavy bucket of scraps. 'I'm coming!' she called to them, but they were making such a racket, as she was slipping in the mud, and the gate of the sty was hard to open.

Eventually they charged at the food with their snouts, wallowing in the scraps. She watched them with a grin. It was then that she spotted Daneen, sitting on the sty at the end of the path, a cap pulled down on his head and resting his elbows on his skinny legs that bore his cut down wellington boots. She waved, as she always did and felt there was so much she wanted to ask him; even tell him about the mysterious letter of Nora`s, but knew it was up to Mick and would try to not to interfere. But she decided she would ask him about the beautiful silk cloth and quickly went indoors and got the roll of material, putting it back in the packaging, that on the back of it, his name was written. The packaging had a stamp on the envelope marked India and it all seemed such a mystery, but she was more interested in making cushions from this exquisite material, but first she would talk to Daneen about it. It had been his and he had sent it to Bridie. And now she could be the one to make use of it.

Wiping her hands on her apron, she picked up the roll of material and went outside to see Daneen, hoping he had not disappeared. She soon spotted him, she waved again and she could see he looked rather solemn as he smoked his pipe and looked deep in thought: his face a mass of tired lines. She would often see him from her top window at night, roaming by the river, wondering, if he was having one of his sleepless nights, bad dreams, he would say, when he would cry out as if in pain.

So she told herself, to be careful as she approached, he looks very touchy, but she didn't want to know his life story. She knew how cagey he could be, when there was any reference to his past. She decided she would leave any delving up to Mick and just tell him about the material.

'Daneen,' she called holding up the roll of material and she sat on the sty beside him.

Straight away his eyes narrowed as he looked at the package of silk material she held onto, and he said in a gruff voice, 'What have we here then, Eileen? I see you have been rummaging about.'

'Yes,' she giggled, trying to make light of it, 'it is the most beautiful material I ever seen. I found it amongst, Bridie's old bits and pieces and it comes from India.'

'That I know,' he said, looking at the material with a sad expression.

'Am I right then, that this belonged to you and you sent it to Aunt Bridie?'

'Yes, and your welcome to it,' he said, folding his arms as if he didn't want to know anymore about it.

'But where did it come from?'

'The Maharaja's Palace,' he said, with a twist of a smile

'The Maharaja's Palace,' repeated Eileen, 'thats a real leprechaun story, now what would you be doing in a palace?'

'You'd be surprised,' he said,

But Eileen was curious, and wanted to get to the bottom of this, not be fobbed off with some story about Maharajas. 'Don't you remember sending it to Bridie?' she asked firmly. 'Wasn't you out East?'

'Goodness woman, won't you be content with it, without making it a song and dance?'

Eileen giggled, but knew he was being as cagey as ever. 'It looks Eastern,' she said. 'It's so beautiful, like it's made of threads of gold.'

'It is threads of gold,' he suddenly, declared.

'What, real gold?' she asked, incredulously, and he watched her as she ran her hand over the golden threads that edged the brocade and the elaborate embroidered birds.

For a moment, he was miles away in thought, then suddenly grunted and pulled off the red, polka dot, crumpled scarf from his neck.

'So where did you find this?' she quizzed him.

'I've already told you,' he said, 'from the Maharaja's Palace,' then told her how he looked after the horses at the palace and Eileen, was beginning to wonder if his story *was* true, as everyone knew Daneen's reputation for looking after horses.

'Well, you were very good with horses, I must say,' she said, 'for everyone in Banturk says, that you could get a horse to do anything,' and just for a moment, his rugged face brightened. It seemed to Eileen, like a ray of sunshine, for he was always so serious. 'I bet you could tell us some stories about this palace,' she said mischievously, but Daneen, hated to be questioned. 'I'd love to hear all about India,' she added, her vivid blue eyes wide with wonder.

'You just enjoy the material,' he said, squinting up through a haze of smoke as he puffed at the pipe. 'Now, have done with it girl and do what you wish with it.'

'Are you sure I can have it then?' she said, as he got up and walked away. 'If it's real gold . . .' But he only waved his arm in dismissal as if he wanted to say no more.' I'll make you some curtains for the shack!' she called after him, but no answer came back.

DANEEN REMEMBERING

Ch.22

Daneen ventured across the small field to the old stables; a place he could hideaway. For a moment he stood looking down at the view, admiring the fertile land and patches of woodland that swept down to the river and beyond, a glimpse of the emerald, green hills. The sun hanged low and a warm glow covered the landscape. How he loved his homeland, it brought a smile to his face, but he was still irritated, that Eileen had encroached on his past: there were things - he liked to keep hidden.

He was thinking about the Maharaja's Palace, that exotic place and the Maharaja, who became his friend. He would have liked to have told Eileen more about that, but he wondered if any of them would believe half of it. They only treated him like an old drunk. He pushed open the creaking wooden door of the stables, that hung off its hinges, then right before his eyes was the line of old saddles hanging on the wall - dusty with age, and he picked up a pair of reins that hung on a hook, remembering that they belonged to the bay horse and could still see her scampering about the field with her chestnut foal.

The old stables, still had straw laying in the corners and the windows still rattled, but he sat on a milking stool, the same one he used to sit on to groom his horse, looking at his old pair of overalls lying in the straw. He was remembering those times, back when he would come to this stable and spend time with his black stallion, grooming the black mane and tail, until they shone. Then, they would go steeple racing in Tralee and would win many a shiny cup, that were still on a shelf in this broken down stable: but they shone no more and were covered with a thick dust.

With the back of his sleeve he cleaned the grime off and polished them up, bringing back the golden sheen and exposing the name of his horse, Black Gem. A tear rose in his eyes, his chest tightened and he swallowed hard as held up the trophy cup, high to admire it, and just as he was looking for a new place to put it, out of the cup something fell onto the floor. It landed in the old sawdust and was now a grimy black and bent to pick it up. He was so surprised to find it, for this had been given to him at the end of the war and he thought he had lost it forever. He smiled as he looked down at the shining medal, shaped like a star; that had been given to him for his bravery and realised that someone must have put it inside the cup. He was recalling then, how he had sent the medal to Bridie after the war.   He had often thought of those childhood days, during the irish revolution, when they were always together and liked to recall that special time, she put the cosh over the troopers head, it would always make him laugh. But he had known that Bridie was not happy, when she did not answer his letters, he was trying to make amends and he wanted her to have the medal.

` So this was where she put it - inside the trophy. He turned it over in his hand, it was the Burma Star, and quite an honourable medal it was too. For a moment he felt proud, but would anyone believe it, he asked himself, that he had won such a distinguished, honour? He was now treated no better than a down and out. With an anger burning inside him, he put the medal in his top pocket. Lot of good it all really did me, he thought, remembering all he went through during the war to get this medal. He thought of his friend Jerry who was killed, and he never ever got the burma star, how unfair it all was, and each time he thought about his friend it brought tears to his eyes. One day he told himself, he would find where he is buried and visit his grave. He was such a fine young man, and knew he would never have survived in the jungle if it had not been for Jerry. This young man on the verge of life, his plane was shot down, his body was burned to charcoal.

With that old bitterness returning, he tried to close the stable door back up, but it only had one hinge and hung on the floor. 'Blooming door,' he moaned, 'everything gone to ruin.' As once the stables, had once been bustling with several horse, but now, it was little more than a broken down old shed, with only remnants of the past. He remembered how Old Shamus and Bridie had always kept the farm going, and when Bridie suddenly went off to join the womens royal artillery, the farm was left to become a neglected wreck.

He strode back to his shack. He pushed the door open. He couldn't wait to get his head down, for that feeling of tiredness was overwhelming.

He wanted to close his eyes and looked around for his bottle of moonshine, and when he had found it, placed it on the bedside table. He was feeling so cold, and that anxiety was sweeping over him; just one of the scars the battles of war had left: they called it post war depression.

He tried thinking of, Eileen holding up that beautiful material and her lovely smile as he lay down his head and closed his eyes, and was visualising her celtic green eyes lighting up, if he had told her about the opulence of the palace: the Maharaja's crown, filled with diamonds, the exotic birds that flew around the great white marble halls; they had all been part of his life, and he would never forget it. But he wasn't sure about telling Eileen, it would sound more like a fairy tale and although, those old times at the palace were during the war, he had been happy there and filled his mind with joy, but his thoughts were also mingled with the harsh memories of war.

These memories - he had been fighting, ever since those terrible times and he still woke up at night, the sound of war crys charging into battle, for those nightmares were always threatening. He would wake trembling, feeling leeches sticking to his body and scratch his skin till it bled. They were all part of the visions that tormented him, as he remembered the attacks from the Jap`s in the burmese jungle, and crawling to the river, trying to get away, the leeches sticking to his body and the screams and explosions, that still rang in his ears.

He felt the nightmare coming on, he was beginning to shake as the old fear gripped him, quickly. He sat up at the end of the bed reaching for his tipple of potcheen, but then the face of a boy came in front of him and he wanted to cry out, for this was the child he had rescued and for a moment he recalled a young man, who was badly injured as he lay by the river side and memories of that day came flooding back . . .

It all happened when he had been on his way to the Maharaja's Palace when he found the boy. He had left early from his post at Calcutta with the British Indian army, where he was sent to train horses for the Burma jungle. The commander in charge had said, `there`s not much we can teach you about horses Daneen`, and when an important assignment came up, the commander turned to Daneen for assistance, asking him to deliver an important despatch to the Mahararja of Bengal. `I know i can trust you the commander told Daneen, who had already made him a sergeant, when Daneen rescued a member of the regiment, during a training campaign. The man had lost control of his horse in the river and the current was strong and they were being washed down the river. It was a quick thinking Daneen who jumped into action and lassoed the horse`s neck. The river frothed and twirled and the horse and its rider were going out of sight and daneen ordered the other men to help, as he managed to tie the rope to a tree, pulling the horse and its rider back to safety. When the Commander heard about the brave deed, he was very impressed,

`Great storytellers the irish`, he grinned and handed Daneen an envelope, saying it was very urgent.

"It has to go by hand and I know, he said, twisting his moustache, with a grin, `you're the fastest man on a horse".

But when Daneen looked over the map, the commander gave him, he could see it was a long way to this palace in cooch behar, but little phased him and was feeling more confident, since he had been made a sergeant, he had been put in charge of the 'stables and the horses' and nobody could tell him anything about handling them, having learnt his skill as a boy working in his grandfather's stables, who would always say: "prefer horses to people, son".

Daneen often wondered if he took after his grandfather, who was a warrior and defied convention, or perhaps it was just the way his grandfather bought him up, as there was danger all around, with the IRA bombings. He had been in the middle of a revolution and a 'runner' for the Tipperary Brigade, where he soon learnt to ride a horse at a speed, taking important messages to the IRA camp. In fact, he wondered if he was doing much the same kind of thing now and when he first arrived at the camp in Barackpoor, Calcutta, he had been given a black stallion. He had a silky black coat and a white temperamental star on his forehead. He was a horse very quick to learn, although very and would grunt and push daneen with his soft nose, as if he understood just how he was feeling. Daneen trained him well and he was the best of all the horses in the stables at travelling through jungle territory. So Daneen was pretty sure he was capable of taking his horse across difficult terrain to take a despatch to the Maharaja's Palace, even though Cooch Behar was a day's ride away.

The commanding general had said: "Get there as soon as you can with the message, the Maharaja will be expecting you".

Daneen guessed it was about the Japanese invasion, that the Jap's were getting into India, for they had already invaded China, and the military were flying in new battalions to fight them. He guessed it would be top secret, so asked no questions and as long as he got it into the hands of the Maharaja who himself was a commanding chief of the Indian army, he would have done his job.

He was glad to be getting out of Calcutta: there were beggars galore in the streets, especially, since the famine of Bengal as the Jap's had stopped the food supplies - importantly, rice coming into India.

The people were starving and he could not stand the sight of the young mothers with babies sitting on the road side, begging for food. Calcutta was a hive of disease, with thousands' of allied troops arriving in the town. It soon became a hub of activity. These servicemen from the United States had recently arrived to fight the Jap's and sat on the steps of the temple and looked sadly at the kids who were asking for food. The Jap's had already conquered Rangoon cutting off imports of rice to India, and Churchill's cabinet had not sent any food supplies and were stopping the ships bringing it in. Mountbatten the viceroy of India had requested food for the workers in industry and a little wheat was sent by Churchill for them, as these workers had to be fed. But food supplies for India were cut and the Monsoon rains fell heavy on the Manipur hills, where tens of thousands of refugees had fallen victim. They were starving and suffering with dysentery, Malaria and Cholera before reaching India and the army had dismantled railway tracks to hamper the Jap's invading.

Daneen was recalling the journey to the Maharaja's Palace and the flooded jungle after the rains, as he crossed the ravines, passing through swampland; getting stuck in the mud. Then patches of jungle with tropical flowers of brilliant colours glowered in the pathways. He could hear the monkeys screeching in the trees, watching them jump from one branch to another. And he had never seen such beautiful birds, which fluttered in the greenery.

He had set out to cross a mountain range and the horse carried a small load. He crossed lands of rice fields. They were almost barren, where men with oxen ploughed. The ploughs pulled by water buffalos worked as usual, where the locals walked in the paddy fields, up to their knees in water, searching for the rice; but the plants were rare to find. This was a land of rice growers and eaters, but the Jap's had stopped the supplies. It was a sad to see the farmers with ox out there in the sun working to find nothing to eat.

Then the flat land, opened up to a great forest area that seemed never ending, until he met a long road, where lines of refugees were all travelling in the same direction, trudging on towards India: some of the old were carried on ox carts and wagons and many people, were bent over, as they carried heavy possessions on their backs - their farm animals walking beside them. They were tired human beings, half starved and in need of medical help.   Mostly were refugees from Burma, but there was little rice even there, for the rice supplies by ship and rail were not getting in. The Jap's had stopped those too. They could be anywhere these Jap's, for they were set on conquering India next, and the British were working to stop them.

As he travelled, Daneen carried a gun in case of trouble and on his horse medical supplies, as well as a tent and a billycan to cook food, in case he got held up in anyway. As he journeyed through jungle areas, up to his knees in swampy marshland, he was relieved to come out to open spaces and he could see the pattern of the Himalayan Mountains in the distance, with the sun going down behind them. He looked up in awe at the snow crested tops on the mountain range. It made him think of home and the blue mountains of Killarney - nothing was more beautiful than them. He looked around at the vast landscape: only the sound of birds of prey crying overhead and the eagle swooped low as if to weigh them up, it gave him a chill, but he patted his black stallion. How glad he was to have him. He was akin with him, as any man would be, and unafraid too; together they were solid - man and beast on a mission.

With the evening sunlight playing on the lush green land, full of tall grasses and winding brooks, he looked forward to seeing the palace and entering the gateway. The afternoon sun beamed down and he stopped to walk the horse to a small river where it could drink. He knew he had to be careful trekking through the jungle area as the Jap's were searching everywhere and nervously he looked around. With his revolver in hand, his horse took a drink. And as he relaxed by the river for a while, he started to think about the poor children suffering during this famine: some of them had run up behind his horse as he left Calcutta and he gave them a few coins. Some rice was being sold on the black market, and this caused fights on the streets, and the police moved in and people were injured. There were families looking for shelter in the jungle and made shelters from bushes and killed wildlife to eat.

He thought how far away from Ireland this river scene was as he stood beside it, watering his horse. He thought of the wild salmon in Ireland in the cool river. Here it was hot, and if the crocs didn't get you the Jap's might.

He sat for a while longer on the bank of a river; that moved swiftly, winding its way down a hill. Feeling tired, he lay under a bush. As he turned his head, under the next bush there was the shape of a man lying on the ground and a sound of murmuring, like from a wounded animal. Going closer he saw it was a boy and the sound came louder from his blue lips. He wondered if he was dying and bending down, could see his body had been beaten, badly. From his leg seeped blood and it looked like he had been attacked with knives. Blood oozed from other wounds on the boy's body.

Just then the boy's bloodshot eyes opened and he gazed open mouth, and held out his hand, crying out in pain.

Was it the Jap's?' Daneen asked, in the little Indian language he knew,and lifted the boys head as he nodded, finding out further that he had been attacked from behind as he was fishing by the river.

'Help!' cried the boy, holding his side and cried out in pain. Daneen noticed how thin he was - probably starving to death, only a boy he thought, on the verge of his teens and decided, he could not leave him to die.

'Your name?' he queried, as he quickly washed the boy's wounds from the river water and bound his leg tight with bandages, that he had in his medical supply.

'I Kimjahvi', the boy murmured, as Daneen washed the blood from his long black silky hair that hung in strands. The boy pleaded with him, not to leave him there, so Daneen lifted him to his feet - his thin legs bending from under him and got him onto the back of his horse, for he would take him with him to the palace, hoping that the boy would make the journey. He was very weak.

He tied the boy behind him on the horse and could feel his breath on the back of his neck as the stallion cantered along. But at least he knew he was still alive. At a quicker pace, the horse galloped towards the palace. The boy's wounds were deep from the gashes of what was probably a hatchet.

He wondered what this Maharaja would say and do. He knew little of this prince - only that he was ruler of the Bengal region of India and a very wealthy influential man. He felt a nervous twinge, doubting the outcome, and wondered if they would be turned away, but Daneen was doing the only thing he felt was right and was going to rely on the kindness of others and he only hoped this Maharaja was a kind man.

His horse was nimble and willing, but it was a long canter up hill and he was slowing down. Soon there was a line of trees in the distance and they were tall palm trees that lined a long drive that led to the palace on the hill. He could even see the palace through the misty sunlight, with its large dome on the roof top that glinted in the sunlight like silver. As he entered the drive with floral borders and flowering cherry trees that dotted the hilly landscape, he breathed in deep, the clear air from the lush green gardens, passing a lily pond where monkeys ambled freely. In the centre of the pond was a fountain where Mandarin ducks swam, and the palace as he got closer, was so imposing with red brick, lines of arched windows and a series of verandas; with the flag of India flying from a glistening pink tower.

He was not sure what the Maharaja would say about bringing the wounded boy along, and there was blood seeping through the bandages and down his leg. He was getting weaker, slumped against his back and looked a real mess, and was murmuring and groaning.

Stopping, he held him up, to give him a drink from his bottle of water; the boy's lips dry and cracking. Daneen managed to part them and the boy sipped the cold water - his dark eyes gleamed fondly at Daneen.

'My name is Kimjahvi,' he muttered, then, his eyes closed having no strength to keep them open.

'We are there now', Daneen said, hoping he could hear him. He wondered if the boy had passed out.

Soon he was at the gates to the palace. Outside were two guards, wearing white turbans, a red uniform and holding crossed swords across their chests. But as soon as he showed the envelope enclosing the message for the Maharaja, that displayed the army crest, they stood aside and opened the gate.

Daneen entered with the horse, the boy slumped on its back, while the guards stood to attention. Soon he was leading the horse along a paved area and the clicking of the stallion's hooves echoed through the line of marble pillars. When two men in long white shirts came out in front of him to take the horse to the stables, they immediately saw the boy slumped over the horse and reached out to help the injured boy, lifting him from the saddle, with anxious faces, `he only a boy`, one was saying in Hindustani, pulling a long white scarf from his tunic to mop the blood from the boys face.

`follow us` they said, as they lifted the boy into Daneens arms and he was guided towards a square entrance hall, with pots of jasmine sending out a sweet fragrance and a central fountain where carp of all colours swam: the water tinkling through the cool opulence of the palace. There were marble statues of previous Maharajas that seemed to look sternly down, as if guarding an arched entrance where a guard stood either side; beside them a black panther in a cage.

Soon a voice demanded for him to enter and the doors opened to a room flooded with light from a glass domed roof. The gilt furniture stood upon Persian rugs. The room shone with pink and gold light, and the walls were decorated with art of golden dragons, religious art, and ancient writings - surrounded by pictures of the mountains of Nepal.

A bell rang at the top of high steps, where the Maharaja sat on a lofty eminence. Two women wearing veils and colourful sarongs knelt beside him with fans.

Daneen walked towards the throne with the boy in his arms and the

Maharaja greeted him, with a graceful bow of his head and outstretched arms in welcome. His deep set, almond eyes looked curiously at the boy. Daneen had expected him to be younger, but this was a older man with a short, greying beard and he stared at him in amazement, for he was dressed like a king: he wore a shiny gold coat and a white feathered head dress with a stunning diamond in the centre. Daneen had never seen such a sparkler, and stared at the encrusted Ruby dagger that hung around his waist. He stood in awe, then, attempted to bow holding the boy.

'Please,' beckoned the Maharaja, with a warm smile and bent over the boy - his black eyebrows knitting.

'Who is this boy`?' he asked, seeing the injuries and was quick to call his servants with a sweep of his arm. Daneen was quick to hand him the envelope with the message from his commander, but the Maharaja was more interested in helping the boy. Within seconds there were the sound of quick little footsteps, servants and medics rushed over to help, at the same time, bowing to their Gracious Maharaja. Daneen wondered what they were all saying in their native tongue and felt helpless, standing in this grand palace, at the mercy of this powerful man, hoping the boy would get the right care.

He watched the servants running backwards and forwards and saw the boy carried off to a side room, while the Maharaja stood looking at Daneen, as if he too, wondered what it was all about.

'He was attacked by the Jap's,' Daneen said, telling him he found him by the riverside, and how he could not leave him, he was in such a bad way.

'The Maharaja listened with a serene smile, his slant black eyes darting from side to side.

'It is okay,' he said kindly, 'we will take care of him,' and shook his head in irritation as he spoke of the starvation in the country. 'It is shocking for my subjects, and we keep requesting supplies from the British Government, but nothing is getting through.'

'It's the Jap's who are to blame,' said Daneen.

'Yes, they started it,' said the Maharaja, with a twist of a smile, 'but the British need to send more ships, and Churchill's cabinet, are not cooperating.'

'Oh,' said Daneen, wondering whether he should voice his opinion any further, on these government policies: he could be out of his league. He could see by the Maharaja's deep frown he was not pleased.

'That boy,' the Maharaja said with extreme disapproval written all over his face, 'is almost, skin and bone. I will arrange for an assignment of rice, to be sent to Calcutta immediately. Hopefully it will save a few lives.'

He beckoned Daneen to follow, as he walked towards his office, his head slightly bowed and his hands folded in a pious manner, he took short little steps. His gold coat trailed across the white marble floor.

His mind was obviously still on the starving people as he told Daneen: 'The paddy fields are bare and thousands are starving. Daneen listened, as he spoke of the hardships of his subjects . . . He seemed to him a very caring Maharaja and when he smiled, the lines around his heavy lidded eyes, crinkled like a fan. There was a pink glow to his chubby cheeks although Daneen felt the Maharaja was weighing him up all the time, as he looked at him with deep curiosity, keeping his staff walking close behind as if in protection.

As they stepped into his office, the room flooded with light, that shone from a tall regency window and Daneen was shown a chair, beside the Maharaja at his black ebony desk, then waited while the

Maharaja read the message, with a serious expression.

Once it was put safely in his desk drawer, he turned to Daneen swinging around in his chair. 'My lineage,' he said, 'the Najanda family, have always been loyal to the British, fighting beside them, going back centuries'. His mood lightened as he talked of military traditions that he seemed so proud of and pointed to a black and white photograph on his desk, displaying smashed buildings, piles of concrete and people sitting on the ground in tears.

'It is the 1934 earthquakes,' he told him. 'My people will never forget it. Such suffering and my father battled to save many lives, then, spent years repairing the disasters after the earthquake was over.'

'He must have been a great man.' Daneen sighed.

'He was,' he nodded, 'he thought a lot of the British and I have always taught my people to keep the traditions of loyalty to the British Crown.'

As the Maharaja wrote a return message, for Daneen to take to Calcutta, he watched him methodically, dipping his pen into the inks, writing in calligraphy, carefully and neatly. Then looking around the room Daneen noticed the portrait on a wall of the Maharaja, dressed in full army regalia, as commander of the Bengal Army. The snow white uniform displayed various, colourful medals and he wore a peaked helmet with high plumage. The light airy office was filled with tall ferns, bric-a-brac, and fans whirred overhead. Around the walls, hung carved elephant tusks, swords and ornate daggers. There were Chinese cabinets with military books and military weapons in glass cases, that Daneen could not help studying, as there were all sorts of guns, even a 'Smith and Wesson' which was his favourite handgun. The Maharaja noticed his interest

'I also have a shooting gallery,' he said looking up from his desk.

'Oh I'd like a go at that,' Daneen said, 'and I'm a good shot.'

'Is that so?' returned the Maharaja grinning into his beard, and agreed to show him later. Then handing him the return despatch, said: 'I'll leave this in your trusted hands.'

As Daneen left the office, he was feeling more relaxed in the Maharaja's company, finding him only human after all. He had told Daneen to go to the kitchens for a meal and there they would direct him to a room, where he can stay. He soon found his way to the kitchens following the smell of curry and the babble of conversation. There he was given Bombay Pie and sat at the table in the cosy kitchen watching the staff.

He soon learnt from the Indian girl in the kitchen, that the Maharaja's full title was Moolah Najanda Jurad Patel, and that he was a very, respected ruler.

'Everyone says he is such a good man, makes acts of charity, his people love him. The Indian girl who everyone called Nighat, told him some of the history of the palace as she cooked, placing a little bowl in front of him: black lentils with a spicy dip and hot bread, all to be eaten by hand with your fingers. 'He is a wonderful man, our Maharaja,' she chatted on. 'You know, his own father Marahaja Sikh Najanda Jurad Patel, had even banned slavery in Bengal. They are a good family - the 'Naj' family.' Daneen liked this young girl. She was very knowledgeable and spoke English well. 'He even visited, Queen Victoria in England,' she said, her bottle green eyes darting to her cooking on the aga stove, explaining, how well, this Maharaja had got on with the old queen. This was all news to Daneen as he dunked, hot lamb dough cakes in the spicy dip. He was thinking of how the young boy was doing under the operation. But Nighat, this lovely young girl, chatted away taking his mind off his worries.

He watched her fuss around all the servants coming into the kitchen, finding out all the gossip; then, watched her knead the bread. 'I make you some onion bhajis, to take with you on your journey,' she offered with a sweet smile. She had olive skin and with a sweet smile made you feel at home. She asked few questions, that Daneen would have liked, but was a mind of information about the palace, and never stopped working for a minute - only to tie her shiny black hair back into a top knot as it fell down on her shoulders.

'I must show you the Great Hall,' she said, wiping the flour from her hands and picked up the corner of her long red sari and led him through a large banqueting hall, holding her finger to her lips, as there were footsteps resounding. 'This is where the officials come to dine,' she giggled.

At the end of the Great Hall, there was a gallery, filled with lines of portraits of ancestors of the Maharaja, all dressed in their finery: turbans studded with jewels, sitting high on the back of a white elephant, on a seat of bright textiles adorned with jewels, under a sun shade. Nighat looked down the line. There was another Maharaja in an orange satin jacket with a high neck, decorated in brocade and tassels, riding a camel.

'Such riches,' Nighat said thoughtfully, who had such a poor upbringing, but was then, fascinated by a picture depicting a Maharaja holding a tiger cub. 'They used to have the tigers as pets, as boys,' she told him, 'walked them around on gold leads. Although,' she added, 'all this was years back. 'This one,' she said, 'he had his own army. Thousands of his troops, helped to fight the Zulus.' Daneen smiled at her naivety, and the way she described each Maharaja with an interesting little bit of history.

Daneen was fully aware of the changing times, for Ghandi the Prime Minister had given a speech asking Indians not to comply with the British, to boycott British goods, and was opposed to helping Britain fight the war, although many Indian troops joined to fight the war- some volunteering. But with all the political talk of Indian gaining her independence, the powerful States of the Maharaja could also be at stake.

These portraits were just like a memory of the past. But, Nighat was just a girl and loved to show the colourful side of the Maharajas. 'I must show you this one,' she pointed to the first portrait in the line. 'This is our Maharaja's grandfather. He was Maharaja Jurad Shikka Najanda. He also served in the British forces. 'Look,' she said suddenly, 'can you see the miniature around his neck? He always wore it. It is a miniature of Her Royal Highness - Queen Victoria.'

Daneen peered with interest at the face of Queen Victoria, on the small miniature, thinking how impressed they must have been with the English Queen.

'And when he had this palace built,' continued the little Indian girl, 'it was bullt in the style of Buckingham Palace'. This made Daneen smile, for he could see the resemblance and the little Indian girl, was so thrilled to have been able to tell someone this, who actually knew Buckingham Palace. 'I wish to go there one day', she said, her big eyes rolling dreamily, and as she took him along the line of ancestors, telling interesting little snippets about all of them, he thought how he would love to be able to take her to Buckingham Palace.

When the dinner gong rang, so light on her feet, she bounced back to the kitchen, lithe like a little fairy in her red sari adorned with stars. He was sorry she was going - her company had lightened his spirits.

That evening, Daneen was summoned before the Maharaja, whose face crinkled in a smile when he saw him. He was an imposing presence, even though he was short, with a protruding belly and strands of his fuzzy grey hair stuck out of the sides of his turban. He was dressed in a high necked thick tunic; that was deep green with heavy brocade edging, he later discovered was an 'Achkan and the gold coat he had worn a 'Sherwani'.'

'The boy is going to be fine,' he said, his penetrating slant eyes staring straight into Daneen's. 'He has come round from the operation'. And Daneen sighed with relief. 'Of course,' the Maharaja said, 'he will need to rest, to get strong again, but he will be well cared for here in the palace.' And he went on to say, how lucky the boy had been, there were many young boys dying on the streets, but he had saved one, at least. 'He will be fine. 'I'll soon be teaching him to ride and I'm sure Nighat from the kitchens' will enjoy his company.

'So do you ride then?' asked Daneen.

'It's my favourite occupation,' said the Maharaja and Daneen's face lit up, for now he knew he had something in common with this grand man, who went on to talk about his stables. 'We will visit them tomorrow,' he said, 'and I'll show you my magnificent stallion. I have just purchased him and would like your opinion.'

Daneen was feeling rather important at this request and looking forward to the visit to the stables, but first, a good sleep in the servants quarters, that were much more luxurious than he had imagined and definitely, better than his bunk back at camp, was what he needed right now. He had a sunken bath all to himself, where a woman came to assist him with a warm white towel to dry him.

Afterwards, he rested on a hammock in the palace gardens, beside him a big red terracotta pot that he flicked the ash in, from his cigarettes, hoping - no one had seen. He was soon informed his horse was being groomed in the stables.

That evening, after the gong rang out in the dining hall, he was going to enjoy a meal with the Maharaja, and the Maharaja sat on a high backed gilt chair, while a pretty girl stood over him with a fan.

Daneen sat opposite the Maharaja, at a cosy table, covered with a snow white table cloth. When the dish of chicken was brought in, alight with a blue flame, the young Indian waiter placed the silver platter in the centre of the table.

'Good appetite' and the Maharaja grinned, pushing the food towards Daneen.

For a while they talked about the war, as on that day more of Europe had been invaded by the Germans. But there was such a peace in this palace: restful like a place of religion, with its tinkling sounds and chiming of gongs, that Daneen felt the war was a long way off. This palace was a world unto its own and outside a different troubled world. He also knew the Maharaja was devoted to his religion, for Nighat had told him how he followed the Hindu ideals and that he took regular devotion at the temple.

As the evening wore on, they drank wine and Daneen was enjoying his company, as well as the fact, he enjoyed an alcoholic drink and several times the Maharaja called for their silver goblets to be refilled. He too was enjoying a conversation that consisted of much horse talk: they talked of different breeds, horse training, as well as racing and Daneen was soon to realise, he was as mad about horses as he was. The Maharaja poured himself a goblet of his favourite wine and Daneen took the liberty of clinking his glass with his, `slainte is tainte` he said and the Maharaja laughed heartily, `I guess that is Irish` he said in amusement. `It sure is grinned Daneen, glad the Maharaja had taken it so well. `it means `health and wealth` he said.

`I can see` said with a swig of his wine `I can learn a lot from you`

`a man after your own heart, I sure am`.

As they enjoyed the wine, tha Maharaja told him, it was from his own cellar and how the land beyond the palace was rich with vineyards. `Perhaps we will ride out there` the Maharaja said and began to tell Daneen about his new horse and admitted that the horse had thrown him.

'Look,' he said pointing to a lump at the back of his head. 'I took the stallion out to jump a few fences and get him into shape, but he threw me off!'

'Perhaps, something spooked him,' said Daneen curiously, and wondered why the horse should do that. 'Or perhaps he is not used to jumping fences.'

'But he should be,' the Maharaja, informed him. 'It is a well trained thoroughbred and I am an excellent rider, because I am the holder of many cups for horse jumping.'

'I would love to help you with the horse, perhaps I can look him over`

suggested Daneen` and see what I can do with him.'

The Maharaja's face lit up in a smile.

Daneen soon learned that this middle aged prince had no children. He had once had a wife, the Maharini Morada Pughet, but she had sadly passed away and since, his life had been horses.

It was getting late, and when the gong rang: time for the servants to retire, the Maharaja dismissed them all and remained and in no hurry to retire himself. He was thoroughly enjoying a companion who could talk about horses, and drinks flowed. Another topic of conversation was playing polo and the Maharaja spoke of the many matches he had won.

'It was in England where I first encountered the game,' he began, 'and I have fond memories of my time at Eton College, that is where I got to love the horses and I was always at the stables. It was in the college grounds and each day I would rush there.'

This made Daneen think of his own grandfather - the blacksmith and thought in a way, he and the Maharaja had walked a similar path.

'I made lots of friends in the world of horses,' confessed the Maharaja, 'and there was a lovely stable maid, I would take for a ride on the back of my horse . . .' for a moment he paused in thought, as if, savouring happy memories of youth. 'Of course,' he continued, pouring another drink, 'I passed my exams - that was expected of me, but I also got fond of the whisky,' he also admitted and held up his glass. 'The boys in the dormitory would smuggle in the whisky and we would sit up half the night talking and laughing.'

Daneen listened as he talked of the good old days at Eton and the British, although Daneen was not a great lover of the British, but kept his mouth shut, as the Maharaja seemed very fond of the them 'I love England. My father was always talking about Queen Victoria.'

'I hear he visited the palace,' declared Daneen, chinking his glass against the glass of the Maharaja's.

'Oh yes, Queen Victoria, our Empress, she loved the Indian people and she had a special Indian servant, that was with her when she was old and alone.'

'So, together they passed the evening with talk of the palace, Eton and the queen. And most of all . . . horses.

The next morning, Daneen looked in on the boy, he had been put to bed in a comfortable room, with chimes hanging from the ceiling, ringing out tinkling sounds, and sweet smelling incense burned from candles in front of a small white statue on the bedside cupboard. Servants were in and out of the room. Nighat sat by his bedside, trying to get him to eat. And at every chance she would sit and watch him and bathe the sweat from his brow. They were about the same age and Nighat found out that his name was Kimjahvi and as the days passed, Kimjahvi began to recover, and Nighat was so joyous.

'I shall teach him English,' she said as she soothed his sores with balm, and made him cool drinks; helping him to sit up, she handed him the cup. Daneen could see she had obviously taken to him, he had the feeling they would be close friends. 'When he is strong enough I will take him with me to the temple. He needs spiritual healing,' she said. 'He has been so ill. Some nights,' admitted Nighat, 'he cried in pain and I held his hand.'

Daneen was glad, the boy was in the capable hands of Nighat; she was like a little angel hovering over him. He wondered how she spoke such good English. He could tell she was more educated than most young girls her age.

'My father is a maharishi,' she explained, 'you know, a teacher - a yoga teacher,' she said, telling Daneen how she was brought up to speak the English language, as soon as she could crawl. 'That is how I got this job', she said jovially and our Maharaja loves the English.' So Daneen was learning a lot from this young girl and when the Maharaja called for him, and told him the doctors were giving Kimjahvi a blood transfusion, Daneen was concerned.

'It's to build him up,' he said, 'he lost a lot of blood and is so underweight.' Then asked, if there was any more that Daneen could tell him about the attack. 'The doctors are curious,' he said, 'the injuries were so bad.'

'I only saw the Jap's driving off in a truck, they were holding machine guns and they just left Kimjahvi to die, after beating him.'

'He was lucky they did not shoot him,' said the Maharaja, dropping his head with a sigh. 'And I will fight with the British, to keep India clear of the Jap's. As for the boy,' he added softly, 'I will look after him, you have no fear, but from now on his name will be 'Naj'.'

'Naj,' repeated Daneen, thinking it suited him. He was pleased the Maharaja had accepted the boy for he knew that he had no right to have brought him here in the first place and relieved the Maharaja had taken him under his roof.

As if reading his thoughts, the Maharaja said suddenly, 'I am glad you have brought this boy to me, for I am sometimes in need of company, ever since my last wife passed away.   She was wife number three and none of them bore me a son. So the boy will be a good companion and like a son to me . . . Well, for a while, until he recovers and decides to leave.' It was clear on his face, he wanted the boy to stay, his expression solemn for a moment, the nod accompanied with a sigh.

At dinner, waiters brought in loins of meat, slicing it up and heating it on a small side table where blue flames flew into the air. The music of flutes played in the background and waiters placed little dishes of food upon the table, but when a young girl in a sari held a small bowl of water in front of Daneen, to dip his fingers in, he wasn't sure whether he was supposed to drink it, instead of wash. The Maharaja smiled, his face crinkling in amusement, then eagerly got on with his favourite subject and that was his horses.

After dinner, Daneen visited the stables, as the Maharaja was eager to show him this new horse. The stables were at the back of the palace, and Daneen looked them over in some amazement, for they were not a bit like the old timber kind, at Tipperary - they were stables, fit for the horses of kings.

'I still like to play polo.' The Maharaja grinned. As they wandered around the stables he pointed out his best horse and talked of some of the happy memories of playing the sport at Eton.

'Tis foine stables you have,' Daneen said looking around in awe, and taking in the smell of the horses, bringing back so many old associations. The stable building was low, with a red tiled roof and each horse in his own individual paddock. They walked along a paved area in front of the stables, stopping to view the horses as they looked over the top of the paddocks. Inside, each horse had its own bales of hay and fresh straw and young boys busied with grooming and cleaning. They came out to a field, surrounded by a white fence, where boys walked the horses around; some horses running free.

A lovely white horse was led out by a boy. It wore a full head-dress with a red high plumed feather, and the Maharaja put out his hand to stroke him, telling the boy that he was not riding him today and handed him back the reins. The boy bowed in obedience and the proud horse neighed and rubbed his head up and down the Maharaja's sleeve, but Daneen could see the defiant look in the stallion's eyes, as it kicked out its back legs, giving a little buck. Then as the Maharaja muttered some soothing Hindu words, patting it gently, the horse grunted and veered back.

'See how magnificent he is,' and Daneen could see the Maharaja obviously adored him. 'He is my new horse, and will be my best racer. I have taken him myself over the jumps, but as I said before, he has thrown me and I just cannot seem to tame him.'

Daneen put out his hand and gently took the reins, looping them through his fetlocks, even though the horse pulled back.

'Don't be nervous boy,' Daneen cajoled him. 'I think you need a bit of the old Irish training'.

The Maharaja smiled, as if he agreed. 'I have heard you have a way with horses,' he said as Daneen walked the white horse around its long tail swishing. He stroked the horse's silky coat and smoothed its long neck, whispering in his ear. He was trying to calm him down, as the horse veered back.

'I would be very pleased to help you with this horse,' he said, 'I can see he is a frisky one. But I need time to spend with him, alone. But tomorrow morning before I leave, I'll hand him back to you, and he will be eating out of your hand. But it must be done slowly, so leave him with me for awhile and I will train him.'

'I would be very pleased,' the Maharaja said, 'to trust you with my 'white beauty'.' So Daneen led the horse back to the stable, the horse's white flanks shining in the weak autumn sun.

The next morning Daneen, tied a rope either side of the horse's reins, pulling it, until the horse became still, unable to move, for Daneen was to show him who was boss. Several times he wielded the whip, cracking it into the air and when the horse was quiet, Daneen mounted him, all the time talking to him in a soft Irish brogue the horse seemed to like. Then he was set free to run in the corral but Daneen was not finished, and with an expert throw of the lasso, it caught around the horse's neck, pulling him back. Tighter and tighter he reeled it in, until the horse was bent to his knees. So when the horse was at his mercy, becoming obedient, he was released and led around the corral and trained to jump fences.

When the Maharaja saw the improvement, he was very grateful to Daneen.

Daneen told him: 'You - just have to let them know who is boss and sometimes a horse needs direction.'

The Maharaja smiled, and when he rode him that day, the horse cleared the fence with ease.

'There would always be a job for you in my stables. You have a talent for horses.'

'There is a war to fight,' Daneen sighed, 'but, how I would sure like to work in your stables. Then there is the boy,' he said, 'I will have to leave him.'

'He will not be alone,' the Maharaja assured him. 'Do not worry, for I promise I will have that boy fit and well looked after for you. We have already had the best doctor out to see him, my own personal physician.'

Daneen was relieved that he could go back to his battalion, knowing that the boy would be in good hands.

Before Daneen left, he went to say goodbye to the boy who lay in his sick bed. He seemed a little stronger and his wounds had been stitched and dressed, and he was trying to pull himself up. As he opened his sleepy brown eyes that were edged with thick black lashes, he looked gratefully into Daneen's. 'You . . . h . . . have saved m . . . my life,' he stuttered, for he was still weak.

He had such a gentle way with him, thought Daneen, who told him he would have to leave the palace, but would come back when he had a chance. But the boy's eyes had already closed and he was soon, back in the world of sleep.

The Indian girl came from the kitchens to say farewell, with a bag packed with food for his journey; her eyes like deep green pools, looked sadly into his, as she was up on tip toes to kiss his cheek, for Nighat was a small girl, but one who had a big personality.

'I have never met an Irish man before,' she smiled coyly.

'We're not a bad lot,' Daneen laughed. 'You just look after that boy,' he smiled, 'and I will be back.'

'That will be good,' she said, running off with a shy smile.

When the Maharaja summoned him, he wondered how he should treat him, for they seemed more like friends, but that didn't stop him from bowing as the double doors opened and the Maharaja came to greet him with open arms, telling him he was sorry he was leaving, but adding: 'We need good men like you that are brave and capable, while this war goes on.'

Then suddenly, he turned and walked towards his office, requesting Daneen to follow.

'I am going away myself tomorrow,' the Maharaja told him, picking up a newspaper that lay on his desk and handed it to him, and pointed at the article, he wanted him to see.

Daneen stared down at the pious face of the Dalai Lama of Nepal, wondering what the article was about?

'It is to do with plans for the improvement of this Country,' said the Maharaja. 'He is a great man and a friend of mine'. He then explained that he was going to Tibet to visit the Dalai Lama of Nepal. He is all for public good, and a very special person, filled with peace and love. There is a place there of holy pilgrimage and at this place in Nepal with the Dalai Lama I am filled with spiritual healing. The last time I visited the dalai lama, we sat looking out at the great hills of Nepal, supped black Assam tea, then went to the temple high in the mountains to pray with the monks. We all need this sometimes,' he said with a far off look in his slant eyes. 'But another reason for my visit,' he suddenly said, in a more practical tone, 'is to recruit men for the army. I am always in touch with recruitment,' he added in a more serious manner. 'It is the Gurkhas I am interested in, that live in Tibet. They are great fighters, loyal and trustworthy. We could do with men like this in the Indian army. And while I am talking of recruitment,' the Maharaja suddenly asked Daneen, 'have you heard of the Chindits?' and Daneen shrugged and shook his head, wondering what he was getting at. 'Well that's what these messages back and forward to Calcutta, are all about. Because there is to be a new group going to be formed to do important tasks and I have given my authority for it to go ahead.'

Daneen was a little surprised at the Maharaja's devotion to recruitment, but evidently he was deeply passionate about it. But Daneen wondered why he was telling him, about these messages, as they were secret and he didn't expect to know anything about it.

'I am telling you this,' said the Maharaja, 'because, I think you would make a good Chindit, and we need one who could be in charge of the horses that can trek across the Burma jungle. There is a place required,' he continued, 'for an `animal transporter` for there will be a hundred mules involved. Daneen looked shocked for this was a lot of mules. 'It is a big operation and there will be three-thousand Chindits in all, but they will be divided into seven columns, but, if you wish, I will put it your name forward to Captain Bailey, who is in charge of the Chindits, telling him you would be a good man to be the animal transporter.'

Daneen wondered what he would be required to do, but anything to do with horses, was just up his street, and he thanked the Maharaja for thinking of him.

'I hope you are not thanking me too soon,' the Maharaja said, 'as this is a special group of men, and training will need to be taken, but no doubt you will pass, as they need men who will be able to trek and take the hard living, but you look fit`. The mules will be led over mountains and have to cross rivers, and will be carrying the weapons and supplies.'

Daneen's mind was ticking over, but it did sound an important operation. He liked a challenge, and the idea of being promoted to animal transporter.

'It won't be easy, but you are the man for it.It is Guerilla warfare you see,' the Maharaja informed him.

'I'll do it,' said Daneen. And he left with the knowledge that he was to become a Chindit and that the Bengal boy would be taken care of by the Maharaja.

JOINING THE CHINDITS

Ch.23

Daneen was sad to leave the palace that day, as he took the long journey back to Calcutta.   When he arrived at the barracks, he went straight to see the commander, who had sent for him. Beside the commander, stood another man by the name of Captain Bailey and as Daneen was introduced to him, he knew he was the head of the Chindits, and that the news had travelled fast.

'I have just received, a Morse coded message from the Maharaja,' said the Commander and it seems you are the man recommended to be our animal transporter. You have a way with horses I hear, and there will be a hundred mules to accompany the men on this mission'.

'And they can be very stubborn,' Captain Bailey said stepping forward, and giving a little grin. 'From my experience in the desert in Israel, the mules get very stubborn, kick out and shed their loads.'

'Oh I can handle them,' said Daneen, 'for there can be a good bond between man and mule,' he said, sticking out his chest, for it was not the mules that bothered him, but the Jap's did.

'Well I hope you realise how dangerous this will be,' Bailey added, 'there will be many hardships. I only want strong, fit men and those that will not be so concerned for their personal safety. For we intend to push the Jap's back, from India. So, do you realise your expectations of a long life, are remote?' and his vivid blue eyes stared into Daneen's as if he was weighing him up for this commitment. 'I ask you,' he said, 'are you up for volunteering for this special mission?' Daneen wasn't sure what he should say, for he wasn't sure whether he would, it was beginning to sound more like a suicide mission, but nodded his head and Captain Bailey gave him a knowing grin as he pulled a map out across the desk.

Daneen liked this officer, Captain Bailey, who had been brought in to do a special mission, but he was an unusual type of commander. It was true he had been made a general, but to look at his attire, he dressed very casual, wearing a green khaki shirt and trousers. He had a long straggly beard - that he constantly stroked and around his waist was a fancy tight belt, with a curved dagger tucked behind it. Daneen could not help staring at it.

'It's an Israeli knife - a Jambiya dagger,' said Bailey catching his eye, 'and all my Chindits by the way, will carry a similar one, - the Gurkha knife.'

Also hanging from his belt was a fly squat and he proceeded to squat flies hovering around the desk and was given strange looks by the other officers. 'I've just come back from Israel,' Captain Bailey continued as he looked down at the map with the others. 'You learn a lot out there,' he said, 'fighting in the desert.'

'It's called Guerilla warfare, broke in the commanding officer and grinned as though he too found Captain Bailey a strange one. He explained that Captain Bailey had got together a small army of three thousand men. 'These are made up of forces from England, and the Burma Rifle Division and of course the Gurkhas. And you will all be trekking with the mules, through the jungle of Burma and the operation is, to blow up the railway. We are calling this operation 'Longcloth' he added, 'for it is the town of Long-Ling that the Jap's had a stronghold. That's what we need to destroy.'

'Of course,' Bailey chipped in, 'the three thousand men will be divided into columns- seven columns to be precise.'

Daneen didn't realise it was such a big organisation and this was the first time Daneen was hearing about what the Chindits' mission actually was, but knew that the Jap's were now occupying the jungle of Burma: it was not going to be easy as this was where the Chindits would be crossing.

'Got to keep the Jap's out of India,' said Bailey, 'they have already invaded Thailand and built a railway to Rangoon, and as you know,' added the officer, 'they dropped bombs on Tokyo and taken it over and the people of China are in a bad way, and we need aid. We have to find a way of reaching them. The refugees are fleeing, trying to get to India and dying on the way,although, some of the Chinese men have arrived on the railway to join our Chindits.'

'That's good,' said the Commander, twiddling his moustache, for above all, we need to keep the Jap's back, and one of the Chindits' tasks,' he added, 'is to disrupt the Jap's from invading, to drive them off, so we need strong, fearless men'.

'Yes, and the only way we will do it,' continued Bailey, 'is to blow up this railroad sky high and to destroy the Jap's strong holding in Longling'. Then on a blackboard Bailey drew a map of the journey the Chindits would make. 'You will operate between two rivers,' he said, and pointed to the river Chindwin and then to the Irrawaddy, 'and you will have to cross them both with the mules. That's where you come in 'O' Rourke,' he addressed Daneen by his surname, 'because horses can be very difficult to get across the river. The mules are primal in this operation, for without them you will have little supplies, but they will carry the radios, medical supplies, weapons, tents, whatever a man needs to survive in the jungle. Of course you will be getting food supplies flown in by plane. They will be dropped by parachute. So that's how you will be living.'

Daneen was wondering if the supplies would even reach them, with the Jap's shooting at the planes. 'I can handle the horses and mules, sir. 'I'll get them across the rivers, I know what obstinate gits they can be.'

'And this river, said bailey pointing to the Chindwin river on the map, has a strong current and the Irrawaddy is four miles wide.' Daneen straight away could see the danger, and looked amazed at the big stretch of jungle between the rivers: it was a very long way to go.

'Of course,' Bailey, seeing the uncertainty in Daneen's face as he stared down at the map, 'it's just a briefing, but I only want men who will be strong and hardy enough. So do you think now you would be one of these men,' he asked Daneen, 'who can be in charge of the hundred mules?'

'Oh I know about horses as I said before,' Daneen jut his chest out, 'and if I've got a good hatchet I can cut my way through the jungle.'

'That's what I want to hear,' the Commander said. 'Here is your leader for the horses, Captain Bailey.'

Bailey came over and shook Daneen's hand.

'Do remember,' added Bailey, 'that, you and all the men, will march on a diet of olive oil and dates'.

Daneen thought, this didn't have much to do with all the expected danger, a lot of good dates would do, and was thinking, Bailey was a little strange.

Bailey was obviously quite serious about the men's diet, and he added in a serious tone, 'In Israel, that's something else I learnt, as we trekked through the desert - dates and olive oil, are most important'.

After three months of arduous training, in Guerilla warfare, Daneen was signed up and wore the traditional Chindits' uniform of a wide brimmed hat and casual clothes. Bailey visited his men in the camp site, telling them that they would be transported by plane.

'You will go with the mules in another plane,' Bailey had told Daneen, and they were to leave at dawn.'

'It's all a bit sudden,' complained the men on the side, as they were getting last minute nerves about being dropped in the dense jungle.

'Now you men,' Bailey informed them, 'are, doing an important mission, and will land in the jungle to disrupt the Jap's from invading India. Right, my men,' he said, looking at his watch, that had a broken strap, so he wore it around his neck. 'You have five hours, sleep then, it's 'Operation Longcloth' and good luck to you all. My heart will be with you.' Then with nothing but the radio contact, he would give us our orders, as we went on our way to the Burmese jungle, mules and all.

Daneen began his life as a Chindit and was flown to Burma with other young men of different nationalities, but they were all Chindits in the same boat, wondering what was ahead of them, and they were told they were to live hard and rough, on little food.

Daneen took over his role as animal transporter, guiding the men with their mules through the jungle. They were sent to target the Japanese depots and to destroy their supplies for the Jap's had stopped supplies coming to India, causing a famine and the Chindits were being sent to be jungle fighters behind enemy lines.

It was a hard life, trekking through the jungle, in this hot climate, with monsoons drowning you and chopping down thick bamboo, to lay across the waters fall, so they could cross, wondering whether there was a Jap sniping in the bushes. They survived on little food, having to cook what they had on a billycan over a fire and most of the men grew beards on these long marches, entering occupied Burma and attacked japanese supply depo`s, rail and communication targets. Through all the hardships, of jungle life, Operation Long-cloth did its job, and North Burma had been successfully infiltrated and this had effected the Japanese' thinking.

When Operation Long-cloth was over and the men were ordered to return home, the Indian refugees, who trudged came in droves trying to get back to India, were just left to their own devices, and the Jap's troops took over their supplies and transport, pushing them aside, but the Chindits were recalled home and Daneen was relieved, for he hated those days in the jungle . . . they seemed endless and he would comfort himself thinking of the beautiful palace, the Maharaja and wonder how the boy was, hoping he would see him again. But he didn't have to wait that long, as when the Chindits' mission was over and the men sent back to their battalion in Calcutta, Daneen was pleased to find out, that the Maharaja had sent for him.

"He is needed at the palace", the Maharaja had told the British Commander and it seemed, what the Maharaja asked for, he usually got.

When Daneen found out he was going to have a new role of assisting the Maharaja with his horses, he couldn't believe it. So relieved to be out of the jungle where, if the Japs didnt get you the snakes would.

Just before he left his barracks in Calcutta, his commanding officer with a beady eye, said: `must be the luck of the irish, he said, somewhat sardonically, but we have decided to let you go, for the time being anyway`, and the maharaja has sent us many good men, `Gurka`s from the Burma Rifles`

`Its to help with training for his horses` Daneen informed the commander. hoping he was not going to snap his head off.

`yes yes, the commander said a little haughtily, ` we know all that, and you will need to return to your station at some point, as the Chindits will be going on a second mission and the next one might not be so easy.'

But Daneen decided he would face that when the time came, for now he was pleased to be sent to the palace and to a new job at the stables. As he set out on his black stallion, journeying across Burma, through forests, swamps and difficult terrain, he would think about the boy and all he went through, and hoped he would remember him.

He needn't have worried, as the boy certainly remembered Daneen, the man who had saved his life who had brought him to the palace, that he found to be a wonderful place and each day there, he became closer to the young girl Nighat, who worked there. They were about the same age and each morning, he could not wait to run to the kitchens to sit and watch her cook.   At first when had arrived at the palace, it had seemed a strange place and he was haunted by those memories in Bengal and of his starving family. He wondered about his poor mother who was so ill and it had been that day that he had gone to the river to try and catch a fish for her to eat that he lay on the bank, and with his hands tried to catch one from but they slid through his hands. It was then that he heard the sound of Jap's voices behind him and then there was darkness as a fist came into his face.

He also had memories of this man, bathing his wounds and picking him up from the ground, for he remembered how he had carried him on the back of his horse and brought him to this palace and he knew this was the man who saved his life. It was Nighat who told him as he lay on his sick bed.

'He will be back,' she said, as she bathed his forehead, for Daneen has promised to return. During those weeks, it was Nighat who was his comfort and as he got better, would limp into the kitchens and sit and watch her, as she talked to the staff as they cooked. She was always bringing him into the conversation and feeding him up, bringing him little bowls of food that she would put on his lap. He loved her warmth, her sympathy, her whimsical smile and those big green eyes would look at him with such concern.

'Now, you are not going to sit there all day looking sad,' she said. 'What you need is a walk around the gardens, the sun is shining and I will take you.'

So once her chores were done, she would guide him around the gardens and he would take her arm as they stopped to look at the many coloured flowers that grew in abundance along the pathways. The Maharaja looking from the window with a smile was glad Nighat had taken him under her wing, as the boy said very little and Nighat would soon get him talking. He was also thinking, that as soon as the boy was strong enough he could help in the stables and he would take him riding.

Soon with the good food inside him, he became well nourished and he put on weight and his sunken cheeks, filled out. No more were his arms thin, but built up with working in the stables, and the more work he did the more, stronger he became. He loved all the history of the palace and would stand looking up at the statues of the previous Maharajas with awe, and ask questions about the dynasties and the religious statues that adorned the palace. He had never seen such statues before, for he was a Muslim and not a Hindu. Although he knew he was different, he loved this place and he settled down to life at the palace.

It often troubled him that his people suffering and the starvation that still existed in his home town of Calcutta, but he never wanted to leave the safe walls of this palace. He and the Maharaja would spend time together at the stables and he would tell the Maharaja how worried he was about his people suffering from starvation and the Maharaja sent extra supplies to Bengal.

The Maharaja had given him a new name-Naj and he had become fond of him and they sat together at dinner like father and son, and spent many hours riding around the palace grounds and along the river path and Naj would breathe in deep, the sweet smelling air, and listen to stories of how the Maharaja had spent his own childhood. As they cantered along, on the, grand thoroughbred horses, he would teach him the names of the plants and the bird life, and he would dread ever going back to the old life, where people were dying of disease and hunger and he felt he could never cope with it again.

When Daneen arrived back at the palace, he could hardly believe how well the boy looked, as he limped towards him.`Tis a foine young man you look, declared daneen in suprise, noticing his long black wavy hair, his dark sparkling eyes with long lashes, that looked straight at him. `You`ve grown so tall` said Daneen and a wide smile broke out on the boys face. It was the first time Daneen had seen that smile and he was so relieved to find the boy a picture of health. From that day on, Daneen taught the boy everything he knew about horses, just as his own Irish grandfather had taught him and Naj was such a willing boy, always curious to know more and more.

Daneen noticed how close Nighat and the boy had become as they went out riding together, they seemed like brother and sister, and she would fuss over him. He could see that the boy wallowed in the care she gave him. Although, he still had his limp, he never let it worry him.

Then one day when the boy needed help to mount the black stallion. 'My leg will never heal properly, but 'I'm glad to be alive,' and bowed his head in gratitude. 'I will always be grateful to you, for saving me and bringing me to this palace.'

He would treat Daneen like his master and when they were training the white Arabian horse in the corral, Daneen lassoed her with that same old skill; the rope swung into the air and fell straight around the horse's neck.

The boy watched in awe. 'Can you teach me that?' he asked.

'I sure can,' Daneen said, throwing the rope in the air again, but with a more serious face. 'Don't keep thanking me for saving you, you are a great help to me with the horses, I should be grateful to you.'

The boy's dark eyes looked down, for it passed over his mind, that perhaps now he was strong enough, it would be time for him to go and how he would hate, to leave this wonderful palace and his friend Nighat. This place was now his home and each day he would look forward to meeting Nighat at the gate of the estate, and she would be waiting there, sitting on the chestnut mare, and they would ride together over the hills, right out to the open plains. They would race the horses and sometimes sit on the sandy banks and share secrets and it was here he had told her about that dreadful day when he was attacked by the Jap's and talked of his parents in Calcutta, as his eyes filled with tears.

'Don't know whether they are alive anymore,' he said. 'My mother was weak with hunger, I could not help her,' he said, 'the Jap's got me.

'You were a good son,' she consoled him, hugging his arm as his long lashes closed over his eyes, 'we will go and find them one day.'

But as time passed at the palace, new memories began to fill his mind and he tried to push away those old visions that still haunted him of men, women and children starving and lying dying on the streets. For now the Maharaja introduced him to another world, the beautiful temple and the sounds of tinkling bells, the cool interior - a place where he would be taken to pray and kneel before his favourite Gods. It was a place of learning, as the Maharaja, would teach him so much about the Hindu religion and the dynasty of his family.

'I would like you to become a Hindu,' the Maharaja told him one day, sitting on his throne in the Great Hall; upon his head a turquoise turban, adorned with pearls and a gold llama coat. 'It is a holy day,' he said, 'a holiday . . . a festival of colour.'

Naj was looking at him in awe and at the colourful wall paintings that surrounded him. There were some of tigers and elephants, and many Gods and Goddesses. The Maharaja pointed to a magnificent wall painting. 'Krishna is my favourite God,' he said with a bow of his head, then asked the boy to sit beside him, pointing to the marble step beneath the throne and rested a soft hand on the boys shoulder as he began explaining the ceremony the boy would be taking.

After Naj agreed he would convert to Hinduism. 'Are you sure?' the Maharaja asked him, 'as you have been brought up in the Muslim faith? It is a big thing for you to become a Hindu. You must have the will, the commitment to study the scriptures and abide by the proper practice.'

'Oh I will,' said the boy, looking up at the painting of Krishna, with a warm smile, for Naj was more than willing to became a Hindu: these people had been so good to him and he would leave his Muslim faith behind.

After that, he often would accompany the Maharaja to the temple to learn about becoming a Hindu. One day the maharaja said to him, 'You know Naj, to perform royal duties, a monarch has to be four- faced like

Brahma, thousand-eyed like Indra and a hundred - hands like Katyayani. Naj didn't know what these meant and his velvet brown eyes looked very serious as he listened to the Maharaja's teachings.

'Don't look so serious young man,' said the Maharaja, with an arm around his shoulder, 'but you never know when I might need your help.'

Naj was a little perplexed but knew what a great ruler this man was and tried to take in every bit of knowledge he taught him.

In the afternoons, Naj would often sit outside the Maharaja's office, a square polished hallway with pillars either side and an inside fountain with blue spraying water, it was so refreshing and he would watch the soldiers of all ranks, going in and out, their boots tapping on the polished floor. He would love to see all the fancy uniforms of the Hussars, with the tall feathers in their hats and they would look at the young boy sitting there in his baggy white churidars and give a little salute. He also loved the ammunition room close by, where there were lines of rifles in a glass case, and ornate swords hung on the wall and he would wander around looking at the collection of ammunition. For Naj, there was so much to see and do, and Naj thought less and less about his old life and each time he thought of leaving the palace, he was filled with anxiety.In fact he was terrified the Maharaja would send him back and asked him when they were out riding.

The Maharaja grinned, seeing the boys anxious face, 'Of course not. I would never part with you,

Naj, You have brightened my life and what a lovely young man you have grown into.' For Naj had developed into an attractive teenager year old, putting on weight and most of his injuries had healed, apart from his leg and still had a limp, but he would always have that: the Jap's knives had severed the nerve.

He would spend much of his time in the day, cleaning out the stables and the Maharaja had insisted that he had a private teacher come in, for further education and the learning of French and English. He also had religious instruction; that was all part of becoming a Hindu. Most mornings he would accompany the Maharaja to the temple, for prayer.

When he wasn't busy with the Maharaja, Naj would go running off to the kitchens to find Nighat and sit there in the warm, watching her cook. He loved everything about this new friend, he could tell her anything. He would tell her about his visit to the temple and she would smile with approval, for she was so pleased he was becoming a Hindu and would talk about her favourite God, Saraswali - the Goddess of learning.

'She is depicted playing the veena.' Naj looked confused. 'It's a musical instrument,' she told him, for Naj was still discovering about the Gods and Goddess' of this new religion. When she asked: 'Who is your favourite God?' he gave a shrug and looked most ashamed. 'Don't look so sad,' she said her eyes wide and sympathetic, 'it will come.'

Often they would sit in the long grass and he told her his dream of one day becoming a man like the Maharaja, who was respected and liked. 'My life in Calcutta was a poor one,' he said, 'nobody had money.'

'You will be a fine man,' Nighat said with assurance, resting her head on his shoulder, then told him of her own life in Calcutta, the daughter of a 'Maharisha' and snuggled up to him.

Before the year was out, the relationship began to get even closer and Nighat developed into a beautiful   teenage girl: together they looked a handsome couple going to the temple together, on special religious days. Naj would take her hand and she dressed in one of her best saris.

'I am so proud to be with you,' he told her one day as they walked home to the palace. They stopped to sit by the duck pond and rest. The midday sun was very hot. They sat dangling their feet in the water. For some reason, this day, Naj could not stop looking at her bud like breasts that were forming, and her olive skin had a pink glow, as her Eastern green eyes looked straight into his.

'Why are you staring?' she asked, but his lips had already come down on hers, gently.

He whispered, 'You are my first and last love, Nighat.' But quickly she got up and ran back across the fields, and he knew he must not do that again.

But from then on she had a new glow about her. `You are my special and true love,' she told him. They would often go and sit by the pond and kiss and cuddle.

One day when they were close together laying in the grass, she talked about her father. 'I do miss him,' she said. 'He is a fine man, but he is old now,' she explained, 'but had once been a Bhakti yoga teacher,' she said proudly.

'A teacher, he must be a quite clever, man,' said Naj with an enquiring look.

She explained how he was a Hara Krishna guru and still preached in the parks.

Naj remembered seeing the Hara Krishna movement in the square in Bengal: they were chanting and singing and he knew from his own new religious studies of the Hindu religion that the Hara Krishna movement came from the Hindu scriptures.

'Your father is a strict Hindu then?' Naj, looked into those soft green eyes as she talked on about her father, and he could tell she loved him very much.

'He is very respected,' Nighat said, 'for his beliefs and work.' But, Naj was wondering, what he would think of him, being raised a Muslim boy.

'Do you think your father would like me?' he asked looking down, 'for I am still a Muslim?'

'Nighat only said with a buoyant smile, 'But not for long. You will soon be a Hindu,' and kissed him softly on the lips, and he no longer thought about what her father wished, for he was lost in a world of love as he held her tight in his arms.

But it was not long, before her father got to know about her close friendship with Naj, for Nighat would often mention him in her letters and when he discovered he was a Muslim, he sent for his daughter to return to Calcutta, telling her she was needed at home.

So it was a sad day for Naj, when they were sitting in the kitchen and Nighat told him, that her father was ill and that she would have to go back home to look after him. He was dreading being without her, and when she left with tears in her eyes, she told him she would be back, when her father improved, but the months went by and she never returned. . .

Naj wandered about the palace, his young face pale and drawn. They had been a young couple on the verge of love and now they were torn apart.

He sat around gloomily and it was the Maharaja who came and said softly, 'I know you are missing your lovely Nighat, like we all are, but you must not fret so.'

The boy seemed in a world of his own and this worried the Maharaja. 'Naj my, Son,' he said a little sharply, that made Naj look up with surprise, for he had never called him son before. 'I know you are fond of Nighat, but she is your first love, and it is always your first love that is the strongest.'

The Maharaja had guessed, there was more to this than Nighat's father recalling her back home, because he was unwell, for he knew that a Hindu man would not want his daughter getting involved with a Muslim.

'What will I do with him?' the Maharaja said to, Daneen. 'He is in love and it's all about their religion. What can I do for him?'

'It's a shame', Daneen had said to the Maharaja, 'because pretty soon he will be a Hindu, and perhaps the father will allow her back'.

But the Maharaja shook his head. 'Perhaps not', he said, 'I know he is a Maharisha - a teacher, and they follow the Hindu scriptures strictly and he will be devoted to his religion.'

'Time will tell,' said Daneen, 'but we can keep the boy busy, get him out on the horses. He needs to get over Nighat'.

But it was weeks before Naj stopped fretting.

'I have decided to send him to Eton,' the Maharaja said to Daneen, 'for Eton is the finest school in England and this will give him a new life to look forward to.'

The Maharaja told Naj his wishes and explained what a great school

Eton was. 'Eton served me well,' he said. 'It was a wonderful place for my life and I hope it will be wonderful for yours.'

It was a wet day when Naj was leaving. The Maharaja stood under his colourful parasol, trying to hide the tears in his eyes, for he had become so fond of the boy's company, he would miss him dearly, but together with Daneen, they waved the boy off, as he was about to depart in a polished limousine, that would be taking him to the private plane to England.

'We will meet again,' the Maharaja told the boy, 'there will be holidays, but there is a war on, so train hard,' he warned, 'and become a good doctor. That is my wish.'

'I will,' said the boy, and thank you both.' He sighed. 'You have been wonderful to me. I will not let you down.' Then looking to Daneen, said softly, 'Let me know if you hear from Nighat.'

'I will,' Daneen told him, and sighed deeply wondering if Naj would ever get over Nighat. It was certainly, love.

'Eton will do him good,' said the Maharaja. 'To get over this girl, he will need to be strong, for great rulers often have five wives.'

'Five!' Daneen was astounded, with a curl to his lip. A harem was not something for any old Irishman.

'So, if the boy is to follow me,' continued the Maharaja in a determined manner, 'any son of mine, has to have their mind on our dynasty, for that may even be at risk in future.'

For a moment, Daneen looked intently at him. 'Do you mean,' he asked, 'that you would, really like him to be your son?'

The Maharaja nodded. 'I think he will make a fine son, but first he must work hard at learning and after Eton I will be sending him to study medicine.'

Daneen could see the Maharaja had it all worked out and he could see many great opportunities for the boy. That's when Daneen also told the Maharaja the news that he too would be leaving, for he had received a message from his commander at the barracks, to return as soon as possible as the men will be leaving on the next Chindits' mission.

'I know,' the Maharaja sighed, 'they are calling this mission, Operation Thursday. The Chindits are being sent to destroy operations behind the enemy lines. It is a much larger expedition - a very special force, and I hear you will be attacking 'Imphal' and it will be a long battle with the Jap's attacking, so do be careful my man,' he warned Daneen.

Daneen was a little thoughtful, as he too had heard this was a more dangerous mission, and more than anything - he was dreading the days in that dim green jungle, where you could hardly see and the days looked like nights.

'Don't worry,' said Daneen firmly, 'we will push those Jap's back and destroy their railroad,' for he knew that was what Operation Thursday was about and it would probably be very dangerous.

`

THE KENNEDY SISTERS

Ch.24

After finding the letter from Nora, Eileen was still curious: there were still unanswered questions, so she decided to pay a visit to the Kennedy

Sisters, to see what she could find out.

The Kennedy Sisters' cottage was on the crest of the hill; it was a solitary thatched cottage with red bricks and she could see the smoke bellowing from the chimney. She pushed young Shamus in the pram up the steep slope and looking back, the village looked like a toy town. She puffed and panted with a small cage resting on the top of the pram. Inside was a cockerel, a gift to keep their brood of hens happy. Also, it was a fine excuse for a visit, for she was determined to get to the bottom of this mystery in the letter.

She hoped they would be pleased with the cockerel for it was not an easy journey, with the bird flapping its wings and rocking the cage back and forth. 'Not far now,' she said to young Shamus, as he giggled at the bird and tried to grab the cage.

As she approached the cottage, the door soon opened, for the Kennedy Sisters, saw everyone who came up the hill.

'What a nice surprise,' Mae Kennedy said, her big brown eyes lighting up with humour at the cockerel on top of the pram.

'Now what brings you all the way up the hill?' she said, lifting the cage inside - a quizzical grin across her uneven features and noticed her high stomach, realising Eileen was pregnant with child again. 'You should be taking it easy,' she chided.

'I'm foine,' Eileen told her, whose complexion glowed after the walk up the hill. 'I hope you`ll be delivering this little one,' and she smiled. 'For sure,' Mae said. `I`ll not retire, while there`s another O`Hara` to bring in the world`.

In the hallway, they talked about the delivery and Mae wrote down dates in her diary.

In the dining room, Eileen was greeted by the two other sisters who sat by the fireside. They looked identical in appearance, with the same homemade tweed dresses and faded red hair, except Babs had no sense of humour, while Lillie joked and smiled all the while.

Mae Kennedy was the eldest sister, tall and stately, her voice soft and musical, but could put you in your place with her clear, grey eyes. Eileen often saw her around the village, in her nurses unform, holding her hat on her greying head of hair, racing on her bike from place to place. On her back a rucksack, with all kinds of medicines for the sick. Everyone would say how caring she was and every Sunday without fail, would walk to church with a stately grace.

The cottage was very warm. A huge block of peat sent out a tremendous heat and a black iron kettle hung over the big fireplace. The cottage had belonged to their mother's family and they kept all the traditional dark oak furniture. It was cosy and the walls were covered with religious pictures. At the far end was a glass patio door that looked out over a blue shadowing mountain. The kitchen was untidily furnished, with a large wooden table and pine dresser.

Soon the tea was being served in dainty china cups and Mae Kennedy, placed a flowered apron around her waist and sliced a fruit cake while Babs Kennedy sat with her hands folded under her apron, staring at Shamus, as he chuckled and held out his arms to be loved.   Eileen lifted her chuckling son into Babs Kennedy's arms and she looked as though she wasn't sure what to do with him. She was not at all used to babies and Shamus soon got bored and wanted to crawl around the room.

Sitting by the fire, they watched the smoke curl up the chimney and Lillie the youngest said, 'I`ll put up the fireguard.' She put her hands over her face and giggled at Shamus, as he pulled the table cloth and the cake toppled from the table. But when Eileen talked of her pregnancy and how she hoped she hoped she was carrying a girl,here were squeals of delight and congratulations. Then they asked where young Mick was, with a knowing glance, for they all knew he did little work.

`I hear from Pat Kennedy that Ginger is helping him on the land` said Mae,

`and he sure needs some help` giggled Lilly,

but Eileen was not going to be rattled, she was hear to find out some home truths.

`It you must know, my mick is a bit upset today,' Eileen said, coming straight out with it, and told them how she had found a letter from his mother and they all looked from one to the other, but at the same time, Eileen was pulling from her bag, a velvet pouch with the brooches she had found. With pleased smiles, they sorted through the sparkling jewellery and each picked a brooch of their choice.

But when Eileen discussed the contents of the letter, warning glances went around the room. On asking them if they could shed any light on this, they said very little, only agreeing in unison, that it was all a bit of a mystery. Then proceeded to chat about the hens and Mae Kennedy cut the fruit cake in slices and handed it out, giving a running commentary on how she made it for the women's guild.

'But I`ll make another,' she said, taking a big bite of her slice and settled her wide hips into the chair.

'So what do you mean a bit of a mystery?' Eileen said, as she waited for a break in the conversation. But no answer came back and Shamus was playing up as he crawled about the floor then tugged away a Babs Kennedy's knitting bag, and she got in a terrible flap as Shamus pulled the line of stitches off the big needle. So Eileen whisked him away before he did more damage, but Babs Kennedy was full of complaints and smacked her lips together in an uncouth fashion, then took up the cage with the cockerel in it.

'What a racket!' exclaimed Lillie, as the cockerel started a chorus of cocker- doodle- doo and Shamus stared to scream at the top of his voice, reaching out for the cockerel's crown.

Then Babs whisked the cage away, with a big red face, her fat hips swinging, and dashed out of the room.

'Take no notice of her', said Mae consoling Shamus as he screamed. 'Bab's gets herself in a real huff.'

'She's an old maid, that's why,' added Lillie 'gone off to feed the smelly pigs,' and screwed up her nose.

Shamus wouldn't stop screaming, until Eileen followed the others out of the door, where Babs was placing the cockerel amongst the hens. It was an amusing sight to see him strutting up and down displaying his feathers and Shamus chuckled with delight this time as the cockerel, cock-a-doodle doo-ed. At the end of the garden there was a chicken coop, a sty with some young pigs and as Babs got inside the smelly sty and poured them mashed up potatoes, they all rushed at.

'She's in litter,' said Bab's pointing to a fat sow and dumped another a bucket of swill on the ground and the pigs rushed again, sloshing it all over the place.'It's her second litter this year,' she said wiping her hands down her woolly jumper, but and as much as Babs tried to offer Eileen one of the new litter, Eileen was adamant, that she wanted no more pigs.

Inside the cottage, they took off their muddy boots, and Babs Kennedy, holding her wide hips, bent to put more peat on the fire.

'I'll do the peas,' Lillie said with a shy smile and sat by the fire shelling them for dinner.

'Got a nice bit of boiled ham for you and Shamus,' said Mae, but Eileen told her she could not stay much longer and went on about the letter, but nobody seemed to be taking much notice.

'So why did not Mick's mother come back to Ireland anymore, can you tell me that much?'

'You better tell Mick to ask Daneen,' mumbled Mae but then that conversation came to a halt, as the two other sisters came bouncing in with new laid eggs for Eileen.

'Take these home for Mick's breakfast,' said Babs handing her a box.

'That's when he gets out of the bed,' Lillie giggled. 'The hens have just laid them.'

But Eileen was not very interested in the eggs or the smutty remarks, she just wanted some answers to her questions and said in a loud voice. 'So what's Daneen got to do with it? It's Mick's mother I`m interested in,' and warning glances again, passed around the room as if too much had been divulged.

Then Babs Kennedy started to talk about the time, Mick came for a holiday as aboy and the atmosphere brightened. She talked of a boat trip down the river and a day at the castle where she had once worked.

'He was very nervous Mick,' she said, as she crocheted some fine lace, 'wouldn't go down to visit the dungeons.' And Eileen had some more tea and listened eagerly to their stories, hoping they would lead into something about Mick's mother.

'I only met Mick, once,' said Lillie, 'he never returned to Ireland again, and when I asked Bridie, if he was coming back for another holiday, she didn't seem very interested.'

The sisters, looked from one to the other, and Babs eventually spoke. 'I think Bridie was disappointed. I remember her saying, that Mick did not look a bit like her brother Tim.'

'So you think that's why she did not ask him back?' declared Eileen with some annoyance. 'Just because he did not look like his father, and poor Mick lost his mother and   was sent off to some orphanage.' The three sisters looked down and did not know what to say, and Eileen's lips were set in a grim line and she wanted some answers. 'Don't you think that's a little cruel?' she said, 'Just when Mick needed his Irish family.'

'We didn't know what to think,' said Mae diplomatically, but her face reddened in a blush 'and Bridie was an obstinate woman,' she added. 'But just think of the legacy that she left him, that surely means a lot.'

Then the three sisters gabbled on, with lots of breathless little gasps, about the inheritance and the land, and what a fine farm it will be one day, and Eileen had to agree how fortunate Mick had been to gain such an inheritance, but that was not the point just now.

The room was getting hot and the fire blazed as Babs threw the peat on. She was a strong, ungainly woman and tossed the blocks of peat with little effort. The heat had sent Shamus to sleep on the sheepskin rug in front of the fireplace and the conversation turned to stories of Irish rebels, that Eileen found very interesting, but she really wanted to discuss Bridie and Mick's mother, and kept trying to get a word in, but then they turned the stories to Leprechauns.

They all had a tale to tell, going on about their Irish heritage. 'Once Irish, always Irish,' the sisters chanted in unison . . . always Irish.' They spoke almost in a whisper, of past Irish rebellions, when the cottage was used by their parents as a safe house for the volunteer groups, who supported the revolution against the British in Ireland.

'I remember one night,' said Mae, 'there was a distant sound of gunfire cracking through the air, then suddenly a bang on the front door and us girls got out of bed, and from the landing, could see these young men come running in and they were shouting about an ambush on the road and that men had been shot. "Got the British truck" I remember them saying, then "blow it up"- Then they sat around the fire talking to Dad about the shootings and how they had got away across the fields, remember that this was a safe house. So Dad gave them a blanket and they were put down the cellar, until the morning light, then they went back down the mountain.

'But I was scared,' Babs said, 'cause I could hear them marching around in the front garden and looking out of the window, saw a young fresh faced young man, smoking and walking up and down carrying a machine gun, then my father's voice telling him to come inside. And when Dad saw me peering around the door, sent me back to bed, saying we should all be very quite. "Stay in your rooms" he warned, "in case the troops came to search".

`And dont you remember` said Babs, `the young man who stood at the back door, keeping a look out, `why for sure that was Daneen, little more than a boy himself`. But the others sisters went quite.

`For goodness sake`, said Babs everyone knows that Daneen was a republican, a real chucky`and Eilleen nodded in agreement, for even she had heard whispers that Daneen and Bridie were revolutionaries when they were young`.

`Its strange` said Eillen how people dont talk about it` and the sisters looked from one to another, as if enough had been said. `and I do remember` said Eilleen `my mother telling me it had been a safe house` she often visited here to see my aunt and my mother also knew Daneen as a boy, she would say, how sad it was, he had such a hard start in life and was pleased when Grandad Spudd gave him a home.

`bound to have a soft spot for him` said Babs, `Daneen being one of her many cousins, shame he`s gone on the garble``

`That what the rebels did, drowned there sorrows, added Mae, `there was a lot of bloodshed in those times`

Young Lillie was listening with Big sad eyes, 'Haven't you seen the memorial stone on the side of the road to Galway? she said softly, It has the names of the brave ones who died that day.'

'Tis strange' said Babs, her eyes rolling in reflection, 'neither our mother nor our father said a word about that night and whenever we questioned about it, they would just put their fingers to their lips, so we learnt at a young age that it was all to be kept secret.

` But don't you remember` said Mae how they used to call us – 'The Sinn Fein Sisters?' This made them all titter. 'And I had many a tumble over that,' she said.

So as they sat under the lamp around the polished round coffee table, it seemed each had a secret to share about this sweet old cottage, with roses around the door; things that you would never believe had gone on and Eileen looked around at the low beamed ceiling and the little door that went down to a cellar and young Lillie, her face full of freckles, in the background was singing in her sweet Irish voice `The Ballad of the Exlle' . . . I am thinking of the many who left the Emerald Isle . . . and as the words rolled off her tongue, a tear drop like crystal ran down her face. . .'

It was all getting a bit creepy, and Babs enjoying the sensation, said, 'That song was a warning, used by the resistance,' and her Celtic blue eyes were wide with anticipation.

Eileen gave a little shudder, feeling the tingle of goosebumps and looked nervously behind her. She was enjoying the thrill of it all, but time was moving on, and so far, she had not found out anything about Mick`s mothers secret as each time she mentioned it, they seemed to change the subject.   So Eilleen just got swept along in the suspense, trying to keep up with their quick irish brogue and forgot all about the baby asleep on the floor. Poor darling, she suddenly said, picking him up and held him to her breast, rocking him to and fro. He soon closed his eyes again, in the cosy warm room.

'Got a bit hot in here for young Shamus,' said Mae with a twist of a smile.

And Lillie giggled. 'Just like it did, for the poor old cockerel,' and held out her arms to cuddle young Shamus. With adoration she looked at him, so Eileen passed the sleepy babe into her arms and turned directly to Mae.

'Is there nothing you can tell me, Mae?' she asked, 'as to why Mick's mother promised Bridie, she would not come back to Ireland? Mick is entitled to know.'

'Might have been a bit of jealousy,' piped up Babs, who said it was about time they all had a glass of Sanatogen. It was her favourite tipple of wine and she disappeared to get the bottle and glasses. 'think the two women both liked Daneen.He was a handsome brute.'Babs eyes seemed to shine, but Eileen had the feeling there was more to it than

277

that. Then suddenly Babs changed the subject, saying `it was time for a glass of sanatogen tonic wine, that was her favourite tipple and went off to get the glasses.

'Better be getting home then,' Eileen said. 'I'm worried about Mick, think he's got depression. He's very sullen.'

'Sorry to hear that,' said Mae, as they all looked down in sympathy.

'It's not been easy for him, being left an orphan.'

And when Eileen got up to leave, Mae came with her to the door and helped her out, with the pram.'I'll come with you down the hill,' she said, putting on her coat. 'The path is slippery,' and looked warily up at the dark rainclouds that hovered overhead. So together they walked and Mae linked her arm through Eileen's, who looked up at Mae`s tall figure, although she had put on weight with age, but she could just imagine her, as a hospital matron, she was very forthright.

'Don`t think, I'm holding out information, Eileen, but I don`t want to involve my sisters in any gossip. You see, I know how gossip can ruin people`s life.' She looked down for a moment, and Eileen felt she had something more to tell her, as Mae clutched her arm and they walked down the hill together. Shamus was fast asleep in his pram, so they could chat away and Eileen wanted to get to the bottom of it. 'The reason, Bridie banned Nora from Ireland, was because Nora was Daneen's lover, and if you must know,' said Mae, 'it was not a pretty situation. I found out one day when I walked in on them, they were wrapped in each other's arms in the cow shed.'

'Eileen gasped in sheer disbelief, hanging on to her every word.

'I tried to tell Nora,' Mae admitted, 'that she was playing a dangerous game. I had often seen Nora from the window, going backwards and forwards to the milk shed. She would be looking around. I soon realised, she was looking for Daneen. He was usually in the stables, or in the paddock walking the horses around. I could see she had painted her lips red and was wearing a low cut blouse, and that afternoon I asked her what she was up to and why she was all dressed up like that just to milk the cows, but truthfully, Nora didn't need to do that, she was so pretty, with her jet black hair and her glowing cheeks. She could attract a man wearing an old sack and she didn't need her face made up. '"Don't be a silly girl"', I'd said to her, telling her to stay away from Daneen. She snapped back at me, that she wasn't doing any harm knowing he was Bridie's fiancé, and continued along her way carrying the milk jug and swinging her hips, and I watched Daneen tie up his horse and they strolled into the shed together.'

'Fancy that,' Eileen said, 'was it just the one off?'

'No, it went on most afternoons, whilst poor Bridie was out with the sheep dog, rounding in the sheep. She could be seen, sometimes from the window, walking across the high field, wielding her shepherds' crook and you could hear the whistle, blow. I used to feel sorry for Bridie, up there on the hill, and not knowing what was going on in the cow shed. And poor Tim, he would never have believed it. Tim was Bridie's brother and Nora was his fiancée. He thought butter wouldn't melt in her mouth. One day I said to Nora: "You must pack it up, because Bridie and Tim will find out and there will be pure war to pay"- but she said she couldn't help it, she loved Daneen too much, and tears were running down her face. "It's disgraceful" I told her anger rising in me, and that Daneen is engaged to Bridie. They are going to get married. But she didn't seem to care, just accused me of being jealous and told me to leave her alone, and mind my own business. "I'm only trying to help I pleaded"- but she didn't look at it that way and glared at me scornfully."Your trouble is" she'd said wiping her tears away, "you have no man yourself and you want to be careful you don't end up an old maid"-This was so hurtful, because I know I've always been known as plain, but to be left on the shelf, to be an old maid, was every girl's dread. `I`m a feminist now`, said Mae and  no women wants to be called an old maid, `she tis, for sure, a little missy`, So I left Nora to her own fate.

The heavens opened up and the suddenly the rain poured down. Eileen stood shivering with the cold.

'Better go,' Mae looked, longingly back at the cottage with the smoke bellowing from the chimney and hurried quickly back up the hill.

'Thank you, Mae,' Eileen called after her, but only a quick wave came back, for the rain was heavy and Eileen quickly put up the hood of her mackintosh and hurried off in the opposite direction. She felt she had been in a whole new world as she thought of all she had been told, but believed the whole truth of who was Mick's father, was not yet revealed and that there was only one person who knew that, and that was Daneen, for he was the man in the centre of it all.

When Eileen's baby was due to arrive, Mae Kennedy was quickly on the scene. On the back of her bike, she carried her carpet bag and ran up the stairs to Eileen's bedroom, running past Mick, who stood there with a gormless expression.

'Plenty of hot water and towels!' she shouted to him.

Before long a healthy boy was born and Eileen rocked him in her arms.

'You can go in now,' Mae told Mick, as he held young Shamus in his arms and took him to see his new brother.

Each day for a week, Mae returned to see Eileen, helping her with feeding the baby and sitting by her bedside. 'I used to do this for Nora,' she said one day and Eileen's eyes widened.

'I never heard what happened to Nora,' she said. 'I would love to know.'

'Well,' Mae told her, sitting back and feeding the baby his bottle; his chubby face so pink as he sucked away, 'it was all a long time ago now,' she sighed, 'but I remember it well. It was a while, before I saw Nora again. I heard she had left the farm and married Tim. By this time the war was in full swing and I joined the London Hospital as a midwife. But like me, there was plenty of young probationary nurses arriving, all thinking of the glamour of being a war time nurse, then getting tired of staggering up and down the wards, with full bed pans to empty, and after each shift, dropping exhausted into bed. It was the uniform,' she stated, 'that the nurses complained of, with its faded mauve and white dress, the collar that cut into your throat and the absurd little cap, held in place by an unreliable pin. . .'

For a while Mae talked of those times during the war in London, and life at the hospital, but Eileen was waiting to hear about Nora. But Mae looked at her watch and rushed off to see her next patient. 'I'll be back tomorrow,' she said, handing the crying baby back to Eileen and dashed out of the door.

But a few days later, they placed the new born baby, named Michael, into his pram and walked along the bridge. 'Some fresh air will do you both good,' said Mae, wrapping the warm blanket well over the baby. They stopped on the bridge looking down at the salmon that leapt out over the rushing water. Eileen was all ears, as they walked slowly along, and Mae continued her story.

'I had only been at the hospital for about a month, when I got the shock of my life, for lying in a narrow hospital bed, was Nora, but she looked ill and extremely thin, despite the fact, she was overdue to give birth to Mick. She just lie there, her eyes closed. The doctor told me she had TB and that they were concerned about the birth of the baby. Straight away I took pity on her, she was once such a beautiful colleen, but now her face was so pale and her thick black hair lay limply on the pillow. I was the head midwife and stood at the end of her bed and weighed up her case, reading the reports and soon informed the nurses, that the baby should be induced.

Then suddenly a weak voice said: "Is that you Mae?" and she opened her eyes and stared at me, with dull listless eyes. "I've got an illness" she said, her voice was flat and tears run down her face, "my baby" she cried, "will it be alright?"- "Yes" I promised, and her thin hand came out to me and I was only glad I was there to help her as it was sheer coincidence I was sent to that hospital from Ireland and I was not thinking about what she had done to Bridie and Tim, only about helping her get this baby into the world. She was so young to have TB. I was told she was alone, that her husband Tim was overseas. When the contractions started, I tried to calm her, she was weak and cramped with pain and kept yelling, "This is my Tim`s baby"- I told her, just take

284

deep breaths and push. It was a rough birth, but I was there to ease her

pain and sat beside her all night, then in the morning Mick was born.

He was a small baby and straight away put in an incubator and tested

for TB. The doctors had already said, that Nora, wasn't strong and the

disease could be progressive, she may not reach middle age. And my

heart went out to her, no matter what she had done.

'Poor Nora,' Eileen said, tears in her eyes, as she rocked baby Michael

in the pram, for he was now stirring and another feed, was soon due.

'So how was Mick, when he was born?' she asked.

'He thankfully was clear of TB,' Mae replied, and Eileen sighed with

relief. 'He soon put on weight, and Nora was a proud mother. I would

sometimes sit with her and help her feed him and we would talk about

Ireland and Tim, who came on leave to see the baby, looking very smart

in his uniform, all his war regalia with shiny brass buttons. He came to

register the birth of Mick. He was very proud himself to be a father and

kept saying he wanted to stay and look after them, but it was war time

and he had to go back, so I told him I would look after them. Nora was

a wonderful mother, and kept saying how much Mick was like his

Father, Tim. I could tell that Nora was adamant that Tim was the father and I never mentioned Daneen and any gossip that surrounded him and her. I was more interested in keeping my word to Tim, and helping Nora and Mick, for as soon as Tim went back from leave, there was an air-raid and blackouts. Many houses were bombed. The streets were in chaos, with piles of rubble, broken windows and closed up shops. At one time a group of badly wounded soldiers were bought in and Nora helped on the ward, giving out the soldiers woodbines to smoke, she would cheer them, with her sweet smile. When it was time for Nora and Mick to leave the hospital, I knew Tim was abroad, and Nora needed help, she was not very strong, so I told her I would look after her and found them somewhere close to live.

I remember taking them through the blackened streets and held a torch as we walked with the baby home. I remember the flying shrapnel, it looked just like red butterflies and many people rushed to the shelter at the underground tube station in Mile End Road. When there wasn't a blackout, the streets were alive with East-enders, and rowdy drunks hung outside the many corner pubs. The narrow back streets, were lined with houses, with broken windows patched up with wooden boards and on the main road a waste-land boundary, with lines of stalls.

The local traders mixed with the many Costas' in bright neck scarves and corduroy trousers, calling out their wares. I was able to get Nora a room in a house that was behind the hospital. It had dreary stone steps to the basement and more stone steps leading to the front door. The house was hemmed in by iron railings and there were constant comings and goings from nurses and medical students who also occupied the rooms. There were four stories in this house and a steep slate roof, under which there was a large attic and Nora and Mick occupied this. Although, the wallpaper was grimy, we soon got it brightened up with paint and coloured posters.I also occupied a room in this house and would call daily to see Nora and Mick - sitting him on my knee and he would give me that shy little smile.'

Eileen had no idea that there was this strong connection and wondered if Mick remembered his Aunt Mae.

'I was only an experienced midwife at the time,' continued Mae, 'and I loved children. I have never had any of my own,' said Mae a little sadly,' but I have great memories of the children I helped during the war years. Eileen noticed, she wiped a tear form her eye as she talked of Nora and the times they spent together. 'It's a shame, but Mick, he doesn't seem to remember me, so I've said nothing. He was very young. But I used to go and help Nora, and visit often. I also got the Red Cross to help her as I worked for them too. London was in a real state of war, sirens going off, and the hospital was packed out with the wounded, after an air raid. Us nurses worked long hours, but when I could, I would go over and help Nora clear up. She would often be sitting about in her dressing gown, the room was usually a mess, but she was an excellent mother. We would often take Mick to the sweet shop on a Friday. There were two shops, one at one end of the street and one at the other. He was only a toddler, but used to play up to go to 'Corams' the one at bottom of the road, but this day, I remember, as we went slowly along, he pulled at my arm and tried to get me to go in the other direction, because he didn't want to go to 'Corams' so we let him choose and off we went, me on one hand and Nora on the other and little Mick toddled between us. It was afternoon and just as we came out of the shop, once he had made his choice of sweets, we heard a big explosion and that's when I saw at the other end of the street, the corner shop was on fire. It had been hit by a bomb. Suddenly the sirens went off and I remember the whining sound of the doodle bug coming over. They were a big cigar like shape and would hang in the sky for about ten minutes before coming down and exploding. So we rushed along to the shelter at the underground station. It was packed out and the sound of bombs exploding all around. Mick was crying and we tried to put the gas mask on his face, but he was too nervous.

'Thank goodness you did not go to that other sweetshop!' said Eileen, her hand on her heart. 'I dread to think what would have happened.'

'It's a wonder,' Mae mused, 'that Mick doesn't remember that explosion. It was such a vast one.Then not long after that, we lost Tim. Although, I don`t think Mick remembers much about his father. He came on leave a few times to see him. Nora was very proud, for he was a pilot and flew one of the spitfire planes that would speed out to intercept the German bombers before they reached the East shore. And I remember Nora was always listening to the radio to see how many German bombers were brought down.

'Is that how he died?' Eileen asked.

'Yes. I remember calling around to the house one day and Nora opened the front door in tears. In her hands was a letter informing her of Tim`s death and how he died, explaining that his plane smashed head on into a German bomber and he was killed instantly. Nora was in pieces, sobbing and crying and dreading being alone, saying she won't be able to cope. She was never, very strong. She was nervous like Mick, but very loving and I wanted to help her. I stayed a while and she rested while I looked after Mick, and felt I needed to tell him about his brave daddy and how he had stopped that German bomber dropping a bomb on England. I don't know whether he even understood, but he went running around, with his toy plane, that Tim had bought him - flying it up and down.'

'Poor Mick,' said Eileen, 'he lost Tim who loved him and then he was to lose his mother.'

'And poor, Nora,' Mae said, 'cause, she relied on Tim a lot, he was a good man. Everyone liked him and his fellow pilots at the barracks, on flying over London one day payed their respects. We watched them from the window and Nora held Mick in her arms pointing up to the planes as they flew overhead: `your daddy`s friends` she told him as they dipped the wings, in remembrance of there friend. Nora was even more lost, without her strong man, and would say, Tim was a true O`Hara brave and bold and my Mick will one day take over from him.'

Eileen could feel the rain spitting down and the baby wanted a bottle.

'It's a wonder you have never told Mick any of this,' she quizzed Mae.

'I was waiting for him to say something, hoping he would have some recollection of me, especially as he used to climb up and sit on my knee, but he never has.

`mind you said Eilleen, my mick would probably have been full of questions, he is like that`

`I make you right there Eilleen` `its better coming from you`. Then with a look up to the dismal sky, Mae pulled up the hood on the pram `poor baby wants his feed`, you had better get back`

Walking back, Mae told her how she remained at the hospital through the war.

'London was not a good place to be and Nora and Mick were evacuated to Norwich, it was the best place for them, the war was getting worse.

'So did you not hear from them after that?' Eileen asked.

'I had a letter from Nora when she was settled in to Norwich with Mick and told me, she was working at the local hospital and they were staying on a farm. So I thought they seemed okay and I continued with my nursing at the London Hospital. Doctors and nurses were badly needed - even young people studying medicine were brought in to help. The bombings got worse and we thought England was losing the war. Many hospital beds were lined up in the corridors with wounded men, and people being brought in on stretchers all the time. Then there were the homeless, as homes were blown up and young families, left on the street. My life was full and I was much needed and we all went our separate ways.Poor Bridie had joined the women's army and Daneen was in India. "Bloody coward" Bridie would say, threatening when he returned, she would make his life a misery.So I supposed that's why Daneen stayed in India. He was gone a long time.'

'Well, that could well be true,' Eileen said, 'because only yesterday I found some oriental material in, Bridie's cottage, from India, postmarked during the war years, and when I asked Daneen about it, he told me, he sent it from the Maharaja's Palace, fancy that.'

'A Maharaja's palace,' Mae repeated in disbelief, 'sounds a bit far-fetched, but nothing would surprise me about that man. I remember when he came into the Kennedy Shop, shouting and carrying on, and they had to call the constable. Blind drunk he was, always causing trouble. And look how he has ended up, seeing life from the bottom of the bottle.'

'But surely,' said Eileen in a soft tone, defending Daneen, 'if you're referring to the affair, it seems more like Nora was the flirt and encouraged him.'

Mae scoffed, for she never liked to hear a word against Nora, she was no longer alive to defend herself.

`I`m just pleased, that Nora found some happiness in the end` she sighed. She died so young, while that scoundrel Daneen, got away with murder.'

'That's harsh,' said Eileen, 'it does take two.'

'But Mae screwed her face up. `He should keep it in his trousers, 'He`s always `hammered`, too fond of a drink`

But although Eileen was shocked to hear about the affair, he wasn't entirely to blame and somehow she felt sorry for him, for at times he seemed a broken man. 'Well . . . perhaps he has leant from his mistakes. We cannot judge a man forever.'

Mae shrugged. 'Maybe, but it's too late now and there's not many men I trust,' she went on, 'and in these affairs of the heart, I'm afraid, the women usually pay the consequences.'

And they both agreed with a far off expression.

'But I'll avoid him like the plague,' Mae said with a grim expression, 'that man did a lot of damage.'

'Oh dear,' Eileen muttered with a sideways glance at Mae, for she was sorry that she mentioned Daneen and thought she had better change the subject.

Stepping over a small stream with stepping stones, together they lifted the pram over, then, carried on down the hilly slope.

'I am just thinking of Mick as a baby in that hospital, said Eileen. 'Did you say he was an overdue baby?' And she started bringing up dates and months. Mae was wishing that she had never mentioned it; after all she was in the trusted position as her midwife and now Eileen was making something of it.

'I'm wondering,' Eileen pressed on with the subject, 'whether Nora got married to Tim in a hurry, cause, plenty of girls did during the war,' sympathetically, adding. 'Lots of girls have to.'

There was silence for a moment as Mae was weighing up what she was getting at.

'I was thinking,' continued Eileen, 'that Mick could have been conceived in the cow shed, when Nora was there with Daneen.' But Mae was looking straight in front of her, remarking how grey the clouds have become. 'Sometimes,' Eileen remarked, 'a girl, doesn't know who the real father is,' trying to dig at the truth. But Mae had gone very quiet until Eileen blurted out: 'Do you think that Daneen is Mick's true father?'

Mae, who rolled her eyes with an impatient expression, then suddenly stopped in her tracks, and said it was time she was going.

'For goodness sake,' Eileen said, with some impatience, her Celtic blue eyes smiling, 'am I not Mick's wife - one of the family? Is this all such a big secret?'

So Mae took her by the arm and said with a whimsical smile, 'There is an old saying,' she said. "It takes a wise child who knows his own father"- and just remember that Nora was my friend.'

'So, you mean,' she said, turning to Mae, 'that we may never know?' and Mae just nodded in agreement. 'Because, if Daneen, is his father,' Eileen said, anxiously, 'that means that Mick is not a true, O`Hara, after all.'

'Now stop your worrying child,' said Mae, 'an 'O'Hara or not, Mick has his birth certificate doesn't he, and no one can dispute that.' With that Eileen gave a weak smile, and they agreed, he may not be an 'O`Hara by blood, but he certainly was, on paper, and Aunt Bridie, knew that.

'The weather is changing,' said Mae, seeing the black and white storm clouds chase by like a herd of stallions to the fire. Then suddenly the rain poured and they were chasing back to the farm, pushing the pram as fast as they could, with the baby yelling for his feed.

MAE REMEMBERS

Ch.25

When Mae got home wet and tired, she sat with a hot cup of tea by the fireside, resting her back in the wicker chair. She was thinking of the baby and recalled . . . how Eileen spoke about Daneen being in India during the war and this oriental material that she had found. It was then, that it brought back to her, something that happened many years ago. . .

It had been that period just before the end of the war, when she had been working in the London Hospital. Nora had gone off to Norwich, and everyone said, it was best she get out of London, as the bombings were bad and it was then that the Americans came in to help as it looked as though we were losing the war.

Mae's mind drifted back to that time, there was so much going on in the hospital, many wounded packed out the wards. Civilians injured in the air raids and soldiers from the front. Mae was promoted to Staff Nurse and in charge of mens surgery, where there was an endless supply of young pilots coming in on stretchers, from the Red Cross ambulances, after their planes were shot down as they tried to protect London from the bombings of the Nazis. Many of the shelters were the only protection for the civilians, but Mae and the other nurses, were kept awake most nights, with caring for the wounded, who cried out in pain. But Nurse Mae Kennedy was much admired for her work and asked to take a team of nurses across the channel abroad ferry boats to bring back the wounded men, who came in on the shores of Dunkirk: there were thousands of them.

Any kind of boat was soon taken, until there was none and men were just left on the shore. Mae and her nurses took as many as they could on the ferry, wrapping them in blankets and fed them hot soup, but alas some were very badly wounded. Some, said, Mae were like Florence nightingale, together with her nurses, bringing so many wounded back from Dunkirk. At the hospital at the time, there was a shortage of doctors, and any young student doctors, were welcome to come to continue their training, as any help was good at such a demanding time. There were some from the Middle East who had been studying medicine at Cambridge and then came and joined the London hospital, studying under the surgeons. One of these young people was an Indian lad, he looked younger than the others, but he was tall and stately. He had been sent to train under a surgeon. He wore a white turban and the traditional 'Angarka` jacket. He had a kind of gentle, patient, bedside manner with the patients, often assisting the surgeon to perform operations. He was known to all and sundry at the hospital as Naj and often relied on Nurse Mae to help aid him with information on the patients.

'Where is Nurse Mae?' he would ask, coming into the ward, and she got to know his Indian accent and he would call her aside to get as much information about a patient due for surgery, as he could, especially, as many young servicemen were losing limbs and Naj would be very sympathetic, but he was very brave and worked hard. He lived in the doctor's quarters and you never saw him out and about, always with book studying. He was such a serious dedicated young man to helping the underdog and especially young children who were left without parents. He would spend hours at their bedsides and pull strings to find them a home to live in.

One day when he and Mae were working together, after an operation on a young lad of twelve or so, who had been in an explosion, stepping onto a mine in the street and the doctors were trying to save his leg, Naj said, to Mae: 'I was once a young lad who nearly lost my leg.'

'Really,' Mae said. 'Are you well now?'

'Oh yes,' said the young doctor, 'my father the Maharaja, got the best doctors for me, but you can see I still have a bit of a limp, but I'm used to it and I don't have pain in my leg anymore.' Many of the staff noticed his limp and could hear him coming down the ward as he dragged his leg slightly, but he would tell them, how he had once been a starving boy on the streets of Bengal and taken in by the Maharaja, who adopted him and was here to fulfil his wishes, to become a doctor and help the sick.

Each day, Naj came to visit the boy at the ward and sit with him by his bed. One day when Mae was washing the boy down Naj arrived.

'Oh don't let me disturb you,' he said, but Mae said he wasn't. He got to help her change the boy's pyjamas.

'That's real nice of you,' she said, and he smiled knowingly at her.

'Do you come from Ireland?' he asked. 'I can hear you have that accent.'

'I certainly do,' smiled Mae, 'and there's a big family of us Kennedys too.'

'You know,' he said,' I have heard that name.'

'Most people have, and we Kennedys are related to Brian Buru.' - one of the High kings of Ireland.

Naj smiled, he wasn't sure who Brian Buru was, but he was pretty sure that the name Kennedy had been talked about sometimes, by

Daneen at the palace.

'Tell me,' he said, 'where do you come from in Ireland?'

'It's Cork,' she said, 'I bet you never heard of that either?'

'Oh yes, I have,' he said. 'I once knew a man who came from there and his name was Daneen, do you know him?'

'Well, Cork's a big place,' she said, 'but I do know someone called Daneen, he used to work on a farm in Inshallalee, loves horses.'

And when she said that, Naj had the feeling that it was the same Daneen that he had been looking for, the Daneen that had saved his life.

'Well where is he now,' he asked, 'this Daneen who loved the horses?'

'They say he is out in India somewhere, no one seems to know much else.'

That fits Daneen I know,' Naj mumbled in broken English.

'But there are many people with this name,' said Mae, 'and a lot of Irishmen love horses.'

'Well if you do see this Daneen from Inshallalee when you return, Nurse Mae, tell him Naj was asking after him and to contact me at the palace in Cooch Bejar,' and with that Naj left.

At the time, Mae had been taken back, to think a Maharaja's son would want to know Daneen and was thinking, he has probably got the wrong Daneen, not imagining Daneen from the farm being pally-pally with a Maharaja's son, but now she was remembering what Eileen told her, about the material from the Indian palace, and it sounded like Daneen was acquainted with the Maharaja's Palace, after all. She had forgotten all about it, never giving it much importance and hurled herself up from the fireside chair, as her sister came to tell her, a woman was in labour.

'You better hurry,' nagged Babs Kennedy, as Mae stretched her tall figure, feeling tired, 'the baby is on its way!'

So dismissing thoughts of Daneen and the Maharaja, she hurried from the warmth of the fire and was soon peddling her bike to the village to deliver another baby.

NAJ AT THE PALACE

Ch.26

When the war came to an end, Naj left the London Hospital and
returned to the palace in Cooch Behar, to find his father was a sick man.
The war had aged the Maharaja and his health was failing. No longer
did he sit on the elephant's back in all his finery, to parade through the
crowded streets on religious ceremonies, when the crowds would cheer
their ruler. It was a long time since he had rode his favourite elephant,
who was now chained outside most of the time and would cry out for
the Maharaja, flinging her long trunk into the air, for the Maharaja had
spoilt `Synobad` the elephant, adorning her with a fine necklace of
pearls and precious stones that he placed around her neck, but now he
was a sick and spent most of his time seeing physicians and the
elephant cried for her master, for `Synobad` the elephant never forgot.

On good days, the Maharaja would lay on a hammock outside in the
sun, with the Indian girls fanning him, his once dark smiling eyes, were
sunken and his thick black hair had thinned. When Naj returned, the

sparkle came back to the Maharaja's eyes, and Naj took his father, out riding in the hills on his fine white horse,but eventually the Maharaja's health got worse and he would lay most days on his bed, under a fringed canopy. Nothing would inspire him to go anywhere and the doctors' said he would die. Naj knew how sick he was, he had seen a lot of death in the hospital during the war and felt he could not bear to lose the man, who was now his father. The Maharaja had told him, that he would be legally adopting him as his own son, and that he would be inherit thousands of acres of land belonging to the estate. This would make Naj feel so unworthy, as the Maharaja had done so much for him, even giving him a wonderful education and he knew he would never have survived if it wasn't for the Irishman, Daneen. He wondered if he would ever meet this man again.

He remembered how this man had bought him from the river barely alive and in and out of delirium, but he recalled that journey through the jungle on the back of Daneen's horse and taking him with him to the palace, and the Maharaja had got the best doctors to get him well. He had so much to be grateful for. As he sat by his father's bed, the servants fanned him and the doctor was in the room checking him and told Naj, his father, the Maharaja, would not last long as he had pneumonia.

That evening as he sat beside his father's bed, the Maharaja awoke and started to tell him of all what he wanted him to do. This was a big estate, and there was much responsibility. He told Naj he had named him as his heir and to take his place, ruling as the next Maharaja.

'You are a Hindu now,' he told him. 'You have been through the ceremony and no one can say you are not a true Hindu and therefore, you have every right to rule as the next prince of this dynasty. So take those reins of administration.'

Naj bent down beside the Marahaja's bed, with eyes filled with tears. 'Thank you my Father,' he said, 'I will do my best to rule.'

'My white Arabian horse is yours now,' said his father sadly. Naj knew that horse was the Maharaja's pride and joy and told him he would care for all his horses.

'Ride him well,' he said weakly, then opened a drawer beside his bed and in a small cupboard got out a medal. It was a George Medal and he told Naj that it was for the Irishman Daneen who had saved him. 'He brought you to me,' he said, 'and this medal is especially for brave deeds, like `rescuing a child. I was waiting for Daneen to return, to give him what he rightfully deserved. But he never returned.'

'I will find him, ' he told his father. 'I will give him this medal.' Also on the bedside cabinet was a photograph in a frame and his father pointed to it saying, 'This was Daneen, just after he brought you to me.' `I remember` said Naj, picking up the photograph looking deeply at the man in khaki dress and wearing a wide brimmed hat: beside him his horse. 'He looks like a Canadian Mounty,' Naj smiled

'No, Son,' the Maharaja corrected him, 'he is a Chindit, and that is the way they dress.

'A Chindit, what are they?' Naj enquired.

The Maharaja smiled. 'If you don't know what the Chindits did during the war . . . you are not the educated boy, I thought you were. For a start they were the 3rd Indian infantry division, but there is a lot more to them, for they were a special force, to penetrate deep into the Burma jungle and survived, just with air drops for supplies. Naj listened to all his father said, and then thought for a moment as he stared at the picture and looking closer could see a badge on the uniform. It was an unusual looking badge, and it looked like it was a Medievel lion.

'I know what that is,' Naj said, to his father, 'it's a Chinte. It is a mythical creature, half lion and half griffin, they are statues that stand outside the temples to protect and guard.'

'There,' the Maharaja smiled and closed his eyes in satisfaction. 'You are my educated, clever boy, after all.'

'So this badge, is the Chinte's emblem, I presume?'

'That's right, Son, they are just like lions themselves, warriors in every sense of the word.And Daneen was a Chindit – the man that rescued you and did not care about the danger to himself.'

Naj looked down, as if in respect. 'One day I will find this man` Papa. And I will give him the medal. I think I would like to take him to the war graves in France. It's a place we should all go, who are able – to pay our respects to the men that died for us. His father only nodded, knowing he had brought up a fine son, one with many morals. He knew he would always do what was right.

'But, Son,' the Maharaja said, 'I hear the Chindits had a bad time on the last mission, the Japanese imprisoned many.'

'I will find him,' whispered Naj, 'I promise,' and with that, his father closed his eyes, as if at peace and smiled and his big hand took hold of his son's hand.

That night Naj did not leave his father, and the night was long, as he mopped the Maharaja's brow, but his mind was going back to that time as a boy when his father took him in. He had a recollection of Daneen holding him in his arms, he remembered how he was wounded and the Maharaja's dark face looked down at him and called for his servants to get the doctor. It was every day after that, the Maharaja cared for him and treated him like a son. He was recalling too, those times when Daneen came and stayed at the palace and taught him to ride, and he knew he was the man that rescued him that day on the river bank. The sound of the mortar fire rang in his ears, he had been fishing by the river trying to get a salmon to eat and the Jap's spotted him and brutally attacked him from behind, then through him into the river, firing their mortar, but he had gone under the water as soon as they fired, and the water had helped protect him from the explosion, even though he went unconscious, but when his body floated to the top, the Jap's had gone, so he crawled to the bank. That was when he heard the distant sound of a horse in the water and then the Irish voice of Daneen as he stood over him. `frigging japs` said Daneen, as he heard them firing in the distance, but seemed unconcerned, they may still be around: just washed his wounds with the water from the river and wrapped his leg in bandages. The pain, Naj would never forget, and remembered going from sleep to awake as Daneen rode him through the forest land, to Cooch Behar.

He knew he had been lucky, there were many starving young men, some wounded and lucky to be alive, just like him, and as he looked at his father lying there, he knew he had been so fortunate to sail to such a safe harbour and if it hadn't been for this man Daneen he would probably have died on the river bank.

He sat with his head in his hands, remembering the Irish voice of Daneen, this tall man with a thin face, who bathed his wounds and whispered, "It's alright boy, I'll take you with me", after that he remembers being well looked after at the palace and grew safe and strong, he would ask about this Irish man, and was told he will return. Then there were the happy times in the stables spent with Daneen, as they rode the horses together out towards the mountains and before long he was riding like a true horse man. He recalled too how his limp would hold him up, but Daneen never mentioned it, never treated him as an invalid, always saying "You're a special boy, the way you survived". Such happy times with his father and Daneen out riding together, although Daneen always carried his revolver, ready to shoot any predators:

`Its the Chindits training` Daneen would say, must be prepared. Thats when he explained he would be leaving, `I will be going back to the chindits, he said and this mission may be a lot worse than the last`, `but I will be back` he added.

The Maharaja was fully aware that Daneen would soon be recalled, and knew how dangerous this next mission would be. `Its named Operation Thursday` the Mahaja said, and as you know, its a mission to blow up a railway further into the enemy lines. `I am afraid for you`.

"But I cannot hold you anymore, as my personal horseman" my dear friend "It is time to go back". And Daneen, knew he must - it was his duty. He hated to leave the Maharaja the palace and the boy, for they had a real bond together. The day he left the boy`s dark eyes were misty with tears and Daneen said, "I cannot remain at the palace forever, it is time for me to go back to my battalion, because I am a

Chindit and I am ordered to fight another mission". The Maharaja could

see how unhappy this made Naj and said to Daneen,

"Perhaps I could say . . . that you are needed here", "as we do not

want you to leave".

But Daneen only said: "It was not easy the last time, but I'm fit

enough to go back and I'll not let the side down". When he mounted his

horse he turned to say goodbye to his two companions, who stood with

sad expressions: `May the road, rise to meet you` said Daneen, with a

wave of his hand, `and they started to smile. `Its his irish tongue again`

said the Maharaja with a broad smile.

And Naj was calling `and may the sun shine warm upon your face`.

`I see he has been teaching you this strange irish language, said the

maharaja as they both stood waving him off, there laughter carried in

the air.

Once Daneen left the palace and was back in the Burmese Jungle the

Maharaja anxiously, listened to the radio for news of the Chindits, as

Operation Thursday was a dangerous mission. He knew it would nto be

easy to blow up the bridge and the railway that ran from Mandalay to

Mitchinawya. Eventually news came that the Chindits had cut the lines, but the Jap's were pursuing them through the jungle and prevented them from getting back across the Irrawaddy: the river, that was eleven miles wide, with a strong current.

'Will he be coming back?' Naj had asked his father as they tried to get radio contact.

'The Jap's have no doubt destroyed the radio contact,' the Maharaja told the boy, and didn't hear anymore for a long while, until it was reported back that the Jap's had got most of them and they had suffered.

It was months later when the survivors returned to India - the lucky ones, but that most of the men were ill and the group had got broken up, so only knew of those who returned.

Naj and the Maharaja wondered if Daneen had survived. When they heard how the men had fought off the Jap's in the jungle and that they had starved and were sick with dysentery and malaria: Daneen's survival seemed slim.

'I will never forget Daneen, the boy had cried to his father, as they longed for news of him.

Then it came in a letter.

Daneen told how he had escaped, leaving the rest of the Chindits as many of the men were going there own way, so he went off alone with his horse to take his chance. . . *I was come across by a local tribesman* [he had wrote] *who fed me as I was starving. . .*

Naj had listened intently to the letter as his father read it out with compassion.

'It is all right, Son,' he said. 'Daneen eventually reached Fort Hertz. That's a remote British military outpost in Northern Burma and they flew him home.'

Naj had jumped for joy that Daneen had made it.

'It is a wonder,' the Maharaja said, 'that he made it through, but he says how upset he is, that his horse starved and died'. Naj knew how he loved that horse and he bent his head in despair:

'But the main thing is,' the Maharaja continued, putting his big arm around the boy, 'Daneen is safe and I hope I see him before I leave this world'.

'Oh father, why do you say that? Your illness could improve.'

'I doubt it, very much, Son. But at least now, the war has ended and we will have peace. It would be so good if Daneen comes to see us. He says that he is suffering with a lot of stress since the mission and I can understand that.'

'But where is he now?' asked Naj. 'I want him to come back'. . .

Naj waited and waited. He would listen to the speeches of Ghandi the Prime Minister, talking to the Indian nation, telling them how the Chindits had succeeded in their mission, and now there was a new road, called the `Stillwell Road' that led from India to China: built by an American Captain Stillwell. And hearing how, the Chindits missions, had made this all possible, and they had returned exhausted from the jungle; although, hundreds of them, had been caught by the Jap's and sent to Rangoon Prison.

'Daneen escaped but why doesn't he come home?' Naj said.

His father's sick face looked at his son. He did not want to hurt him. `He knew how much he loved Daneen. 'War does things to men, the old Maharaja,' said, 'takes them in different direction. Perhaps one day, he will just come walking back through the door.'

'I hope so,' said Naj.

'Just remember, he is a brave man,' the father said. 'Those Japanese, shot and wounded many men and Naj could not help wondering if the Japs had got Daneen. He would always remember those happy out riding with Daneen and then coming into that cosy kitchen and Nighats arms out to greet him. She was someone else, he had lost and would dream of seeing again.

The night his father, the Maharaja passed away, Naj was far away in his thoughts of Nighat, visualising her sweet smile before him, that he did not hear his father's breath change and when he looked in to his face, he knew his father was dying.

After he passed away there was a large funeral service, people lined up outside the palace in tears and walked in processions through the streets. There were many letters of condolences from officials from all over the world, including Queen Elizabeth the British Queen and visits from other Maharaja's who were related to his father.

When the Will was read, Naj was told, he had been officially named, as heir to the estate, where he would inherit the Maharaja's great wealth and lands. But Naj had had no doubts, that this would come to pass, for the Maharaja had told him, that he was his true adopted son, but nothing would replace this wonderful father he had come to love and it took Naj a long time to recover from his father's death. He grieved heavily.

He would spend much time at the temple, remembering when they knelt there together and what his father had taught him, he had also come to love his Hindu religion: it seemed all he had to turn to now, that his father had gone.

But the day came when he got stronger again, just like he had as a boy at the palace when he first came there, and he knew he had to do what his father had wished. And so Naj claimed his right as Maharaja Najanda the Third and the great ceremony went on for weeks. There were parties in the streets and festivals and Naj was taken through the streets on the back of his father's favourite elephant 'Synabad' and he personally put the jewelled necklace around her neck and sat high on a plinth on her back, wearing sparkling robes of shining pink and his father's favourite turban encrusted with diamonds and emeralds and the people cried out: 'Our, Great Prince of Bengal!'. But since the end of the war, the status of the Maharaja`s of India was now changing and Naj knew there was much work to do, as dynasties were being threatened and titles taken away. It was now Naj's place as the next Maharaja and it was a different world, for the great Maharajas of India.

The state, headed by Ghandi was to seize the riches of the Maharajas and he was defying the British and against the British rule of India, for he was seeking the freedom of India and had the backing of Mountbatten and there became lengthy disputes between the State and the Maharajas' status. Some of them were having their lands seized by the government, and although, Naj was not one to worry about riches, he was glad of the protection of the status he now held, for since coming to live at the palace as a boy, he had been brought up, to go regularly to the Hindu temple with his father and leant his ways of respect of the past and pray.

Before his father died he had told him to rule as he did, with goodness and humanity. He had talked to him of taking a wife, saying how he could have five if he wishes. `I do not want you to rule alone` his father had said, `you will need someone beside you`. But so far this was a wish of his fathers, that he had not yet fulfilled, there always seemed so much to do, in these changing times for the dynasties and there was much unrest between the Hindus and the Muslims. People were being massacred and the president Ghandi had gone to prison. Since independence, there was fighting over territories. Muslims banded and fought back the Indian soldier, and many were killed on the streets. Naj hated war and killing and had it in his heart to be a surgeon. He had never forgotten what he saw and learnt under the surgeons at the London Hospital and it was his wish to help the sick. So he moved some of the statues in the Great Hall and opened it up as a training centre for medical students and medical research and progressed with his degree to become a doctor, as his father had wished.

There was a lot of responsibility now for the young Maharaja all around, there was much talk of the political climate beginning to change, if India was given independence and divided into two sets of territories, and he wondered to himself, if he would be the `last Maharaja' to rule.

The years had passed and Naj had taken his rightful place, sitting on his father's throne,

but he knew there was something he had to do and that was to return to his childhood home in Calcutta and try to find out what had happened to his family. He also thought, it was about time he looked around for a wife, like his father had wanted, but there was yet a more important promise he had to fulfill and that was to find Daneen. This Irishman he had never forgotten, who had rescued him and give him the medal just as his father had wished. But he wondered if he was still alive, as he never came back to the Palace like he promised. He hoped he was still alive, as it was well known, that many of the chindits had been imprisoned in Rangoon, that many had died. But he would try to find him and perhaps Calcutta would be a place to start, after all, that was where Daneen, had been stationed and it was also the home town of Nighat, that beautiful young girl he had fallen so in love with - It would be a dream come true to see her again.

DANEEN THE DOWN AND OUT

Ch.27

Although Daneen had got back from the Chindits' mission, having escaped from the jungle, he was not the same man after the war and certainly not the one Naj had known, for he had been through the traumas of war, seeing so many of his friends being captured by the Jap's and tortured, and even died in that terrible prison - Rangoon, at least he had survived that, but those months trapped in the jungle, dodging the Jap's, the starvation and disease had taken their toll. The army doctor had diagnosed `combat stress` for he was troubled by nightmares, that not only occurred at night. He would suddenly get the shakes, and it would all come back.

Daneen was a very troubled man and not sure where to go, when he was discharged from the army. He thought of going back to the palace, that wonderful place of safety, but he heard it on the radio that the Maharaja had passed away. He seemed his only friend and alli. He was even more distraught. He knew it would not be the same at the palace anymore, that free and easy place, especially the kitchen where that lovely girl Nighat worked, and she had said she was going back to Calcutta to look after her father, so she would no longer be there and the boy – well perhaps he had been sent off to school in England, that's where the Maharaja had said he should go . . . to Eton just like he did. So Daneen wasn't going back to the palace and he certainly wasn't going back to Ireland and feeling distraught he decided to remain in Calcutta.

When he was discharged from the army, he wandered the streets, wondering what to do, where to go, and often a state of confusion came over him and he would hear the sounds of the jungle, they would start with the crys of the birds, the screech of the monkey, then they would mingle, the sounds of guns and the crys of the men, sometimes calling his name and he would hold his hands over his ears, trying to block out these sounds, as they got louder and louder and seemed to all join together banging in his head, until he could think no more. Like a frightened child he would run into a doorway and sink to the ground, shaking from head to toe until it subsided. Then feeling drained and weak he would ask himself, `where was he was going, where was he. It was like he had been in another world. These bouts happened daily and he never knew when they would come on him. The army doctor had given him pills, but it was a drink of alcohol that would help him more and he got to sitting in doorways with a bottle, getting so drunk that he would not feel these traumas that took over his whole being.

Eventually, when the army station became empty of servicemen, he had to leave and had nowhere to live, he was not capable to work and constantly seen sitting on the streets smoking dope, that he acquired from the rest of the homeless of Calcutta. Eventually, he joined all the other down and outs, who lived under the arched bridge by the river, waking most mornings feeling dehydrated; his tongue like the texture of sandpaper. He would rub his heavily veined hands together, trying to get the circulation back in them, then looking for his bottle at his feet, finding it empty, would then hobble down the road to where there was a collection of small shops and try and nick a bottle off the shelves.

Cider laced with whiskey was his favourite drink and one particular afternoon, he successfully, got away with two bottles grabbing them from the shelf and hiding them under his dirty white kurta and loped away. Smiling to himself, that no one had caught him, he could hardly believe his luck, as he usually got a boot up his back or a bucket of water thrown over him as he tried to leave the shop with a bottle. But today no one had noticed, they were all too busy gossiping about a down and out who was thrown himself in the river.

It was a desperate way of life, he knew that, so many men who had fought in the Burmese jungle, were never the same again. He tried not to think about this soldier who had died, he was so much younger, but had been tortured by the Japs. Daneen shuddered, he could feel the old shakes coming on, the haunting sounds of the jungle, he just wanted to get back, to sit under the arches and drink his bounty, it was what he needed, the only thing that cheered him up. Some of the time he slept in the park and doorways, even though the police moved him on, calling him a bum. He still had feelings about his situation, he knew his life had reached its lowest ebb, but felt he had to keep going.

There in the back of his mind were the Emerald green fields of Ireland, that swept down to the sea and the soft brogue of the people rang in his ears. He hated the gabble of the Hindustani language, but he knew he could not go back, not yet - not in this state, and there no way out. But at least he had his drink for the day, as he hobbled back to the river to hide himself under the bridge, with his bounty.

After drinking himself to oblivion, he would often scream out at night as memories of the last Chindits' mission - Operation Thursday came into his sleepy brain. One particular memory would haunt him, when he found himself sinking in the mud, with snakes crawling over him and would wake yelling out. 'Get them off!'

'Cut it out!' the other down and outs would shout back, some old soldiers, who had also suffered mentally from the outcome of war, some dressing like the local Indians, in baggy trousers and turbans. Some were United State's soldiers, but their accents and white skin, would give them away, as they raved in drunken binges. They had all stayed in the mission some nights, but they were all drinkers and smokers of dope, all sorts of drugs, whatever they could get their hands on. People would pass them and sigh.

'What a state', others would say.

It was one day when a girl passed and he looked up, his eyes red and his face pale and with his grimy hand wiped the sweat from his brow.

'My goodness,' she suddenly said, and straight away he knew the voice, for it was Nighat the Indian girl from the palace who would often say in loud, English words: 'My goodness'.

'Is it really you?' she said, kneeling down to talk to him, as he sat his back against the bridge wall and looked miles away as he smoked a pipe, the smell of hashish rising in the air and she knew he had become a drug addict. It took some convincing but he took her arm and she took him back to her humble house in Calcutta that at least got him off the streets.

'Father', she said as she entered the house with Daneen, 'this man needs help. He is a fine soldier and worked in the palace with me.'

The girl's father was bent over and walked with a stick, but he had been a fine Maharisha; a man with healing powers. He believed that yoga and meditation would help to heal Daneen. The house was a crumbling white stone house in the hills and a bed was made up for him in a glass lean too, where he could look out at the garden and many plants grew and brought back memories of the farmland in Ireland with its many crops.

As time passed, Daneen took over the task of growing vegetables and herbs and fixed the house and Nighat always kept a cooking pot on the stove. She made the place a happy home, with her sweet ways and she was lithe and full of spirit, now a young woman and not yet married, but somehow with looking after her father and helping him in his teachings, she had met no one of real interest to marry. Sometimes she would dream of Naj, the boy at the palace, even though it was so long ago. but in her heart she had never forgotten him and wondered if she would ever find a love like his again. She now had another to look after, as well as her father, there always seemed someone learning on her and at least Daneen was improving, since he had come to live at the house..

Less and less Daneen needed the weed to smoke, but he was a damaged man and even Nighat found him hard to cope with. He was often bad tempered and unhappy, although she did her best to lift his spirits and even got him a donkey, as he kept yearning for a horse. Nighat was able to do a deal with a farmer and a white donkey arrived. It was not at all like the stallion he had once owned, but he would pretend it was, and with glazed eyes, ride the donkey around the yard, then eventually, taking it onto the streets. Then often going off on the booze and would be seen on his donkey shouting and yelling about the Jap's and Nighat would have to find him and bring him home.

As time passed, her father became more bedridden and Nighat had to spend more time caring for him and although a kind old gent, and a quiet serenity about him, he was getting tired of Daneen's drinking and shouting sessions.

'It is about time,' he told his daughter this man went back to Ireland. You have helped him enough'. For not only did they take him in, they had worked to get him off the dope, that he had been so addicted to.

Her and the father, had often taken Daneen down to the Ganghi, and washed his body in the healing waters and prayed. 'He is better than he was,' the father said firmly, 'he no longer goes down to the river to smoke the dope with the down and outs.'

'No, but he goes on terrible drinking binges. He says he cannot sleep without it.'

'Well, that even - you might never be able to change, Nighat,' said the wise old man.

Nighat often used to talk about her time at the palace. Daneen would listen to her rambling on about the young man. 'I remember how you brought him to the palace and we became great friends.'

Daneen too, would often think of him and remembered how the boy and Nighat used to flirt together, chasing around the gardens, being much the same age: a relationship that developed into teenage love.

Nighat had come to work at the palace as a young serving girl when she was twelve. And although she had to leave when her father got ill and return to Calcutta to look after him, as she was needed at home, she was very sad to leave the palace and especially to leave Naj, but when she was settled at home, her father had told her, that she should forget the boy in the palace, because he was a Muslim. There had been bad feeling between her and her father for a while, as she found it very hard to forget Naj and had even told her father that he was taking up the Hindu religion, but her father was not interested. He was not a Hindu from birth. So she asked Daneen one day, about Naj, who said he had remembered the Maharaja sending the boy to Eton in England.

'It is so sad the Maharaja passed away', she said, 'Naj must be very lonely without him', and her big green eyes filled with tears. 'Perhaps he will visit Calcutta one day, for he also came from this town'.

'Perhaps,' agreed Daneen, who hoped not, as he would not want the boy seeing him in this state, he felt little more than a wreck of a person.

But Nighat kept a little lamp shining for him in her heart, she would think of him every day but she knew she must follow her father's wishes. One day her father told her, she should take a husband `We need a strong man to help he said, I am not so young anymore Nighat`. Then asked her if she was pure.

'Of course,' she answered with a huff, 'no man has touched me'.

'What about that Muslim boy?' he asked.

'No, father,' she said, with some impatience, 'we were just children.

'And what about Daneen?' he asked with a quizzical glare.

This shocked her more. 'No. Of course not! Goodness father, he is too old .' How could her father ask her such a thing or even think this of her?

'That means nothing in India,' he said, 'old men and young girls get married.'

'Well, I don't want to marry any old man', she said with some defiance and Daneen, is only a friend.'

'That is good', muttered her father.

'And I love him as my friend – like he is brother.'

'You love everyone my child', her father grinned; pleased his daughter was untouched. It was now confirmed, she was a virgin. She had looked him in the eye and not hesitated in answering. He had every faith in Nighat that she had told him the truth.

'So Daneen was just your lame duck,' chuckled the father, in more humorous spirit. 'As a girl you were always bringing home a lame duck. But now,' he said, 'I have to look to finding you a husband, and I will betroth you to a good young man.'

She banged down the pots as she cooked, for Nighat wanted to choose her own husband and all she ever dreamed of was to be with,

Naj. Sometimes she had to remind herself, that he was a station above

her, living at the palace, for Daneen had told her, the Maharaja had

treated him like his own son, but she remembered when he was an

injured young boy from Calcutta. She even knew the street he came

from. It was a poor district, and now it was little more than a slum since

the Jap's had blown up half of it with their bombs.

Ch.28

NAJ GOES TO CALCUTTA

. The years had passed and Naj had taken his rightful place, sitting on his
father's throne,

but he knew there was something he had to do and that was to return

to his childhood home in Calcutta and try to find out what had

happened to his family. He also thought, it was about time he looked

around for a wife, like his father had wanted, but firstly, there was a more important promise he had to fulfill and that was to find Daneen. This Irishman he had never forgotten, who had rescued him and give him the medal just as his father had wished. But he wondered if he was still alive, as he never came back to the Palace like he promised. He hoped he was still alive, as it was well known, that many of the chindits had been imprisoned in Rangoon, that many had died. But he would try to find him and perhaps Calcutta would be a place to start, after all, that was where Daneen, had been stationed and it was also the home town of Nighat, that beautiful young girl he had fallen so in love with - It would be a dream come true to see her again.

He often felt lonely, with a whole world of responsibilities upon his head and shoulders and found himself thinking of his real family. He did not forget or shrug off that he came from Calcutta, it was all in his past that he felt shadowed by and needed to look into. but he still felt a humble boy, one whose name was Patel, the same as his fathers, the late Maharaja. He knew it would not be difficult to find them he thought.

So he went to Calcutta, dressed in Western clothes. He still walked with a limp and did want to look too elaborate, wearing the long white button through shirt, and a white cap and left his black silky hair hanging loose under it: hiding every aspect of being a prince, as he wanted to walk the streets to find the street where he used to live. He had a recollection of it, but heard the area had been bombed. It was by the square in Calcutta. He remembered how he used to sit on the wall close to the market as a boy and get a bit of pocket money by helping the stallholders pack up their wares, he must have been about 11 then, for soon after that, the war came and everybody seemed starving, there was no food to sell and Calcutta was filled with army personal and men trying to keep the peace.

As he got off the train at Calcutta, he could smell the air, with that same spicy aroma. He was used to the fresh air of Cooch Behar now. There were young boys in the square playing football and he remembers doing the same and he remembered all the colours of the market place, the bright vegetables on the stalls and the yards of materials of vivid fabrics hanging up to sell and the noise of the hawkers, the rattle of the ox cart. But now it looked a shadow of itself, a dowdy place, void of the bright colours. A cart with livestock and chickens jumping out came rushing down the street pushed by young men wearing kurtas, and wielding sticks.

It seemed the market place was not so safe anymore and the bombings of the war had caused much destruction to some of the houses and rubble still remained in piles around the town, although their was re-buildings of a new cinema and town hall.

The centre of Calcutta, with its many buildings was a hive of activity with the people trying to get on the tram running up the tramline that run along the town and big wagons rolled down the road clearing debris.

He walked about, trying to find the street where he used to live, for the war had changed much of the appearance of places. He was looking for the corner shop that stood at the entrance of his street, remembering how he used to always be running back and forth with errands for his mother, but he could not find that corner shop, with its many stalls outside, for it was no longer there: a bomb had blasted it away. Eventually, he found the street he used to live, there were apartment blocks either side and each apartment was tall, thin and crammed against the next. On the small balcony's, lines of washing hung down and Naj watched a hawker who stood, calling his wares, that he carried in a basket, then suddenly a woman would call from the balcony above and let down a long string and he would send the basket up containing food. The hawker made his way along the apartments, his customers calling and waving down to him.

He wandered along the narrow street, looking up for something familiar or someone he knew. Either side were two storey apartments; some still had their windows boarded up, protecting them from broken glass and some flats were half blown away with piles of debris lying at the entrance. When he came to the end of the road, he looked for the apartment where he used to live, remembering it was the last apartment block in that particular street, but even though he walked up and down again, just to make sure he had got his bearings right, the fact was that the building was no longer there. He found out from the hawker as he stood nearby selling his wares, that the apartment had been destroyed by the bombing, it no longer existed.

The hawker was an elderly man and he looked sympathetically at Naj. 'Was there someone in particular you were looking for?' he asked. 'I've known a lot of people in this area', he said, 'been selling here since I was a boy, even before the Great War.'

Naj felt suddenly anxious for in his heart he felt that his family had gone up with the bomb and to hear of them suffering would have been too much. 'My family,' he muttered quietly.

The hawker gave a sympathetic smile. 'Sometimes it is better not to know, but I tell you boy, that when that building went up, it burned for days and I don't think there were any survivors. The Jap's dropped one of their massive explosives, right on the top of it.'

Naj gulped, and bent his head as if in prayer.

The man placed a consoling hand on Naj's shoulder.

'You are right,' Naj said, 'I can only presume my mother and father are no longer alive.'

'What was there name?' the man asked, reaching for the basket that was coming back down from the apartment window above.

'It was Patel,' Naj whispered.

Straight away the hawker said, 'Not Mrs Patel with the white hair and always buying nectar for her bees?' And Naj knew that was his mother for on the veranda at the back of the flat, there was a beehive, and mother loved to cultivate them and the family always had fresh honey. He was speechless for a moment, thinking of his mother and he had to choke back the tears and nodded.

'She was a good woman,' said the hawker in an understanding manner and gave Naj a pat on the back. 'Visit the Ganges, boy,' he said, 'it will cleanse your spirit. You can pray for your family. I remember your mother, always smiling, but not very strong.'

Soon the hawker was on his way with a cheery grin and picking up the money from the basket as it came back down on the string.

So that was it thought, Naj, letting the tears flow as he walked further along the street and felt sad thinking of those memories of his childhood, and his mother and father, and each step was like a milestone, reminding him of so many more. Suddenly he was at a crossroads, and a bike went by, ringing its bell and scooted around him. He had to pull himself together.

All he wanted was a place to put his head down, he was thinking of going to the temple to pray, for he needed some comfort, some solace, just needed some peace from this noisy street, his head was in a maze. For he had seen and heard enough, so decided he would find himself a hotel, it was now getting late and he wanted to get himself settled for the night, and decided in the morning he would find the temple.

At the crossroads, he thought of which way to go, it all looked familiar, with the rickshaws crossing the streets and people shouting, aware he was in the midst of traffic: the sound of car horns hooting, carts crossing his path, and men rushed erratically around with barrows, some with farm animals on the back trying to sell their wares. Walking close to the river, he saw there were men sitting under the bridge, smoking peace pipes, some staring into space and looking as though they were on drugs. Some were European, although some wore the traditional Indian Kutars and turbans, although recognisable by their white skirts. Others were soldiers, wearing their old khaki uniforms, and a passerby referred to them as 'Old Soldiers' damaged. 'Jap's got hold of them.'

So this was Calcutta now, he thought, a place filled with the debris of war, the grimy streets, homeless people. He was glad he was not staying and pushed through the crowd to get back to the station, but the crowds were thick, as there was a man on a donkey causing a riot. He was going round and round the square on the donkey, which he whacked with a stick and shouting in English about the Jap's.

'He crazy,' an old Chinese lady said, telling Naj how she was a refugee from Burma. 'We walk many miles to come to this place . . .' Going on about her long journey of survival to reach India, but Naj was staring at the scene before him. He could see this man on the donkey was a European and he asked the woman why he had not gone back to his own country.

'Lots of them here,' she said, 'they gone crazy, some blame it on the Jap's.'

He watched the man, who was reminiscent of a cowboy with his wild horse, the crowd were laughing at the display as the donkey was kicking out his back legs and the man was yelling, and it didn't sound like English, but an Irish accent, that Naj recognised - had heard before. He stared in disbelief as the man shouted and waved a gun. It was a sad crazy sight, and it was then as the man on the donkey turned his way, and looked straight at him, he thought for a moment the face reminded him of Daneen, that man who had saved his life. But how could that be he? He was asking himself. Daneen was such a proud character, and just as he was about to take a closer look and limped across the square to investigate, the man took off at a speed on the donkey giving it a hard whack and they went much too quick for him to follow.

'Where does he live?' he asked the old woman, who had walked beside him. She only shrugged. Naj wondered, if he would ever know if that was Daneen or just someone who resembled him? This man he had just seen, was unshaven-had a beard and his hair was longer and dishevelled. His face looked gaunt and he was thinner.

It troubled Naj, as not only had he lost his real family, who had it seems, disappeared after a bombing, he kept wondering if that poor mad man could have been Daneen, for if it was, he should have helped him, just like Daneen had helped him as a child. For this man whoever he was - was a sick human being, damaged by war it seems. He kept thinking of his parents and now there was this vision of Daneen's face before him, and he kept wondering if that poor man could have been him. 'You have got to pull yourself together', he told himself, deciding what he needed, was a rest.

He felt he wanted to go to the temple, to pray, to find some solace, so for the time being, he would just find himself a hotel, somewhere quiet to get off these noisy streets. He just wanted to get a bed for the night; his head was in a maze. He had seen and heard enough of Calcutta, but he remembered the temple was by the square and he would try and find a hotel near that.

In the square the lights came on and there was a hotel just opposite the temple. The entrance was lit with floodlights and a limousine was parked outside, he had to get off these streets, and the place looked ideal. He knew it would be a long night, filled with visions his lost family. He had always hoped they had survived the war and wondered over and over what had happened that night of the bombings, and went to sleep visualising what could have been, tossing and turning and hearing his mothers gay voice and remembering standing on the veranda and the buzz of the bees. It had all gone, he told himself as he closed his eyes and cried. He was woken early by a young boy wearing a kutar and bare foot, carrying a tray of tea, and a vase of flowers upon it and he thought he would take the flowers to the temple as an offering.

'Thanking you,' he told the boy who bowed and held out his hand and Naj put a coin there. He did not eat but put the naan bread, meat and herbs that were on the tray into a bag - for these he would take to the temple as an offering, too.

Leaving his sandals outside the temple, he entered the coolness of the white building: the tall statue of Vishnu the supreme Hindu God was before him. Soon, he was following a queue of people as they went towards different statues to kneel in worship to. He soon found a place to pray; his head in his hands and knelt down on the prayer mat.

Naj repeated prayers to his favourite Gods, chanting many mantras. He made an offering of flowers to his favourite God, Krishna. When he came to the priest, he poured water over his hands. Afterwards he sat quietly in the temple, thinking of his parents. His eyes were closed, but when he opened them he saw in a queue of people who stood by a statue of an idol that there was something familiar about a young girl, who wore a shawl over her head. Perhaps it was the upright way she stood, or even the way she held her hands in pray, they were small and gentle and for a moment, he was thinking they were just like Nighats hands and tugs of excitement pulled inside of him as he wondered if it was her. For a while he watched spellbound, not taking his eyes of this young woman, who stood so demurely and he noticed how she wore her hair, he could just see the long black plat that hung down her side, almost to her waist and he was waiting for her to turn, so he could see her face, for if it was Nighat, how blessed he would be, to find her again and prayed to his God that it was.

Then suddenly she turned to go towards the priest, receiving a blessing, Naj saw her face and knew immediately it was her. Her cheeks were a little fuller, but as she looked up at the Priest he could just see those eyes held in that same strange reverence. She hadn't changed a bit, it was Nighat, the girl from the palace, although a little older, a mature women, but still her skin as fresh as a daisy. He remembered how he would sit and watch her make cakes and they would go riding on the ponies together, and lay in the long grass sharing their thoughts and dreams. What comfort she gave him, when he was so ill and he had grown to love her. When she left the palace, he had been heartbroken and soon after sent to England to Eton. For a moment he was thinking what a coincidence, that she should be here, but perhaps he had all the time been hoping to see her, for he knew this town was where she lived. He sat back and watched her, although now, a young lady, she was still small, but so pretty and lithe and he knew the flickering of love was already in his heart. He decided he would go outside and wait for her to come out, smiling for the first time, for he was thinking of what she would say, when she saw him.

He sat on the wall, feeling better after his blessing from the priest: his faith always restored him. He decided that on the way back to Cooch Behar, he would go to the Ghanges and make an offering and pray again for his parents. He was also sure, that as the adopted son of the Maharaja, he wanted to always be loyal to his memory, to do his duty, serving as the next monarch.

He felt now he could go on, go forward in life, he had laid his ghost to rest except for Daneen and he was a man he had to find - he had told his father he would. But where he did not know, then the vision of that man on the donkey came before him and he kept telling himself, that it was not him, but could not be sure. He was just sitting wondering this, when Nighat stepped out of the temple into the morning sunlight, her long pink sari glowed in the sun and she flicked the long scarf across her shoulder.

She was just about to walk past him, when he stepped forward and smiled, greeting her.

'Hallo Nighat. I thought it was you.'

'Oh!' she said suddenly, with the shock of surprise, and stared at him for a few seconds, before her face broke out into a smile. It was a wide infectious smile, that always made his heart leap,

'Oh it is you,' she said, 'it really is. And a Hindu, at last, I am so pleased, But Naj, what are you doing here in Calcutta?'

'It is a long story,' he said taking her arm, 'let us go somewhere for a cup of our favourite tea.' Then looking around the square, could see nowhere, but his hotel in front of him, so Nighat followed him there, where they sat in the cool lounge surrounded by palms and silver tea trays.

'This is lovely, this place,' she said, looking around at the splendour of the brocade drapes and tall rubber plants, and twisted the ends of her long black plat in a nervous manner, as she could feel Naj`s eyes upon her, for they were   roaming over her face, from her high forehead, her green eyes, to that perfect roman nose and those wonderful full red lips.

For a while, she sipped her tea and smiled sweetly every now and again and he started to laugh at her.

`you have grown into a beautiful young women` he could not help saying and I have thought of you often Nighat, wondering what happened to you.' and reached out his hand across the table.

She looked up into his soft brown eyes and gave a knowing smile `I know she murmured, `I have thought of you too`. Then sitting back, in a relaxed manner told him about her life with her father and that he was sick man 'He has no one else but me to care for him', and he can be very awkward, she almost grinned. `and then there`s Daneen, she added, 'I've also been looking after Daneen.'

With that Naj almost dropped the teacup. 'Did you say Daneen?'

Nighat explained how she had found him down and out and taken him in. He listened for while to the long story unfold, of how Daneen had been injured mentally in the war and when he was discharged from the army where he was stationed in Calcutta, could not cope with civvy street.

Naj sat back thoughtfully in his chair. 'Don't tell me he was the man I saw in the square yesterday, on a donkey shouting and yelling about the Japs?'

'Yes that was him,' said Nighat with a smile, then sighed. He has been driving me mad lately, going out on the donkey getting drunk and my father has been getting very fed up with the shouting. But we have helped him,' she said, looking down with a sad expression.

345

'I'm sure you have', Naj said taking her hand in his. 'It was very good of you to take him in. But I would never have believed,' he said, 'the man would end up on the street like that.'

'Well that is war,' said Nighat, in a wise way, 'that is what happened to many a brave man.'

'That is right,' agreed Naj and was thinking how he let him go, that he should have approached him yesterday and gone with his instinct when he saw his face.

'You said you saw him . . . Daneen,' said Nighat. 'Did you speak with him?'

'No,' answered Naj and shook his head. 'And he was soon gone.'

'It's a shame you didn't talk to him there and then. Perhaps you could have even taken him back to the palace and got your doctors to help him. He really does need help.'

'Of course I will,' Naj said. 'I will do whatever I can for him. He can come back with me later when I go. That is if he isn't as stubborn as a mule-and will return to the palace with me.'

'But that is not possible,' said Nighat in a gentle voice, as she knew she was breaking sad news, 'you see . . . Daneen went last night, and he left a letter. I saw it this morning and was so upset, that is why I came to the temple. I felt so worried and unhappy, because I do not know what is going to become of him now.'

'What do you mean?' Naj said. 'He has left a note, but where has he gone? What did the note say?'

'It just said, he did not want to be a burden any more, but he would never forget me and my father for all the help we gave him. He had written, that he loved us and one day would come back to see us, but that he was going back to his homeland of Ireland.'

'Ireland,' repeated Naj, 'of course, the place he was born.'

'Well, perhaps he will find peace,' said Nighat. 'I certainly hope so.' There were tears in her eyes and Naj clenched her hand.

'I loved that man too', he said, 'he saved my life remember'.

'Well . . . perhaps we will meet him one day again', Nighat said. 'I just hope he gets better'.

'Do you know where in Ireland?' Naj asked.

Nighat gave a shake of her head. 'No, not at all, he never spoke of it very much, but he never lost that Irish accent, used to shout in this strange language. He said it was Gaelic, whatever that is.'

'And he was very well known in the streets here,' laughed Naj. 'I remember now, I think he comes from County Cork in Ireland and I will go there to find him. Would you not come with me?' he asked with pleading eyes, for he was smitten with her all over again.

'That would be lovely,' she said, shacking her head, 'but at the moment my father is looking for a husband for me, he thinks it is time I was betrothed.' and perhaps he is right, she grinned, I am getting past my prime`.

'Nonsense,' said Naj looking her straight in the eyes. `you are as lovely, as when you were a girl`. and I`m still single he said, never found anyone as lovely as you Nighat.

`I can see you are the same charming boy, that you was at the Palace`, she jested, surely, she said coyly, a maharaja can pick who ever he wants to be his bride, even have five wives`.

`That may be the case, he said, with a teasing smile, but I have not found anyone I want and stared straight into her green eyes, until she had to look away with a blush,

`Oh she said` then you really are still a free man, or should I say King.`

For the next couple of hours, they had a meal, of lentil salad, with naan bread and rice. He wanted to hear about her life with her father, soon realising it was full of responsibilities, as they talked about the division of India, the new territories and the troubles between the Muslims and the Hindu`s. `Its been terrible she said, these last years,`I have had to keep a special eye on my father, he goes and preaches his muslim religion in the market`, he is so outspoken and these are still troubles times.

`I need to protect him she said`, I often go and sit close by:

Naj, listened to her words, he knew only too well of the political upheavals over the past years, the kingdom had been under much theat and there had been bloodshed, when crowds of muslim`s had rebelled in the streets. He could see Nighat, was just the same as she ever was, loving and concerned about her father, always being the little mother, like she was with him, when he was an injured boy at the palace. So they talked about those times, reliving those times they rode out on the horses and sat by the lake`.

`so you remember, he said, I had come from Calcutta, well, I came to find the place I lived as a boy`and sadly she shook her head.

`It`s all been bombed to the ground`. he said

'I know she murmured, but you have a special place in the world now,' she told him, when he looked sad, 'and your parents would be so proud of you.'

'Nighat,' he said, 'you are such a beautiful girl, not only on the outside but also on the inside.'

'How can that be?' she giggled.

'Because of your goodness', he said, 'here', he tapped the sides of his head, 'and in here,' he punched his chest where his heart was, three times to demonstrate that goodness.

They said farewell after spending many hours together. She cried at the station and he held her tight in his arms. 'I have to visit the Ganges on my way home,' he told her, and afterwards I shall write to your father, and I will tell him that I am now a Hindu and I am also the Maharaja.'

'Will you really,' she said, 'because then he may allow us to meet. You do still want to meet me . . .'

'The train came chugging into the station. 'Nighat, of course we will meet. I have never forgotten you, so - you do not get betrothed to anyone, do you hear?'

'No your majesty,' she said giving him a bow as he boarded the train back home. Then as she looked at him with pleading eyes, he could not help pressing his fresh strong lips down on hers. The kiss only lasted a few moments, but there eyes sparkled with love.

`Dont forget he said, tell your father to expect to hear from me soon` but her wondrous green eyes looked down,

`Remember, my father has plans for me, I am worried, she said ` I do not want to . . . cannot, go against him.

'But I am a Hindu now,' said Naj firmly, do not be afraid Nighat, 'there is no reason to part us.' And the hope came back to her face.

'Perhaps, he will listen, but you are not Hindu from birth,' she sighed. 'Well you are a Maharaja now, and maybe that will change his mind.' A guard blew the whistle for the train to depart.

'That's right,' he grinned, 'and you can be my Maharini. Just leave it to me.' And as the train pulled away, she was smiling brightly, for in her heart, she knew he loved her. Naj was still waving from the window as he watched her walk back up the platform, with her quick little steps, and he knew that he would dream of her lovely presence all the way home.

As he relaxed back in the train, he was glad to be leaving Calcutta behind as the town flickered by the window and could see the green fields, where the suns rays shone down on the pickers on the paddy fields. He was already missing Nighat and her bright personality, always a tale to tell, and now she had told him all about Daneen, he may never have known that this madman in the square was really him, if he had not met up with her and having that glimpse of happiness with her again, had compensated, taken away some of that sadness that was in his heart for his late family. But how would he help Daneen he asked himself, It seemed the terrors of the war had turned him almost mad. At least he had seen him again, even though he wasn't the man he had been before. He closed his eyes with a sigh, thinking that one day he would go to Ireland to find this man, but now he had been left with many responsibilities, for the kingdom he had inherited was plagued with insecurities. There were many threats to the dynasty that his father had been so proud of and how he wished he could hang on to it all, for his sake.

Yes, he thought trying to drift off to sleep, he must build this kingdom, make it strong, for his father had entrusted him with so much and he felt he needed a wife beside him, one who was strong, who had seen a lot like him. Yes, he smiled to himself, Nighat was his woman, and he was her man. He was so happy he had found her, it was like she had dropped from the sky, the angel that she was and he knew that Nighat would make a fine Queen.

THE GANGES

Ch.29

The train slowed to a stop, arriving at the River Ganges, that was at the foothills of the Himalayas and when Naj got off the train at Varanasi, the mountains of the Himalayas towered above him. The white topped peaks were the source of the River Ghanges, and this sacred river, was a place of worship, where so many people came to bathe, to cleanse themselves of their sins. Some came to make offerings, others who were sick came to the healing waters and families came to cremate their loved ones, placing their ashes in the Ghanges, in the hope of existence when life on Earth was over.

As he walked from the station, there were many little narrow streets, cramped with shops, selling everything and little children ran around and begged. The colours of the place almost blinded the eye, with its bright materials for sale and there were monkeys jumping over the rooftops, then suddenly running down and stealing a handful of food from the stallholder. He gave a little Indian boy a coin and others ran up behind him, then there was a cow and a bull in his path and he waited until they moved, for they were soon being fed by a woman in a long sari from her front door and she placed a row of beads around the white bulls neck.

This was a sacred bull Naj knew that, and he stood for a while watching in adoration. But he could hear the bells chanting from the river bank and smell the burning smoke from the funeral pyres, so he knew he was nearly at the banks of the River Ghanges. All around, the maze of smoke was rising in the air and filling his lungs as he got nearer, and the sounds of tapping bells, the beat of drums and the sounds of mantras being prayed and chanting. There was a preacher with a crowd, who was preaching the Gospel, amongst Christians.

You never knew what came up before you as you walked along, with dancing in the street, and Buddhists sitting quietly in meditation. It was like a misty colourful world all unto its own. He passed a man playing a flute, sat down on the ground and out of a basket a snake came rising: a cobra. He stopped to watch this. It reminded him of his childhood, often seeing this in the square at Calcutta. The old man looked up with a grin, he looked very old and he wondered for a moment, if it was the same man, only older. On the corner as the street opened up to another narrow causeway filled with shops and balconies of flats with people standing watching the burning flames from of the funeral pyre on the river. By a large statue of Buddha, there was a man selling garlands of flowers, and he stopped to buy two, for he would use these as his offering.

As he came out to the banks of the river, he could see a line of crumbling temples stretch before him and the crowds on the side of the river, some were sitting cross legged, little clothes, perhaps a kutar, eating a bowl of food in front of them; pigeons flying back and forth for the crumbs. Many were bathing, ducking their heads and disappearing into the dark waters for a few seconds, and coming up as though refreshed from the water, that was the colour of brown and some people were praying, as they stood up to their waists. Others were drinking the water and women stood washing their clothes, then beating them on the rocks at the side to get them clean, or hanging them in a line tied to a post. Every place you looked there was something going on in the crowded river, that was afloat with flowers and ashes and the hissing sounds from the burning of bodies that came suddenly from behind on the dock, where white doves were set free, and loved ones were cremated, the bodies being set afire and laments from those mourning their dead relations. And the hissing went on endlessly and the people prayed and some called for salvation.

Naj sat watching a man on the dock who was cutting some young boy's hair, shaving his scalp and he got up to join the queue, for he knew this ritual when one made an offering of one's hair to the river: it was a way of giving up your ego. This he felt was something he needed to do. He was feeling even sadder about his parents as he saw the funeral pyres all around, the giving of immortal life into the next for the dead. He did not have the bodies of his family to cremate and commit to the River Ghanges.

He bent his head feeling their loss and threw the flowers out onto the river. The sky gleamed with rainbow colours and there were many rowing boats taking people out to make their offerings in the deeper water. He watched the rowers, thin little Indians, wearing kutars and a turban, not looking strong enough to row such a long boat, filled to the brim.

He decided he would not go in the boat. He wanted to avoid the crowds. He would make his offerings by wading through the water, but first he would wait for the barber and have his head shaved.

It did not take long. There was a line of people and the barber was very skilled with the razor, that he skimmed over your skull and soon Naj, in his hand he held his own black silky curls and in a small dish that the barber gave him, he placed the hair and let it float out on a dish, with a lighted candle. This would be an offering he was proud to make, for he felt he had been so fortunate to survive and now he had even become royalty, yet his wonderful parents were gone from him and he could only hope that they had come to the river and prayed in this wonderful place of goodness, and before he walked into the waters, he removed his kutar, his head now bald and stepped down into the healing waters for he remembered the words of his father told him 'that the flow of the river represents the nectar of immortality'.

And when he came out, feeling refreshed from the blessings of the water, he did not feel embarrassed about his shaven, bald head. Many of the passengers had the same, having made their offering to the blessed waters from the boats and as he closed his eyes to go back to his life in Cooch Behar, where he was to undertake the ceremony to become `The Maharaja' he decided he would now go forward, remembering his parents with deep affection.

UN-COVERING THE PAST.

Ch.30

Back home with Mick, Eileen was waiting for the right moment to tell him about her visit to the Kennedy Sisters, but decided, the least said about the love affair the better. She had made a special dinner of boiled ham and new potatoes, placing a lace cloth on the table, bread and butter and young Shamus and Michael were settled early in their twin beds and beside them a cot, with their baby sister Noreen.

'Looks a fine meal', said Mick, pulling in his chair. But there was a tired look about his eyes.

'I showed Daneen that material from India,' began Eileen, 'but Mick didn't look interested, just sat gloomily, in deep thought. 'And guess what,' Eileen continued, 'a Maharaja gave him it.'

'Poppycock,' Mick snapped at her. 'A Maharaja,' he huffed.

'Sometimes I think you don't believe anything he says. After all, he did serve out in India.' But Mick only shrugged in a bored manner.

'Well, I'm thinking of asking Daneen to babysit one evening, almost shocking Mick from his sleepy mood.

'Him, babysit? You're joking! He would be on the drink. I'm not leaving the children with him.'

'But he is so fond of Shamus, the boys really taken to him`.

``cant think why, said Mick, and sat up from his dinner a questionable look in his eyes.

'He just wants us to be happy,' Eileen said, in a cajoling manner, trying to prepare him for what she was about to say, then with a hand on his, she told him about her visit to the Kennedy Sisters.

Mick listened with great interest about his birth in the London Hospital and his face lit up with a surprised smile, then got very sad hearing about his father Tim's death and his mothers hardships and when Eileen mentioned Daneen his face flushed scarlet. But Eileen rattled on, in an excited fashion, brushing over the parts about his mother's affair with Daneen.

`Don`t you remember your Aunt Mae?' she said, she could see, Mick looking very gloomy. 'She used to sit you on her knee.' And told him about the time, Mae with Nora took Mick to the sweetshop and a bomb was dropped in the street. But he was far away as if trying to take it all in although, admitted, he did remember a big explosion.

`So did you find out,' asked Mick, 'why my mother was banned from Ireland, cause that don't make sense.'

But Eileen only sighed and shook her head.

'Some trouble no doubt,' said Mick, 'between Aunt Bridie and my mother, like to know what.'

Eileen was thinking, she should at least prepare him. `think your mother and Daneen were larking about in the cow shed together, something like that,`'she declared.

'What you mean, larking about!' exclaimed Mick,. He got up and paced up and down wanting to know more, `so what`s that all about, was there something going on between them`.

But Eileen's courage deserted her. `now don`t make a mountain out of a mole hills Mick, you know what women are like,' she said in a flippant manner, 'they get jealous, make something out of nothing.'

But Mick's face showed he was not convinced; his expression deftly serious. `'there's more to this than meets the eye` he said grimly

'For Goodness sake, exclaimed Eilleen, `It was all such a long time ago,' 'best let sleeping dogs lie and placed a tender hand on his shoulder. But Mick was in deep thought; with his hands clenched inside his trouser pockets.

Now Mick she said,' trying to cheer him up, 'what about asking your aunt Mae over for dinner?' thinking, it might be better coming from her.

'And from what I hear,' she went on, your aunt Mae was very good to you when you were small.'

But Mick didn't look very interested, just stared out of the window, towards the shack, trying to piece it all together.

'Strange,' he suddenly said, 'I've often wondered why Aunt Bridie didn't leave Daneen the farm, he had worked on it for so many years., he must have really upset the old girl'. He was full of questions, and when Eileen looked at his bewildered face, it pulled at her heartstrings. She came beside him, her arm around his shoulder, handing him a hot cup of tea.

'Don't want that,' he said, almost pushing it away, 'get that scotch out, you're keeping for Christmas.'

For the next hour, Mick sat drinking and getting up and sitting down, mumbling he needed to have a good talk with, Daneen.

'But be kind,' warned Eileen.

'I've never been unkind to him! The cantankerous old git he is.'

'He's just like most Irishmen,' Eileen said, 'likes a drop of the hard stuff.'

'Always drunk, you mean.'

`   `well now, and you best remember how touchy, he can be in drink' she said dreading any confrontations between the two men. Then with a sideways glance Eileen reminded him, how Daneen changed once Shamus was born.'It seemed to calm him down a bit.'

'What you mean?'

'Why Mick` she smiled enigmatically, 'Don't you recall how he used to shout and scream when you first came here, then he got a lot better when we had Shamus, even helped on the land`

Mick looked thoughtful, then poured another glass of whiskey and swallowed it down. A little woozy, his eyes rested on the sleeping babe in her cot as he walked over and stood staring down at her, with a deep frown, wondering who she resembled.

'Just thinking,' Eileen folded her arms, 'how strange it was hearing all about your mother from, Mae. I could just picture her, so pretty and naive, sounded a little nervous Mick, just like you.' But he was hardly listening as he stood by the cot, his mind miles away. 'Just think,' continued Eileen, `what she must have gone through, in the London blitz, and none of this would have come out if we hadn't found that letter, and you know who you have got to thank for that, don't you?'

'Who?' Mick queried with sudden interest.

'Why, Oikey of course. He was the one who found the letter, hidden in the lining of that tattered bag, don`t you remember? Just shows you how things can come out in the end and it's, all down to Oikey.' But Eileen was not sure this pleased Mick, his mouth turned downwards in a grim line and he gave a hostile glance at the pig who lay in front of the stove.

'Thought he would have something to do with it,' Mick said, dolefully, 'got a lot of thinking to do tonight, I`d like to know more about Daneen and my mother.

So Eileen gave up trying to defend Daneen, for in her heart, she wondered if this man was, truly Mick's father. And she left Mick to his thoughts, as he sat head bent, shaking it from side to side, as if he did not know what to make of it all and Eileen noticed the little muscle in the side of his neck twitching.

THE MAHARAJA VISITS MAE

Ch.31

The train passed through a range of mountains that shone in the hazy sunlight, a thousand colours, and then passed a tall castle, surrounded by the lakes. Naj looked around at the cool greenness of the countryside and could understand why they called it the Emerald Isle. It was not a comfortable journey, with hard wooden seats and the train was slow, stopping to remove a cow off the line. The carriages were almost empty, except for a few nosy housewives with shopping bags who looked him up and down, giggling amongst themselves at his attire and their dogs sniffing around him. He was wearing a colourful, brocade kutar, with long loose pants and around his waist an ornamental belt with a jewelled stud. He was dressed as a Maharaja and wore his title with honour, since his succession to his father's throne and determined to follow his wishes.

It was a wet day when he arrived at the station of Banturk, although it was June and the air warm outside but the red and gold brocade coat was getting wet and the hem of the white silk trousers trailed on the floor. He wanted to know where to get a taxi and looked around. All he could see was fields and mountains, but soon the station master, Paddy Mac was at his side and looked him up and down with a curious eye, for he had never seen a man dressed in this fashion at his station before.

'Are you looking for a taxi?' he asked, staring at the black turban and wondered why a man like this should be visiting Banturk, checking his ticket with much caution. Paddy was a short man, with bushy whiskers and his large grey eyes peered from under his station master's cap in a suspicious manner. 'Who is it you have come to see?' Paddy Mac asked with a squint. 'What address have you been given? Perhaps I can help.'

Naj told him he was here to see Mae Kennedy.

'Oh,' Paddy Mac said, with surprise but some relief. 'She's our local midwife and a foine woman.' There was now a broad smile on the station masters face, but he was wondering if he should get on the phone and warn her.'That's her cottage beyond,' he said, 'at the foot of the mountain,' and pointed to a blue ridge of mountains, where a white mist hung on the peak. 'It's a long walk up the track, so you'll have to get a taxi up there, but Mickey burns the cabby will take you, knows the road off by heart.' Naj was finding this Irish accent hard to follow as Paddy Mac mumbled his words. 'I'll let him know you're here,' he said, scuttling off to the red telephone kiosk outside the small station, all the time peering through the window at Naj at he talked on the phone.

Naj had the feeling he was telling the whole village he was here.

Naj was glad when the taxi arrived, after being barricaded with questions from this old station master, who had a thick Irish brogue, that was almost incomprehensible, but Naj placed a crisp note in Paddy Mac`s hand and he looked at it as if it was gold, never being tipped so much.

As the taxi drove up the track towards the white cottage, he could see the smoke bellowing from the chimney. The countryside looked damp and dew sparkled on the Emerald green fields and he gave a shudder with the cold, being used to living in a hot climate.

It had been a last minute decision to take a plane to Ireland to try and find Daneen, as he still had the medal: the George Medal that he told his father he would give him. He also felt he had to get it settled before the wedding, as his marriage to Nighat would be a big affair and celebrations continued a few days after the initial ceremony, so to find Daneen was something he had to finish, for his father's sake and his own. In his heart he had always wanted to find him, to thank him for all he had done for him as a boy.

It had been a fluke that he had managed to get hold of an address, as his father's old friend, a first class surgeon had visited the palace. Naj knew him well, as he had studied under him at the London Hospital, during the war years, when his father had sent him there and he had never forgotten all the surgeon taught him. He was an elderly man, but had a fine mind and when Naj asked him if he remembered Mae the nurse who also worked in his team in the hospital, he said, he would never forget her, "A fine Irish nurse", he said, "did a lot for the wounded, who were injured in Dunkirk".

So Naj explained why he wanted her address in Ireland and the surgeon said he would ask his secretary to search the records of past employers. "It is a long time ago", he told Naj, "but I am pretty sure I can get you the address".As the surgeon left, he picked up his walking stick, tucking wisps of his iron, grey hair, back into his turban, then stopped to view the statue of Naj's father, that stood by an inside fountain at the entrance of the palace. "You have done your father proud", said the surgeon, looking up at the statue of his friend, I can see his great pride and that sense of fun in his smile. We will remember him", he said, "a benevolent ruler, kind towards the poor, ready to protect the weak", and Naj nodded with a knowing smile, for had not this great man he spoke of had taken him in.

"I remember", said the surgeon, reminiscing about his friend, " we had so many good afternoons spent in his little summer house, he used to like to picnic there, and sometimes he would make me my favourite curry. The surgeon was still smiling at the happy memories he had shared as he stepped into his limousine, waiting outside the palace.

It was only a week later when Naj received a letter from him with the address of Mae Kennedy in Ireland.

'I am going to Ireland', he had told Nighat who was busy with the guest list for the wedding. 'There is something I must do there'.

Nighat immediately sensed how important it was to him and wrapped her arms around his neck.

'I will miss you', she had whispered, her sparking green eyes gazing into his. 'Have a safe journey'.

So without delay, he was flown to Ireland and arrived at Cork airfield. From there he caught a train to Banturk. But he was not expecting the station to be such a remote place, never having been to Ireland before and was finding the whole scene odd, as the taxi travelled higher and higher up the mountain road. The rain was beating on the windscreen, but he rolled down his window to admire the view.

'It is a beautiful place,' he sighed, 'but wet and damp.'

'It's always raining this time of year,' said the taxi driver, and took the opportunity to find out information. 'I hear you're here, to see the Kennedy Sisters.'

'That is correct,' Naj gave a quick reply, but then had to listen to a long description about the local horse racing event, from the chatty driver, that Naj only half understood, the man's Irish brogue so thick.

On arrival, Naj got out of the cab, holding his coat from trailing in the mud.

'They're a fine little team those Irish sisters,' was the cabby's parting shot, 'talk to one and they all join in.'

Naj thanked him with a wave of his hand, there was so much he didn't know about this place, except that the people were so nosy and all seemed to know each other's business.

Before he had time to knock on the iron door knocker of the cottage, there was a face at the window and her eyes opened wide, he could hear her calling, 'There's a strange young man at the door.'

Naj smiled to himself, and he didn't want to shock her. `Its him` called Lilley with a wide eyed expression. Soon the three sisters stood in the hall staring, and he wondered when he was going to be asked in and suddenly an arm came around his shoulder and a woman with tears in her eyes and fair hair mixed with grey, said: 'Naj is that really you?' and he stepped inside to a big fire burning in the range and the Mae took his coat. 'It's beautiful,' she said, looking over the elaborate colours.

Soon they were chatting, mostly about the journey from India, and hot tea and biscuits were served by one of the sisters, but he soon realised what the taxi driver meant, for as soon as he explained how he had come to find Daneen, they all repeated his name one after the other with a wide eyed expression. He wondered if he had dropped a clanger. Mae was soon talking of the old times in the hospital and the surgeon.

'I remember how you helped the injured soldiers,' Naj said.

'It was many years ago now,' Mae said, 'and I recognised you straight away. I always remembered you as that bright teenager who was so willing to help. I can't believe that you are now a Maharaja.'

Naj told them about his father and that he had chosen him as his successor.

'Oooh!' Lillie exclaimed, 'real royalty,' asking if she should curtsey.

'We are so proud to have you here,' Mae jumped in before he had time to give Lilly an answer, though she curtsied anyway, 'but why, have you come all this way, is it only Daneen you're after seeing?'

He could see they were guarded about Daneen, and told them he had a war medal for him.

'A war medal!' they all repeated in unison, sounding surprised.

Lillie started to giggle. 'I'd never imagined Daneen getting a medal.'

'He'll have to clean himself up first,' Babs chipped in, sternly.

'You mean,' declared Naj, 'you had no idea that he was commended for his bravery?'

'Bravery . . .' Mae gave her sisters a warning look to hush. 'We know little of his life when he went to war,' she added.

'Well I best leave it for him to explain,' Naj said, 'but I will tell you one thing, I have also come here to thank him, as he saved my life as a boy. I was starving on the streets of Bengal, It was the time of the famine and when I got attacked by the Japs, Daneen took me to the Maharaja, who got me the best doctor and I survived.'

'Goodness,' they all repeated, one after the other, and Naj smiled at this for his lovely, sweet Nighat always used that word – Oh goodness.

After that,' Naj continued, 'the Maharaja took me in and made me his adopted son. So I have a lot to thank Daneen for.'

The sisters looked from one to the other, in dismay, very surprised to hear this news about Daneen.

'I am only hoping that you can tell me where to find him.'

'But are you sure this is the same Daneen, we know?' asked Babs, sceptically, 'for the Daneen we know, is not much of a hero.'

'Now be quiet,' Mae chided her, 'this young man has come all this way to find him. Who are we to judge?'

Naj shook his head in dismay, these women obviously had a dim view of Daneen.

'It is the Geroge Medal,' Naj reminded them with a determined air. 'It is a medal for Bravery and one he much deserves.'

For a moment Mae paused in thought . . . 'I did hear,' she said, 'from Eileen Kennedy that Daneen had stayed at a palace in India during the war, so there could be some connection.'

'This is so,' Naj said, 'and I would say, there are not many men around here, who served in India with the name of Daneen. He must be my man,' he decided with a grin. With a far off smile, he quickly drank down his tea, then put the dainty teacup on the table and asked for the address, where Daneen was staying.

Babs was soon writing down the name of the Eileen's farm. 'Daneen is living there,' she said, 'the farm is not far from here,' and handed him the directions. 'Eileen will make you very welcome,' she added. 'Will you be going today?'

'No tomorrow,' he said, 'for today I need rest and I am looking for a hotel for the night, could you please recommend one?'

'Why don't you stay here?' offered Mae with a bright smile.

'No, no,' Naj shook his head, 'I will be better at a hotel, but I thank you.'

'Well there is always the Blue Crest,' she told him, 'that's in Cork town and a taxi could take you straight there.'

'That will be fine,' Naj gave a nod and held out his hand to Mae, clasped her hand in his, and Babs went to call on the landline, for a taxi.

For a moment Mae rested her head on his shoulder and he gave her a little hug.

'You were a wonderful nurse,' he told her, 'you taught me so much, I have never forgotten you.' And Mae felt so proud, as this majestic young man, kissed her on both cheeks.

'So will you be going to see Daneen tomorrow,' Lillie chuckled.

'There`ll be sparks flying, when you do,' laughed Babs.

'Tomorrow morning is fine,' returned Naj, wondering what they were finding so funny. 'I would appreciate it, Mae, if you would tell them to expect me around eleven. I hope that will be okay, because, I plan on flying to Normandy tomorrow. I have a plane waiting at Cork airport and I need to get home.'

'A private plane,' they all muttered, one after the other, with an impressed air.

'I am going to be married,' he told them, and the sisters eyes widened with interest, wanting to know more.

'Have you known her long?' asked Babs.

'Is it an arranged marriage?' Lillie wanted to know before Naj could answer, Babs.

'No, and yes I have known her many years,' he replied, 'but it was sad, because we were teenagers when we met and fell in love and it has taken me all this time, to get her down the aisle, as you would say.'

'But why?' asked Babs curiously.'

'It is a long story,' he said, 'but let's just say a young girl in India, will not go against her father's wishes.'

'Didn't he like you?' Lillie asked, and Mae gave her a nudge whispering, 'Don't be nosy.'

'It is okay,' Naj said. 'It is no secret, we came from different religions, but when her father died she was free to marry me.'

'That's good,' said Lillie, 'it's a bit like the Catholics and the Protestants, here I suppose.'

'Exactly, although, we are now, both Hindus,' said Naj.

'What's her name?' asked Mae. Naj got out a photograph of Nighat, who looked beautiful, her hair in long black plait, her green eyes sparkling above a turquoise shawl.

'Her name is Nighat, but soon she will be given the name 'Prem Aditi' and she will be my 'Maharani.'

'Ooh,' Lillie said, 'makes me go all funny,' and wondered what it meant.'Is she going to be your queen?' she asked.

'Exactly,' Naj smiled, and wanted to laugh at Lillie, for she as green as grass, but he loved her fresh faced beauty.

As the taxi pulled up, he made his farewell, and there were many blessings. He had found them so endearing. 'Will I see you there tomorrow, Mae?' he asked her, will you be at the farm?'

'I don't think so,' she said a little nervously, 'me and Daneen don't always see eye to eye.'

'Really,' he said, 'that surprises me. You are such an easy person to talk to, but then,' he added, 'I do remember even as a boy that Daneen can have his awkward little ways- especially over horses.'
As soon as he left, Mae was on the landline, phoning Eileen, to tell her the news.

'This is all a shock,' Eileen kept saying, 'you actually mean a real Maharaja is coming here tomorrow? Well what do you know? She gasped. 'And to see Daneen . . .'

After hearing the news, she could not wait to get off the phone. She was suddenly in a flap, as she was not going to have a Maharaja visiting the shack where Daneen slept. It was such a mess, and for the rest of the day she was cleaning the floors, polishing furniture, kneading pastry for the base to make a special cake, as well as cooking dinner for the men when they came in.

ARRIVAL OF THE MAHARAJA

Ch.32

When Mick arrived home, he found Eileen all in a fluster. She kept moaning about the pigs and they were pushed out of their cosy place on an old blanket by the aga and shoved outside for Mick to give them a bath.

'Can't believe he is coming here,' she said to Mick, 'and you better make sure that Daneen is here too, and tell him to put on a decent suit and have a bath.'

'Okay.' Mick grimaced as she went on and on, about the Maharaja coming to the cottage.

`I can`t see why this important man, should even come here to see Daneen remarked Mick, why he is nothing but an old drunk`.

`now stop that talk said Eileen, I have told already told you, that he knew worked in a Palace in India, but you never believed me, well now I here he is getting a medal, so you better watch your P`s and Q`s.

`what bloody medal`,

`because he is a war hero, thats what, the Kennedy sisters told me, the Maraharja thinks the world of him`.

`well would you believe it, scoffed Mick, he is now a bloody war hero`, what next`.

`I`ve no time for this Mick, said Eillen with some irritation, `you are always running him down, and shoved a bucket in mick hand, telling him the pig sty needs swilling out.

`And I dont want the maharaja going anywhere near the old shack, she said` `Daneen never does any work in there. It probably stinks.'

As soon as Daneen ventured up the path and heard the news of the Maraharja coming to visit him, he was taken by surprise and very sullen, telling Eileen `he wasn't going to put any suit on`.

He was still a secretive man and in his heart, Daneen was afraid of the past coming out, revealing the time, he had been a down and out in

Calcutta and what would Eileen think about that? She could be very fastidious. Daneen as much as he would love to see Naj again, would be glad when the visit was over and decided to say as little as possible. He was also pretty sure, Naj knew about this time in his life, when he was out of his mind and had spotted him in the square: a crazy drunkard mad man on donkey.

'I'll be in the shack,' he declared with a deep frown; his broody eyes darting from side to side, thinking, how to avoid as much of the visit as possible.

`what and not say hallo` said Eilleen, sweeping around him with the broom

'Well, that I'll do,' Daneen said, with a sideways glance at Mick, as they were not the best of pals. Eileen had tried to bring them together, in her more practical way and at one time, when the crops fetched a good price at market, suggested to Mick, that he should offer Daneen a weekly wage for helping him on the land. But Daneen got very offended and put down his tools:

'Don't try to buy me off, Lad, he said `this land is part of me and there's no compensation for that.' With that he had marched off and from that time on, seemed to go back into his shell and rarely turned up to help with the crops, instead went off on the booze with Davey Jones.

So this particular day, when the Maraharja was expected, Eilleen wanted a good atmosphere for her special visitor.

`so make sure you two oafs get on together, today, she said squinting her eyes at the two men, `it wont hurt you for one day`.

``to be sure, shrugged Daneen, with a sly look,. `but I'm not missing the horse fair, Maharaja or not, and that starts at twelve. Don't want to be late, otherwise, there won't be a seat,' and grumbled on about needing to work on the high fields and that he wouldn't be around much to entertain this Maharaja.

'Eileen listened to him, with her arms akimbo, sighing in frustration, thinking, he was as obstinate and selfish as ever.

'Well, you be pleasant to this man,' she snapped at him, her face flushed with annoyance, 'after-all, he has come all this way thousands of miles from India to see you. Don't you realise he is royalty?'

But Daneen only shrugged and strolled off. 'If he wants to see me,' he repeated, 'I'll be here in my shack. I told you, can't stand all the old chit chat.`.

Eileen gave a deep frown, annoyed at Daneen's stubbornness.

'Now Mick,' she said, putting her foot down, 'that shack is a disgrace, you will have to tell him again. He cannot have the Maharaja going up there.'

'Okay,' Mick said, feeling worn out with the whole situation. He wasn't worried if the Maharaja saw the messy shack, he could not care less.

But Eileen's womanly pride was foremost. 'No way will the Maharaja visit that old shack,' and proceeded to go around with a duster, then suddenly, ran to the oven as steam poured out, as the bread was burning. There was a lot of clanging of the pots and pans and shrieks from Eileen.

'Relax woman,' Mick said, 'you'll wear yourself out.'

'I'll not rest till this place is spick and span for tomorrow, and fit to receive the Maharaja in to,' she said, banging the hot bread pan down on the table, 'he'll be coming here and not to the shack ' and marched up to find Daneen, the broom still in her hand and banged on his door,

'make sure you come up to the house in the morning she said |I'm getting the best china out` and stuck out her chin in a determined manner, and even Daneen knew not to defy her.

At midday the Maharaja arrived at the cottage, he walked down the path, like an apparition wearing white and gold: a high necked gold embroidered jacket and white loose silk pants; his white turban bearing a gold feathered plume.

'He is here Eileen,' shouted as she looked from the window and quickly took off her apron.

'Welcome,' she said, opening the door wide, but could not help staring at his grandeur. The front door opened straight into the living room and Daneen and Mick sat looking very smart. Mick's hair was plastered down with brylcreem and Eilleen had given Daneen a suit and tie to wear, against his wishes as he preferred his old jumpers. Eileen had got out her grandfather's pocket watch from the dresser and pinned it on to Daneen's waistcoat. This was all to make a good impression on the Maharaja and Eileen had worked and nagged all the previous day and that morning. She herself looked just right in a woollen blue dress and wore cork shoes having discarded her old slippers. Young Shamus was now school age and wanted to wear his green cub suit, with badges, but looked smart and was well behaved, unlike his young brother Michael. There was a real racket going on as they introduced themselves to the Maharaja, as young michael started crying at seeing the sight of this man, who to him looked a little odd.

'I have upset the child,' said Naj with that warm smile and Mick was quick to pick Michael up and place him in the play pen with his baby sister who was only a year and started hitting her brother with her bottle.

`what a beautiful boy` he said looking at Shamus in his Cub suit`,who was tall for his years, with deep set Irish eyes and Naj was thinking there was something about him, that reminded him of Daneen.

'Please sit down, here next to Daneen,' Eileen said, going to the cooker to get the hot cakes out and Daneen looked up at the young man, whom he had not seen since a teenager. He noticed how he still had that limp.

'It's good to see you again, young man, or should I say 'Your Royal Highness.'

'Oh don't be so silly,' Eileen called over, knowing Daneen could be sarcastic when he wanted to be.

'No, please call me Naj, we are friends. I hope you remember those old days at the palace. It is such a long time ago.'

So they had tea and talked of the changes that Naj had made, like his medical school that he ran there in the palace and how the status of the Maharaja's of India, was not the same.

'What, you don't ride about on big elephants with a crown on?' Eileen said.

'No,' Naj chuckled, 'it is not so grand anymore, not since the division of India. But Eileen didn't know much about that, and didn't really want to, she was never interested in politics of the world, only what went on in her own Irish village. 'Even the decor is not so grand,' Naj said.

Daneen was quiet and listened with a far off look on his face as if he was recalling that lovely palace where he had spent many happy times with Naj and the previous Maharaja. `me and your father had a real craic` said Daneen with a grin, although Naj wasnt sure what `the craic` even meant.

'Still got the old stables I hope.' said Daneen. 'Me and your father, spent many hours with the horses.'

'My father loved horses,' Naj sighed. 'And of course I have kept the stables.'

'They were grand,' Daneen said, 'unlike the ones we have here, all falling down.' And Eileen shot him a look as if to say, do you have to say that?

'And you Mick,' the Maharaja asked him, 'do you like horses?' Naj was trying to draw Mick into the conversation as he sat quiet and hardly said a word, but Mick answered, that he had enough work to do on the land, without the worry of horses to look after.

'He has enough work alright, when he is out of the bed,' Daneen piped up, and Eileen gave him a glare, as to why he should say that, and embarrass Mick by putting him down.

Naj tried not to let his amusement show. 'I can see you are still the straight talking man you used to be.'

'Of course, why shouldn't I be?' Daneen said, rather abruptly. 'but I haven't got all day to sit and chat.' He took the pocket watch from his waistcoat in a superior manner. 'By the way, there is a horse show in Bantry, and it starts at twelve, and I don't want to miss it.'

'Now that's not nice Daneen,' Eileen said, telling him off, in a school ma'amish way, 'as Naj has come all this way to see you and you want to be going off, elsewhere.'

Daneen only shrugged, he did not want all the past brought up for Mick and Eileen to jabber about. Then to their surprise the Maharaja got up from the chair, put down the cup on the table and looked at his watch that shone gold on his wrist.

'Would you mind if I came with you?' he asked. Daneen looked up with surprise as he was trying to avoid any chit chat and just wanted to get off to the horse fair for a drink with his mates. 'The taxi is still waiting outside,' Naj said, 'we can ask him to take us both there.'

Daneen was taken back, as he was ready to make his getaway, but when he looked up into the soft eyes of the Maharaja that smiled at him knowingly, he suddenly softened. 'Well I hope you like gambling 'cause there's some good horses racing today, and I won't be rushed.'

A sudden smile broke out on Naj's dark face. He would not be deterred. 'That sounds good,' he said, 'I love horses. Don't you remember how you taught me to ride? It would be good to go together.'

'Whenever you're ready,' Daneen said, resigned to the situation. Even Eileen was finding it amusing, as she knew Daneen was planning on going without him. Then suddenly remembering the Maharaja put up his hand.

'Before we go, I am almost forgetting what I came for, because there is something, I must give you,' and he searched into a carpet bag beside him. 'You see my father gave it to me years ago, and I promised my father I would give it to you.'

As he got out the small velvet box, there was a silence in the room, even the children were quiet. Daneen, Mick and Eileen waited in anticipation, as Naj opened the box and took out a sparkling medal of the George Cross holding it up. 'This is what you earned, the highest honour of all, for bravery, such as rescuing a child, for you rescued me.' There remained a silence in the room and Daneen's eyes were filled with unshed tears.

'I have come all this way, to give you this, a well earned honour, for I remember that day, you picked me up from the ground, on your way to the palace and took my injured body with you.' Naj pinned the medal onto the lapel of the suit, Daneen was wearing. 'You saved my life. It was my father's wish, that you should you have this`.

Daneen went to speak, but the words seemed stuck in his throat . . . 'Your father . . . the late Maharaja was a fine man,' he said softly, 'always working for the progress of his country and helping the poor.'

Eileen and young Shamus gathered around to admire the medal and Mick stood with a look of disbelief `do you mean` he enquired `that Daneen rescued you from the Japaneze`.

`You mean you dont know, the story, said Naj,, `well perhaps Daneen will tell you, because surely, you know how brave this man was in the war,' Naj praised him, but Daneen only laughed.

'There's a lot they don't know,' he said with that same obstinance. 'They just think I'm an old drunk.'

`what a thing to say, eileen exclaimed with some embarrassment, and was just about to ask Naj, about the time Daneen rescued him, when there was a sound that caused the Maharaja to cringe. 'What is that?' he said, as the pig scuffled and whined at the back door.

'Oh, that's only Oikey,' Eileen said, giving Mick a nudge to go and shut him up.

'Who is Oikey?' the Maharaja enquired, as the sound was deafening any conversation.

'He's a pig,' Daneen informed him, 'and a good one at that.'

'Well let me see him,' Naj said, 'in our country we value such animals.'

So against Mick's wishes, Daneen opened the back door and Oikey rushed in and knocked the coffee table flying with the best china on it and when he saw the Maharaja, sat down in front of him as if in homage. It was almost unbelievable to Mick when Oikey sat quietly, like a pet dog would and allowed the Maharaja to pet him.

'Well, would you believe it!' Eileen was saying with a wide smile. 'I have never known Oikey to be so good with strangers. Suddenly there was the sound of a car hooting outside and Daneen rushed to the window to see the taxi driver waving.

'It's time to go,' he said to Naj, 'if you want to go to the horse show, the taxi can't wait any more . . .'

With that the Maharaja quickly made his farewells, with a shake of his hand to Mick and an Indian custom kiss on Eileen's hand, thanked them for their hospitality, and Daneen rushed him out of the door.

The horse fair in Bantry was full of local people and the steeplejack racing had already began. Daneen went to stand by the rail and started cheering the horses on out loud, having seen his friend Joe trying to race to the finishing post. Before long the Maharaja was joining in and then afterward they viewed the horse in the paddock, the steam rising from the thoroughbreds as they circled around.

'He looks a fine horse that chestnut.' Daneen could see why this horse won it.

'Find out if it's for sale,' Naj said, not wasting anytime, for he could see that Daneen still had his love of horses and he wanted to do something to help this man who had done so much for him.

So when the horse was auctioned off, and Naj became the new owner, he gave the papers to Daneen and told him, it was his. So Daneen with a proud smile took the reins and tied the horse up outside the beer tent, where all his pals came shaking his hand in congratulations, for Daneen now owned a race horse and the winner at that. At first Daneen was not ready to accept such a gift, but when he saw how adamant Naj was, he could do little else but accept.

'You need a start,' Naj said. 'I can see that and you have so many skills and handling the horses, you must not lose the skills. Suddenly Daneen had dreams of doing up the old stables for the chestnut horse and even rebuilding the place, for now he had a race horse and it was a good start. There was no end to the races the horse could win, and could bring him in a fortune. So Daneen was feeling a lucky man and downed pints of porter in the beer tent, celebrating with the locals.

Naj was pleased to join in and it was then Daneen told Naj that he was getting married to Nighat, the girl who used to work in the palace. This was a great surprise to Daneen who said, `your starting late, your father had many wives, but in the end I think he preferred his horses`. Naj laughed, he knew how true that was.

`I had no time to take a wife, said naj, building the dynasty back up, I owed that to my father. Also I have become a doctor, passing my exams in these last years. there was little time for women`.

`Nol time for women ara, grinned Daneen, to be sure, i wish i had kept away from them myself,  nothing but trouble`

`not all, said Naj, Nighat is special.

`Ill drink to that said Daneen, ordering more drinks to congratulate him, saying what a fine girl she was, for how could he forget when Nighat took him in and all her care, trying to get him off the drink and drugs and he suddenly went quiet and evasive, for those were times when he was a down and out and he didn't want any discussion about that: it filled him with shame, and although, Naj, with a shrewd glance was quite aware of what Daneen was hiding, still continued to talk of his love for Nighat and told Daneen how he had never forgotten Nighat when they were teenagers at the palace and of their friendship. He told him how he found her in Calcutta at the temple. She had turned into a beautiful woman.

'Beauty is as beauty goes,' said Daneen softly, 'and she is one beautiful girl,' then rushed off to the bar for another drink.

So on the way back home, Daneen was fired up with booze and filled with the excitement of owning a race horse. He was grateful to the Maharaja and they talked of old times again at the palace their time with Naj's father.

'He was a great man,' Daneen slurred, and Naj asked him why he never came back to the palace to see him.

'I couldn't,' he said, 'sometimes, the war changes men.'

'Couldn't or didn't want to,' Naj retorted with a hurt expression. They were silent for a while. Daneen sat with a far off expression, his eyes red veined with alcohol, and a wide grin on his face, but he was determined he wasn't going to admit how he had lost his sanity after the war, and only for a moment, did he glance shrewdly at Naj, wondering, if he was going to bring up about that time, when he rode the donkey in the square, acting like a lunatic, as he was pretty sure Naj had seen him.

'So, whatever happened to you?' Naj eventually asked, 'you just left the palace one day and I never saw you again. It was only my father who told me you had been recalled on a second mission.'

'It was the Burma Campaign,' Daneen drawled, 'we were being returned to blow up a bridge.'

'I did not know the details,' admitted Naj. 'I only know I waited each day for you to return, like you had promised.'

But Daneen only shrugged, the alcohol gave him a warm feeling. He didn't want to go on explaining the details of the Burma Campaign that only brought him down, for at that time he was a sick man and only wanted to hide himself. 'It was a different world after the war,' Daneen muttered, 'and I eventually heard your father had passed away.'

'And that was a difficult time for me,' Naj said, bowing his head, 'my father was sick and not the same man.I was hoping you would return . .

. see him before he passed away, but eventually I lost him.'

Daneen wasn't sure what to say, for he did not want to talk about that time, after the war, when he had been a raving madman: angry and traumatised. The palace was the last place he wanted to go. He preferred the arches of Calcutta, where he could rant and rave and smoke drugs and shut the rest of the world away.

They were nearly at the cottage, as the taxi drove through the white mist on the hills, with just a glimpse of the Blue Mountains. They both knew there were unsaid words, but also, that they had a bond, something time and distance could never change.

'Are you coming in,' Daneen asked, when they pulled up at the cottage, for Eileen was waving from the window. But the Maharaja only waved with a smile and said to Daneen in a mysterious tone: 'There is something I would like you to do,' and Daneen wondered what else he wanted to know. 'I am flying to Normandy later. It is the day, the anniversary of the war and I want to pay my respects to the men who died. Daneen was thinking this was something, he had always wanted to do. 'I wondered, if you would like to come with me? My plane is waiting at Cork Airport to leave for France.'

Daneen was taken by surprise at the invitation, but thinking what an opportunity this would be to visit the graves of the men, who had suffered in this war, to pay his respects, there were so many good men that he knew and had been lost, and with a few pints of porter inside of him, he was ready for anything. 'Why not,' Daneen said, as if raring to go.

'But I am leaving tonight, if that is all right with you, then, we would have all day tomorrow to visit the graves.'

'I'll come alright,' Daneen said. 'There are graves I must visit. I want to pay homage to those friends I lost.'

Naj smiled, it was as he had thought it would be, for the Daneen he had known and trusted had a lot of feeling for humanity. Had he not rescued him as a boy, lying there wounded in the Bengal Jungle. Yes - this was the real man he knew.

'Good man,' said Naj, 'can you leave now?'

'Wait there,' said Daneen with a smile all over his face, 'I'll just pick up a few togs.'

Eileen looking pleased to see them arrive, came out to greet them but Daneen went rushing past and up the path to his shack to get some clothes. He was looking forward to his trip on a private plane. 'Now there's a foine greeting,' said Eileen with arms akimbo.

'I won't be a minute,' he called.

A few minutes later when she saw him return with his suitcase, she wondered what was going on. 'Where you off to?' she asked.

'I'm off to France,' he simply said, and Eileen stood at the door looking dumfounded and full of questions. 'I don't know what you're up to,' she nagged as he got back in to the taxi. She turned to the Maharaja. 'Won't you at least come in for some tea?'

'No,' the Maharaja smiled and took her hand and kissed it gently. 'It has been my honour to meet you and I hope we will meet again, but I have a lot to do and need to be back in India in a few days, I have a wedding to arrange.' He got into the taxi, but Eileen had one eye on Daneen, sitting beside as him with a supercilious grin on his face, as he seemed to be acting very odd, talking about flying off to Normandy in France.

'Is this true?' Eileen said as the taxi driver turned the key of the ignition on, 'are you really going off to France?'

'Yes, my dear,' the Maharaja answered gently, 'but all you need to know is, that Daneen and I, have some unfinished business. Just remember that Daneen is a war hero.'

With that the taxi pulled away and Eileen was left a little gobsmacked, wondering what France had to do with it. And when she told Mick, he rolled his eyes. 'It's just a lot of hoo har what I've seen today, I'd prefer to believe Oikey than them.' From the window Eileen could see the taxi getting smaller and smaller as it travelled back down the hilly roads, and she knew that this visit from the Maharaja was something that the village would be talking about for weeks.

OFF TO NORMANDY

Ch.33

It was a small red and white plane that waited at Cork Airport and planes landed and took off as they walked across the tarmac, the noise of the engines filled the evening air. It would be late evening when they got to Normandy, Naj had told Daneen and a hotel was already booked. There was a Indian pilot to greet them, having been waiting around for hours for his master the Maharaja to return and there were just a few seats, where Daneen and the Maharaja would sit and watch the TV screen in front of them.

'Just relax,' Naj told him and get yourself a drink. There is a bar in the corner.'

It was all luxurious and Daneen closed his eyes for a while with a glass of whisky in front of him on the little table as the small plane soared up into the sky; cutting across the beams of light from the tarmac below. In the background Daneen could hear the babble on the radio and the Hindustani voice of the pilot being directed across the Irish Sea towards England. Before long, he could see the white cliffs of Dover and the rolling green fields of Kent, where his friend Jerry had lived.

'It's the garden of England,' he said to Naj. He started to think about his friend Jerry who had been a close companion during the Burma Campaign. He smiled to himself thinking of this man, always jovial, and although slight in build, he could easily walk the forty miles a night and was the best trekker through the jungle he had ever known.

Jerry had come from a village in Kent and from a horse breeding family and he became a keen steeplejack jumper; so he had a lot in common with Daneen. They both loved horses and became pals straight away. Jerry was young at seventeen to be called up in the army and he was just making his way in the movie industry as a stunt man, he could ride a horse, by standing on its back and do a back flip at the same time. He also rode a motorbike, spinning on it in the air.

"Thought I was going to be a stunt man in the movies", he complained to Daneen when they first met, "but instead, they thought I would make a good Chindit, whatever they are supposed to be". Daneen would marvel at his abilities when they were deep in the jungle and lost. Jerry would watch the monkeys picking the fruit and follow them swinging from tree to tree, bringing back fruit to eat. Daneen was surprised to hear he was half French, as he didn't look it.

"I've got my mother's fairness", he said, "but my father's big ears", he would laugh, flipping a finger behind them. His laughter was contagious and Daneen would never forget him.

As the plane soared across England, he looked down at the choppy water of the English Channel; as the little white frothy waves rolled across the sea and in the distance the land of France. Miles away in his own thoughts, he finished his whisky and continued to watch the waves on the sea, just visible through the headlights of the plane. He was looking forward to his night in a posh hotel and tomorrow, to see the war graves in Normandy. He wondered if his friend Jerry would be buried there. He had often wondered what they did with his remains, as evidently his body was badly charred, like the others that died, on the plane that had crashed into the hills over France.

They had been on there way back to England: it was a supply plane, sent down into the jungle and took back some of the wounded men. It was getting difficult to land, with the sniping Jap's and it was sheer luck if the plane landed. The men had put a large sign 'LAND HERE' in a clearing and the pilot had spotted it.

Jerry had not wanted to get on the plane, but he had been wounded. He had been hit with a bullet in his shoulder and no more could he swing through the trees and plod through the boggy land, filled with tributaries that were getting harder for Jerry.

"I'll be alright he would say", the pain written on his thin face, and

Daneen was worried he was going to get gangrene in the wound. He had been very unlucky when a Jap, shot at him, from the bushes. So when the news of a plane was trying to land in a clearing, there was a lot of excitement amongst the men and they gathered the wounded that would go for the return journey.   There were supply boxes coming down on parachutes and men rushed to get them, when the plane landed safely.

Daneen had told Jerry that he should go on it, but jerry argued the fact: he was staying, the wound would heal, but Daneen got his way and Jerry was aided onto the plane: its engines still running, the propellers spinning, causing the trees to bend. There was little time, as the Jap's could spot the plane and shoot it down. Daneen waved his friend off, as he climbed up the rope ladder. He would miss him, but at least he would not die in this jungle from the wound-well that was what he thought, but it was the next day the radio operator told the men, that the supply plane came down over France and there were no survivors.

Daneen had to live with the guilt of losing his friend, all because he pushed him to get on to that plane.

Daneen shifted restlessly in his seat and drew a deep sigh as he thought about it all.

'Are you all right?' Naj asked looking over at him from his seat across the aisle.

'Sure,' Daneen muttered, 'just some old memory of my friend who died - we were in the jungle together.'

'Well, perhaps we will find his grave in Normandy and you can pay your respects to him.'

Daneen certainly hoped so and with that closed his eyes to sleep for the rest of the journey. The sun was going down but they were over the mountains and going down the other side.

'It won't be long now,' he could hear Naj saying, 'we will be there and you can get a good night's sleep in the hotel.

But Daneen was hardly listening, he was still thinking of those days in the jungle as he drifted off to sleep. Deeper and deeper sleep pulled him, the sound of the plane engine humming, became further and further away in the world of sleep. He was tossing and turning as that old song was in the background: a song the men sang as they marched single file through the jungle. It was a song for their commanding officer Captain Bailey. Some would laugh at him and say: "Who'd he think he is, Lawrence of Arabia with his dagger in his belt?" But all the men loved him, even when they became half starved, trapped for months in the jungle, and the Jap's were here, there and everywhere, yet the song was still in their hearts, singing and chanting it as they marched along . . ."Won't you come home Bill Bailey, won't you come home. . .

Daneen twisted and turned, the sound of singing was getting louder, ringing in his ears and he was trying to wake up, but something was holding him down and the footsteps of the men, he could hear, over and over. . . He was choking back tears as they rose in his throat as he recalled how they marched, trying to keep up their spirits, singing that song - that was for their leader. There were times when he visited the men at camp and the men would chant the song, often behind his back but Bailey would laugh. He was aman of courage, Will Bailey, always urging them on.

"Don't give up men. You must get to Mandalay - to blow up the railway". So the men were marched forty miles a night; they did not want to let their commander down and above all they wanted to get the railway blown up and stop the Jap's once and for all. They all hated the blood thirsty, Japs, for they would suddenly spring out in the jungle from nowhere and would shoot down the men.

Even as they marched through the night, the jungle was lousy with them and they would kill at the drop of a hat, just as they would die at the drop of a hat, for their country. They were a strange, fearless lot. We would hit back, there were shoot outs. The Gurkhas would cut their throats with their curved knives. They were excellent fighters, but there were too many Japs and no way out.

The starving Chindits had no more supplies, they had come to a halt, because no other supply plane dare chance another drop, for the men had ventured out of the supply zone and the planes were being shot at by the Jap's. There were no more supplies of food, or medical aid, they were on their own, in a dark wilderness, and behind every tree a Jap could be waiting to snipe. The song still rang in his ears and the vision of the drawn faces of the men, as they marched in the tropical heat, with their packs on their backs, carrying shovels and machine guns, and leading their mules. Some men dropped with weakness; but there was no time to nurse them, the orders were that if any man couldn't get up, he would be left behind, for the operation to blow up the bridge and place the booby traps was their mission.

Suddenly instead of the singing, Daneen heard an explosion and the fire of a bomb blast light up in front of him. He woke with a start. And the realisation that the Chandits, did achieve their mission, after all: they did blow up the bridge and he had seen how it all ended. The men had crossed the Chinwin River and planted booby traps on the railway line that ran from Mandalay to Mitchinawya and when it blew, it cut off the Jap's supply train. But some Chindits were killed and as he relived the past, he was sweating and trembling:

 as he always did after one of these nightmares. He tried to pull himself up to get to the whisky on the table in front of him and managed to take a large swig, feeling the hot liquid pour down his throat, and memories were still flooding back to him, that would not leave him alone: explosive lights in his eyes and voices of the men and felt himself, being pulled back to sleep, as if water was flooding over him, for those that survived had to now get back to the river that was eleven miles wide. They tried crossing the river in inflatable boats and canoes, but the waters were swarmed with Jap's and gun fire pursued. Some men swam for it, and the mules had to be taken across. Some were lost, as they floated off dead down the river, or dying in the water. Others were tied up to the boats, until they tipped over and the mules drowned. It was a pitiful sight. Those that made the crossing, just hid in the reeds, others crawled onto the muddy banks, slipping and sliding in the thick mud and clinging onto the branches; mud blinding their eyes. Everywhere you looked there was a Jap coming out of the greenery, shooting who they could down. The wounded lay on the muddy banks, and the river to take them, for the current was strong and the waves swept over the bank. It took three months to get out of the jungle, as the men were trapped by the Jap's and had to keep making diversions to get away from them. Aimlessly they walked with aching legs, feeling any minute, they could give up and drop to the ground.

It was only the memories of Nora that kept Daneen going. He would allow the memories of Ireland to sweep over him and think of those times running across the cornfields with her, her raven hair flying behind her and smiled to himself as he recalled how she would run to him and he would catch her in his arms and swing her into the air, her full red lips pressing down on his "Be careful", he would say to her, "someone might be watching and you are betrothed to Tim".

"No, no, darling", she would insist, her arms around him, "it's you I love", and they would make passionate love. Over and over he would recall those wonderful memories, as he trekked in the jungle in filthy conditions and tears would often rise in his chest when he thought of Tim his friend, who had been killed and how he had betrayed him, but he learnt to push away this sad memory and only think of the good ones, when he and Nora were together, for his life could end any minute in this dangerous jungle: there could be a Jap around the next tree to shoot him down. So as he hacked his way through the thick evergreen, he would recall her warm kisses and her loving ways. And how they romped in the hay and she would creep up behind him, as he groomed the horses, putting her arms around his waist.

"You should not tempt me, you hussy", he would smile.

"But I can't help it", she`d giggle, "each time I see you I want to be with you". So he would take her in his arms, trying not to think about Tim who was working out on the fields. These were precious memories, to see him through, and each time he thought of them making love, it would give him strange stirrings of excitement in his belly, just like a kid looking forward to a party, for she was the woman he loved and he always would. But when the war came, he knew it was the best way forward, for him to leave, for he did not want to keep hurting Tim. He was his good friend, who had taken him into the farm and given him work. He should get away, and leave him to his happiness with Nora. It was best he went to war and try and forget her, her life was with Tim, who owned half the farm and had a lot to offer her, whereas he had nothing; nothing except his horses and his riding. Often, he would close his eyes and imagine cantering with the black stallion, across the emerald green fields, almost smelling the sweet, damp air of Ireland.

At times he would think of Bridie and how he must have hurt her, for she had her heart set on them getting married and them running the farm together and he would beat himself up, wondering why he didn't have the sense to leave well alone, for Bridie owned half the farm and Tim the rest. He could have had a good life at the farm with Bridie, raising horses, but now he and Nora had gone and spoilt it all. He would wonder if Bridie would ever get over it, for the truth was out, she had found out about his affair with Nora, and now she would chuck him on the street. But he knew he would never forget Nora, the love of his life and when he was in the burmese jungle, when the real dangers began and tested any man to his limits. It was then, he would bring back the lovely memories and they kept him going, as it was months, fighting to survive, the torments of the Jap's, and the diseases, that threatened their lives. The men became sick and when they were dying, they were told to just keep going, to get home and that they should leave the dying behind. At times, were told to shoot them, when they were in pain, giving them a bullet in the back of head, to put them out of their misery. Such degradation, such torture in this terrible jungle, and many did not survive. Some were his friends and he would always be haunted by these brave men, who fought for their country and suffered these terrible hardships, some starved to death, and most men lost their own body weight. Some took a chance and went to a village for food, asking the locals to feed them, but the Jap's were waiting and closed in, capturing the men taking them to the prison in Rangoon: there they suffered terrible conditions, and hundreds died in these camps and he had already decided he would never let the Jap's take him, if he could help it, after hearing how they tortured the men.

But it was an order to eat the mules that disgusted most of the men, for most - loved their mule, but because they were starving were ordered to eat them. This order came from headquarters. It was the hardest thing for many as they cooked the flesh of their mules over the fire. Some wrote poetry about them and cried, as they had become so fond of them, for they had carried their loads and trekked beside them. Conditions could not get any harder and some men went their own way, often getting lost in the jungle.

They were splitting up and going their own way, starving with hunger, yet he could not kill his own mule and took the dangerous paths out, hacking away at the bamboo, where Jap's could be waiting to blow you up with a grenade. Eventually, reaching a village, stumbling onto a shack made of straw and bamboo and begged for food and a woman took pity on him. She was part of a bronze aged tribe, she had a strange look, where her neck extended with rings around it, but her black eyes were kind and with the rest of the women of the tribe,cleaned the infected the sores on his legs, using a leaf dipped in their own jungle medicine: their dark hands so soothing. They never spoke much. Their language was of the `Kayan` tribe and they knew little of the western world, but this black skinned woman, fed the mule, hid him in her house and for weeks he stayed there delirious whilst she nursed him back to health.

As soon as he was able, a young tribesman, led him from their camp, that was hidden deep in the jungle and from there he made my way to an outpost, and with that feeling of feeling safe, was flown back to India. he could still hear the cheers of the people as a group of us men came off the plane, for the Chindits had returned and all across India was hearing the news of the Chindits, who had blown up the railway, stopping the Jap's taking over China and   treated as heroes.

The Chindits were unimpressed. They were bedraggled, weak men, trembling with ill health, some so injured they would never be the same again. Fortunately for those who had survived, this happy welcome could not replace their suffering. They would be scarred forever. The cries of the people were ringing in his ears, over and over and the noise would not stop. . .

It was only when the gentle hand of the Naj tried to wake him, that Daneen realised he had been dreaming.

'What is it?' Naj was saying, you have been calling out a name.'

'What name?' he muttered.

'Keowana, who is she?' asked Naj smiling. But Daneen's eyes were shot with tears, as he knew that was the name of the motherly tribal woman who helped him. 'You have been shaking,' Naj said, 'that I was wondered if you were having a fit.'

'No, it's combat stress,' he said with a sad smile.

'I did not know you suffered with that,' Naj said, his sleepy brown eyes filled with sympathy. 'Can I do anything to help?'

Daneen only shook his head. 'Only, if you can take away memories,' he said.

Naj's dark eyes looked anxiously back, but he wasn't sure what he could do. 'We are landing in ten minutes,' he said suddenly, as the pilot called out to put their seat belts on.

THE WAR GRAVES

Ch.34

As they pulled up at the cemetery, there was a stone archway, with the words inscribed - 'Their Names Liveth For Evermore'- On walking through, a crowd of people were also going in: most of them veterans in uniform, decorated with a line of medals across their chest. Some walked with sticks, others in wheel chairs, some walked like Daneen upright - like a soldier, but they were all men that had fought in the First and Second World Wars. There was a coach parked close by and others were stepping off to join the stream of people, including Naj, the Maharaja in line and beside him, this tall, stick like man with a sour face, followed the crowd along the path that led to the visitors centre.

This was an arched white building and above it flew flags of different nations. All around the neatly cut lawns were rows and rows of headstones with white crosses. All religions and Nationalities were catered for and Daneen noticed the Star of David above some of the headstones. The graves stretched for miles, and outside the visitors centre was a war memorial with many poppy wreaths laid upon it and the words inscribed – They gave their unfinished lives so others could be free-.

'Let us go and look in the visitors centre,' Naj suggested. He wanted to know more about this battle on the beaches of Normandy, that he had heard so much about. Inside there were photographs of the thousands of men on the beaches at Dunkirk. Tour guides explained how they had suffered.

'On land and sea and air,' the words from an audio recording rang out, 'these men who died for their country. . .'

'I can't believe this could happen,' said Naj, 'all those men waiting for a boat to get home and being shot at by the enemy.'

Daneen scoffed, he had little faith in the authorities, and was thinking of all those young men of little more than seventeen who had died to save their country. 'They were kids some of these heroes,' he said with a sardonic air.

'Perhaps your friend is listed here,' said Naj, 'let us find the book of references.'

'But I thought most of the Chindits were buried in Burma,' said Daneen, 'although some were taken to be buried with our captain out in Arlington, Virginia.'

Naj looked at Daneen with some surprise. He was a man of few words, but not an ignorant one. 'But I thought you said, this plane came down in France.' said Naj

Daneen shrugged. 'Well a lot of the casualties of war, were brought from across the battlefields and placed to rest here.'

They moved along the marble hallway, along the walls photographs of yesterday depicting some of the men and the battles. Soon they came to a long list of names on the wall above them and Daneen stood searching for anyone he knew. Beside them was an elderly man in uniform looking up at the list and pointing with his stick.

'Found him,' he suddenly said with a broad grin, towards Daneen. 'That's me mate.' He had a coarse Cockney voice. 'Glad I've found him 'cause, there's thousands of graves out there.' Daneen viewed everyone with suspicion and glared at this big man, with a red face and thick bull neck, but two humorous grey eyes peered back from a mop of red and grey hair under its cloak of grease.

Then suddenly over the audio system, came the sound of an Irish song, Daneen recognised immediately. It was 'The shores of Normandy' and was quite surprised as the old man, stood as if to attention as the song rang out over the great hall and they stood in silence listening to the words.

'You an Irishman?' the old man eventually said, with a wide grinning face and stared straight at Daneen, who didn't seem to want to talk. 'There's a lot of Irish graves on the North side,' the old man continued, but Daneen only shrugged with a lofty air, continuing to look up at the list for his friend Jerry's name.

'Perhaps we haven't got enough information,' said Naj as he searched, bending his head back to see right up to the top of the list, for the name of Dupont.

The elderly man also stood looking up, close beside him. 'Do you know what area?' he said in a nosy fashion. 'It's a big cemetery, there are many plots.'

Daneen didn't like being questioned. 'Let's go,' he said, giving the man a black look. 'We can look amongst the graves,' and walked right by the old man with a lofty air, although Naj gave him a polite nod as he passed by.

'He was only trying to help,' he told Daneen.

Outside in the fresh air, they walked amongst the gardens, the sounds of a bugle playing in the background. Along the paths, they passed groups of veterans who stood over graves and placed wreaths. It was a fresh day, the sky was grey and the grass a little damp. Along the way there were maintenance men, and gardeners tended the graves and green lawns. There were lines and lines of white crosses and inscriptions on the graves and they stopped to read the meaningful words - from a mother to her son 'His heart was purer than gold'. Then suddenly there came a familiar voice behind them, it was the same old man and recognised his voice.

'Ain't yer found yer mate yet?' he asked curiously. 'My mate's buried over there,' and pointed to the churchyard, 'just sorry it took me so long to come here,' he added, and Daneen looked at him with some interest, wondering why. The old man looked down, resting on his stick. 'Some never come to the graves,' he said, 'can`t face it, too many bad memories.'

'But at least you have paid your respects now,' Naj kindly said, and the old man's eyes shot with tears.

'Perhaps it will bring some closure,' he muttered, 'but . . . I'll never forget my friend Pierre.'

Naj was wondering, if he should help the old man along, for he had been so jovial, but now he had a long face with downcast eyes, then he suddenly looked up to the sky, taking a deep breath, as if pulling himself together and now he spoke in a brave fashion. 'What's yer mate's name? Perhaps I can help you find him. Was he Irish like yerself?' he asked Daneen with a little smirk.

'No.' Naj answered for Daneen, standing tall in a dark blue velvet coat and matching turban with pearl studs. 'He had a French name, 'Dupont.'

'Well, why didn't yer say,' said the old man, with a grin, displaying a line of white teeth that looked to be his own and not dentures.'French, aye,' he muttered and paused in thought and stuck out his chest. That was when Naj noticed the collection of medals that adorned his uniform, there were many, including the George Cross medal, that was one of the highest awards in the face of the enemy. 'Now if he was French,' the old man declared with some knowledge, 'he might be in the churchyard, with me mate 'cause he was a French Resistance Fighter and that's where they put him. Had no kin, you see, but it's a small churchyard, bit individual if you see what I mean, but Naj was already weighing it up, looking over at the churchyard; its small grey stone steeple, just visible over the high brick wall. 'That's where they put a lot of the missing,' the old man said, 'worth having a look.'

'Thank you,' said Naj, holding out his hand to shake his.

'My name's Bob,' the old man said, 'hope you find yer friend. Good luck.'

Daneen followed Naj towards a churchyard, pushing open the rickety gate, finding the garden was a overgrown and some of the gravestones marked with age. There was a mixture of nationalities, their names inscribed on the gravestones, as they wandered around. Stopping in the churchyard, they leaned on the wall, looking down at a view of rolling hills: the valley all shades of green, with a row of tall poplar trees in the distance. Close by was a grave of a Royal Enniskillen Fusilier and Daneen thought how this young man would like the view below, it was so reminiscent of his homeland of Ireland. 'Here lies a man of my own heart,' said Daneen, 'and only young when he died.'

There were many graves of brave young men, whose lives had been taken by the war and he felt, that he had been lucky to survive the horrors as he did.

'I do not know what happened to you exactly, out in that jungle,' Naj quizzed Daneen, as they walked around, 'but it must have been pretty bad, the way it has affected you.'

Daneen only grinned, accusing him of doing his doctor bit on him, as he was quite used to the fact that Naj was a doctor of some standing, but Daneen was not ready to talk to any `shrink` as he called them, after all, what would these outsiders know about what he had been through. Had they ever had to kill a snake and eat it while it was still warm, just to survive in that dark jungle, that affected your sight, as you constantly viewed the world through darkness, finding your way around- only the moss on the trees to hold on to, to get your bearings.

He remembered how his mate Jerry, used to find roots, grubs and insects to eat, as they were starving, refusing to kill their mules, like so many of the Chindits had to. It was Jerry who had saved his mule when travelling across the Irrawaddy, it was eleven miles wide and the mule came loose from the rope and was going down the river at a speed, towards the rapids, when Jerry jumped in, leaving Daneen to man the boat and Jerry`s strong, lithe body fought the current, until he got close enough to the mule to guide him back. Daneen remembers being forever thankful to him for that. He felt a lump in his throat as he walked along the path looking for Jerry's grave, for this young man had given his all to him. He wondered if he would have survived without this friend for he knew a lot of tricks on survival and the jungle was lousy with Jap's, ready to shoot. During the night, was the only time, you could move forward, without the Jap's behind you, as the Japanese troops were suspicious about advancing after dark. But in the daylight, Jerry showed him how, to make a booby trap for any nosy Jap hanging around, and this was done, by laying a trail with two lengths of bamboo - bent back taut and held by a trip wire, and any man stumbling into it would be shorn in two when the bamboo sprang viciously back and they smiled to themselves, when they got a few Jap's and would watch from behind the bushes, cheering when one got caught in their snare.

As they wandered alongside the graves looking for where Jerry Dupont was buried, Daneen was giving up hope and sighed. 'Don't think he is laid to rest here, perhaps he was taken out to Virginia, to where

Captain Bailey was buried.'

'I do not think so, somehow,' Naj was optimistic, 'after all he was only a private and not of any exceptional rank.'

Daneen stopped in his tracks, with an angry glare, ready for a row there and then, but he suddenly heard Naj declare, 'I've found it!' And Daneen went rushing over to the grave that was at the beginning of a long row of graves, with many French names and Jerry's grave was the first. 'He would like this position,' said Naj, his velvet brown eyes shining. 'Your friend Jerry, is at the front of the line.'

Daneen stood still and stared down at the name engraved in the stone: Jerry Jack Dupont - and all he could mutter was: 'They have put him with the French resistance fighters and dropped down on his knees. Naj wasn't sure what to do and stood beside him, as the rain started to drizzle, for the grey clouds were becoming darker and it looked as though it was going to pour down. Naj could only watch as Daneen pulled from his pocket the medal, holding it for a moment to his lips.

'Jerry deserves this more than me,' he said, and pushed a hole into the earth with his finger and placed the medal in the ground. Naj watched as Daneen covered the glittering Burma star, sweeping the soil over it with the side of his hand and patted it down with his fingers. 'It's okay now,' he said, 'it's where it should be. The Burma star was given to us Chindits after the mission, and when I saw how some of the other men suffered, like my friend Jerry, I never thought I deserved such a medal. So I sent it to Bridie in Ireland, but she didn't want it.' Naj was wondering who Bridie even was but didn't ask, as Daneen looked at breaking point: his hand was shaking. 'I sent it to her,' he said, 'even though she did not deserve it, but Jerry does, for he was there and gave his life.'

Naj had never seen Daneen like this before. Standing over the grave, his head bent in reverence. He read the words from the gravestone:

Jerry Jack Dupont 1928-1944

Served in the Chindits division

Died 5th June l944 – lost his life in a plane crash in France.

'You know,' said Daneen in a hoarse voice. 'I heard his body was unrecognisable, charred to cinders. My poor, dear friend,' he croaked, 'he was burnt alive, when that plane crashed.' He cried out, 'If . . . only! I had not forced you to go on that plane, you could be alive today!'

'If . . . is a little word,' said Naj sadly, 'but it means lot.'

'I remember, Jerry kept saying, "I'm not leaving . . . the wound will heal", but I almost pushed him onto that crowded plane, filled with other wounded men, to be taken back to England to the hospital, but alas,' cried Daneen, 'they never got there!' Then with his head in his hands, Daneen started to weep. 'If only I had not pushed him to go,' he said as the sound of hard dry sobs escaped from his lips. Naj's fingers gently touched Daneen's shoulder.

'If . . . he had not got on that plane,' Naj attempted to comfort his friend, 'who knows what other fate,' he said very quietly, 'could have befallen him. He may have survived as you had or he may not have, in that treacherous jungle.' Naj took a step back, his eyes downcast, finding it overbearing, he could see that Daneen was still filled with guilt about his friend and left him to his tears, but they seemed to never end. His sobs could be heard all around the small graveyard.

Suddenly Daneen slumped over the grave, resting his head down as if it was a pillow, shedding many tears of anguish. 'I'm sorry Jerry,' he sobbed more quietly, 'I should have listened to you.'

Naj had no idea how to console him, apart from kneeling beside him, with a hand on his shoulder. But Daneen cried on; salted tears ran down his cheeks as he softly said his friend's name. Naj felt he couldn't bear it any longer and tried lifting him to his feet. But as obstinate as usual Daneen would not move, folding his arms around himself tightly, lying on his side and just kept talking about the war with one hand on Jerry's gravestone.

Then all of a sudden from the other side of the wall, the voice of Bob, the old man could be heard, his round head with a military cap poked over the flint stone wall. 'Want any help mate? I can see he's in a bad way.' But that was the wrong thing to say about the proud Daneen, who didn't want his sympathy, quickly wiping away his tears with the back of his hand, shouting: 'On your way!' and shook his fist.

'He will be all right,' Naj told Bob, taking a firm hold of Daneen's arm. 'Now, let's get you home.' He told him to calm down as he called the old man names.

'Nosy old git!' he roared and Naj was quick to frog march him from the churchyard.

However, the equally obstinate Bob was still lingering around, with a sympathetic look on his face, but he wasn't being frightened off by any means and followed the two men from the churchyard, walking slowly behind them. There was something he wanted to ask them and when Daneen was calmer, the old man approached Naj.

'I am going to the Normandy beach,' he said, 'and wondered if you would both like to come.'

'I think we are going back to the hotel now,' Naj said,' holding Daneen by the arm, 'but I thank you for offering, kind, sir.'

Daneen had looked glum and broody, but to Naj's surprise declared: 'I'd like to go, never seen the Normandy beaches, so many suffered there.' And he shrugged off Naj's arm.

'Okay,' Naj said, 'but I thought you were not up to it.'

'Course I am.' For the first time Daneen gave the old man a mischievous grin.

'How are you getting there?' Naj asked, Bob.

'I have a car parked at the back of the churchyard and could do with the company.'

'But it is going to be wet on the beach,' Naj said, wondering if they should go. He wasn't sure they got on too well.

'The rain will clear by the time we get there,' the old man looked up at the sky.

'Why how far is it?' Naj asked as they walked towards the car.

'About an hour,' he said, 'but I've got nothing else to do, and it's worth seeing while I am here.'

So in the capable hands of the old man, they were driven in his shiny red Volvo out towards the coast. On the journey there, Bob related his own story of why he was there, telling them as they sat in the back, that it was a woman who brought him here today. He then passed a photograph of her for Daneen and Naj to see. 'I meant to come earlier to find my friend's grave,' he confessed, 'but somehow I couldn't do it. I just didn't want to think about, all that had happened. You see I was also in the French resistance during the war. I didn't get through the medical for the army core and was very disappointed, but when it looked like old Hitler was going to win the war, I was called to serve in France, and worked with the resistance. I spoke good French, you see. That's where I met my comrade Pierre,' he told them.

'So where does the girl come in to it?' Daneen asked, staring at the photo of a pretty blonde girl in a dance dress. 'Is she French too?'

That's when the old man told them, that this pretty Simone was his friend Pierre's, sister and they got very close. But it was one night when their resistance group, had blown up a Nazi truck in the village square, that Simone got caught. 'She tripped in the street and the Nazi grabbed her and took her off, her screaming. I'll never forget it,' he said, 'and friends had to pull me back. From there she was sent to a camp and I never saw her again and it was also that night, that my friend Pierre got killed . . . He was shot trying to run away.'

'That was sad,' said Naj, 'losing two good friends that same night. The old man nodded from the driving seat at the front, and glanced back at them over his shoulder.

'It broke my heart,' he said. 'You see I had fallen in love with Simone and I never stopped yearning for her, not even after the war.'

'So this is Simone,' Daneen gave a sympathetic nod, holding up the photo. 'She looks a real cracker.'

'She was,' the old man admitted with a hearty laugh, 'but guess what, that's what's brought me back, because I suddenly heard from her last year. It was through an organisation that finds lost friends of war time and I was amazed when I had this letter from her and she asked me to come out to see her in France.

The two men in the back were sitting on the edge of their chairs, as this was astounding and sounded an interesting story.

'So have you seen her yet?' Daneen asked curiously.

'Not yet, going to meet her tonight, taking her to dinner and goodness knows what else,' the old veteran said cheekily, 'although, she is getting on a bit now, like me.'

So for the rest of the journey the two men at the back were entertained with memories of Simone and the old man, when they first met in France. It sounded like love at first sight and a true love story if it worked out for them both, Daneen thought, and made the journey there quicker and very entertaining.

BEACH AT DUNKIRK

Ch.35

At the beach, moods seemed to change, for there was a sad atmosphere in the air as they stood on the low sea wall and looked out across it to the grey sea beyond; the waves rolling in to the shore like white horses. Daneen was standing there, thinking of all the men that waited on this beach: poor bedraggled soldiers, trying to get home to English shores.

'I remember being here,' the old man announced, 'it was like hell on earth . . . this whole beach, covered with soldiers and trucks, dying and wounded men laying in the sand.

'You mean you were actually here, at Dunkirk!' said Naj with surprise. 'Did not the resistance fly you back from France?'

'No, I was not waiting around to be captured by the Gestapo, they had taken over our village near Bordeaux, and I wasn't going to be questioned and tortured by those bastards. So I dressed in civvy`s and because I spoke good French, hid the fact I was English and by a series of lifts in cars, I got to the coast of France. I was planning on getting on a boat back to England, but I didn't expect Dunkirk to be the hell hole it was. So I was trapped. It was only by sheer luck, that I was able to get on one of the overcrowded rowing boats. It was a terrible journey. The boat was heavy with too many men. Some wounded died on board, others exhausted dropped into the sea, but I was a lucky one. I did get back, where so many of the men on this beach didn't.'

Daneen stood looking out at the sea, imagining what it was like at that time, perhaps, on a level, with his terrors in the jungle.

'You've never been back since, then?' he asked of the old man.

'Never,' he said, bending to pick up some sand from the beach, placing it in a bag. 'I'll take this home and remember those men who died upon this sand.'

'You must be a hero,' Daneen looked at the old man with fresh eyes. He had not realised what he had been through.

'Hero,' scoffed the old man, 'whatever, but you will find the veterans are reluctant to call themselves heroes.' And Daneen knew just what he meant.

Along the beach came a group of old soldiers, their medals glinting in the hazy sun. They talked as if sharing memories, for they all had a common bond and nodded as they passed. One took off his army cap and said out loud with a little salute: 'Here's to the men who did not come back.'

Through the dark grey clouds there was a ray of white light that looked like a ladder to Heaven, as it shone down to meet the horizon. The old man sat on the beach, looking out to sea, the sound of the rolling waves seemed loud in the background. Daneen and Naj sat beside him, the trio all equally silent as if reflecting on the past.

'So what was your part during the war?' the old man eventually asked Daneen, turning to face him, but Daneen kept his head down, as if not wanting to speak.

'Oh I see, it's like that is it, so bad you can't even talk about it. Well if you want my advice,' giving Daneen a soft pat on the back, 'I'd talk to someone, because that's what I had to do.'

Daneen looked up, staring straight at him.

'Yes,' nodded the old man, 'you know I'm right. I was the same, but it was a woman who helped me and I knew when I heard from Simone, that here was the key. For many evenings after she contacted me, we talked on the phone about our experiences.

'But I don't need no fancy woman to get me talking,' Daneen obstinately and Naj's face crinkled with amusement.

'Perhaps it wasn't so bad for you then,' the old man said shrewdly, trying to draw him out.

'What you mean, not as bad for me? You don't know half of it. It's the same in the village in Ireland where I live, they treat me like an old drunk, that I never did a brave deed, if only they knew all that I went through.'

'Well if you don't tell them, how are they to know, that you are - really a war hero. I take it that is what you are?'

'I'm not no - bloody hero,' snapped Daneen, 'my friend Jerry was the one who deserved all the respect. I would never have survived that jungle if it wasn't for him-'

'Oh so you was in the jungle, not Burma,' the old man said in surprise, 'well if you was, I take my hat off to you, because I've heard the Burma Jungle, was hell on earth.'

'It certainly was,' returned Daneen.

Naj was relieved they were agreeing about something and gave the old man a knowing smile, for Daneen seemed ready to talk.

With a deep sigh, Daneen began telling the old man about how he became a Chindit, and Bob, looked very impressed.

'Guerilla warfare,' he said, 'they kept the Jap's at bay alright.'

Then Daneen told him of the time, that they were dropped by plane in the Burmese Jungle. 'It was 1942, I was stationed out in India, when it all began . . .' And the old man relaxed, laying down on the sand resting his arms behind his head, ready to listen. He soon heard all about the time, Daneen spent in the jungle.

'. . . It was when China was being bombed,' Daneen went on, 'they were being invaded by the Jap's, and they had to be stopped from getting into India, so us Chindits were sent to fight them off. I remember,' he said, 'how the refugees from China were travelling across Burma, to India, and they were suffering all sorts of degradation from disease and famine, but they had to get out of China. . .'

And Naj was listening to every word with great interest. 'Is that when you found me?' he interrupted, wanting to hear about the time that Daneen rescued him. So Daneen relayed that story of how he was on his way to the Maharaja's Palace assigned with a message for the Maharaja and came across Naj injured as a boy and dying by the side of the river, after being attacked by japs and he rode him across the plains to the palace with him on the back of his horse, and there he was nursed back to health.

'That's when the Maharaja adopted me,' Naj said proudly. The old man looked from one to another, he had noticed there had been a bond between the two men, but now he knew why they were connected.

'That was a stroke of luck,' the old man said, in his forthright tone, 'instead of dying on the streets, you end up king of the palace.'

'It wasn't quite like that, but I will always be grateful to Daneen,' Naj said. 'I owe him my life.'

'Some debt,' the old man said softly, but Daneen was more interested in relaying his story about Captain Bailey, and the men he picked to be his Chindits. 'We were known as a penetration group,' he continued. 'Some were from the British Army and some were Gurkhas. There was even the Chinese, and we were all trained in guerrilla warfare. But it was no picnic, crossing the Burma Jungle by foot, carrying weapons on our backs, and yet we were told by Bailey to eat dates and take cod liver oil. He was a real eccentric, that one. Daneen gave a deep sigh as he started to relate the time he was sent back for the second mission. 'It was in 1944, he began and this time we were to blow up the railway that ran from Mandalay to Mitchinawya. We had to get across the great river of Irrawaddy, taking our mules with us, a hundred of them, then continue through more jungle until we reached the Chindwin River and that was lousy with Jap's but we managed to plant the booby traps on the railway lines.'

'You make it sound easy,' the old man said, 'but I'm sure it wasn't.'

'It certainly wasn't,' gulped Daneen.' It was horrific, bloody terrifying.'

'But did you blow it up?' Naj wanted to hear the rest of the story.

'Course we did,' grinned Daneen, 'mission accomplished, but there was a lot of hardship and suffering, 'cause when we tried to get back over the river, the Jap's were everywhere and shooting the men down and we were told that any man who was injured, we would have to leave.'

'Leave?' repeated Naj. 'Leave behind. I can, not believe that.'

'Oh it's true boy,' the old man said, his sharp eyes looking straight at him, 'that's the way war was, dog eat dog.'

Daneen look down, as he sat on the sands, hugging his legs, looking like the traditional pixie. 'No, it wasn't easy to have to leaving the wounded and the bastard Jap's kept coming, we would be slipping in the mud, hanging onto branches, trying to get out of the river to get away from them and the poor mules, some we lost. They floated off dead down the river and our wounded men were dropping like flies and had to be shot in the back of the head. . .'

For a few moments, the three men were silent as they took in the shock of that extreme action.

'How terrible,' Naj sighed, 'how could you shoot your own men?'

'Had to,' Daneen stated, 'it was orders. We could have just left them to suffer in agony and bleed to death, or be shot at and put out of their misery by the Jap's instead-much like an injured dying horse, you have to shoot it so it dies quickly else it will suffer in pain and it's no use to anyone alive if it can't get back up on its legs again . . . but it was orders, we couldn't carry the wounded and we had many miles to get back, through the dark sweltering jungle. We had not eaten for days and many of us were exhausted and losing our own body weight. Most of us had dysentery or malaria - all were sick. In the end we were told we had to eat our mules or we would die.'

And Naj looked at Daneen, in astonishment. 'I can, not believe that,' he muttered, his Eastern eyes sad on hearing this.

'That's war,' the old man repeated. 'Somehow, I knew your story would not be pleasant.'

'If it's any consolation, Naj, we, I mean me and Jerry we didn't kill our mules and eat them. Neither of us had it in our hearts to,

'So how did you get back?' asked Naj, his face looking a shade paler, etched with sympathy for all those men and mules.

`Not all got back,' Daneen answered, dropping his head with sadness, 'but I was one of the lucky ones and when we arrived back, all of India was hearing of the survival of the Chindits, the men who blew up the railway and stopped the Japs taking over.

'There you go,' said the old man, 'you were heroes. I knew you were.'

'But as you say, we heroes are reluctant to accept that, for I remember some of those great men, who never came back, like my friend Jerry who was shot, by one of those sniping Jap's, and many of those Chindits that fought beside me in that jungle, survived by eating grubs, even snake, and had diseases, with leeches crawling over them.'

'Go on,' the old man said, as Daneen had suddenly gone quiet, finding it hard to speak further. `Get it out of your system,' the old man, placed a gentle hand on Daneen's shoulder.

'Those, bastard Jap's,' Daneen said at last, 'they tortured the men, putting them in terrible prisons, like the one in Rangoon. Rat holes they were.'

'It all sounds so terrible,' Naj said, 'all what you must have been through. You should wear your medals with pride.'

'That's right,' said the old man, ''cause, I remember the pictures on the news - reel, those men looked like walking skeletons in those Jap camps.'

'Many did not survive,' Daneen bent down his head as his voice croaked.

'Strange lot those Jap's,' the old man shook his head from side to side, 'I hear killing means nothing to them'

Naj stood up and shook the sand off his long robe, and looked at Daneen and the old man who sat close together. Both had tears in their eyes, but both looked as though they had gained a friend.

'You don't want to be late for your date,' Naj said loudly to the old man, who was far away, mumbling in conversation with Daneen, as though he was now invisible.

'Date?' repeated the old man, his toothy grin returning. 'My goodness,' he said getting to his feet, 'my pretty Simone will be coming to the hotel soon.'

'You sure she's still pretty,' Daneen quipped in jest, 'after all it was many years ago you knew her.'

'Get away with yer,' the old man chuckled, helping Daneen to his feet, 'I'll ask her if she`s got a friend for you, if you like.'

Naj was wondering if he would ever get back, these men were getting on like a house on fire.

But soon the old man was walking back to his car, his stick aiding him along, with short quick movements, eager to get back as well. 'Don't want to keep her waiting,' he said with a saucy grin.

He soon dropped Naj and Daneen back at their hotel and addresses were exchanged.

'Let me know how your date goes,' called out, Daneen as the old man drove off quickly to his hotel a few streets away.

THE CONFESSION

Ch.36

Eileen was waiting at the door of the cottage as the taxi pulled up. She was hoping that the Maharaja would be coming in for tea and had the best tea service out, but he only rolled down the window to speak, while Daneen rushed out from the back seat of the taxi, and hurried down the path to the shack.

'Well that's a foine greeting,' called out Eileen, with her arms akimbo.

'Well that's our Daneen for you,' the Maharaja smiled warmly.

'Won't you come in,' she cajoled him, 'I have a nice cream sponge to eat.'

'No, my dear,' he said beckoning her closer, 'but there is something I must tell you about Daneen.' So she listened with a deep curiosity as the Maharaja told her how Daneen had broken down at the gravesides of his comrades. 'Watch over him,' he said. 'Perhaps it was all too much for him to relive the past, the way he did, and I believe it was something he had not been able to talk about till now. For we must remember,' the Maharaja added with his head bowed, `it was a terrible time, for those men`.

I had no idea Daneen suffered the way he did said Eilleen her blues eyes flooding with tears.

`They were very dangerous missions` said Naj

'he`s never told me` she confessed, 'and he drinks so heavily . . . perhaps, to blot it all out.'

'Exactly, and well, that is why he is a war hero, and we must not forget it.'

'Don't worry,' Eileen said waving the taxi off, 'he will be treated like the hero he is.'

Mick stood beside Eileen, waving the taxi off. He had listened to their conversation, with an un committal expression on his face, but as soon as the Maraharjas Taxi was out of site, his face changed `So now, he said with a sardonic grin `we have to treat Daneen, like bloody royalty it seems`

`Oh don`t moan` said Eileen with a sigh, `The Maraharja is a good man and for sure, so is Daneen, so you had better get used to it Mick, cause all the village will soon know, that he`s a Hero, especially with Babs Kennedy spreading the gossip`

¬`seems there is a lot I don`t know about the man, admitted Mick, whether he is some bloody hero or not, I could not care less, but I would like to know what exactly went on between him and my mother, before he went off to India on his spree.`

`Oh your not still on about that now Mick`.

`Yes he replied, I am and I`m going to have a word with him, hero or not, he can still answer a few questions. `

`up to you` she shrugged, looking at her watch, you`ll probably catch him working on the high fields with Ginger  and it wont hurt you, to get stuck in and give a hand`.

`I intend` to said Mick and went rushing off `

``Be kind` said Eileen

`I`m always kind, he called back, but I`m fed up with always being the last to know anything around here`.

He then disappeared out of view and Eileen went into the house with a sigh. It was time to cook for the children and Shamus was calling her from the window. She was looking forward to an afternoon sitting around the arguer, with the children and doing her knitting. It had been such a busy time lately, full of excitement and yet there was a little smile on her face as she was thinking of the Maraharja and his wonderful visit, it made her feel so important, then she thought of Mick all stewed up and Daneen acting the war hero. `What a site for site for sore eyes she chuckled`. Of course she hoped it would all end happily, for Daneen could be very feisty and Mick was all worked up.

Up on the high field, Mick looked all around for Daneen, but there was not a sign of him, there was only young Ginger, sitting up the front of the lorry trying to plough the field.

`where`s his lordship` Mick asked immediately

`Heard, he`s up the Farmers club, with Davey Joe, complained Ginger, getting hammered`.

`fed up with waiting` he said, shacking the swet from his thick red hair as the afternoon sun beat down.

`can`t resist a good old binge, can he, said Mick, suppose you`ve heard, he`s a war hero`

`news, spread like wildfire in these parts` said ginger, and Daneens up for the craic, getting free drinks, the crafty ole fella`

`typical` said Mick, heaving himself up into the lorry and slumped beside Ginger, moaning that Daneen was not around, as he was all fired up and ready for battle with Daneen.

For a long time, there had been so many unanswered questions and nobody seemed to be straight forward, they always had a good story to tell, but would beat about the bush when it came to anything else. He wondered if he would ever really get to know these people, even though he had been in the country for many years, would he ever discover the truth about this man, who one minute was little more than the local beat nick, when he arrived, then he`s told he was once living at a palace in India, and now he was a war hero. He was like the original mystery man. These thoughts turned in his mind, while he worked with Ginger, all the while, giving it a lot of thought, what happened in the cow shed, trying to weigh up the rights and wrongs of his situation.

When the lorry broke down, Mick poured the petrol in, while young Ginger tried to get the lorry started - revving the accelerator with his foot erratically, until clouds of smoke appeared, then moaning about Daneen going missing, and that he would be left all day to do the work on his own; his hands all black with oil.

`You're a lot of blagguards, the lot of y'is,' he said, then rushed from one job to another trying to get them finished.

The afternoon sun was hazy and flitted in and out on the high field, last season's bundles of wheat lay wet in mud and bags of seeds were left around the half ploughed field, in an un-orderly fashion. In the end Ginger, threw down his cap. 'I'll be jiggered, yer ain't got an ounce of work in you today Mick O`hara. I`m going home,' he declared. 'You can all go to the birds.'

Mick was not sure what he meant about the birds, but he had to admit he was in no mood for work. It was hot and he felt irritated he had not spoken to Daneen.

He watched Ginger going across the open fields, but he did not care, he was happy to just sit for the next hour by the stream to try and relax. He was soon gazing down into the big silver pool and saw the salmon laying lazily at the bottom, for this was where the salmon spawn. They're travellers, he thought, they`ve come all the way across the sea to their place of birth, back to where they came from, just like you. Mick was far away in thought, thinking over what Eileen had said, his thoughts only broken when occasionally a salmon leapt out over the water.

Going back towards the cottage, the sun shone in an red glow bright above the mountains, he looked at the glowing sky, a promise of a good day as he walked towards home. At the cottage he noticed Eileen standing at the kitchen window as he passed, he was sure she knew where he was going. She gave a little wave as he walked past and down the narrow wooded path to Daneen's shack. So as Mick approached, he did not know what to expect.

The shack stood a little way back from the river edge, it was built up on piled railway sleepers, and the small broken window at the front was mended with brown paper. Red Virginia Creeper grew amongst the weeds that climbed up the walls: a neglected air was about the place with pile of unwanted muddy boots left outside, old rusty buckets and a battered arm chair.

'Daneen,' he called, 'are you there?' But there was no reply, only silence, except for the sweet song of the birds and the trickle of running water from the stream that ran down the hill side and emptied itself into the river. Mick pushed the rickety old door and it swung open and the smell of soot, and smoke, and alcohol assailed his nostrils.

'Daneen,' he called into the half darkness of the room, but no one was there. Mick looked around, it was a strange sort of room. It was the first time, he had ever stepped inside, Daneen had never invited him, to his shack, that seemed entirely Daneens Territory and Mick dared not encroach on that. But now he was inside and looking around, he was not surprised it was so untidy. There was a wooden table with remains of a meal, a battered old stove and on the wall were pictures of landscapes, but one picture took Mick's eye. It was a painting of a young girl, there was something vaguely familiar about it, as if he had seen it before.

She was very pretty with raven coloured hair like the style of Eileen's, it hung down in long sausage curls on her shoulders, she wore a pink dress and a winning smile: that smile he knew well, it reminded him of his mother, her sweet smile as she waved goodbye to him; it was the only hint of beauty left in that face ravaged with disease.

He felt that old feeling of melancholy sweep over him and sunk down into the horsehair armchair. On the table beside him, was a photograph album and he rested it on his lap and stared down at the face of his mother. Then looked at the two men who sat either side of her on that log, he knew one was Daneen as a young man: and he stared at the photograph for ages, as he could not believe, how much he looked like himself, It was like looking at himself in the mirror, for he had the that same long nose, slim head and it was frightening, although Daneens, skin was now the colour of dried bark, with deep welts that lined his sunken cheeks.

As Mick looked at the photograph, he could see Daneen was not the good looking young man, he used to be and Mick put it all down to the drink, for everyone knew he was a drunk. But they would also say how he had been to war, but Mick could just imagine him being a drunken bum, back then as well. Sad, he thought, as he sometimes, felt sorry for him, but he was such a cantankerous old git and hoped he would never get like him. Then looking closer at the other man in the photo, realised, it was definitely the same man in the photograph that always stood on his mother's mantle piece - it was for sure Timothy 'O`Hara.

Mick placed the album back on the table, then shutting the door, went outside to look for Daneen.

Going round the back of the shack he walked through the copse of trees that nestled on the bend of the river and then he spotted him, hunched up holding his knees like one of the traditional Irish pixies, his rod was set up beside him and he just stared into the green frothing water.

Mick approached him quietly, not wanting to startle him and sat himself down on the mossy bank beside him, but he had no need to wonder what to say to him, for the man turned, his eyes like steel giblets looking straight into his.

'Well now, if it's not himself,' he said, his voice a deep rolling brogue, his eyes were red rimmed. The smell of alcohol almost knocked Mick back, as Daneen took another swig from the whisky bottle beside him.

Mick could see he was lousy with drink; he looked dusty and unkempt, his green dungarees stained, his droopy moustache was straggly and lightly gingered from the many pints of porter.

'I suppose you've come to ruck me,' said Daneen, 'for not turning up at the field.'

'No matter,' said Mick wanting to keep things calm, for that all seemed unimportant now and Daneen looked suspiciously at him.

`Have you come to see the war hero, then lad`, Daneen enquired. `must be some reason why your here`. There was a supercilious grin on his face and his head swayed from side to side.

'And how is our Shamus?' he asked with a sarcastic tone, his eyes half closing, his voice slurring and Mick could see the man was drunk and didnt want to tangle with a drunken man and would try to get him home, before he fell into the river.

'Now come on, Daneen,' Mick said firmly trying to get him to his feet. `It's time you were getting home, the sun's going down.'

'I'm not going anywhere,' Daneen roared, leaning on Mick to get up and poor Mick was shoved to the ground. Daneen's soft doleful look had now changed and his eyes narrowed in a mean expression. In a vain attempt he tried to retrieve a cigarette packet from his jacket pocket that lay on the grass and started to sway from side to side. The packet was squashed when Daneen managed to grasp hold of it.

Mick looked on afraid as Daneen tried over and over to light the woodbine cigarette and puffed it wildly trying to ignite the flame. All of Mick's efforts to make him sit down again were in vain and poor Mick followed the drunken Daneen as he staggered in a sideways direction close to the river edge. Mick dared to catch his arm to pull him away, but all he got was abuse. A lot of shouting and screaming and pulling and pushing went on until Daneen slipped and he went foot first into the rushing green water, but Mick had caught him by the arm and heaved the man back onto the river bank. Apart from a foot full of water, Daneen was fine, but poor Mick's nerves were shattered,

'What are you trying to do, drown yourself?' Mick said, puffing and panting, he knew if Daneen had gone any further into that river the current would have taken him.

'Calm down boy,' Daneen slurred, and shook off the water from his leg. 'If the river had got me, I would not give a damn.'

The cold water had sobered Daneen up some, he pointed to the water that swished and gushed fiercely on its journey down the green hills.

'I have been sitting here wondering whether I should throw myself in, and then you come to save me boy. You would all sure enough be better off without me,' he confessed. His face was pale and pensive and he sat with a drooping head.

'What a thing to say, Daneen, why should we want to get rid of you?' Mick tried to pacify him. This was so unlike Daneen to think about killing himself. From the corners of Daneens eyes a line of salted tears trickled down his cheeks, Mick turned for a moment with embarrassment, and Daneen sat, head in hands.

'Now what`s up with you?' asked Mick with concern, but he knew he had to tread softly: Daneen had many sides to him.

'Has something happened to upset you?' Mick asked `thought you would be pleased, your now a honourable war hero`, Mick could not help saying.

'Codswallop,' returned Daneen sitting up and reaching for his bottle and wiped the tears from his face, with the back of his red rough hand. His voice cracked as he exclaimed: 'Have you not worked it out by now? The whole village has been talking since you came here.' Mick was not sure what to say and Daneen looked at him shrewdly. 'I've heard from

Babs Kennedy,' he said, 'that your Eileen was asking questions.' And Mick could not deny it.

'And I heard,' Mick admitted bravely, almost blurting it out 'that you was seen in the cow shed with my mother'

But Daneen only roared with laughter. 'Bloody, women, that's what it is,' Daneen said, 'that big mouthed Mae,' 'Trouble tis,' he said, 'the women get bored, got nothing else to do but gossip, putting two and two together and making three.'

'Go on Daneen,' said Mick, wanting to hear the rest of the story, with one eye on the strong liquor.

'Well, sit beside me,' said Daneen, giving the ground beside him a hard pat, 'I'll try and explain,' he slurred. But Mick wondered if he could explain anything in his drunken condition.

'You see those fields yonder,' Daneen said, his eyes suddenly looking dreamy, and a soft smile crossed his face, as he pointed to the expanse of meadow land.

'Well at one time,' Daneen continued, 'there was corn planted, as golden as the setting sun and I can just see your mother and I running like wild things across the land, her hair falling loose, it streamed out behind her like a horse's mane.'   Shirty shirty

Mick breathed a soft sigh. He could just imagine his mother at that very moment and listening to Daneen talking about her, visions of that mother he loved came before his eyes. Daneen talked about the time, he taught her to ride and Mick sat hanging on to every word, his eyes gazing at the sunset in the distance that sent a pink and red glow over the sky. But he was also wondering how well Daneen knew her, and quizzed him with a critical eye.

`Yes Mick, confessed Daneen, I certainly knew her, I loved her truly, and I can see her now, her eyes glinting in the sun and smiling at me with those dimples each side of her cheeks. She was the prettiest girl in the village but highly strung,' his eyes lighting up a little. 'Her mood would change with the wind, but I would have made her my woman, there and then . . . only she was engaged to Tim 'O' Hara,' he added. 'and what a fine young man he sure was. He was my pal alright and I knew how much he loved your mother, but she seemed smitten with me, telling me one day that I was the one she loved. I tell yer, it took me by surprise and I did not want to upset my mate Tim. So I told your

mother I wanted to travel and see the world, but she took little notice.
Then one day, she came along, to milk the cows, swinging her bucket,
with that sweet smile and we stood chatting in the cow shed. She
looked so pretty I recall, and we larked around as we usually did.

`I bet you did` said Mick with a sardonic grin,

`Tis for sure, young Mick, you can imagine the rest, your a man aint yer`
`and as Daneen roared with laughter, displaying his yellow stained
teeth, Mick was glad he did not talk about the event, he could not bear
it:

'So you were lovers?' said Mick, gritting his teeth, for he could not
imagine his pretty mother, with this rough looking man. 'Or was it just a
romp in the hay for you, didn't you want to stick with her, do the
honourable thing?'

'Honourable?' said Daneen furiously. 'I wanted to fight for my country
to joined the Irish Guards` You forget it was the outbreak of the war.'

But Mick sat gloomily thinking about this situation of Daneen with his
mother in the cow shed and it didn't please him. He was thinking what a
blagguard he was, sleeping with his friend's girl, and any minute now,
he felt there was going to be a big row. He was thinking, he had better

go home and was feeling wet sitting on this bed of damp ferns, and could just picture his steaming meal on the table. But Daneen was in a talkative mood and sat hunched in a world of his own, a half smile on his face - like an old man looking back down the road: memories of Nora floating before his eyes. But Mick only stared coldly at him, until Daneen's red veined eyes turned away and he reached for his bottle.

'After that, declared Daneen, yer mother cut all ties with me and went off to England. I heard she had gone off to England to join Tim, who was stationed there.' Mick was wondering if his mother just took the better man and ran- and he also wondered, if she could have been already pregnant.

'And I was waiting for my papers for the Irish Guards, Daneen went on, `things were happening so quickly, remember that war had been declared, lots of young men were leaving the village, volunteering for the forces, and there was little time to dwell on things back home and little time for goodbyes, so I packed a few things and left, sailing to Liverpool on the next boat and the next thing I heard, your mother and Tim were married and they were expecting a baby.

It seemed to Mick that Daneen had it all tied up in a neat parcel, yet what about poor Tim, Daneen seemed to have few recriminations about the fact he had betrayed his friend.

'So as far as you were concerned,' said Mick looking him in the eye 'this baby was Tim's.'

'What is a man supposed to think,' Daneen said emphatically, 'they had married and there was I, wrapped up in fighting the war, men were dying for the rights of their countries. But Mick was not impressed, just stared down at the water as it seeped higher over the mossy bank.

'Look boy, it's no good you looking at me like that,' he said hoarsely, 'cause I never knew nothing about you. All I knew was Nora married Tim and then they had a kid, which is the norm,' Daneen raised his hands.It was only when old bull Pat Kennedy, said one day: "I should look at young Shamus 'cause he's just like me.'

Mick shuddered, his hands were sweating. 'What are you saying?' he demanded. 'Is that why you came to help me with the high field?' his throat dry, but the words came tumbling out.   There was so much he wanted to ask him, but he was too angry to speak and instead, just sat wondering, why he was bringing Shamus into it. He dreaded to think that his lovely Shamus, looked anything like this derelict old man. He wiped the sweat from his brow, he felt like running away, especially when he looked at Daneen sitting hunched up on the bank, his trousers wet, his long face almost reaching down to his knees, puffing away at his woodbine, what a state he looked, but he didnt even feel sorry for him, as he thought of people he had betrayed.

There was a silence between them for a while, the only sound; the tinkle of water running from the river. The evening was cooling down and there was a cool mist descending on the green hill: the sun was down, fighting against time in the evening shadows.

Mick's thoughts were suddenly interrupted, when Daneen, declared:
'You probably know, that Bridie and I were engaged`.
 Mick shook his head in disgust, so not only did he betray Tim, but he also left poor, Aunt Bridie in the lurch.
``We were to be married in the spring,' Daneen admitted with a regretful sigh.

Mick just wanted to tell him what a dirty scoundrel he was, but bit his tongue and sat with his head in his hands.

'It's no good you judging me boy,' Daneen said, with sudden anger in his voice, 'Bridie made me pay alright, and even after her death she had made me pay,' he added with a sneer, 'for I hoped one day your aunt Bridie would forgive me and leave me some of the land I worked so hard on.

'Well I suppose things happen the way we make them happen,' Mick muttered unsympathetically, but Daneen only sneered, his face red and he poured more whisky down his throat.

'My poor mother,' Mick said shaking his head, wanting to get to the truth, it was all very enlightening, and suddenly turned and looked at this drunken man, wondering miserably, if he was his father. He certainly hoped not. What sort of man betrays his fiancée, his friend-brother in law to be and it seems- deserted his mother.

For a while Mick sat quiet, trying to piece it all together and thought of the man that was on his birth certificate as his father. There was always an air of mystery about this Timothy 'O'Hara and his family in Ireland. He recalled when he was about three years old and saw the photograph that stood on the sideboard of Tim in his army uniform. He used to look for ages at this man with red curly hair, in khaki, holding a rifle, and one day, his mother clutched the photo to her bosom and screamed and cried, that he had been killed.

"Was he my daddy"?' he had asked, but there was no answer, only the sound of her sobs. . .

His thoughts were suddenly broken as Daneen searched for his bottle on the bank, then poured more drink down his neck. He was thinking how despicable he was, glaring at him as he puffed at his woodbine cigarette.

'So where were you when my mother needed you?' asked Mick accusingly. `when I was born`

'I told you, fighting the war, like a lot of men`out in India, most of the time`.'

`What in the Maharaja`s palace,` said mick with a sneer`

'Well, if you take that smirk off your face I'll tell you,' said Daneen with a cold glare.

And went on to tell him how he ended up in the British Indian Army working with horses and eventually got a job the Maharaja's palace. 'I liked the people he said and stayed on after the war, those days at the palace were some of the best times of my life,' Daneen confessed with a far off look, 'and how I loved looking after the horses, they've always been my world.'

Mick was looking at him with disbelief.

'You forget boy,' grinned Daneen, 'that I learnt all about horses from my old grandfather, when I was a boy, and the Maharaja soon realised there wasn't much I didn't know about them. That's when, he asked me to train his own horses and I lived in an old timber hut beside the stables, and with a few of the locals to help, I kept the stables in order. I used to groom the horses and exercise them - some of them were real wild. Only I could handle them and trained them to behave, and do as their master says.'

'My old grandfather,' sighed Daneen, with memories flooding back, of the days of the Irish revolution, and he wondered if Mick would ever be brave enough to throw a grenade like he did - he doubted it. So Daneen chatted on about the stables his granddad used to run. 'They were the biggest in Kilkarney,' he said, 'and he even trained them up, for a millionaire, who raced them. I was sure glad to be with Granddad, for when I was a boy in the orphanage, they used to send me to him on school holidays. Then I got to stay with him. He was a great old man, God rest his soul, he taught me all he knew and when he passed away there was only Bridie, but I did not forget all he taught me about the horse trade.'

For a moment Mick felt sympathy for Daneen, for he himself had been an orphan.

' . . . was at the palace some years,' Daneen continued with a far off look, but Mick was looking at him, narrowing his eyes, for he could only think of his poor mother being alone, when Tim got killed, with a baby to bring up and Daneen never bothered to return.

'Didn't you ever wonder about my mother?' he asked.

'Course,' Daneen answered cautiously, 'but England was a long way off boy, never knew what went on. It was only bumping into a corporal from Banturk, that I heard that Bridie had gone off to join the women's land army, "a bitter woman" he said, and told me Nora and Tim were happy with a son. . .'

Of course Bridie was a bitter woman, Mick thought, betrayed by her fiancé she was on the verge of marrying.

' . . . But when the war ended,' Daneen carried on, 'I thought better of returning home, for I knew Bridie would be on the warpath, so I thought if I survive bloody Hitler, I'll stay on in India and there was a woman here, working in the stables with me, and after the war, she went back to Calcutta, I went with her.' For Daneen found this story easier, than telling Mick that he had been stationed in Calcutta and ended up a down and out on the streets. He had suddenly gone very quiet.

'How many blooming women did you want?

You soon forgot about my mother and Bridie and likely got yourself a harem,' Mick said. Daneen did not answer, he had clammed up. 'How many bloody women did you have?' Mick goaded him, his brown eyes glowing with anger. 'Sounds like you lived it up, when my poor mother was working nights at the hospital and left with a child to bring up. And did you know,' Mick continued with a hostile tone of voice, 'that, my poor mother had TB and went to an early grave.'

Daneen looked down. 'I never knew why she died so early, but now I do.' He shrugged miserably.

'No thanks to any help from you,' snapped Mick. 'You were having too much of a good time in India, by the sounds of it.'

'So that's it is,' Daneen snapped back at Mick, 'you think I was having a good time out in India, well,' pointing a finger at him, 'that's because you know nothing about war!'

'So just tell me . . . why did you come home?' asked Mick with some impatience, for he was walking around and slapping his legs to get the circulation back into them.

'If you must know,' said Daneen, 'as the years went by I started to miss my homeland of Ireland. I would think of the old peat fire and would long to breathe in that fresh moist air. I guess I'd had enough of the hot climate of India and living in a land that was not my own. Ever since I was a young man , Bridie's farm had been my home. I had no family as such, my grandfather had died and Bridie's father gave me a home and I worked on his farm, so this place was my roots. At one time I used to dream of owning part of this meadow land, dream of me and Bridie running it together, building the farm up, making it a grand place. But as they say - the best laid plans of mice and men, Mick, for I fell in love with your mother and so my plans went out the window.'

'But that was of your own making,' Mick said not daring to look at Daneen, he was still seething inside: he was disgusted, how one man, can cause so much hurt and just hid out in India, afraid to face the music. He was showing himself to be a real coward.

'So what happened, when you did return? I don't expect Bridie was too pleased.'

'You're right there, lad, she was always a strong woman, but there was a coldness about her. They say she served as a gunner, standing beside the men and giving the orders to fire the gun. It was dangerous work and the loud sound of the guns were deafening. She was always a bit deaf,' he added.

'She must have been a brave woman,' remarked Mick.

'She sure was,' sighed Daneen, 'that I know for sure, but also a treacherous one,' he stated. 'Nevertheless, the farm was run down when I came home, she had lost interest in it and her hearing was bad, used to spend her time fishing instead. After she set about me with a shovel, saying I had destroyed her life, how she would never forgive me for being unfaithful and chased me down the road, with a shotgun in her hand. But I still came back and we had days of recriminations and tears. She eventually calmed down, and I made her an offer to work for nothing to get the place in shape, she was glad of the extra hands, but she treated me like a dog at first, but I guess I was hoping in time she would forgive me one day, but it seems she never really did.'

`So what did Bridie say about my mother and me?' Mick enquired.

`She never mentioned your mother, except when she first took me back on. She said: "Nora is dead and I never want her name spoken near me and as for my poor brother he died in the war". - With that she walked away and I never dared to mention your mother's name again. After the years passed we did settle down to become friends again and we ran the farm together. The struggles of Ireland, we would talk for hours about, for we remembered the times of Michael Collins and the signing of the Anglo-Irish treaty, although, old Ireland was partitioned, and Northern Ireland is still controlled by the British, but me and Bridie, we always wanted Ireland to be a free state. We even went on a few campaigns together, demonstrating at the border in Derry. There were crowds marching and I can still remember Bridie waving her gun at the British Troops as they drove by, she had a lot of guts, we were brought up like two peas in a pod. She always wanted to go to Dublin to march in the Saint Patrick's Day Parade and we agreed to take her, as her health was beginning to fail and it was then, she said to me – "the land will go on with you, Daneen". But now I realise that all the time she meant the land to go to 'your son' and I suppose, the land is going on with me, in a strange sort of way. Just a little trick of Bridie's, a way of making me pay for my mistakes I suppose. I see it all now, although, it's taken me a while to accept it, as I worked hard for Bridie,' he muttered. 'I thought she would have at least left me some . . . land.'

'Well, perhaps she thought you did not deserve it,' said Mick, rubbing salt in the wounds.

But there was as sad look on Daneen's face as he spoke about the day Bridie died.'I only heard of your existence when Bridie was on her deathbed,' he said. `she was not very old, but her hair had turned iron grey, she was so thin. 'so I called the priest for her to have the last rites and afterwards with little breath and tears in her eyes she spoke of the time when Nora and myself broke her heart. It was then she told me about you. "Nora has a son", she murmured . . . "a fine nephew" I think they were her last words,' said Daneen, dropping his head into his hands, a tear escaping through his fingers and down his face. But Mick's face hardened, feeling he deserved any pangs of guilt, after what he did and was remembering his Aunt Bridie with some affection. He knew little of her in his childhood and realised now, how his mother and Bridie must have thoroughly disliked each other.

He sat quite for a while and thought how sad it all was and what a waste. He shuddered with the cold and looked over at Daneen holding the bottle up and draining out the last dregs. A cold breeze blew and dark clouds now obscured the sunset. Daneen stretched and got up from the damp grass, looking bedraggled.

'I know you're judging me,' he scoffed. 'So what, I lived the day, survived the war and came back from India with nothing.'

'Yes, not a pot to piss in,' jeered Mick and old Bridie took you in.'

'That's true enough, but I can't understand why she never told me.'

'Told you?'

`About you` he said in a hoarse voice.

But Mick only shrugged, as if he couldn't care less. 'Come on,' he said turning to face Daneen, who seemed suddenly like an old man, 'I've heard enough for one day, it's time we were going,' but Daneen refused to budge, declaring, he was fed up, with his bitterness and smashed down his bottle of whisky, onto a rock on the bank, the glass splintering into the air.

`You don't know what it takes to tell you all this boy and you would never understand all I had been through. War is no picnic.'

Nervous: Mick jumped and got to his feet, his backside was getting cold and numb, sitting on the damp grass and he thought he had better keep his opinions to himself, otherwise this confession of Daneen's could turn nasty, he knew it didn't take much for Daneen to turn.

`Now let's get you home, Daneen,' Mick said gently, 'I'm feeling a little tired myself.' That was an understatement for Mick, as he felt a terrible tiredness seep over him, and he felt so cold.

He managed to get Daneen to his feet, more willingly, although he kept bending to look for his bottle that he had dropped in the grass. In his eyes there was an empty gaze as he rambled on about how beautiful Nora was.

'Oh how I wish she was here now,' the old man said, his head falling to one side. `Suppose you think I'm a stupid old man,' he mumbled as Mick got him to his feet, but his legs went from under him.

as he rambled on about the war, raising his arms and screwing his eyes up, looking in the distance, as if he could see the enemy. 'Bastards!' he yelled aiming a rock and Mick was beginning to get more nervous, as Daneen was shouting about the Jap's. He could see Daneen was on the verge of one of his rages:

` if you knew`, sneered Daneen`half of what I went though in the Burma campaign, you would understand. You only think of me as an old wreck of a man, who never did anything of any value in his life. I was in charge of a hundred mules to get them and the men across the widest rivers. Weeks on foot trekking through jungles, through mud and by swamps` and all Mick wanted to do, was get Daneen back to his shack. 'It's getting late,' he said, 'we can talk tomorrow,' but Daneen, was roused up and started shouting again insisting that he wanted another drink.

'Bloody Jap's!' he roared toppling over. Mick wondered, if he was losing his senses and tried to help him up. 'Let go of me!' he yelled, then started to spar up to Mick and clenched his fist, although he did not seem to know what direction to point it in. Daneen was very riled up, shouting at the top of his voice, insisting that he wanted another drink.

Mick stood back as Daneen swayed and eventually collapsed on the ground and started to shake, calling out about Burma and the Jap's and finally passed out.

Mick was not a strong lad, but somehow he carried him back to the shack, the man's thin body resting on his back, like a sack. He put him to sleep in the old bed with the dirty linen and the old man muttered: 'I thought Bridie might leave me the land, but now I know what she meant. . .'

'What's that?' Mick leaned closer to read Daneen's lips.

'She said, the land will go with you . . . and if you're my flesh and blood boy . . .' he murmured, 'I'd say, the land is going with me alright.' Mick looked down at Daneen, no longer full of bluster, but lay there with an enigmatic smile. Mick pulled the blanket over his shoulders.

`Thank you, Son,' he finally mumbled closing his eyes.

On the way out from the shack Mick lingered for a while, feeling sad, he picked up the photo album and sat with it on his lap, looking at the photo of his mother, thinking, how happy she looked with the two men. He looked again at the face of the young pilot, and then back at Daneen – yes: this man is my father - he finally thought with a sad smile.

Ch.37   DANEEN A HAPPIER MAN

Mick walked back up the pathway towards Eileen, looking forward to seeing her. The smell of cooking assailed his nostrils as he entered. He was so pleased to be home, although, Eileen was complaining that Mick had been a long time, but she noticed how pale and serious his face was and wondered what was wrong.

'What's up with you?' she cajoled. 'You look frozen to the bone.'

Mick sat hunched over the fire not bothering to pick up the baby as he crawled around his feet.

'It's Daneen,' he admitted, 'he was blind drunk and telling me stories.'

'What kind of stories?' asked Eileen with curiosity, but Mick was tired and feeling emotionally drained, he never could cope with people very well.

'He was drunk out of his head, `fed up with his carry on`.

`As you like Mick,' she said, helping him off with his damp trousers and putting a blanket around his legs. 'I can't think how you got so damp and cold.'

When Eileen put the steaming meat pie onto the table he only nibbled at the food while she fed young Shamus.

`Well now,' Eileen said to the babe, 'your father's in a deep black mood, has Uncle Daneen upset him?'

He half smiled from his gloom as he looked up at her smiling

questioning face.

'So Mick 'O'Hara, won't you give me a clue at least?'

'Daneen . . . told me he loved my mother and called me his son,' he

confessed gloomily.

Eileen was silent for a moment and worried by the forlorn look on

Mick's face.

'Well now, Mick O`Hara, I have heard a similar story but `but its a

wise child who knows his own father, so they say! 'and it's no good you

letting all this upset you,' she added firmly. 'Don't you think you had

better make the best of a bad bargain, if Daneen is your very own father

and just get on with it. He`ll sure enough help you on the land and he`s

so fond of the children, might make a fine grandfather. But Mick sighed

heavily, as if he was not ready for all this, although, Eilleens celtic green

eyes were sparkling with a lively interest,

`There`s something you should see` she grinned and went rushing off to

the dresser, pulling down a letter from the top shelf,

`look what I have found, she said, handing it to Mick, it was tucked inside an old book of aunt Bridie`s all about India`.

Mick unfolded the old newspaper article and looked down at it with surprise, for on the front was a picture of the maharaja on an elephant and who was leading the elephant, but Daneen, his face smiling out towards the camera, a tall lithe figure with fine white teeth.

`It`s him`, said Mick, feeling a tear rise to his throat, for he was realising how he had failed to believe the truth,  that all along his lovely wife had told him, how Daneen had lived at the Maharaja`s palace and he had failed to belief any of it.   As he read the article, he looked down pensively and Eileen waited beside him with a smile, never ever daring too say. `I told you so`, but just rested a gentle hand on his shoulder.

`How old it is, she said, the paper is so brittle with age, but how wonderful for us all to keep, a lovely memory. `Perhaps Naj would like to see it`.

`This Maraharja on the elephant`` said Mick, `he looks very grand in his jewels, he must be the one, who took Naj in.  It says how he was Cheif Commandant of Military forces and that he got Daneen to join the Chindits, because he was a wonderful horse man and that he was also his friend, who took care of his own horses and trained them` 'es darling said Eileen `it is all so revealing, and look how handsome

Daneen is, in the picture he can only be about 40`.

yes` and I must have been only a small boy at the time, just like our

hamus`.

He looks a real king the old Marahaja said Mick, seems hard to believe

how he adopted naj and now he is his heir.

yes smiled Eileen, just as Naj had told us`.

`But he was not even his own blood` sighed Mick, as if he still found it

hard to take in`

`yes said Eileen with a knowing smile, but truth is sometimes stranger

than fiction` and I can only guess, the old Marahaja, must have loved

Naj very much, and needed an heir.

Mick knew that she was right, as he looked up at her smiling face.

`But in the end darling, she added stroking his hair, `Tis an old saying,

for sure, that blood is thicker than water`, and Mick suddenly felt a rush

of emotion as he rested his head on her breast and cried.

`I`m sorry I doubted you Eileen, I should know your the wisest women I

know.

For a while he sat in a dream by the fire and watched the smoke curl up the chimney, the logs blazing in the grate. When Eileen mentioned the article, she giggled and said, `I`m not surprised, I always knew there was more to this man, than meets the eye`` and for the rest of the evening, was on the phone to the kennedy sisters, talking about Daneen and the Marahaja of Bengal. `Daneens is in the newspaper` she said to her many cousins, and he`s a war hero`. .

Mick would cringe, being fed up with hearing about it. But there was little he could do. With a deep sigh, he dozed by the fireside, thinking about Daneen. This man who was his father, telling himself how unfair it was, that his mother struggled alone, while daneen lived at a Maharajas palace in Inida. Then he thought how Daneen was only a young then, not much older than himself, who wanted his freedom and didn't even know he had a son. But would he ever change he wondered - this selfish, drunken man, who had little morals and he had worn him out with his drunken confession. Mick closed his eyes with exhaustion, wondering whether he would ever get used to the idea of Daneen being his father.

But the next morning Mick went to the shack and picked up the old man from his bed and with no arguments took him to the fireside at his home with Eileen.

'Here father,' he said, 'you will no longer live in the shack, you will be here with us and my home is your home.' Eileen looked on and thought what a long statement it was for her Mick to make.

Daneen with a hangover said very little, only looked up at Mick with a surprised expression and stared through blood shot eyes, nodding in agreement as Mick continued. 'You will be looked after here with us,' and Daneen knew it was up to Mick now.

Since that morning a lot of the old fight seemed to go from Daneen and sometimes after dinner, he would sit with Shamus and ramble on about the war, and grab his toy gun and together they ran around the room. `We`re the Chindits`, Daneen would tell him.

Eileen would look at him in a quizzical fashion, as if weighing him up, thinking he seemed a different man, somehow, not so aggressive in manner and more approachable, thinking the Maraharja need not have worried, for Daneen seemed to have it all under control. Although Mick said, `he seems a bit quite, do you think he is alright`,

'Course he is,' his wise wife, Eileen said, 'he has laid his ghost to rest., although Mick was not sure what she meant. He would often give a little sneer, when Eileen would talk about Daneens many adventures: ` `But don`t you see, Mick said one day `what a selfish life, he has led`.

`Now Mick` she said, putting down the baby in the playpen, and stood in front of him, hands on hips: `How can you say that, she declared, `for Daneen, has paid for the mistakes he made, like we all do in life. `dont you see` the good in him, how from a lad, and born an orphan, he fought in the irish revolution, and how he suffered in the war in Burma, Yet, got a medal for bravery. Perhaps many men lived because of him.

Mick just stood nodding his head, he could see Eileen was on her orange box, she never did like Daneen run down. He should realise to keep his mouth shut.

And she said, her celtic green eyes blazing, `Daneen lost the two women he loved`. And then, she said with a roll of her eyes, he lived in a palace and was friends with a maharaja`. So you may say, he led a selfish life Mick, but he gave a lot in other ways, so don`t be too quick to judge someone like Daneen, he is a man who lived his life to the full. With that Eileen picked up the baby and walked out into the garden, to where Daneen was sitting. Mick watched her hand the baby to him and then they all sat together on the bench, the evening sun shining down upon them.

On other occasions, Daneen would sit and mellow out by the fire and talk about his time in the jungle. It was as if, he was bringing it all out in the open, something he had buried inside of him for years. There were no more nightmares, he was a happier man, although, there was still a bitter streak, but a man that was more ready to accept his destiny. And Mick it seemed suddenly became a man, for the right or wrong of it, young Mick now had found the father he never had, as Mick had also laid his ghosts to rest. He and Eileen never talked much about it; she was always more for doing than talking was Eileen.

She went into town and bought Daneen some new working boots and sat and knitted him some warm socks and in no time she had the little shack all cleaned up. Daneen never stopped her, he was quite content to let Eileen take him over, although he still hid his drink under the bed, but Eileen never said a word, only insisted when he looked after the children that, he dare not touch a drop, and he never did when he watched over his own grandchildren..

From hence the land flourished: it was not only Mick's now, it was half Daneen's, because that was what Mick wanted. They worked together as father and son and when they came in tired from the fields, Eileen would take off their boots and put them by the fire guard to dry and fuss around them, both.

When Eileen and Mick had Noreen baptised at the church, calling her Noreen Mae after Mick`s mother, the woman Daneen held so dear in his heart, and his aunt Mae, who was also asked to be `Godmother` and stood proudly at the altar in a nice navy suit with a white blouse and on her lapel was a medal for her services during the war and all the village heard how she had worked tirelessly in the hospital during the blitz caring for the wounded soldiers.

After church, they all went back to the cottage for a feast laid out on the kitchen table and Daneen got on the drink, then sneered at Mae saying: 'She might have a big medal, but she also had a big mouth,' but Eileen soon put him in his place, pointing out Mae`s commemoration and placed the new baby in her arms.

For the rest of the evening, Mae sat talking to Mick, with young michael on her lap, just like she used to do Mick as a boy. They were now a happy united family and one that grew and prospered, although sitting in front of the fire was old Oikey, he had followed Daneen in and refused to move. For Mick, this was the only fly in the ointment, for he not only had to contend with Oikey glaring at him as he sat toasting his nout in front of the fire, but Oikey's wife selena as well, who was very

at and the pair were now joined by the piglets, who were growing fast

nd took prime position beside Oikey. Mick wondered what the future

vould bring, for now there were eight of these pigs. Young Michael

oved the playful piglets and would pull at their tails until Eileen told

him off.

Eileen had made a waistcoat for Oikey and a turban that fit snugly

around his ears with a small plume. Mick had scoffed. 'Won't last long

n the mud,' he muttered and rolled his eyes.

'Well, Oikey is a sacred animal in India and he is sacred in this house

too,' said Eileen with her hands on her hips,' and Mick chuckled.

And as for mother pig Selena, she wore around her neck a frilly collar

that Eileen had also made, from the Indian material she had found in

Bridie's cupboard.

'She looks a real tart in that,' smirked Mick.

'To be sure,' returned Daneen, 'but Oikey will take his pride of place

now,' he said as the pig placed himself beside him in a protective

manner, but the same old beady eyes would watch Mick with a sneer as

if to say:

'Well I'm glad it's all settled at last'.

As time passed in the homestead and the little pigs grew into big ones Mick began to think- 'Well if you can't beat them join them. So in the end even Mick and Oikey became friends for it seemed more than anything that fate had willed it that way.

THE MAHARAJA'S INVITE

Ch.38

It was a month later when the invitation came. Eileen was about to take the smelly, spicy envelope from the postman.

'All the way from India,' he said. 'I bet it's from that Maharaja,' his piercing eyes looking down at the envelope, 'people are still talking about it.' Eileen looked at him with an impertinent air.

'Let them talk,' she said with a sharp, 'Thank you,' as she snatched it from his hands. He was waiting for her to open it. 'If it is from his lordship,' she said in a haughty fashion, 'I'll soon be finding out,' and she went inside and shut the door in his face. Then sitting herself in front of the fire, Mick beside her at the table, she opened the invitation and her face lit up, telling Mick that they had been invited to a ceremony at the palace and danced around the room, the invite in her hands.

'A ceremony,' Mick huffed, 'in India. Can't be going there,' he stated.

'And why not,' Eileen frowned. 'For goodness sake, look at this card,' she said, 'turning it over in her hands, 'it's beautiful,' she added, staring at the words written in gold calligraphy. She was full of excitement, but Mick was unimpressed and picked up the new baby from her cot as she cried.

`It says it's from- His Royal Highness Maharaja Najanda Patel. What a mouth full!' She giggled as she read out the words:

MAHARAJA MOOLAH NAJANDA PATEL AND NIGHAT MAJINARDI REQUEST THE PLEASURE OF MR AND MRS MICHAEL O`HARA AND CHILDREN AT THEIR MARRIAGE ON AUGUST THE 4TH AT THE TEMPLE IN COOCH BEHAR, WHERE THEY WILL BE MARRIED ACCORDING TO `SIKH RITES`.

'Sikh rites,' repeated Mick, 'what's that?'

'Don't know,' shrugged Eileen, 'must be one of their rituals. I've heard, they have a ritual, where their garments are tied together as they circle around a fire.'

'What,' Mick said with a shake of his head. 'I'm not dancing round any fires.'

'Not you silly,' Eileen said, 'the couple getting married, but I'm warning you, the wedding could go on for three days,' and Mick looked very gloomy. He didn't want to have to put up with a lot of Indians with their rituals and moaned about not understanding a word in their language. But Eileen was reading the P.S that said, they would be collected from home, then driven to Cork Airport on the Friday and returned a week later.

'Where we going to be staying?' groaned Mick 'and a weeks a long time to be leaving the farm, there would be no work done.'

'As if you worry about the work,' she snapped, 'cause, it says here, we will be staying in our own quarters in the palace. Goodness! I've never even been out of Ireland and now I'll be going to India!'

'Now hang on,' Mick said firmly, standing his ground, 'it's a long way to take the children.'

'Don't be such a fuss pot,' she said, 'where's your sense of adventure.' And Mick knew he was beat - she was already discussing what she would wear and what present to buy.

Also in the envelope was another card addressed to Daneen. 'It's for the man, himself,' said Eileen, joyously. `He can help with the children,' and handed Mick the invitation.

'I'll take it to him now,' said Mick, eager to get away from the pressure of all this talk of going to India. 'He is in the high fields planting the corn seeds.'

'He will be thrilled to be going.' Eileen grinned, still half in a dream.

But Mick wasn't so sure. 'You never know with him,' he said, 'it's a long way.'

'Not, for him,' Eileen said most profoundly, 'all the places he has been. He is already a well travelled man.'

'Beats me why he ever came back here,' shrugged Mick 'could have stayed in the palace, even become a Maharaja.

'Don't be so silly,' Eileen said, 'and this place is his roots, and I don't think he will ever leave, especially now, you are truly father and son.'

With that Mick looked content, knowing he could never win and went to find Daneen.

As he walked to the hill he was thinking of this palace in India, it was a whole other world. Perhaps Eileen was right - where was his spirit of adventure? But he wasn't sure about wearing a turban . . . he would have to say no to that. He quickened his pace up the hill, he could see Daneen now, driving the tractor, and could just hear him singing, as his voice was carried by the wind. It was that old rebel song of Ireland. 'Ballad of the Exile' and for some reason it was choking him up . . . and as he hurried across the field to meet his father, he found himself singing along.

487

Printed in Great Britain
by Amazon

28926900R00274